STONE COFFIN

STONE COFFIN

Kjell Eriksson

Translated from the Swedish by Ebba Segerberg

MINOTAUR BOOKS
A THOMAS DUNNE BOOK ≈ NEW YORK

A THOMAS DUNNE BOOK FOR MINOTAUR BOOKS.
An imprint of St. Martin's Press.

STONE COFFIN. Copyright © 2001 by Kjell Eriksson. Translation copyright © 2016 by Ebba Segerberg. All rights reserved. Printed in the United States of America. For information, address St. Martin's Press, 175 Fifth Avenue, New York, N.Y. 10010.

www.thomasdunnebooks.com
www.minotaurbooks.com

The Library of Congress has cataloged the hardcover edition as follows:

Names: Eriksson, Kjell, 1953– author. | Segerberg, Ebba, translator.
Title: Stone coffin : a mystery / Kjell Eriksson ; translated from the Swedish
    by Ebba Segerberg.
Other titles: Stenkistan. English
Description: First U.S. edition. | New York : Minotaur Books, 2016. |
    Series: Ann Lindell mysteries ; 7
Identifiers: LCCN 2016010566 | ISBN 9781250025517 (hardcover) |
    ISBN 9781250025500 (ebook)
Subjects: LCSH: Lindell, Ann (Fictitious character)—Fiction. | Women detectives—
    Sweden—Fiction. | Mystery fiction. | BISAC: FICTION / Mystery & Detective /
    Police Procedural.
Classification: LCC PT9876.15.R5155 S7813 2016 | DDC 839.73/8—dc23
LC record available at https://lccn.loc.gov/2016010566

ISBN 978-1-250-14467-6 (trade paperback)

Our books may be purchased in bulk for promotional, educational, or business use. Please contact your local bookseller or the Macmillan Corporate and Premium Sales Department at 1-800-221-7945, extension 5442, or by email at MacmillanSpecialMarkets@macmillan.com.

First published in Sweden as Stenkistan by Ordfront

First Minotaur Books Paperback Edition: December 2017

10 9 8 7 6 5 4 3 2 1

STONE COFFIN

Prologue

The lizards darted in and out of the wall, lightning-quick. They were celebrating the sun, which would be rising out of the sea in half an hour. A morning ritual.

The stone wall could easily have been in Ireland. The stone was different, but the style of it was the same. Stone on stone, haphazard at first glance, and yet so beautifully functional. The wall rose to a height of one and a half meters, encircled the garden, and along one edge of the property, linked to the wall of a building.

The gray expanse of the fiber cement roofing tiles was framed by dark vegetation. A couple of palm trees, a citrus tree, and a couple of midsized trees he did not recognize. He had collected a few of their brown seedpods, shaken them, listened, and fished out a couple of dark seeds. They looked poisonous. They lay in his palm darkly gleaming, almost metallic, like mystical messengers, and for a moment he had the impulse to toss them down his throat.

Poisonous? No matter. They were beautiful and he would save them to plant later.

The rain began suddenly. The drops gathered in the undulations of the corrugated roofing tiles. They gleamed as they left the roof and fell toward the ground. They glimmered just as they were about to drop. He had the notion that they were a melody played out on a keyboard. A dance across the keys. Soundless music. He—tone deaf—was blinded by the beauty of their fine music.

Pull yourself together, he thought, and in that moment the rain stopped.

The sea washed in over the beach. Yesterday evening he had tried to figure out the pattern of the unceasing movement of the waves. Was there a pattern? Seven small waves and one large? At some point everything grew very still, a resounding silence, as if the sea were holding its breath. Two, three seconds, nothing more.

A flowering creeper resembling a morning glory encircled his feet. He sifted sand through his fingers and looked out over the water. A container ship was huffing in the distance. He made plans but was too tired to be rational and too disoriented in that scene to find any peace in it. Exposed, he thought, I am exposed on this beach, and it is here that I must make up my mind.

But instead of making any decisions, he went to the little bodega that also doubled as a bar. A shack made out of wood and sheet metal, resting up against a tree and with a view of the road. Ramón, "The Baker," held out his hand across the packets of chewing gum stacked on the counter.

A white-haired man, his face deeply lined, was watching him intently. There was a woman sitting across from him. She wore a tight-fitting green dress.

He ordered a beer, sat down at the other table, nodded at the old man, and lifted the cold beer bottle to his lips. If I could only stay like this, he thought, here at this table. The water came from the mountains and the salt from the ocean.

"Good," he said, and he knew that he was going to get drunk. As long as he kept drinking, the Baker would keep his establishment open.

He signaled the Baker that he should serve beer to the old man and the woman.

We are the new conquistadors, he thought, and sighed.

"Problems?"

Sven-Erik Cederén nodded and raised his bottle. He had been to this country five, six times, but he had never been here alone before. Each visit had shifted his parameters. The first couple of times he had sought out the usual tourist places, drunk rum, and watched the women, but without taking any initiative. Now he went to the Baker, mostly sat quietly at his table, and drank Presidente.

"How long are you staying?" the Baker asked.

The couple at the next table turned around and looked at him inquiringly, as if his answer was of the greatest import.

"One more week."

The old man raised his bottle.

"I will buy some land. Just outside Gaspar Hernández."

"That's a village of idiots," the old one said.

"What does your country look like?" the woman asked.

He started to give the usual response—the cold, the snow, the ice on the lakes, the forests—but then he stopped. He wanted to express something more.

"We live . . ." he started tentatively, "we live a fairly good life."

He began to talk about his daughter. He started on another beer. The Baker opened a bottle of rum and poured him a glass. He rested his arms on the counter. Sven-Erik looked at him and they smiled at each other.

"Do you miss her?"

"Of course."

"There is something else that you miss more," the Baker said.

"One always misses one's homeland," the old one said.

The Swede shook his head.

"You miss a woman."

"Perhaps."

What had he done? Could it be fixed? No. He could only patch it up. He was the sinner who had repented too late. For almost forty years he had marched to the beat. Now he was falling out of line. He was scared. If only he could sit in this shack, drink beer, and talk with the people who came by. The Baker and his shop would give him absolution.

He was afraid, but not for himself. Lies! Of course he was afraid of the sentence. He escaped to a bodega full of beer, Pringles, and chewing gum.

He kept on talking about his country. What do I choose to tell? What do I know about Sweden? Should I talk about life in Uppsala-Näs, the Edenhof golf course, about my colleagues, lectures at the business association, the tiled bathrooms, and the dock that I spent a hundred thousand kronor to renovate?

He glanced at the woman as he talked. She was between twenty and thirty. Her arm rested close to his. Maybe he could. The wad of bills in his pocket. The cock that swelled in his pants.

He took a sip of his beer. The Baker looked at him and nodded.

✦

One

"Come up here on the road! You're getting your shoes dirty!"

The girl tore off a last flower and held the clover flowers up to her mother.

"Four leaves means good luck," the girl said.

"We'll put those on the grave."

The woman arranged the flowers, peeling away a withered leaf.

"Nana liked clover," she said thoughtfully, looking off at the church and then at the child by her side. One day, she thought, you got only one day together on this earth.

Six years and one day ago, Emily was born, and the very next day her grandmother died. Every anniversary of her death they walked to the church and laid flowers on her grave. They also sat on the low stone wall for a while. The woman would drink coffee and her daughter some juice.

The walk took them half an hour. They could have taken the car but preferred to walk. The slow trip to the church enabled reflection. She had loved her mother above all else. It was as if Emily had filled in for her Nana. As one love slipped away, another arrived.

She and her newborn had been transported in the Akademiska hospital to the unit where her mother lay in a state between consciousness and sleep.

The little girl had been lifted into her arms. At first it looked as if she thought yet another burden was being added to her already ravaged body.

The woman guessed that the baby's scent brought her mother to life, because her nostrils widened suddenly. The gaunt, needle-riddled hand patted the tiny bundle in her lap and she opened her morphine-obscured eyes.

"I want to run the last bit," the girl said, interrupting her mother's thoughts.

"No, we'll stay together," she said, and right before she died, she realized that she might have saved her daughter's life if she had let her go.

The car struck them both with full force. The child was thrown some ten meters and died almost instantly. The mother was thrown forward and the front left wheel of the car ran over her body. She lived long enough to grasp what had happened, that she might have been able to save her daughter. She also had time to note that the car swerved and slid as it accelerated and disappeared in the direction of the church.

"Why are you killing us?" she whispered.

✦

Two

Ann Lindell was savoring her colleague's good mood. Sammy Nilsson had read the horoscope of the day with a serious face, but when he arrived at the final line, ". . . and why not give in to love's invitation that comes your way today?" he burst into laughter.

"Love's invitation," Lindell said. "That's something."

"Maybe Ottosson will offer you a cup of coffee," Sammy said. "I think he's working on you."

Ottosson was the unit commander for Violent Crimes. He had called a meeting for nine-thirty, and both Lindell and Sammy thought he would likely announce a reorganization of the unit.

Everything seemed to be undergoing reorganization. The community policing initiative that had been introduced with great fanfare lay shot and gasping. It was going to give up the ghost at any moment. There was talk that the community policing in Gottsunda and other far-flung areas would be relocated to the Fyrislund industrial area. "Community" was likely to gain a new definition if Commissioner Lindberg got his wish.

"How are you doing? I hear rumors that you're seeing someone."

Lindell looked up abruptly. Sammy thought she seemed almost frightened.

"Seeing someone? No way."

"Didn't you hook up with some guy?"

"I went out and partied with the girls."

"I heard something else."

Lindell smiled. "Don't believe everything you hear. It was just one time."

"And one time doesn't count?"

Lindell just smiled in reply.

Ola Haver walked up to them. Lindell saw in his face that something had happened, but he sat down at the table before he started to talk.

"We have a hit-and-run," he said. "Two dead."

"Where?" Sammy asked.

"Uppsala-Näs."

"Any witnesses?" Lindell asked.

Haver shook his head.

"Someone who drove past the scene called it in. One of the dead is a child. A little girl."

Haver was white as a sheet.

"Shit," Sammy said.

"Maybe six years old."

Lindell checked the time: nine-twelve.

"I'll call Ottosson," she said and got up.

Love's invitation, Lindell thought as she jumped into Sammy's car. Hardly. These were the kinds of invitations that came their way.

She glanced over at Sammy as he turned onto Salagatan. He swore quietly about the traffic, drove up Sankt Olofsgatan, and stared furiously at the driver who came from the right and forced him to stop.

Haver was in the backseat talking on his phone and Lindell heard that he was getting information directly from the patrol unit on the scene.

Wednesday, July 14. One of those summer days that promised so much. The valley sloping down toward Lake Mälaren was flourishing with vegetation. The field grasses were tall. In some plots they were even gathering the first harvest. At Högby a man had left his tractor by the side of the road and was taking dignified steps through the clover and timothy grass that almost reached up to his waist. For a moment, Ann Lindell had an almost physical recollection of Edvard. It could have been him walking across that field and running his hand across the top of the sheaths. A stabbing sensation. Everything was over in a moment, and yet it wasn't. He was there. In the landscape. Even after half a year, Edvard Risberg existed as a shadow inside her. She heard his words and felt his hands. No one had touched her like he had.

A deer buck peeked nervously out of the edge of the woods, up toward the Lunsen forest. The sun was shining straight into Lindell's face, but she did not fold down the sun visor in the car. Instead she let her face bask in the rays. Edvard, are you walking by the sea?

One kilometer up the road, a woman and her daughter were lying next to a ditch.

Haver said something that Lindell didn't quite catch.

"It's probably Ryde," Sammy said. "He's the only one who drives such a rusty Mazda."

And so it was. Eskil Ryde, the forensic specialist, was already on the scene. He was leaning over the ditch, one hand running through his thin hair, the other gesticulating.

One of the uniformed policemen waved on a minivan. Lindell caught sight of something in the ditch as she climbed out of the car. A child, she thought and glanced at Sammy. They exchanged the briefest of glances.

Ryde lifted the gray blanket. The girl's forehead was cracked. Åke Jansson, the second uniformed officer, was sobbing. Haver put an arm around him and Jansson balled up his hands. Lindell brushed his shoulder as she went to kneel next to the girl's body. She didn't really see it, only the tiny legs sticking out, the right hand with light-pink-painted nails, the pattern of the red dress, and the blonde hair that had been colored just as red.

Lindell straightened up so fast she felt dizzy.

"Do we know who they are?" she asked of no one in particular.

"No," Jansson said. "I've searched for a pocketbook, purse, or something like that, but there's nothing. They must live in the area. The truck driver who spotted them thought they looked familiar. He drives this route daily."

Lindell had already registered the presence of the truck that was parked some thirty meters away.

"Stay the hell away from my bodies," Ryde said.

"I wanted to know who she was," Jansson said, insulted.

"Maybe they were on the way to the church," Haver said.

"The girl had picked flowers," Ryde said.

"How do you know?"

"Her hands," Ryde said.

Four police officers circled around a child's body. Ryde gently pulled the cover back into place.

"Let's take a look at the woman," he said.

The woman had been beautiful. Her hair, the same shade as the girl's, was cut short and added a touch of toughness to her face. Not much toughness left now, but Lindell could see that she had been the type of woman that you noticed, that you listened to. She thought she could read self-awareness and will in her features, even though a sharp rock had cut into her chin as if the woman's lip had been pierced by a ring with a blackened jewel.

There was gold in her ears; she wore a substantial gold ring on her left ring finger, and on her right hand a silver ring with precious stones. Her nails were well groomed. "Probably five hundred kronor," Lindell noted. Those nails had carved patterns in the gravel between the lush green of the ditch and the black, cracked asphalt.

Her dress was khaki, summery thin with marks from a car tire across the narrow back.

Her eyes were blue, but her gaze was broken.

Lindell looked up and let her gaze wander. Summer lay like a warm breath over the landscape. There was absolutely no wind and the sound of a motorboat carried from the lake. A man came walking along the willow allée leading to Ytternäs farm. He walked slowly, but Lindell saw that he was attentive to the gathering of cars parked along the road. Here comes the first gawker, she thought and quickly turned around.

"Identification, that is the most important thing. Who is the minister around here?" Lindell asked and looked over at Sammy, who shook his head.

"No idea," he said. "I'll go up to the church. There may be a bulletin board."

Lindell walked over to the truck. According to Åke, the driver was sitting up front, and as she drew closer, she saw his face in the rearview mirror. He opened the door and slid down from his seat in a seasoned and yet stiffly awkward movement.

"Hi, Ann Lindell from the police. You were the first on the scene?"

The man nodded and shook her outstretched hand.

"Do you recognize them?"

"I think so."

"Sorry, what was your name? I forgot to ask."

"Lindberg, Janne. I live up there," he said and pointed.

"So you've seen them before?"

"Yes. They often walk along the road. I think they live up toward Vreta Point, but I don't know her."

"She was a beautiful woman."

Janne Lindberg nodded.

"You were coming from home and headed into town? When was that?"

"Around nine."

"Tell me what you saw."

"I saw the mom first. Then the little girl."

"Do you wear glasses?"

"No, why?"

"You're squinting."

"Because of the sun."

"So what did you do then?"

"I checked to see if they were alive." The man shook his head. "Then I called."

"And it wasn't you who ran them over?"

The question made him flinch and he stared at Lindell.

"What the hell," he got out. "You think I would run over a mother and child? I'm a professional driver, damn it."

"It's happened before. May I see your cell phone?"

"Why do you need to see that?"

"I want to see when you called us."

He sighed and handed it over. Lindell selected "Recent Calls" and saw that Lindberg had made the call at 9:08 A.M. Before that he had made a call at 8:26. She also wanted to check "Incoming Calls" and see if Lindberg had received any calls shortly before the emergency call. And sure enough, someone had called at 8:47.

"You got a call before you dialed 112. Who was that?"

"A guy from the asphalt gang. I drive asphalt but had a little problem with the car this morning. He called to check to see if I was on my way."

"So you were in a hurry this morning?"

"Yes, I should have been at the plant a little after six."

"Wasn't it the case that you were stressed, got a call, lost your focus, and didn't have time to swerve?"

"Lay off! I haven't run anyone over my whole life!"

"May we contact the guy who called you?"

"Of course."

"You understand that you have to stay here. We have to examine your vehicle. I don't think you've hit anyone, but we have to check it out. Okay?"

Janne Lindberg nodded. "I keep thinking about that little girl," he said.

The man that Lindell had spotted in the allée had almost reached the truck by now and she decided to wait for him. He had a slight limp.

"What's happened?" he asked. "Did someone hit a deer?"

"No," Lindell said. "It's a hit-and-run."

The man stopped abruptly. "Is it Josefin and Emily?"

His voice cracked.

"I saw them on the road," he said. "Is it them?"

"We don't know. Perhaps you can help us."

The man started to sob.

"I saw them on the road. I knew they were coming today."

"It was a woman and a little girl. Could it be them?"

The man nodded.

"Will you help us?"

Lindell took a step closer to the man. She was touched by his weeping and obvious despair and she was also feeling close to tears.

"That's her," the man said when Lindell raised the gray cover.

His face was ashen and Lindell feared that he would faint.

"Let's go sit in the car. Then you can tell me what you know."

At that moment, Sammy returned. "The minister is on his way," he said as he stepped out of the car.

"I don't need a minister!" the man said.

"He's not coming for your sake, " Lindell said soothingly.

"Can you come over?" Ryde shouted. He was crouched down by the woman.

"Talk to him," Lindell told Sammy and walked over to Ryde.

"I don't think she died immediately," Ryde said. "She dragged herself along the road toward her child. See?" He pointed to a faint trail of blood on the roadway.

"She broke her nails," Lindell said.

"She wanted to reach her daughter."

Lindell kneeled and stared down intently. The woman's hand was slender. The stones in the silver ring glittered. Lindell saw that the skin on the index finger had been worn away.

Ryde crawled closer and bent his head to get another angle.

Lindell could barely stand to observe the remnants of skin left on the road. The two officers looked at each other, bent over a woman's beautiful hand on a sunny June morning.

"It wasn't an accident," Ryde said and got up to his feet.

"You don't think?"

Ryde looked around before answering.

"It was daylight, a straight and decently wide stretch of road," he said finally.

"You mean this was murder?"

Ryde didn't answer but got out his cell phone. Lindell remained standing where she was. The girl had picked flowers, she thought. She looked over at the gray cloth that covered the little one. The mother had not managed to reach her. How many meters were left? Seven, eight?

A car appeared. Haver flagged it down and Lindell took out her phone.

✦

Three

An initial meeting and review at the police station took place at shortly after six P.M. A dozen officers from Violent Crimes, a few from Surveillance, and a couple from Forensics were present. Sammy Nilsson led the meeting.

"What do we know? Josefin Cederén, thirty-two years old, living in Vreta. Emily, six years. It was her birthday yesterday. We know that they were on their way to the church where Josefin's mother is buried. They went there every year on this day. Several of the neighbors have confirmed it. Ryde, what did the pathologists say?"

"It was a passenger car. At least according to the pathologists, that's what the injuries indicate. Death must have been instantaneous, at least for the little girl. She was thrown in the air and must have died at the moment she hit the ground. There were some signs that the mother may have lived on for a short while after the accident."

"Okay," Sammy said, "as you know, the husband, Sven-Erik Cederén, is completely MIA. As is the car, a blue BMW—99 series—with sunroof and all the extras. Haver checked with Novation, where he bought the car. With cash, I might add."

"Where does he work?" Lundin asked.

"MedForsk. It's a company that develops pharmaceuticals. High-level research. A relatively young company, a spin-off from Pharmacia. Sven-Erik Cederén never showed up to work today. MedForsk has some twenty employees and we have talked to all of them. No one has seen him."

"But we know that he left for work as usual," said Norrman, who had been in charge of the door-to-door questioning in Vreta. "He left shortly after eight o'clock. We've talked to about twenty neighbors. The one who lives across the street said a few words to Cederén around seven. Both of them were out to pick up the newspaper."

"And he said he seemed completely normal," Berglund added. "They talked about the usual, weather and wind. According to the neighbor, Cederén was like a clock."

"Where is Lindell?" Beatrice asked.

"With Josefin's father," Ottosson said.

"Does he live in town?"

Ottosson nodded.

"And in Vreta. Josefin Cederén was actually born in that county."

"Apart from that, it's probably mostly moved-in outsider shits," Haver said.

"What do you mean, shits?" Ottosson asked.

"Okay," Sammy said, "we know that he left Uppsala-Näs as usual, but that he never turned up at work. Where did he go?"

"His summer house," Lundin said.

"They don't have one."

"Arlanda," Haver suggested. "He knew that his wife and daughter were going to walk to the church, waited somewhere in the bushes, ran them over, and left the country."

"We've checked," said Sixten Wende. "No Cederén has left via Arlanda."

"A lover," Beatrice said.

"We've put out an APB on him as well as the car. I'm sure we'll at least know where the car has gone within a day. That's no ordinary ride."

Ottosson's certainty stemmed from thirty-five years on the job, of which the last twenty had been in Violent Crimes. Cars had a tendency to turn up. People were trickier.

"He may also have been hit," he went on. "I have trouble imagining that he would first wipe out his family and then disappear."

"People have done worse things," Wende said.

"I know. But to run over your own child, isn't that too much?"

"Maybe he was out of his mind?" Sammy said.

"But the child," Ottosson insisted.

"Beatrice will take on the family's finances, assets and debts, insurance, the whole thing. I want a complete briefing tomorrow. You can have Sixten on this too," Ottosson said, turning to Beatrice.

When Ann Lindell wasn't present, there was some confusion about who should lead the conversation. Sammy had the psychological advantage, as he worked the most closely with Lindell, but on the other hand, Ottosson was the boss. Ottosson, however, often sat quietly during meetings, completely confident in Lindell's ability to pose the right questions and assign tasks in a sensible way.

"What's the motive?" Ottosson asked. His role in the meeting could perhaps best be defined as the engine, weighing the arguments, asking lots of questions, forcing his colleagues to sharpen their thoughts.

"Jealousy," Haver said. "Maybe Josefin had found someone else."

"I think she was pregnant," Beatrice said suddenly.

Everyone's gaze turned toward her.

"When Ann and I examined her, I thought I could tell."

"How could you tell?"

"Her belly. Breasts. Especially the breasts. She just looked pregnant."

"What did Lindell say?"

"She doesn't have kids," Beatrice said.

"That's so fucked," Haver said emphatically.

"Well, we'll soon find out what the circumstances are," Ottosson said and turned to Beatrice.

"Could you see if there's any more information available?"

She got up reluctantly and left the room. At that moment Riis walked in. They met in the doorway without exchanging glances.

Riis had few friends, and everyone else had to think long and hard about whether it was worth it to be friendly to the grumpy detective. Beatrice had been one of the first to abandon any attempt at cultivating a collegial relationship or even collaborating with him. "Riis is a grumpy old man in a transitional age," she would say. "He hates us all."

Riis sat down and everyone waited for what he had to say.

"Well?" Ottosson said finally.

Riis opened his notebook with a sweeping gesture.

"Cederén was a man with vision," he said and looked up. "He wanted to do something with his life. He was successful, not least in terms of material wealth, he is probably unhappy, and he is very dead."

"Dead?"

"Mentally dead," Riis said and sighed.

"Are you jealous of his money?" Haver said calmly.

Riis shot him a quick glance, smiled, and continued.

"He has just bought a house in the Dominican Republic, if anyone knows where that is. It is a country in the sun, and that's where Mr. Cederén wants to go. He does not want to live in Uppsala-Näs. He also plays golf. He came in first in the most recent tournament at Edenhof."

"Get to the point," Ottosson said.

"I think he ran his family over with his car and fled. He wanted to play golf in the Caribbean."

"I'm happy to go there and check it out," Wende said.

Ottosson turned and looked at him as if he were seeing him for the first time.

"Two people have died and all the two of you can do is talk shit," Haver said, convinced that Riis was simply counting the three days until he went on vacation. He was more than happy to turn a summer murder over to his colleagues.

"In my opinion," Riis went on, "the Cederéns are well-to-do, stable, well-adapted, and social. Neither of them has had any run-ins with the law before. Nothing that we have found in the house so far indicates anything unusual. There was tasteful art on the walls—or what I believe to be fine;

it didn't actually depict anything. There were thick carpets, a lot of glass, and fine magazines. As it should be, in other words."

"The classic question: Was there an answering machine?"

Ottosson leaned forward to look squarely at Riis, who was leaning back in his chair.

"No messages," Riis said.

"A calendar? Address book?"

"We haven't found one yet. He must have it."

"What do we know about his work?"

Ottosson was trying to regain control after Riis's harangues.

"There was something," said Riis, ignoring the change of topic. "There were no flowers, not a single potted plant. Can you believe it?"

"Because of allergies, perhaps?"

"Who is allergic to plants?"

An unfamiliar silence broke out, as if everyone were trying to imagine a home without plants.

What a group, Norrman thought. Here we are sweating away, with Ottosson sitting there like Jesus with his beard and mild face. Who is Judas? Who is Peter? Who is Thomas?

"There are thirteen of us at this table," he said, breaking the silence.

They all looked around.

"His work," Ottosson repeated.

"MedForsk is a so-called star performer engaged in very advanced re-search. Everyone that we have talked to is understandably in shock, but behind the feeling of unreality and anxiety, there was a strong sense of self-confidence, wouldn't you say, Ola?"

Haver nodded.

"Yes, the place breathed success. Like a soccer team that has won enough times to feel basically invincible. Like a unified team headed into the finals, convinced they were going to win. Like an assumption."

"Just like us," Riis said. "A winning team."

"They're about to go public. What does that mean? Money? There might be a lot at stake. I'm bad at that kind of thing," Sammy said.

"'This happened at an unfortunate time'—one of them let that slip," Haver said.

"Can there be a connection to the company, or is this a family drama, pure and simple?"

Ottosson's question was left hanging.

"Did Josefin Cederén have any connection to the company?"

"There's certainly a lot of questions," said Wende, who had come out of his shell. Earlier he had tended to sit quietly during meetings and to speak only when answering a direct question. Ottosson wanted to hear new voices but was at the same time slightly irritated at Wende's new role. I just miss Ann's voice, he thought, that's all.

"We'll have to work through them one by one, or rather, at the same time," Sammy said. "I think we have a pretty clear idea of our assigned tasks. It's Wednesday today. Molin stays on MedForsk and works his way through Cederén's computer and paper files. Fredriksson is on Vreta. Within a day we should know everything about the Cederén family's finances and private relationships; we should have mapped out all of Sven-Erik Cederén's movements today and at the very least have located the car."

The meeting ended. Ottosson stayed behind, in his seat, studying the forensic team's photographs, turning them over one by one. He muttered something inaudibly. "Can you run over your own child?" he asked himself. The girl would have been starting school in the fall.

When he reached the picture of the edge of the road, with the woman's hand outstretched and the lines that her fingers had etched into the gravel, he imagined her struggle. How she had dragged herself.

Ottosson felt a headache coming on. He felt heavy, not just in his head, but in his entire body. That morning he had felt happy about the beautiful weather, the approaching summer, and the early morning meeting scheduled with Sammy and Lindell. He had just been given the green light to raise their salaries.

✦

Four

A gull was sitting at the very end of the dock. It appeared to be using the water as a mirror, admiring its whiteness, the faint curve of its beak and the sharp gleam of its eye. Its head turned slightly, as if it heard Edvard's steps or as if it just wanted another angle on its reflection.

Pride, Edvard thought, that is what it sees. He sat down on the bent trunk of the pine tree. The light-brown bark often offered him a little extra warmth, but today he didn't need it. It was almost twenty-five degrees. Absently Edvard rubbed his knee. The fall from the ladder had resulted in a nasty abrasion, which smarted.

The gull seemed unaffected by his presence. Perhaps it recognized him. You are sitting in my spot, he thought, but that's all right. Go ahead, look at your reflection, dream a little. There was a sense of thoughtfulness about the bird that appealed to him. Maybe he's pleased with the day, digesting a fish, savoring the sun. Or else it's the direct opposite: He is melancholy, he has lost something. Perhaps he dropped that fish.

Edvard didn't want to interrupt, but he was also slightly irritated that the gull was lingering so long on the dock. He coughed discreetly but this didn't help. The gull stayed put.

Edvard waited. Viola, the old woman who owned the house that he lived in, had put dinner on the table and they were about to eat. He wanted to stand at the end of the dock for a while first.

Suddenly the bird took off, flying out over the bay; some droppings splashed into the mat green water below. Edvard immediately stood up and walked out on the dock. For a moment he had the impulse to jump in but decided to wait until evening. It would be the first swim of the season.

The temperature of the water here around Gräsö Island in northern Uppland had long hovered around fifteen degrees, but now he thought it had risen to seventeen, perhaps even eighteen.

Squawking, the gull was now barely visible as a smudge across the water.

It was moving toward the mouth of the bay and the open sea. Edvard wished for the same—to be able to lift off.

The dinghy tugged sleepily on its line when a faint breeze blew in. It was not a strong burst, more like a puff or a breath. Perhaps it was the flapping of the gull's wings carrying across the water.

Edvard Risberg stood as far out as he could, his toes hanging off the edge of the dock, like a diver. He stretched his arms up toward the blue sky, stretched all his limbs, and looked out. The sounds of human activity could be heard from the other side of the bay. Probably a vacationer setting things in order. He lowered his arms and took a deep breath.

Standing on the dock gave him a deep sense of satisfaction. It was his, erected on the ice at the end of February, now sunk into the mud. Inside the dock was granite, part smooth, rounded stones collected on the shore, part sharp pointed pieces shattered by the ice.

It resisted the wind and the sea and kept the nor'easter in check. Victor's two boats and the dinghy rested peacefully inside its protective arm. Tons of stone. Timber. It held steady, built by Victor and Edvard and Edvard's two teenage sons, Jens and Jerker.

Victor had built many docks and stone-filled cribs in his day, but this was likely his last. He had risen to the challenge as never before, seemingly indefatigable.

The process had taken a full week, and the boys had been there the whole time, sanding boards, nailing them down, and screwing in bolts. They had carried stone, and finally at the very front of the dock facing the sea, they had attached a brass plate, engraved with the date and their four names.

One afternoon they had put on their hockey skates and taken off across the gray ice, skating almost all the way to the mouth of the bay. Edvard had watched after them, happy and proud, but also nervous about the cracks and fragile edges of the ice. They had returned, their cheeks blazing. Edvard had made a fire and grilled hot dogs on the beach. Viola had come down with coffee and hot juice for the boys, just as at the Studenternas stadium when the home team Sirius was playing in town.

Jens had reminded Edvard about the bandy games, about the times when they had packed grandfather Albert into the car and headed into town. His voice had been like it was before. For the first time in over two years, the boy had spoken unreservedly with Edvard. He had been eager but interrupted himself when he saw his big brother's face. Jerker had not said anything, just stared out over the ice.

The boy had given his father a quick glance and stopped. Edvard went over to his older boy, stood very close to him. Victor had kept talking and was putting more wood on the fire, but even he fell silent at the sight of the two of them. Edvard wanted to say something, break two years of isolation. He saw the defiance but also the repressed longing in his son's pained expression. He knew that he had to take the first step, so he put his arm around the boy.

They stood like this, completely still, silent. Edvard knew that words could wreck everything and struggled not to break into tears. There had been enough tears. He just wanted to hold his son. If everything was going to hell, at least they had this moment.

"You've grown," he said and let go.

They ate several hot dogs. Viola, feeling cold as usual, complained about the wind and stepped closer to the fire.

"Rubber boots are cold," Jens said. Viola chuckled and muttered something. Victor had pulled over a large pine stump that he threw onto the blaze. Dusk was sneaking up on them and the temperature fell as it grew darker. They all drew closer to the warmth.

"We'll probably see the stars tonight," Jens said, and Jerker flinched as if he had been hit. It made him think of Edvard's stargazing in Ramnäs, and he did not want to recall that time for anything in the world. As a first measure after Edvard moved—or rather fled—Marita demolished the old outbuilding that had functioned as the observatory. Jerker hated clear starry evenings and nights as much as Marita had.

Edvard suggested that they play cards instead, so they did. They had spent the whole week together and had built a dock that was the sturdiest on the entire island, at least according to Victor. One week, and then the boys had come out some weekends during the winter and spring. Slowly but surely they rebuilt their relationship and Edvard could experience some of the old joy with his sons.

This weekend they were headed back to Gräsö Island. Edvard knew that they took the bus out to the island in part just to be nice. Under

Jerker's grumpy exterior and Jens's sometimes nervous prattle, there was a touching impulse to please. It was Edvard's life force.

After Ann left him, he had sunk deep, convinced he would have to live alone, aided only by Viola's care and his work, which allowed him to sleep heavily at night. But now he had a brighter outlook on life and his own existence. It was as if he had regained his place in the landscape.

He had also resumed his contact with a couple of his old friends from the time he was a farm laborer, especially his associates from the union. Fredrik Stark, who was the same age as Edvard, politically active, and a landscape gardener, had been out to visit on several occasions. He had stayed a few days, working on his computer and reading several long extracts aloud when Edvard came home. He claimed that he was writing a novel, and Edvard was alternately irritated at and envious of Stark's confidence.

He had called Ann in a burst of optimism and a sense of hope that she might still be interested. He did not know if they could resume their relationship or if they could live together, but the one thing he had learned during those dark winter nights was that he did not want to live alone forever.

Would she call him back? And if not, would he try again?

✦

Five

The man sitting across from her was scratching his head. He had done this almost incessantly since she had entered his kitchen.

An old American box clock was ticking on the wall. Lindell's parents had one just like it. In fact, there was a great deal about Holger Johansson's kitchen that reminded her of her childhood home in Ödeshög. The smell, the fifties décor, the pattern on the waxed tablecloth, the old cookie tin on the counter, and the embroidered tray cloth.

They had a great deal on common, but one thing set them apart: death. Holger's kitchen would never be the same. From this point on, his furniture and household items, the vases, the prints on the walls, and all of the small things that a person collects over the course of a life would lose more and more meaning. They would eventually gain a layer of dust and grease, sadness and old age.

The objects would lack significance; he would hardly notice them. He had aged fifteen years in one day. Emptiness and sadness had suffocated this man, this father, withering away in front of Lindell's eyes.

"She was my only child," he said.

Lindell gripped her pen hard and wished she had brought someone with her. She knew from experience that she was more emotional, more easily affected by another's grief if she was alone. Her mind simply worked less well.

"Did Josefin and Sven-Erik have a happy marriage?"

"I think so," he whispered.

He stared out the kitchen window.

"No fights?"

"Who doesn't fight?"

"Were you close?"

He nodded. His hand fumbled helplessly over the wax tablecloth.

"What do you think of Sven-Erik?"

"He . . . worked a lot. Josefin sometimes complained. Since he got that new job he was gone even more. Went here and there."

"Business travel, you mean."

Another nod.

"He has disappeared, you know. Where do you think he could be?"

He did not respond.

"You can't think of anywhere in particular?"

"That would be Spain. He always traveled there."

"Where in Spain?"

"I don't know. He just said Spain."

Lindell was quiet for a moment. Holger Johansson's neighbor could be seen in the garden. It was a woman who was in the house when Lindell arrived. She sensed that they were not simply neighbors and was glad that the man would not be completely alone.

The woman was busying herself with the summer flowers and looked up at the house from time to time.

"Can you understand that Emily is dead?"

He stared at Lindell with a bewildered gaze and she knew what his next sentence would be.

"A six-year-old. What had she done? If only it had been me in her place. Thank god Inger isn't alive," he said, and Lindell knew he meant his wife. He fell silent and looked back out the window.

"Lately something was up. They would come up here, not every day, but often. She would take the stroller. She liked to walk. Then they started to bike. Sometimes they came by every morning. Vera and I have a cup of coffee every day at half past ten."

"Did something change recently?"

"That was my impression. Jossan—Josefin—seemed more distracted, I guess you can say. As if something was weighing on her. I asked her once. She just smiled and said that everything was fine, but a father sees . . ."

Holger Johansson huddled over the table. It was as if Vera sensed it because at that moment the front door opened. Without even looking at Lindell, Vera walked up to the man and laid her arm around him. Lindell fixed her gaze on Vera's hand resting on his shoulder. She leaned her forehead against his graying head. Her hand was covered in liver spots, and the weeds that she had pulled at so frenetically had left green streaks and stains. Lindell stared at her hand and her thoughts raced between her home in Ödeshög and the little girl in the ditch. There was also Edvard and his old Viola in the house on Gräsö Island.

She got up very slowly and laid her hand on the woman's shoulder. Vera looked up, expressionless. When Lindell turned around a last time, she had straightened her back. She was staring out of the window. Lindell followed her gaze. The mock orange shrub in the garden was blooming.

The man scratched his head and Lindell caught sight of abrasions through the thin, back-combed hair.

Lindell drove out of the yard and almost ran into one of the fence posts. After fifty meters she braked and came to a halt. Unable to rid herself of the image on her retina, she whimpered silently as she thought of the girl's mangled body. Inside she was in turmoil. A murdered child—she regarded this as a murder—was worse than anything else. She had seen a child's corpse only once before. At that point she had been a police trainee, around twenty years old. It was fifteen years ago. That time it was a confused mother who had strangled her baby in a crib. Terrible enough, but this was worse. Was it the summer, the valley idyll, the girl's delicate limbs sticking out from her dress, and the fact that she had been picking flowers?

Lindell rolled down the window. She had not eaten anything since her morning coffee and felt miserable. It was six o'clock but still a beautiful day. She took some deep breaths and her nausea receded somewhat.

She already hated Sven-Erik Cederén. Where was he? She looked around as if he were to be found somewhere nearby. Was he holed up somewhere? Would he be watching the news tonight?

Why kill his wife and child? There was only one motive and it was jealousy.

"I'm going to find you, wherever you are," she said, her teeth clenched, putting the car in gear and starting off down the gravel road.

Then it struck her that he might not be the guilty one after all. Why assume this? she thought. It only blocks the lines of deductive reasoning. He might also be dead. She drove slowly, crawling along the narrow road. Perhaps he had been a witness to the accident, had found his wife and child along the side of the road, and had become so distraught that he left.

It sounded unlikely, but nothing could be assumed. Too many mistakes had been made as a result of preconceptions.

She knew that the meeting was already under way but decided to linger a while longer in Uppsala-Näs. It was unusual for her to be absent. She didn't like to miss any information and was committed to being a team player, but right now the meeting room seemed like an oppressive bunker, with the same tired faces saying the same things.

She wanted to think, to be left in peace. She did her best thinking at Café Savoy, because even though she wanted to be alone she also wanted to have people around her. She liked to sit there drinking her coffee, maybe reading the paper, but above all observing the clientele. People were her stock-in-trade, to study and seek to understand. At the café her brain rested but was also working at full capacity. She could recall several times at the café when she had identified connections and had had crucial insights into investigations, with the conversations of the mothers, the loud screeches of the children, the discussions of the tradesmen, and the rustling of newspapers as background.

Lindell drove in the direction of Villa Cederén. She had a feeling that

Fredriksson was still there. Maybe also Berglund. That was all right. Both of these gentlemen would let her walk around as she wished.

A small group of curious onlookers had gathered on the road outside the house. They tried to look casual, as if it were their habit to congregate there, but their hungry gazes betrayed them. Maybe I'm being unfair, Lindell thought. They might be good friends of Josefin and Emily, and their gathering here a reaction to the shock.

She swung into the driveway, got out, and spotted something that she had not noticed on her quick visit earlier in the day. Right next to the flagpole, almost hidden behind the lilac bushes, was a doghouse. A bowl with dried food remnants was to one side of it. Lindell crouched down to peek inside. She saw a blanket and some chew toys.

No one had mentioned a dog. She remained standing outside the kennel. The voices of the neighbors on the road could be heard, and Lindell decided to get to the bottom of this immediately.

A waft of scents of the early summer struck her as she walked out onto the road. She steered her course toward a man who was standing with a packet of mail in his hand.

"My name is Lindell. I'm with the Uppsala police."

The man shook her hand. "A terrible thing."

"Are you a neighbor?"

The man nodded, dropping a newspaper and a couple of letters at the same time. Embarrassed, he quickly picked these up, glancing at Lindell.

"Do you know if they have a dog?"

"Yes, a pointer. Isabella."

"He takes it along sometimes," a woman interrupted.

The man took a step closer to Lindell, as if to shield her from the woman, and told her eagerly about the dog and the Cederén family's routines.

It turned out that the dog was difficult. Josefin Cederén had never taken to it and it was a source of annoyance for the neighborhood. Outside, alone in its house, it would howl mournfully and long. Inside, the pointer chewed everything—rugs, curtains, and flowers. As a result, Sven-Erik Cederén often brought it to work. He was the only one who appeared to be able to handle the animal.

I should take the time to stay and listen, she thought, but her urgent need to be alone drove her to politely deflect the questions of the curious neighbors.

She returned to the yard. Fredriksson's car was parked in front of the main entrance. He had returned and was now starting to resume his old form. After a heavy fall and the winter's murder hunt, he had taken sick leave. No one believed that Fredriksson would return to the unit, but he reappeared in time for a complicated gang rape. Even Ottosson had looked astonished.

Fredriksson's presence at the morning meeting had set off an unusual silence in the room, as if a dead man had returned. Ottosson had coughed and stood up. A collective smile spread among the assembled officers. Sammy had pulled out Fredriksson's old chair.

Now he was reviewing a pile of papers in the living room. He looked up quickly and with an expression akin to relief. Perhaps he thought it was Riis who was coming back.

"How is it going?"

"There's plenty of papers."

"What are they?"

"Old documents, the kind one ends up accumulating."

Fredriksson leaned back in the sofa and rubbed his eyes. "I think I'll have to get a pair of reading glasses."

Lindell sat down across from him.

"We'll have to put out a search for Isabella," she said, and walked once around the room.

"Who is that?"

"The dog."

Fredriksson made an effort to return his attention to the papers, but then sank back on the couch.

"If you look around, what impression do you get of the Cederén family?"

"Wealth," she said simply.

"Yes, wealth, but something else too. It's messy and not a little dirty. Behind all the artistic glass pieces, there is a ton of dust, there's dirt under the rugs, the kitchen is sticky, and the bathtub is grimy."

"So?" Lindell said.

"A house of almost two hundred square meters—neglected. We know that Josefin was a stay-at-home mom. She had been home since the girl was born. Whatever she was doing all day, it wasn't cleaning."

"What does *that* mean?"

"I don't know. People are different. I wouldn't have been able to stand this mess for a single day."

Lindell was quiet. His observation gave her no ideas.

"I think she was unhappy," Fredriksson said. "She allowed one of the finest houses in Uppsala-Näs to go to the dogs."

"She had other priorities," Lindell said tartly.

She didn't like Fredriksson speaking ill of the dead. Tossed in the ditch at the side of the road, on her way to her mother's grave with her daughter, though separated from her by several meters at the moment of death. Josefin Cederén had not even had the chance to give her daughter a final hug. An untidy house, yes, but now she was dead.

"I don't think she was happy here," Fredriksson resumed. "That tells us something."

"But it may not have anything to do with her death," Lindell objected.

"That's true, but it's a question mark."

"There are many question marks in people's lives," Lindell said. "We happened to be dropped into this."

She got up and walked out to the kitchen. Fredriksson's observations were correct: The kitchen was sticky. There was a large open space with a freestanding island, the massive beech top of which was covered with kitchen utensils, a couple of plates with dried yogurt on them, an open tub of margarine, and bread crumbs. She must have been planning to clear this away after visiting the grave, Lindell thought, but the fact was, the kitchen verged on disgusting.

Who would clean now? Her father?

Lindell walked upstairs. The girl's room was full of stuffed animals. The double bed in the master bedroom was unmade. A white pajama top had been thrown on the floor. A couple of slippers peeked out from under the bed.

She walked over to one of the bedside tables and picked up a book. An American novel. On the other table there was a folder full of notes that Lindell assumed had to do with MedForsk. She flipped through the pages. Tables of explanatory text—some in English, some in Spanish. Occasionally in the margin there were hasty notes, scribbled in pencil in a difficult-to-read hand—a question here and there, a couple of exclamation points.

Everything had to be examined, page by page, in the hopes that there would be something that would explain why he had slain his family. Or was he lying dead somewhere too? Was there a third party that had slaughtered the entire family?

And in that case, where was he? Lindell thought of the dog. A pointer. Was that a spotted kind?

She stood there with the folder in her hands. The front door opened, and she assumed that it was the technicians returning after a quick meal.

There were two other rooms on the second floor. A guest room with Spartan furnishings; a sewing room with a sewing machine, a dressmaker's dummy, and a table draped in black cloth. Lindell pulled out the uppermost drawer in a dresser that looked out of place with its baroque style, marble top, and curved legs, and carefully looked through the bits of fabric. The next drawer was filled with paper—sketches, from what Lindell could tell. At the back of the drawer, under some patterns, there was a blue book with a linen cover. Lindell opened the book to the first page and immediately realized that she had found something that would help her understand Josefin Cederén, because it was her book. She deduced this both from the fact that it was hidden in her room and also from the handwriting.

It was a diary beginning at the end of May 1998. The first entry read: "After a year of uncertainty I now know everything. I can't say that I am surprised, but it hurts so much. Perhaps I am the one to blame."

The handwriting was clear and easy to read. Lindell turned the page. A person's innermost thoughts, recorded over a period of two years. The last entry was dated the fourth of June.

There was sadness in the blue book. Josefin wrote in it instead of cleaning.

Lindell kept searching the drawers for other notebooks but didn't find anything else. Either this was the only one or Josefin had stored her earlier diaries somewhere else.

She brought the journal with her and went downstairs.

"I've got some reading to do tonight," she said and showed her find to Fredriksson, who was still sitting at the table.

He looked up. "I wish that I could find some personal notes, but these are simply documents from his work. I need a medical researcher to translate."

Allan Fredriksson looked fresh and alert despite his recent illness.

"I'm glad you're back," Lindell said.

There was a time when he had not met her gaze. Now he looked at her with a smile and nodded.

One of the technicians came out of the kitchen. Lindell had taken a second look at him earlier. He was in his thirties and had that appealing blend of strength and softness that Lindell liked. "He's married. *Happily* married," Sammy Nilsson had said when he noticed her look.

"We're sorting through the trash and the only item of note is the remains of an airplane ticket. All of the rest is an ordinary collection of refuse. Would you like to see the ticket?"

They went out into the kitchen. Lindell could not help sniffing the scent of his aftershave or whatever it was.

He held up a piece of paper with a tweezer.

"I think it's the back of an airplane ticket," he said. "There's a handwritten note that says eight twenty-five. Other than that there is only the name of the company. British Airways."

Lindell looked at it without expression.

"Keep it," she said and left the kitchen.

"Think I can take one?"

There was a bowl of candy in the living room. Lindell was extremely hungry, and the sight of the candy made her mouth water.

"Maybe they're laced with poison," Fredriksson said.

Lindell twisted off the wrapper of a Marianne. Normally she didn't eat candy, but right now the treats were irresistible. She took one and then another.

Fredriksson looked up. "You should eat some food instead."

"I'm hungry, but not at the same time. Candy is exactly what I needed."

"I don't think people need to eat more than bananas," Fredriksson said.

"Bananer." Lindell chuckled.

She held the journal in her hand. She knew that there were threads she could start unraveling. What had pushed Josefin to start to write? The inner pressure had become too great and she had been forced to write down her anxiety and despair. What had she sensed and then become convinced of? She would find out tonight.

As Lindell left the house, she bumped into Berglund and Haver. They were going to assist Fredriksson.

"At least until ten o'clock," Haver said.

"Go home to your girls instead," Lindell said.

He had become the father of a little girl in May. But Haver simply smiled. They briefly discussed the outcome of the morning meeting.

Lindell called Ottosson and let him know that she would not be coming by. She was going to read the journal.

The neighbors were gone, the road empty. A couple of ducks flew in a wide arc over the house, and there was a scent of summer.

But something didn't add up. Lindell thought of Josefin's well-groomed nails, painted and polished. She seemed attractive and clean, even in death. The house stood in stark contrast to that impression, more than a little dirty and unkempt, almost disgusting. She had to have been a woman who placed a great deal of weight on appearance; her closet and shelves were filled with clothes, beautiful and most likely expensive. She sewed a great deal, taking her inspiration from fashion magazines, and her makeup table was covered with all kinds of jars and products.

Why didn't she keep the house clean? The Cederéns would never have been able to invite people over. What was their social life like? Lindell had an impulse to pay a visit to Josefin's father again but decided to wait until the next day.

Her nausea had increased on the trip back to town and she stopped at a McDonald's and had a hamburger.

She managed to get home and into the bathroom right before it came over her again. She crouched over the toilet and cursed herself for not taking care of herself. She drank a little water from the tap, rinsed her mouth, and rested her brow against the cool porcelain. What a day. Yesterday all routine office work and a meeting about the new organizational structure. Today a decimated family.

Holger Johansson's lacerated scalp appeared in her mind. Did he have eczema or had he scratched it during the day?

She threw the journal on the floor in the entryway. She stepped over it and walked into the kitchen. The light on the answering machine was blinking, so she pressed the play button. The first message was from Ödeshög. Ann had started to realize that her parents were no longer in the prime of life and that she could get a phone call about sickness, or even death, at any time. But this time it was only the usual words from her mother—"How are you? Everything is fine here"—and then some details about which flowers were blooming in the garden.

The other message brought her to her knees. Edvard's voice sounded as if it came from another age, another world. She knew it so well and yet it sounded so foreign. "Oh, god," she breathed, and sank onto the chair.

He sounded happy, and this made her heart beat faster. She stared vacantly as he talked of Gräsö, passed along greetings from Viola, and talked about work. At the end of the message, his voice grew lower, his tone more hesitant, as if he was unsure of how to sign off. There was a quick good-bye and then it ended.

Give up, she thought. Leave me in peace. She replayed the tape and listened to it again. His voice. She could imagine him standing in front of the window overlooking the bay, a sunny Roslagen landscape. Or else he was sitting in the wicker chair.

He had talked about his work, mostly about his work. Repairing a barn. Where did all this work come from? He built things, spending his days breaking and bending, lifting and heaving, cutting and fitting, living with others, laughing and having cups of coffee, leaning up against a red-painted wall. His hands. Lacerated, scarred, and sometimes so rough that they made a sandpapery noise when he rubbed them against her back, sometimes with fingertips worn so smooth that you wouldn't have been able to get a good set of prints.

She could hear his heavy steps on the stairs. His exchanges with Viola. She could feel his breath.

Ann pulled over the telephone and selected number one on speed dial. Ödeshög. Mom and Dad.

"Yes, I'm fine. There's a lot of work right now."

She did not want to talk about the Cederén case. Her mother chattered on.

"Yes, maybe, but there's just a lot going on right now."

The closest neighbors, Nisse and Ingegerd, had had a grandchild. A boy. Four kilos. As her mother talked on, Ann opened the refrigerator and peered inside.

"In July and half of August," she said and took out the margarine and caviar spread. "Of course. I'll come then. I promise."

No bread in the house.

"I miss you too. Give my love to Dad."

At the very back of the cupboard there was half a packet of hardtack. "Fiber," she muttered and made herself four pieces spread with caviar, picked up the milk, and went out into the living room, returning to the entryway to pick up the journal.

Now she was adequately supplied. Her belly screamed for food and her head ached. She took a couple of bites, poured the milk—it was Edvard who had taught her to drink milk—and leaned back in the armchair.

The blue journal was resting on the table. She was curious but still felt some resistance. Josefin's journal had not been written for public consumption. Now her notes would be pored over. Her clothes, photos, medications, and trash would be systematically sorted, examined, and evaluated.

Ann crunched on the crackers, looked around the room, and decided she should clean more often.

She herself didn't have any diaries. Not even from her teen years. The only piece of writing she had saved that could be considered private was a letter. It was from Edvard, written in January. At the end of the Christmas holidays, she had left the island and also him. She had been too much of a coward to tell it to his face, but the way she disappeared had clearly indicated that it was for good.

A couple of weeks later, he had sent her a letter. Hands trembling, Ann had read it. She had not imagined that Edvard could write so passionately. It was as if all of the words that he gathered in his self-imposed isolation had welled forth and spread across the pages in front of her. Even the fact that he owned stationery was astonishing. But he must have borrowed it from Viola.

He wrote that he loved her, but that it was too complicated to live so far apart. Now he did not want to see her anymore—as if she had not been the one who had left. He was going to focus on his work and his two sons. This was certainly news to her. Jens and Jerker had hardly been out to the island during the past two years, and contact with their father had been sporadic at best.

She couldn't eat the last piece of bread, but licked some of the roe topping. Now for the journal.

She read it for half an hour before she put it down. There were twenty-five pages to go, but she already had a possible motive for Josefin's death. Why Emily had been killed was still unclear.

Josefin had written that the only thing she was sure of was that Sven-Erik loved his daughter above all else.

Thoughts of Edvard kept returning for the rest of the evening. For long periods of time, things had been wonderful. They had made love with an intensity far beyond what she had experienced before.

He had taught her a great deal. That serious gaze. Thoughts roamed like lost dogs through her landscape of thieves, murderers, and other violent perpetrators. He had made her a better police officer. Perhaps it was his language that most fascinated her, the words borne by a life so close to the earth and green, growing things. He gave name to that which she many times did not see or reflect on. He reawakened her own background and language in her. The dialects were different, but she could hear her own and her parents' language in his.

They had met once—her parents and Edvard—and after their initial nervousness, a certain feeling of kinship had emerged. Her father had taken Edvard out onto the plains and driven with him down the narrow lanes. God only knew what they talked of, but when they returned, it was as if they were old friends.

They had lingered by the car, looking out over the land. She and her mother had stood in the window, watching them.

In the car on the way home, Edvard had said that her father carried a rift within him, and Ann had wondered what he meant. Edvard had been quiet for a long time—she had learned to wait out his silences—but shortly before Södertälje he had embarked on a rambling account of life on the plains of Östergötland and all the villages and settlements that he and Ann's father had driven through. Her father had pointed out the long-shuttered shops where he had delivered pork and beer for twenty-five years. By now most of them had been turned into private residences but were still easily identifiable by their storefront entrances and large windows. Occasionally a sign—Arne's groceries—could still be made out.

"You were spies, in other words," Ann inserted.

"Exactly. We spied and your father told stories. It was there, in his stories, that the rift was."

"No one cares about his old delivery routes. Do you know I often accompanied him in the summer?"

"You told me that the first time we met . . . no, the second, don't you remember? When we walked down that old road. You told me how he used to sing in the car. That's why I fell in love with you."

Then he fell silent. Was it the memory of that old road, of his earlier life, that overcame him? She assumed so, and they did not speak until they reached the roundabout at the southern entrance to Uppsala. The visit to Ödeshög and the car ride back home became one of her most beautiful memories of their time together.

Nothing more was said of the rift, but she had a feeling she knew what he meant. That was Edvard. He read the landscape and people like nobody else.

Her father's delight in seeing his old delivery locations, the obligatory honk as he drove up to the entrance or loading dock, the faces of the country grocers in the doorway, the talking, the jokes, the clinking of the fully loaded beer crates and the clatter of the empty ones—everything that gave the trips meaning was relived during those Sunday hours.

Edvard had observed all this, but also something more. A rift. How her father walked around in his old memories. Edvard understood these things. She missed this, missed his intensity, his gaze.

She got up out of the armchair. Should she pour herself a glass of red wine? She smiled to herself and decided instead to have more milk.

The blue journal was still open on the table and she would read more. About the rifts in Josefin's life.

✦

Six

"Day two," Ann Lindell wrote in her notepad. Then nothing else for a long while. And then the number one.

"Can you live with this, Sven-Erik Cederén?" she said out loud and wrote his name on the page.

Security had been increased in the nation's airports and harbors. A national alarm had gone out yesterday morning, but had not yielded anything. Everyone knew how easy it was to leave the country. Perhaps he had gone to Kapellskär, taken the boat to Finland?

"Lover" was the next word. She stared at it. "Love." After reading Josefin's diary, Lindell knew that there was another woman in her husband's life. Who she was and where she was, it didn't say. Either Josefin herself did not know or else she did not want to write down her name. She hated the woman, that much was clear, and perhaps she did not want to give her a name, a shape.

She was only mentioned in passing. Josefin and Sven-Erik's relationship had circled around this woman, although he did not know that she knew. Or did he? Had they quarreled about her? Lindell did not think so. There was nothing in the journal about this. She was simply present, a boulder rolled through the dirty, elegant house in Uppsala-Näs, carried up the stairs, the stone that Josefin stumbled over. She compared herself to the other woman, scrutinizing her husband and his reactions.

Josefin had tortured herself over it. The knowledge that there was another had worn her down. At the same time, she had been pregnant. The journal said as much and the autopsy confirmed it. Sammy Nilsson had come back with the report that stated that Josefin had been in her second month.

Was it another man's child? The diary did not say, but the whole text led to the same conclusion: that Sven-Erik was the father. Lindell remembered one of the sentences quite clearly: "How could he go from her to me?" Lindell wondered how she could receive her husband in bed, make love to him knowing full well that he had a mistress, but sensed that it had been a desperate attempt to win him back. Perhaps a child would save the marriage?

Lindell took out the list of MedForsk employees. Nine names in all, of which three were women. All in their thirties. The whole workforce was young. No one over fifty, most of them between thirty and forty.

Lindell decided to question the women. The preliminary work that had been done yesterday had yielded nothing out of the ordinary: "He seemed fine" and "I didn't notice anything unusual." Lindell noted that Wendell had conducted the interviews and had also had time to type up the reports. There were photographs of all of the employees. That was impressive. He must have worked into the night.

She wrote down the women's names as she studied their pictures. All three were attractive. Two blondes and one with henna-colored hair. Weren't most affairs job-related? Lindell picked one of the blondes.

MedForsk was located on the outskirts of town, in an area where Lindell had almost never had reason to go. Even the street name was new to her. Here they were, the start-ups in IT and medical research. All housed in nondescript buildings, like a parade of boxes in yellow brick. These were supposed to be the city's future, with company names and logos discreetly placed on the side and above the entrance. There was no way to guess what lay inside.

Lindell cheered up when she saw a company name for a business that she could place: *Lasse's Auto—Everything for Your Car.* She wished that was where she was headed. A car lift and walls hung with tools, the sound of an angle grinder and the sparks from a blowtorch—this was familiar to her.

Instead she found herself in foreign territory. The reception area of MedForsk seemed deserted. Behind the unmanned reception desk, there were three doors—all of which were locked—and a small seating area. That was all. Not a sound, no signs of human activity, and Lindell thought perhaps the entire workforce had decided to stay at home.

A woman suddenly turned up from behind a door, quickly closed it, and then turned her eyes inquiringly at Lindell.

"Ann Lindell, police, Crimes division," Lindell said, and held out her hand.

She recognized the woman from one of the snapshots. She was the one with henna-colored hair. Just like the surroundings, the woman's hand was chilly. Her eyes revealed nothing, partially concealed behind a pair of glasses.

"Yes?" she said in a somewhat baffled tone, as if she were at a loss to understand what the police were doing at MedForsk.

"I'm investigating the accident that occurred yesterday."

"I see."

"And Sven-Erik Cederén's disappearance."

"I've already been questioned."

The henna-haired woman pulled her slender body together and looked even more inaccessible. The blue dress with the narrow silver belt brought out something snakelike in her persona. Her arms were folded under her small breasts.

"I know. We're gathering additional information."

"But you've already been out here. A truckload of police officers showed up here this morning."

"We're trying to get a better picture of the company."

The woman walked around the reception counter and picked up a thin notebook with hard covers. The pencil that was attached to the cover bore visible chew marks.

"We've divvied up the work, and the three women at MedForsk fell to me."

"Fell to you," the woman repeated.

"I could start with you, if that's all right."

"I'm actually somewhat occupied right now and I'm also supposed to watch the desk . . . but we can go to the kitchen."

The woman made toward the nearest door, punched in a code, and held the door open for Lindell.

The kitchen, which was strikingly relaxed in its furnishings, was located in the center of the building. On their way there, Lindell saw some offices as well as a room behind a glass door that she took to be a laboratory.

Lindell took out her notebook. The woman across from her sat at the edge of her seat, her legs pressed tightly together, staring at Lindell.

Her name was Sofi Rönn and she was thirty-five years old. Lindell already knew this, but she let Sofi talk a little about herself. She had been employed for five years. She was, in other words, one of the veterans. Her tasks were administrative in nature and had nothing to do with the research.

"How would you describe Sven-Erik Cederén?"

Rönn sat quietly for a moment. "He is a skilled and driven researcher," she said finally.

"Driven in what way?"

"He works night and day," Rönn said and gave Lindell a look as if anything else was nonsense. "He arrives early and leaves late. He travels a lot, going to conferences, and he has a wide circle of contacts."

"Is he well liked? I know it's a bit silly to put it that way, and I understand that you wouldn't want to speak ill of a coworker."

"He's liked. We all like him."

For the first time, something else broke through her chilliness. Rönn's shoulders sank somewhat and her gaze wandered from Lindell's face to a point in the middle of the room.

"Did you know Josefin Cederén?"

"Yes, she came by occasionally, but that was all. We didn't interact much."

"Did you interact with Sven-Erik?"

"What do you mean?"

She glanced swiftly at Lindell.

"In private, I mean."

"We met at events through work, nothing more. Is that what you mean?"

"I don't mean anything in particular, just if you ever met with Sven-Erik and if you were a part of his life, so to speak."

Silence. It slowly dawned on Sofi Rönn what Lindell was after with her questions, and she stared back at her coldly.

"Sven-Erik and I have nothing to do with each other in private," she said curtly.

"I'm trying to gather some information about him beyond his professional life. Work we can map with relative ease, but it's harder to uncover someone's personal life. A coworker often becomes a good friend. One confides in good friends. Has Sven-Erik said anything that would explain his disappearance?"

Rönn shook her head.

"It doesn't look good," Lindell said. "His wife and six-year-old daughter Emily—I'm sure you've met her—are the victims of a heinous hit-and-run, and the husband vanishes without a trace. It doesn't look good."

She let the words sink in for a couple of seconds before she went on. "Some people think he killed his own family. What do you think?"

"Never," said Rönn quickly and without hesitation.

She removed her glasses but kept them in her hand.

"Never," she repeated. "He would never have done such a thing. Not to his own child. Emily was a wonderful little girl."

Her icy demeanor was slowly melting. Lindell didn't speak, letting her gather her thoughts. Rönn wiped her cheek.

"He loves Emily. He's always talking about her."

"Does he love his wife?"

"Why wouldn't he love her?"

Lindell gazed back at Rönn. A couple of people walked past the closed door to the kitchen and laughter echoed down the corridor.

"Lately he seemed a bit out of it, you could say."

"Do you think it was anything to do with his marriage? Did he say anything specific?"

Rönn shook her head, but it was clear that something was weighing on her mind. Her initial standoffishness had vanished. She clearly wanted to talk and Lindell had no reason to hurry her.

"He traveled a lot and he may have met someone. I don't know."

"Tell me more."

"He's changed."

"Where did he go in his travels?"

"We have a daughter company in Málaga. UNA Médico. He often goes there."

"And you think perhaps he met someone there?"

"Maybe."

"How has he changed?"

Rönn squirmed, stroking her hand over the already smooth fabric of her dress. Her nails reminded Lindell of Josefin." He used to be so nice. Always chatty and making jokes."

Rönn slipped into a dialect that Lindell mentally placed in Hälsingland. She made a few notes on the page and checked the time.

"He's been quiet. Doesn't say very much. Mostly stays in his office. He hardly ever comes out even for a cup of coffee."

"Was it after a trip?"

"Yes, more then, but he's changed overall. He's more irritable."

"Have there been any conflicts at work?"

A new pause. Lindell wished she had something to drink or maybe snack on.

"Sven-Erik and Jack didn't get along so well."

"Jack is the boss?"

Rönn nodded. "They started the company. Jack is the CEO. They each own half. They had a fight. We could hear them sometimes—it's a small workplace."

"What did they fight about?"

"I don't know. There was just irritation and tension in the air."

Before Lindell wrapped up the conversation she tried to get a better sense of the other employees at MedForsk. Rönn went through each one systematically and explained their position. Lindell was starting to appreciate the at-first-so-frigid woman's thoughtful speech. She measured her words carefully, but Lindell had the impression that she was trying to give as accurate an impression of the company as possible.

In response to a direct question about whether Cederén could have had a relationship with one of the other two female employees, Rönn immediately dismissed the idea.

"Absolutely not," she said sharply. "I know Lena and Tessan very well.

Lena for at least ten years—we used to work together at Pharmacia, and Tessan is happily married. She's pregnant and on cloud nine. She and her husband have been trying for several years. Neither one of them is the type to have an affair, and definitely not with Sven-Erik."

"Why not with him?"

"Because he isn't their type."

"What kind of type is he?"

Sofi hesitated again.

"He has a melancholy temperament that can be hard to bear. Most of the time he's pretty cheery, but then he's suddenly just the opposite."

"He seems outgoing, plays golf, that kind of thing."

"He is good at golf. In the winter he sometimes takes golfing trips. I think his putting is a way to escape the pressures of work."

A melancholy temperament. She had studied his face in a staged family photo she had found in the villa. It was one of those pictures that men place on their desks at work. The happy family. He looked extremely contented, his arm around a well-dressed, well-groomed Josefin, his daughter on his lap. Could this man be unfaithful? Yes, most definitely, Lindell thought. Could he mow down his own family? Yes, perhaps, under great pressure and with uncontrolled emotions. Anger, jealousy, and blazing hatred could change almost anyone. Lindell and her colleagues knew this all too well.

She posed the question to Sofi, who dismissed it as absurd.

"Then why has he disappeared?"

"I don't know. He might have witnessed the whole thing and gone into shock."

"Thanks, you've been an enormous help," Lindell said and got up. The woman stopped her with a gesture.

"There's one more thing. I think that Josefin was pregnant."

"Yes, she was. Do you think that someone else could have been the father?"

Sofi made a face that Lindell interpreted as meaning it was impossible.

"How did you know she was pregnant?"

"Josefin told us last week. Jack held a little party; we had had a break-through in the lab and we were celebrating. Josefin didn't drink anything. I made some joke about it, and she told me straightaway that she was having a baby."

"Did she seem happy?"

"It's hard to say. She said it without any enthusiasm. You know when you get all bubbly, in between the vomiting, when you can't stop smiling."

Lindell nodded. She thought about the blue book. There Josefin had written down her mixed feelings about the baby. She wanted to have it but frequently found herself arguing for an abortion. She didn't say this straight out, but her doubts were expressed so strongly that the thought must have occurred to her. "What if he leaves me?" she had asked herself a couple of weeks ago, on May 22. The third of June she had noted: "Tonight I'll tell him. We have to make a decision."

A short time later she was dead. Someone had made a decision.

Lindell also talked with Lena Friberg and Teresia Wall before she left MedForsk. It was exactly twenty-four hours since Josefin and Emily had died.

Lindell longed for a chocolate biscuit at the Savoy, but when she had almost reached the café, she decided to eat some real food instead and thought of a lunch place that Haver had mentioned.

She drove to the end of Börjegatan and ended up parking far too close to a crosswalk. The place, Brostugan, reminded her a little of the Savoy. The interior had not been updated for a while and imbued her with a feeling of comforting familiarity as soon as she stepped through the door. She heard a construction worker order cabbage rolls and decided she would have the same thing.

She sat down next to the window. A television was on, with the volume turned down. It was tuned to a cooking show with a chef who had an almost tragicomic look. Ann watched his lips and tried to deduce what he was talking about. Definitely not cabbage rolls.

Contrary to her habit in public places of studying the people around her, she hunkered down over her meal with an intensity that surprised her.

When she got her coffee, she summarized her visit, taking out her notepad, jotting down some observations and thinking about what Teresia Wall had told her. The eighth of June, CEO Jack Mortensen and Sven-Erik Cederén had had a spectacular quarrel. Sven-Erik had just returned from Spain. Although he had been unusually tan, he looked worn out—"majorly hung over," as Teresia had put it.

The two men had confronted each other in Jack's office. Their agitated voices could be heard all the way to the kitchen. Teresia had not known what the fight was about. She had asked Jack about it, but he had dismissed her question with irritation and simply muttered something about "Sven's damned doubts about everything." Teresia had a theory that they were fighting about MedForsk going public. The company was entering a phase of significant expansion and needed big money. Maybe Cederén had had misgivings about the shape these plans were taking, because the next day Jack shut himself up in his office and worked feverishly. According to the general consensus—there was a great deal of talk at the company these days—he was putting the finishing touches on the prospectus. A press conference was scheduled for June 16.

The day after the quarrel Cederén had not shown up to work. He had called Lena Friberg about an upcoming meeting with a consultant regarding some technical equipment.

People came and went at the café. There was laughter. Clearly there were a lot of regulars because nods were exchanged and short questions about work were met with equally short, sometimes ironic, responses.

Haver is right again, Lindell thought. She would return here. Here there was the life, everyday life, that she needed so desperately. Real people with real jobs, dressed for work with the tools of their trade in their pockets and company logos on their backs and chest pockets. People who had not killed anyone.

But who may hit their wives regularly, she thought disloyally.

Axel Olsson came to answer the door in his bare feet. One big toe was severely deformed and both feet were wet. He was emaciated, with an ascetic face and large hands he did not quite seem to know what to do with.

"Excuse me," he said guiltily, "my wife is resting."

Cederén's father excused himself frequently.

After he had put on some socks and slippers—while he rambled incoherently about foot salts and a visit to his doctor—they went into the living room. People often received her in the kitchen, but Axel Olsson quickly pulled the door to that room shut and with a restrained gesture led Lindell deeper into the apartment.

The air was stale. The furniture had once been petit bourgeois in that way that Lindell recognized so well. The large chest with inlaid wood in the doors, the coffee table and the vaguely dark red sofa, a bookshelf with a limited number of books and a proliferation of glass bowls, photos, and souvenirs, a couple of worn armchairs, and a stand with a droopy foxtail fern.

Lindell examined the photos while Olsson apologized. There was the son, the daughter-in-law, and the grandchild, in several editions. A dozen older photographs in brown oval frames that Lindell assumed were dead relatives took up an entire shelf.

"Is Sven-Erik your only child?"

He nodded.

"I haven't had time to pick up," he said, "but please have a seat."

For his own part, he went and stood by the door to the balcony.

"That's quite all right. I know you have other things to think about right now."

"My wife is feeling poorly."

"You have lost a grandchild and your daughter-in-law. I understand," Lindell said.

Olsson looked confused and picked at the fern, shaking it with an unexpected ferocity that sent a shower of yellow leaves onto the floor.

He and his wife had already been visited by the police the day before and had at that time denied any knowledge of where their son could be.

"Have you heard from Sven-Erik?"

"I don't understand this."

"I know you have been thinking about this ever since you heard the news. Has anything occurred to you about where he might be?"

Olsson closed his eyes. He looked as though he was sedated.

"Sven-Erik hasn't called?"

He opened his eyes, fixed them on her, and said very slowly, "He doesn't call us very often."

Lindell got the feeling that at any moment he could fall asleep standing up.

"He has a lot to do," Olsson added. "We always tell him that he's working himself to death."

Olsson walked up to the closest armchair and placed his hand on its back. He cricked his neck back as if he were going to give a speech.

"He wasn't happy," he said. Realizing he was talking about his son in the past tense, he immediately corrected himself.

"He *is* unhappy. It's that job of his."

"Was he happy with Josefin?"

Olsson started. It was as if the mention of her name gave him renewed vigor. He moved around the chair and sat down, leaning toward Lindell and looking straight at her for the first time during the conversation.

"She put pressure on him, you understand. She always wanted more. That house, cars, and new clothes. Sven-Erik couldn't say no."

He stopped as quickly as he had begun and looked down.

"Did they fight?"

"Everything had to be the best. Sven-Erik could never disagree. He had to work. She wanted new things. Fight? I don't know. Not that we saw."

Nothing in Josefin Cederén's journal had indicated a difference in attitude between the spouses with regard to lifestyle and money. She had not expressed any objection to her husband's way of life, with the exception of his infidelity.

"Was Sven-Erik faithful to Josefin?"

"Is anyone claiming otherwise? Is it her father? You should know that he never came here for a visit. In the beginning we invited him and Inger, but they never accepted or behaved like normal folk. He was so full of himself. Now I guess he's blaming it all on Sven-Erik."

Olsson sank into a heap, sobbing. "I can't do this."

It was as if he had used up all his power. Lindell just sat and observed him. His hands were pressed together between his knees. The stale air was starting to get to her. She stood up without making a sound. A large photograph of Sven-Erik Cederén in a graduation cap was prominently displayed on the bookshelf.

She wanted to put her hand on Olsson's shoulder, say some comforting words, but she couldn't manage it. It was possible that his son was a murderer, so Lindell couldn't assuage the father's pain, and perhaps she didn't really want to. There was something about his person that made her feel not so much distaste as dislike.

She closed the door behind her and knew that there were countless questions she should have asked, that she should have spoken with the woman who was behind one of the closed doors. Perhaps she was sitting silently in the kitchen? Lindell tried to imagine her: large, heavy, thinning hair with a grown-out perm, full of sorrow mixed with helplessness and perhaps anger. Mostly a wordless grief. "Feeling poorly," her husband had said. Lindell tasted the word. "Poorly."

Once she was out in the fresh air, she called Sammy Nilsson, who could relate that the review of MedForsk's business documentation was taking considerable time. The connection to the daughter company in Spain was not completely clear. The two companies pursued many of their activities independently, but the majority of the laboratory work took place in Spain. Most of the documents were in English, but many were in Spanish. A translator had been called in. Sven-Erik Cederén was the one who managed the communications in Málaga since he knew the language.

Beatrice had checked on the insurance. Both Josefin and Emily were insured through Skandia, with Sven-Erik as the beneficiary. The amount was in the millions.

"How are their private finances?"

"Good," Sammy Nilsson said. "There are shares for about half a million, mostly in pharmaceuticals, loans for nine hundred thousand, bank resources for half a million, and as much again in interest-bearing securities."

"Not bad," Lindell said and thought of her own meager assets. "No acute situation, in other words."

"No, and no significant financial events recently. Just the usual amount of activity—regular deposits and no large withdrawals. We're working on Sven-Erik's credit cards right now. Sixten is looking into that."

"Anything from the house?"

"Nada. No other personal materials."

Lindell heard voices in the background on the other end. A telephone rang and one of her colleagues laughed. Riis mocking someone, most likely, she thought.

"Having fun?"

"Berglund is making a fool of himself. He just won ten thousand on a lottery ticket he found in his car."

"Found?"

"He had forgotten about it," Sammy said. "What about you?"

Lindell talked through her visits.

"Where is he?" she asked.

"Overseas," Sammy said.

"Maybe Spain?"

"I'm betting on the Dominican Republic. We're trying to sort out that house business. The translator is helping us with the papers."

"Sounds good, Sammy. Give my regards to Berglund."

She hung up and looked back at the airless multifamily building where Sven-Erik's parents moldered. She was almost certain that Axel Olsson—possibly also his sickly wife—were observing her from a window.

What substance might there be in his talk of Josefin and her desire for a lavish lifestyle? Lindell did not believe him. Her wardrobe was large but not notably expensive. Beyond all the dust, her home had been relatively normal.

It was obvious that the parents had not seen eye to eye. Perhaps it was the differences in their backgrounds. Josefin's father had apparently been a higher-up in the Swedish Social Insurance Agency. She didn't know what profession Axel Olsson had practiced, but she assumed it was something blue collar. He had muttered something about the other's airs of superiority, that he had been made to feel inferior, but having met Josefin's father, Lindell had trouble imagining him being patronizing. It all probably stemmed from some old disagreement. They had not continued to see each other socially, that was all.

Ottosson, Wende, and Beatrice were sitting in the lunchroom with a man she did not recognize. She guessed it was the interpreter, and this was immediately confirmed.

When he introduced himself as Eduardo Cruz, she felt herself transported back a couple of years to the time when she was investigating the murder of the young Peruvian refugee Enrico, whose brother had had the same accent.

Beatrice, who was always observant, noticed her reaction and began to describe the results of her and Wende's mapping of the Cederén family's personal finances.

Lindell, who had already been briefed on most of this by Sammy, listened distractedly. From Enrico and Ricard, her thoughts went to Edvard. He had called.

"What do you think?" Ottosson asked and looked warmly at her.

"I didn't really catch all that. I have to get a snack," she said and got up.

She returned with a cup of coffee and a chocolate-covered biscuit and Beatrice made a comment about blood sugar.

"We've finally managed to get in touch with the Dominican Republic," Wende said. "We had problems getting our fax to go through."

"What's the time difference?" Ottosson asked.

"Six," the translator said.

"Eduardo has translated the reply, and it appears that Cederén bought land in the northwestern part of the country, not far from Haiti."

"Land?"

"Yes, no building, just land, more precisely two hectares. He paid eighty-five thousand dollars."

"He hired a firm by the name of West Indies Real Estate in Sosúa," Beatrice said.

Lindell did not want to start speculating about what this might mean while the translator was present. Instead she asked if the fax had yielded any additional information.

"Sven-Erik Cederén has been there in person on several occasions, most recently the fifth of June. That was when the deal was transacted and Cederén transferred money from the MedForsk account to the Banco Nacional. Eighty-five thousand dollars."

"How much is that?"

"About eight hundred and fifty thousand kronor," Wende said.

Ottosson stroked his beard.

"So now MedForsk owns twenty thousand square meters of Caribbean land," he said. "Why?"

"Handelsbanken has confirmed the payment," Beatrice said.

"Thanks so much for your help," Lindell said to the translator. "It's likely we'll be in touch again."

She stretched out her hand.

"Where are you from?"

"Chile," Eduardo Cruz said, and stood up.

Lindell gazed after him.

"He reminds me of Ricardo," she said, and this was the first time she had brought up his name to her colleagues.

His death, how he had thrown himself out of a window when the police arrived. This had been a taboo subject in her presence. No one had wanted to open this wound. They sat quietly around the table until Wende broke the silence.

"Jack Mortensen had no knowledge of this affair. Or so he claims. He was under the impression that Cederén had been in Spain."

"That's what everyone at MedForsk believed," Lindell said.

"What a mess," Beatrice said.

"Is this the heart of it?" Lindell asked of no one in particular.

"The Caribbean," Wende said.

"Maybe he was planning to move there with his lover," Lindell said.

"Who is that?"

Lindell leaned back in her chair.

"We'll have to check all flights again, track his flights, review passenger lists. She may be there somewhere. If they really were planning to flee to these warmer climes, I'm sure she must have accompanied him on an earlier trip."

"But why pay with funds from a company account?" Ottosson objected. "He should have fudged it."

"He's a man," Beatrice said. "He thinks he's invincible, that he can do whatever he likes and he'll pull it off."

Lindell shook her head.

"Do we have anyone here who knows Spanish?" she asked Ottosson.

"Riis, maybe," he said, and chuckled. "He's got a place in Spain."

"Should we send Riis to the Dominican Republic?" Beatrice said excitedly.

"I'll go there with the Chilean," Lindell said.

Once she was back in her office, Lindell sat with her notepad, doodling and sorting the information she had received. In front of her on the table were several folders with information about MedForsk and the Cederén family's personal finances, as well as transcripts of the interviews.

It was already a considerable amount, but she knew that this collection would grow even more before the investigation was concluded. She was impressed by her unit's effectiveness, despite all the turbulence in the building. She knew she was working in a good group.

And at the bottom of the pile was a memo from the police chief: "Questions about the necessary restructuring of community policing." She read this heading several times before she tossed the whole thing in her bottom drawer. It would take a while before she would be able to get to it. Most likely there would be a new memo within a short period of time that either fully or in part completely reversed the earlier conclusions and suggestions.

The last time she had seen the chief he had been in uniform, on his way to some reception. He loved his uniform. If only he would spend as much time on the Uppsala division's actual problems as he did with his uniform.

He called, she thought, and as so often happened, her mind wandered to Edvard. There were now longer stretches of time between these thoughts, which she saw as a sign of health, but he was still there. If she called him back, she would be lost, she knew that. All it would take was hearing his voice. "No, you silly goose, you're not a lovesick teenager."

"Your hands," she said aloud and smiled.

She removed the wrapper from a piece of chocolate that she had brought back with her and decided not to call. He could stay on that island with his beautiful hands and his heavy thoughts.

It struck her that MedForsk's Jack Mortensen would have to be interviewed again, and she searched around for the number to the company.

Mortensen was out on an errand, Sofi Rönn—who answered the

phone—announced. He wouldn't be returning to the office. Lindell was given his cell phone number.

"One more thing, since I have you on the line. What do you know about the Dominican Republic?"

"Nothing really," Rönn said. "Why do you ask?"

"I was just wondering," Lindell said, and then decided to tell her about the fax from West Indies Real Estate.

"That's news to me," Rönn said. "Why would he buy any land there?"

"You haven't heard anything about the company planning to build a new facility in that location?"

"No, not a word, and I think I would have heard something if anything was in the works."

Lindell thought so too, because Sofi Rönn appeared to know almost everything about MedForsk and its employees.

"Please keep this information to yourself," Lindell said.

"Of course. It'll stay between the two of us," Rönn said, and they ended the call, both convinced they would have a great deal more to do with the other in the near future.

Lindell dialed Mortensen's cell phone number but was greeted by a recording. Lindell introduced herself and asked him to call her as soon as possible.

There was a gentle knock on the door. Ola, Lindell thought immediately. And so it was.

"It took a bit of digging, but I've finally uncovered information about Cederén's credit cards," he said and laid a dozen printouts in front of Lindell.

"Three different cards: a company card—a Visa—one MasterCard, and one Hydro card."

Haver sat down.

"I've tried to filter out what I believe to be unimportant. Those transactions are marked in green, most of which is personal business. We have business charges, including flights, and those are blue. Then we have meals—white—and the rest are red."

Lindell glanced at the top page and observed what he had just told her: colorful dots by every line.

"I've mapped his gas purchases on a map and have listed the foreign transactions separately," Haver went on.

He grabbed the pile of paper and started to spread the pages across Lindell's desk. Lindell peered at the map.

"Most of the gas was bought at Hydro by the western edge of town?"

"Yes, if he followed the 55 home, it would be the nearest gas station. But he has also stopped at the station by the E4, on Råbyvägen and along Öregrundsvägen."

"And restaurants?"

"This is what I was thinking: If he had a lover, they would probably have gone out to eat a couple of times. I've marked all the charges where I believe it's a bill for two people."

Lindell smiled. "You like this, don't you?"

Haver looked up. "There are twenty restaurant visits for two at eight different establishments the past two months."

He stopped and waited for Lindell's reaction.

"Let's visit all those places with a photo of Cederén. We might get lucky," she said finally. "Can you keep working with the lists? I think we've got something here."

"Who can I take with me?"

"Talk to Ottosson. He'll have to figure that out. You can give the foreign transactions to Beatrice and Wende. They're working with Spain and the Caribbean connection."

Haver closed his folder. "You can keep the lists," he said. "I've made copies."

"Hey," Lindell said as Haver opened the door. "Nice work."

He nodded and closed the door softly behind him.

Ann got up and went over to the window. She burped unexpectedly and her mouth filled with the taste of cabbage rolls. She didn't like the current situation. What if he had managed to make his way out of the country?

She stayed by the window for a quarter of an hour. Her body felt heavy and she had a faint headache. Edvard.

She remembered his first visit in her old office. His careful questions, his worry, his concern about who the dead boy was that he had found, how he had looked at her and taken her hand as they parted. Already then, after only ten minutes, there was something in his eyes that she could never forget. It was something in his gaze, a kind of hunger, an undercurrent of daring mixed with insecurity. A boy's eyes, but a man's gaze.

She knew where he was but didn't go to find him. She knew his number by heart but didn't call him. Was this a form of masochism? She had left him and chosen loneliness, work, and perhaps the hope that she would find someone else. But as yet she had not found anyone to replace Edvard.

She knew now what it was that had impelled her to leave the island. It wasn't the practical problems—him on Gräsö, with some unspoken loyalty to his aged landlady; her in Uppsala, with her work. No, it was his inability to steer his own life. He simply allowed things to happen. To all outward appearances, he had casually dropped his two sons and no longer had anything to do with them. He had laid his life aside and merely existed in a state of absentmindedness and passivity.

Even though she knew—and she found this even more infuriating—that this life pained him. How many times had she told him to break out of his isolation, to resume his contact with Jens and Jerker. To become active somewhere, where his frustration over the state of things could find expression and meaning.

At first she had thought that it was her presence that made him hesitate, that he was ashamed of his sons or that he didn't want to confront them with her. After all, they had first met her as a detective in a murder investigation. They had been suspects, but had been freed of suspicion. And yet their involvement had indirectly led to Eduardo's death. Even more crucial to take ahold of these boys.

But she wasn't the sticking point. That much she had figured out. Edvard was simply not up to the task of living, and she did not want to be pulled into this silence and repressed suffering. She wanted to live completely and fully. Her job was depressing enough as it was without having to deal with heaviness the moment she came home.

"But," and she cursed herself, "here he is. Why did he have to call and record his damned message?"

"And look at you," she told herself, her brow against the windowpane, "here you are moping around.

"But without Edvard. Without his eyes, hands, and lost love. You pour two glasses of red wine into yourself almost every night. Go out with the girls and get drunk, falling into bed with a man that you hardly remember what he looks like the next day. What kind of life is that?"

Her inner monologue was interrupted by the sound of the phone, and it occurred to her that she had been allowed a full fifteen minutes of peace with her thoughts.

She lifted the receiver. It was Jack Mortensen.

✦

Seven

Ola Haver immediately set his plan in action. He managed to tear two officers away from Patrol and four from Surveillance.

They came together for a meeting after only an hour, the lists of restaurants in front of them. Haver was pleased to be able to leave the station, and it was clear that the others felt the same way.

"I can never afford to go out to eat," said Malm, who was from Patrol. "So I guess this is the only way I can do it."

"There are eight places in all," Haver began. "Svensson's Orient at the Saluhallen; a Greek restaurant across from V-Dala; Trattoria Commedia, the Italian joint around the corner; the Wermlands Cellar; two Chinese joints on Kungsgatan; Fowl and Fish in Tunabackar; and Kung Krål by the Old Square. I suggest we each take one. There are seven of us. I'll take both of the Chinese restaurants. They're practically next door to each other."

"I'd like to take the Wermlands Cellar," said Valdemar Andersson, who was from Surveillance. "It's so expensive I'd never get there otherwise."

They parceled out the other establishments, each equipped with photos of Sven-Erik Cederén, Josefin, and the three women at MedForsk.

"First we'll show the photo of Cederén and see if any of the staff recognizes him. If they do, we'll ask about any female companions. Try to get them to remember some detail—appearance, clothing, anything—and whether they appeared intimate with each other. Try to get them to describe the woman first and show the pictures later. Okay?"

Two of the investigators exchanged a glance, which Haver caught.

"Old hat, I know," he said with a smile. "I'll give you each my card in case any of the restaurant staff thinks of something later on and wants to call."

Soon the seven-person group fanned out across the city. The sun was shining brightly, the sky was blue, and the streets were bathed in light. They walked quickly. All of them were thinking of having a beer—at least a light beer.

In many ways it was a task that corresponded to what the public thought was police work: going around to businesses, showing a photo and trying to evaluate people's reactions, watching memories surface, seeing doubt and also distrust. It was the fictional version, underscored by American police movies and television series, but it was also their own dream of how their work could be: clean, sharp, smart, and relatively straightforward.

For once they had a chance to leave their paperwork and move among the people. They also had the possibility of exercising real skill or just having the kind of luck that led to the unraveling of a knot or even the whole case. In spite of the restructuring that they preemptively dismissed, they wanted to do a good job. They wanted to have breakthroughs. Quick, perceptive insights. Luck, a lot of luck.

All of them walked with light steps except Magnusson, who was on his way to Svensson's. He turned his head nervously side to side when he reached Sankt Petersgatan, looking up toward the center of town. As he passed Dragarbrunnsgatan, his senses grew even more alert. This was the part of town his son tended to hang out in.

He desperately wanted to avoid running into him. Erik suffered from several varieties of drug dependency, and Magnusson suspected he was also HIV positive. There was nothing left of the Erik he had loved.

Once he had gone down to the intake area and observed his son. He had hardly recognized him. The colleague who had tipped him off about his son being brought in had stood a couple of meters away. When Magnusson turned away from the two-way glass, they looked at each other. The odds weren't good. Both of them knew it. "I'm sorry," the other had said.

Relieved, Magnusson passed the Domkyrka Bridge. Erik didn't usually go west of the Fyris River.

Svensson's was closed. Magnusson gave the door a couple of shakes and pressed his face against the glass. It was supposed to open in half an hour and he was convinced that the staff was already there, so he banged on the door one more time.

A man appeared, pointing meaningfully at the sign. Magnusson took out his ID badge, pressed it against the glass, and was let inside.

Three waiters studied the photo, no trace of the initial nonchalance in their faces.

"I recognize him," one of the men said. "He's been here several times."

Magnusson watched him strain to remember more.

"He's been here several times, is always complimentary about the food."

"What about you?"

The other two shook their heads.

"He was here with a group of people once. I remember it because one of the women spilled a bottle of wine."

Magnusson took out the shots of the women from MedForsk.

"Was it any of these?"

"Her," the waiter said quickly and pointed to Teresia Wall. "Maybe," he added.

"Has he ever been here with only one woman?"

"It's possible. I'm not sure."

Magnusson held up a snapshot of Josefin. "Do you recognize her?"

The man looked at the five photos on the table and let his gaze wander from one to the next.

"I have a memory for people," he said. "I think he was here at the end of May, but not with any of these women."

"Do you remember anything?"

The man stood quietly.

"What did they eat? How were they dressed?"

"I think the woman had something like sushi. Not meat, at any rate."

"Was she a vegetarian?"

"No, she ate fish."

Magnusson waited, letting the waiter try to coax the images from his mind.

"She was blonde, I remember that much. Long blonde hair. Something blue as well. Maybe a wide headband or her dress."

He looked unsurely at Magnusson, who nodded. The waiter smiled.

"This is hard," he said. "What is this about?"

"How old?"

"Maybe thirty or thirty-five. Fresh-faced. If I saw her again, I think I would recognize her. I do have a memory for people," he repeated.

"Could it have been the fifteenth of May?" Magnusson asked after peeking at the list of Cederén's credit card purchases.

"It's possible."

Sven-Erik Cederén was known at two other establishments, Akropolis and Trattoria Commedia. It turned out that he frequented these places several times a week for lunch, something that many MedForsk employees corroborated. Often many of them accompanied him there. No one, however, was able to identify Josefin or recall an unknown woman at Cederén's side.

When Haver considered the information, it was only the visit to Svensson's that had yielded anything, even if this was regrettably thin: a blonde woman in her thirties who ate fish but not meat, fresh-faced, perhaps with a blue dress.

"There must be tens of thousands who would fit the bill," Haver said.

"That many fresh-faced ones?" Magnusson said.

Haver realized that he had overlooked something important.

"How stupid," he said. "We should have asked for an account of any temporary staff. There must be extra hands at a place like that."

"And most likely paid under the table," Magnusson said.

"Can you look into it?"

Magnusson made a face that Haver interpreted as a yes.

Sören Magnusson tackled it immediately. As he had imagined, most places denied having any temporary employees. You're lying, he thought bitterly as he received his fourth negative answer in a row.

The last one on the list, however, the Wermlands Cellar, came up affirmative. Certain evenings and sometimes on the weekends they had a young woman come in. She was studying French at the university, the kitchen manager said, and worked as much as she could. She was good, so he called her in any time they were short. She had worked some ten or twenty evenings during the spring, he believed.

"Can you see if she was working on the twenty-second of May?"

It took a while before he returned to the phone.

"Yes, she was here from six o'clock until we closed."

"Do you pay taxes for her?"

"What the hell do you mean?"

"Just joking," Magnusson said and explained the reason for his question.

Afterward, Magnusson looked down at what he had written down: Maria Lundberg. He dialed the number that the kitchen manager had given him and wished desperately that she would pick up. He was really hoping to have something to come back with.

She answered immediately, at first clearly taken aback. She sounded very hesitant.

"Did you get my number from the Wermlands Cellar?"

"Yes, and I'm from the police."

"How do I know that?"

"You don't, but we can hang up, you can call the station, ask for me, and then we'll see where you end up."

It struck him that he lived in a society full of suspicion.

"That's okay," she said. "If all you want is to show me a couple of pictures, that's okay."

He came by the student apartment area some twenty minutes later. Maria Lundberg was outside her front entrance, waiting.

"Are you Magnusson?"

"The one and only. Sören Edvin Magnusson," he said and smiled. "Here's my badge."

The young woman examined it and he examined her. Twenty-five, short hair, and a bit of an underbite. Magnusson had a weakness for underbites. His first love had had one.

"That's okay," she said.

"What have you been through that you don't trust people who call and want to see you?"

She looked at him and he sensed something like fear.

"I was raped three years ago," she said. "Where are the photos?"

"I'm sorry, I didn't know," Magnusson said.

"No, you can't tell on the outside."

He took out the snapshots, showing her the one of Cederén first. Maria nodded at once.

"Him, I know," she said firmly.

"Are you sure?"

"Completely. His name is Sven-Erik. I don't know his last name, but his father-in-law's name is Johansson."

"How do you know all this?"

She smiled. "Now you're curious, aren't you?"

Magnusson was impatient and did not notice how beautiful she was when she smiled.

"Yes, I am," he said in a controlled voice.

"Earlier I worked part-time for the elder-care services. Johansson—Holger is his name—was one of the clients, and he had just been widowed."

She fell silent. Magnusson looked at her with something close to gratitude.

"He was so sad. Mostly he just sat at the kitchen table. We helped him with food and laundry. He wasn't in such a bad way, just depressed. Then a neighbor woman started to help out and then we weren't needed anymore."

"Did you meet the son-in-law?"

"Yes, a couple of times."

"And you've seen him at the Wermlands Cellar?"

"Yes, one time. It was about a month ago. He came in with some girl who wasn't his wife."

"You've met her too?"

"The wife, yes, several times."

"Can you describe the woman?"

"Blonde, attractive, probably someone with money."

"What makes you think that?"

"Her clothes."

"Did Sven-Erik recognize you?"

"Yes, he looked really embarrassed, so I knew it probably wasn't his sister."

"Did he say anything?"

"Just some general things. I asked a little about Holger. But you don't intrude on the guests."

Magnusson took out the photo of Josefin. "Do you recognize her?"

"That's his wife," she said immediately.

He took out the shots of the other women from MedForsk.

"None of these," she said. "What is it that's happened?"

"We don't really know yet, but we're looking for him."

"And his lover."

Magnusson nodded.

"I want you to sit down and think about this properly. Try to remember everything about that woman even if it doesn't seem important. Write it all down. May I call you tonight?"

"Are you hitting on me?" she said in a serious voice but smiled at the same time.

"You bet," Magnusson said.

✦

Eight

Kåbo was a part of the city she rarely visited. There was no bustle here, the clientele that caused trouble on the streets and squares, stabbing each other, drinking, dealing drugs. How many violent offenders had been seized in this area the past ten years? From what Lindell could recall, there had been only one such incident. A retired physician had thrown his wife through a glass door in a drunken haze but had been sober enough to stem the flow of blood. Otherwise she would probably have died.

He had been released on probation and probably still lived there with his frightened wife.

Behind the exteriors of these million-dollar houses there were probably other things that happened that the Violent Crimes unit never heard of. Lindell studied the houses as she slowly drove through the neighborhood. Beautiful gardens with lilacs on the corners, hedges of privet or spruce, rose-bushes, expensive paving, buxbom spheres, and rhododendron in the shade.

The upper classes lived behind these hedges, fences, and walls—in part the old upper crust, those with noble names or weighed down by generations of academic merit, but increasingly the new, successful elite from the worlds of data, consulting, and pharmaceuticals, as well as physicians, lawyers, and pilots. In short, people with money. Friends of the police, who with their votes demanded law and order, more police, and harsher action.

One thing they had in common was that they all complained about their taxes, but they did not appear to be suffering. Often along Kåbovägen, Rudbecksgatan, and Götavägen, there were a couple of parked cars in the driveway, and neither was exactly a rust bucket.

On all of these streets carpenters and workmen of all kinds were engaged in frenetic activity. Houses were demolished, rebuilt, and renovated. Diggers created ponds, containers were filled with old kitchen materials, while small trucks backed in bringing new equipment and landscaping companies carted in bricks, Öland stone, cobblestones, stone meal, and soil. The women who could be seen were either housecleaners or the kind that hung curtains and discussed interior design with the woman of the house, who was often harried, in a professional career, and active.

There were exceptions, of course: those who had lived here for a long time, perhaps happened upon a dilapidated house for a cheap sum, before the party days of the nineties when taxes were lowered and home prices rose like a shot. These houses were transformed more slowly and often by the homeowners themselves.

"Would it be nice to live here?" Lindell wondered to herself as she crawled along Villavägen. A couple of women were loading cleaning equipment into a Mazda. "Probably under the table." Lindell had heard talk of Polish cleaning women who went from mansion to mansion at lower-than-market wages.

It's beautiful, but I wouldn't want to live here even one day, she thought and kept an eye out for the street she was looking for. She took a couple more turns; then Jack Mortensen's house appeared.

The house was a strange mixture of Jugendstil and functionalism. Ugly, Lindell decided, who preferred old Victorian-style houses with intricate details, turrets, and spires. A not-too-ostentatious Volvo was in the driveway. Lindell parked on the street.

The first thing that struck her was the beauty of the garden. A small path that led from the gravel driveway was bordered with roses, not yet in bloom but covered in small buds. A sea of perennials encircled a seating area where a pergola, coated with vitriol so it looked antique, rose almost threateningly over the greenery. But its appearance was deceiving; it served only to support a variety of vines, among them a fragrant flowering jasmine. The main entrance had stone steps lined with evergreens on either side, like soldiers in neat rows. The porch in front of the door was as big as Lindell's bedroom and inlaid with black slate, with terra-cotta planters filled with summer flowers that had not yet reached their full zenith. And yet it made a magnificent impression. Lindell simply stood and took it in.

"Beautiful, isn't it?" she heard a voice from above.

MedForsk's Jack Mortensen leaned over the wrought-iron railing of the balcony above the entrance.

"Very," Lindell said. "You must be Jack Mortensen."

"I'll be right out. Go ahead and have a seat on the patio," he said and pointed. "I've already put the coffee on."

Mortensen soon emerged carrying a tray laden with cups, saucers, a coffeepot—all of fine china, Lindell noted to her astonishment—two folded napkins, a plate of scones, and a pot of jam.

"I thought you might be hungry."

The pastries were golden-brown and warm.

"The jam is made from cornelian cherry. I get it from my brother in Denmark."

"You're from Denmark?"

"Yes, but I have lived in Sweden since I was ten. My parents divorced and my mother and I moved to Sweden. She's from here."

The jam was delicious. Despite the robust serving of cabbage rolls, Lindell would have been able to finish all the scones on the plate.

"Do you have any more information on Sven-Erik?" he asked, and the almost honey-smooth voice with which he had begun the conversation was replaced with a more businesslike tone.

"No, unfortunately. We're trying to establish his social network," Lindell said and wondered exactly what she meant by that.

"Social network?" Mortensen said thoughtfully. "I don't think he had much of one. Sven-Erik was by and large a solitary figure. There's the golf course, of course. That was a case of mutual affection. The greens become extra velvety when Sven-Erik swings his three-iron. The golf balls just love to be hit and putted by Sven-Erik. They go where he wants them to. He had a low handicap, in other words."

Why the ironic tone? Lindell wondered. She had trouble following his artful formulations.

"Do you play?"

"No, that's why I have employees," Mortensen said with a half smile. "Well, yes. I've tried it, but it's not my thing."

"Then what is your thing?"

He smiled again. Lindell wished he would stop smiling.

"I'm partial to gardening," he said and waved his hand toward the greenery.

Lindell nodded.

"I also collect textiles. My mother is the driving force in that enterprise, but we have become united on that front."

"Textiles?"

If Mortensen picked up on the faintly mocking tone in Lindell's question, he ignored it.

"Particularly from South America and Southeast Asia."

Lindell knew nothing of these matters but tried to look interested.

"Do you know where Cederén is?" she asked after a brief pause.

"The gods only know."

"Has he gone abroad?"

"Hard to believe. Where would he go?"

"What about the Dominican Republic?"

Mortensen picked up his coffee cup, took a sip of the now-cool drink, and put the cup down again in a slow movement. He shot Lindell a glance before he replied.

"You've learned of Sven-Erik's purchase of a piece of Caribbean paradise. Honestly I have no idea why he did it."

"Have you asked him?"

"Yes, we have discussed it, and he could not give me a satisfying answer."

"Golf, perhaps?"

Mortensen tilted his head as if to say: Why would anyone be stupid enough to buy land for golf?

"It's a riddle," he said. "Have another scone."

Lindell obeyed his command. The crystallized sweetness of the jam reminded her of her mother's gooseberry pie. A faint puff of wind brought
with it a whiff of jasmine and something that Lindell thought was mock
orange. She took a bite.

"He paid with company funds," she observed and put down the pastry.

"That's what worries me."

"Did you ask him why?"

"He said he didn't have enough in his account at the time, but that he
would transfer the funds at once."

"And has he?"

"No," Mortensen said.

"Worried?"

"Of course. Sven-Erik is a brilliant researcher and also, for some years
now, my friend. We started the company together, but he appears to
have lost his footing recently. Buying the land was an expression of that."

"Do you believe he killed his family?"

It took a while for Mortensen to reply. He looked out over the garden as
if the answer could be spotted between flowering bushes, over the top of
the fluttering white butterflies and the industrious pecking of the small
birds. Lindell watched him, how his expressions changed during his inner
dialogue.

"Yes," he said finally. He turned back to her and leaned forward. "Unfortunately I believe that something terrible has happened to Sven-Erik."

Lindell felt his breath across the little patio table. She grabbed her coffee
cup and leaned back, drank some coffee, then put the cup down as carefully as he had done earlier.

"Terrible?"

Mortensen nodded.

"In recent days he's been quite confused. I and several others have tried
to talk with him. I even called Josefin a couple of days ago to talk."

"What did she say?"

"She understood immediately what I was talking about, but she is very
loyal."

"So she didn't mention anything that could explain his confusion?"

"No, she said it could be due to his workload, but he's always worked
very hard."

"Did he have a lover?"

Mortensen gave up his assertive stance and sank back against his chair; a new silence took hold. Is he thinking or is this acting? Lindell wondered, but she did nothing to speed up his answer.

"I don't know, maybe, but why leave someone like Josefin? A fantastic woman. She was beautiful, intelligent, and a wonderful mother. She gave everything to her family, she . . ."

He broke off and gave Lindell a pained look. She thought she could see the glint of moisture in his eyes.

"I've been thinking about it constantly," he went on, his head turned away. "Why kill them? What's happening in the world? Nothing is certain anymore. We have worked together for so long to ease people's suffering, to develop cures for the most painful diseases, so I have trouble grasping how he could be guilty of something like this."

His earlier ironic and worldly tone was replaced by a questioning and remarkably weak voice. His face was equally altered. The lines in his tanned forehead deepened and he looked around in bewilderment.

Lindell observed him. Keep talking, she thought, but the air was filled only with the chatter of birds. The sun had shifted during the course of their conversation and now peeked out from behind the corner of the house. Lindell pulled her hair out of her face and savored the warmth for a moment.

"Can Josefin have had another?"

Mortensen started. "Never," he said emphatically. "She was faithful."

"How can you be so sure?"

"I am sure," he said simply, and Lindell sensed that the conversation was starting to draw to a close. But she still had to ask some questions about Sven-Erik's habits. She had to get a better profile of the disappeared man if she was to have a hope in finding him.

Mortensen told her about the Cederén family's vacation travels and something about work at MedForsk, but after she asked him if he knew that Josefin was pregnant, he closed up like a shell. He denied any knowledge of it, and Lindell did not believe him. Why, she wasn't sure, but something about his reaction indicated that he knew more about the relationships in the Cederén household than he wanted to tell.

"Tell me about Spain," she said finally.

He responded with a verbose account of the daughter company. Much of the practical work took place in Málaga. There were some fifty employees at the two facilities and this number was steadily growing.

They concluded the conversation as if on an agreed-upon signal. Mortensen stood up, gathered up the china, brushed the crumbs from the table, and replaced the lid of the jam.

Lindell closed her notebook. She hadn't written many words. The taste of the cornelian cherry lingered in her mouth.

"I would show you some of the textiles," he said, "but I'm a bit pressed for time. I have to leave. Perhaps you'll come back? I think you would appreciate the pre-Columbian pieces. They are so beautiful, preserved for centuries. I could also ask my mother to stop by. If she has an audience, she can hold forth for hours."

"Maybe I will."

"I hope so. I have more jam too."

Mortensen smiled, and now his smile looked more genuine. Lindell wanted to pat him on the cheek. He radiated loneliness. Or perhaps more a kind of helplessness before her, the cleared table and the massive contours of the house—as if he didn't know where to go with his tray.

"I'll be in touch if I think of anything. Do I have your number?"

Lindell wrote down her home phone number and gave him her card, which he studied.

"You're young to be leading a murder investigation," he said, as if her age were listed on the card.

"You're also leading something akin to an investigation and we're about the same age."

He gave her a quick glance.

"Thanks for the appraisal," he said, and it sounded so absurd and innocent that Lindell had trouble holding back a laugh.

Lindell knew he watched her as she walked down the path and past the car and turned by the massive granite post out onto the street.

Her face was warm and she felt that summer had really arrived. This did not cheer her up. In fact it was slightly unsettling. For the first time in several years she hadn't planned anything.

Last year she and Edvard had gone to Denmark, driven around Funen and Jutland, sometimes camping and sometimes checking into little inns or

B and Bs along the road. They had gone swimming, seen art exhibitions, and eaten. She gained three kilos those weeks. Nothing had worried her. She had kept her cell phone turned off most of the time and had called home to Ödeshög only a couple of times. Edvard had been unusually relaxed. She remembered his laughter and his playful mood as with a great deal of splashing they threw themselves into the icy waves of the North Sea. "Happiness" was the word that came to her as she took out her car keys.

What would she do this year? Go home to Mom and Dad, that was already decided, but she couldn't stay in Ödeshög for four weeks. At most, three or four days. It struck her that no one had asked her what she was going to do over the summer.

She felt slightly disheartened as she slipped behind the steering wheel. The meeting with Jack Mortensen had brought something to life that she wished for all the world wouldn't bubble up. Definitely not during work. In the evening, at the kitchen table and in front of the television, or more often when she crawled into bed, she could take it. Then she could treat it, perhaps lessen it with a glass of wine or—with a massive effort of will—plan the next day's work in order to repress the thought. It was the loneliness that Mortensen had displayed. He had his garden, his successful company, his collection of textiles, his mother—Lindell found the use of the word "Mother" depressing—but he could not conceal his loneliness. He breathed it. That was what she had sensed across the table.

She expected him to call—in fact she was almost certain of it—and was unsure of how she felt about that. Two lonely souls consumed by their jobs, what did they have to say to each other? Or else she was wrong. Perhaps his asking for her telephone number was genuinely motivated by the thought that he might come up with something of interest.

She was decent-looking, she knew that, and men looked at her. Mortensen had studied her left hand in order to determine that there was no ring. This was normal—she did the same thing herself—but now it irritated her. What was he thinking?

She turned the key and suddenly had the conviction that the car wouldn't start.

✦

Nine

Gabriella Mark knew a lot about fungi, at least the ones that plagued her vegetable garden, and yet she hesitated. The attack she saw before her was irreparable. These were her most beautiful plants of the new type of cauliflower with firm heads, relatively small but incredibly delicious. Now she had to remove them, but she hesitated.

Why hadn't she seen it earlier? Maybe some of the plants could have been saved. How she had worked: making careful preparations, moving seedlings and pots, working manure into the cleaned-up beds, acclimating plants, alternately airing them and covering them up with old rugs when an evening chill came creeping from the stream. And she had deceived that treacherous draft but not the fungus.

She pulled out the deformed heads with rapid movements. One by one they ended up in the plastic bag by her side. The bag would end up in the garbage can. The fungus was destined to burn up in the public furnaces and not contaminate her painstakingly maintained compost.

She stood up and grew dizzy. When she opened her eyes, stretching out her hand as if to find something to steady herself against, she knew that he wouldn't come. He should have come yesterday but hadn't even tried to contact her. With each passing moment it grew more and more likely that he would never come.

She had proudly shown him the cauliflower. He had laughed, leaned over carefully—concerned for his suit—and said something about the vegetable counter at B&W. He liked to tease her, but she knew he loved her vegetables.

"Butter," she said out loud.

An almost unnatural warmth lay over the earth. Spring conditions had been ideal, without a night frost since the third of April. Now came the heat. It steamed from the windows. The small wedges she used to prop the covers open for airing were pushed up all the way, which made the rows look like a sea of flat, clumsy, shiny creatures with their mouths ajar. They chirped like living things, exhaling and inhaling. The condensation from the glass dripped slowly over cabbages, onions, carrots, and turnips. The latter she had already harvested once, tiny tender goodies.

She knew it. He would not be back. The feeling of rejection stabbed her in the heart. He loved her, she knew it, as if that fact could console her. It made the whole thing even more idiotic.

She grabbed the bag and dragged it away. Her gaze was focused and she was taking calm breaths, just as the psychologist had said she should. "No flitting, just focus on what you are doing," he had said. "Take it in whatever order you like, but don't lose your grip."

Her leg muscles worked as the bag skipped across the gravel yard. Beads of sweat dropped from her brow. She understood that her gardening had a therapeutic function. All this systematic picking and sorting. She could never consume everything she produced. Especially now.

Emil, the squirrel who had kept her company for almost two years, was sitting by the flagpole. Mostly he was naughty. She knew that he raided the bird's nests, had caught him sitting on the nest under the dormer of the old laundry. So what, he came back, he was her friend.

Gabriella smacked her tongue a little at him as she usually did. Emil looked up and scrambled off.

She leaned the bag up against the garbage can. The guys would most likely take this one as well. She could pay them in radishes.

The lid of the mailbox was open. She realized that she hadn't brought in the morning paper. She immediately saw the photos on the first page, read the headline, and collapsed onto the low spirea hedge that surrounded the property.

When she returned to consciousness, blood was the first thing she saw. The dizziness returned and she had to struggle to maintain her bearings. A branch from the hedge had sliced a long cut into her arm. She stared stiffly down at the blood, which was beginning to clot.

To crawl to her feet, grab the detestable paper, and stand up took her half a minute. She walked toward the house, took the stairs in five slow steps, and pushed the door open with a whimper.

She washed her wound and saw that it was not as serious as she had initially thought. "I don't want to get a scar," she muttered and examined it more closely. Then she tied a cloth around her arm. The mirror was no comfort. She leaned over the basin and then backed out of the bathroom without looking at her reflection.

After having a glass of rhubarb juice, she sat down in the kitchen. The remains of her breakfast were still on the table and she shoved them aside with her uninjured arm.

"I have to take something," she thought but did not rise. The sweat came in waves, the heat rose in her body, and she felt as if she were being lifted out of the kitchen. She closed her eyes in order to ease her vertigo. Her mouth shaped itself into an O and she pushed the air out of her lungs, inhaled deeply, then breathed out again. Most of all she wanted to scream, but she continued the breathing until she found herself back at the table. Her fingers scraped the tablecloth. The crumbs from breakfast were still under her hands.

She opened the newspaper and in one sitting read the long article, which contained a description of the sight that had met the reporter and photographer. There were also comments from the police, residents in the area, and neighbors.

A drawn-out scream filled the house. It felt like a relief, but the scream also scared her.

"He's dead!" she screamed and realized that her love had not been enough, that he would never walk down to the water with her, never call out her name. Never again. When it struck her that she had not given a single thought to the dead woman and her child, she felt ashamed at first, but his image immediately rose again before her teary eyes.

"I don't want this anymore," she mumbled and made her way to the bathroom. At the very back of the cabinet were some old pills. She had kept them as a reminder, looked triumphantly at them, certain that the time in which she had needed them at night was over. Now she took one and then another. A couple of blue oxazepam slipped in along with them in her haste.

"He can't be dead," she whispered.

✦

Ten

Lindell took the route past the Savoy. It was an enormous relief to walk into the café. Her stomach was still full of scones and sweet jam, but she needed this time to think.

After a moment's deliberation she switched off her phone and sat down with a hot cross bun and a cup of coffee. A group of construction workers rolled in, but luckily they preferred to sit outside by themselves in the beautiful weather. Lindell had the room and her thoughts to herself. Left behind on her table was a copy of *Året Runt* magazine, which she flipped through listlessly.

She summed up for herself what Mortensen had said about Cederén. He had believed that Cederén had been responsible for killing his family. He if anyone should know his colleague and long-standing friend. Or were they friends? There had been a tone in his voice that she hadn't liked and couldn't interpret.

Was Cederén really capable of running over his own flesh and blood? Lindell felt increasingly doubtful about this. If he hadn't, where was he? She was sure that there was a connection between Uppsala-Näs and his disappearance. The women at MedForsk had also talked about the change in his mood, that he had tended to stay in his office and no longer took part in coffee breaks and that he had been abrupt and angry recently. Why? Was it Josefin's pregnancy? Problems with his lover?

Lindell took her first bite of the pastry and tried to imagine the scene in the Cederén household. Josefin pregnant and alone with Emily in the large, messy house; he unfaithful to her and preoccupied with a large amount of work. In addition, he had purchased land in the Dominican Republic. Riddles inside riddles.

She knew that the answers had to be found at MedForsk. "Money," she mumbled. The company was facing sweeping changes and was expanding. Perhaps there had been conflicts about the direction. But why Josefin and Emily?

Had Cederén simply not been able to manage the stress, privately and professionally, and become unhinged to the point of murdering his own family?

Lindell allowed herself half an hour at the café. An older woman with a walker came in, and the waiter brought her a cup of coffee and a shrimp sandwich. If the old woman had trouble walking, it was clear that her appetite remained intact. She polished off the sandwich in a couple of minutes. Lindell watched the brief meal with fascination and then got up to leave. The woman concealed a burp behind her napkin and Lindell smiled at her.

Sammy Nilsson, Beatrice, and Wende were sitting in Ottosson's office.

"We tried to reach you," her boss said.

"I've been thinking," Lindell said and sat down.

Beatrice observed her from where she was sitting. Lindell felt her gaze and didn't like it.

"We think that MedForsk may have cooked their books," Sammy said. "Molin has found some inconsistencies. It seems like they may have transferred funds to Spain without paying taxes here in Sweden."

"How much are we talking about?"

"We think maybe three million, maybe more."

"Have you talked to the Financial Crimes unit yet?"

Sammy shook his head.

"Then we have a mysterious transaction with a company on some island somewhere, a tax haven."

"I see," Lindell said with a sigh. She had trouble with finance. It became too technical, too many numbers. She had problems interpreting her own pay stubs.

"We'll ask Molin to do a brief report," Ottosson said. "Then we'll have to evaluate how we proceed. It may not have anything to do with our investigation."

"Molin is never brief," Beatrice said.

Lindell was quiet. She didn't want to get stuck with a financial crimes investigation. The FC unit could do that.

"Maybe we should connect with Bosse Wanning in FC?"

Ottosson's question hung in the air.

"At least he's someone who's possible to understand," he added.

Lindell nodded.

"Let's put Bosse and Molin together and see where it leads."

She paused, glancing at the clock on the wall. She wanted to shower. And she wanted to eat again. She wanted to sleep. She wanted to call Edvard. Anything other than this airless and stuffy room, the sticky T-shirt, and the feeling of being behind on everything.

"Anything new on Cederén?" she asked.

"Nope," Sammy said, "even though the entire building has been on it."

"He's holed up somewhere," Beatrice said with a sharpness in her tone that was unusual.

Lindell left the station shortly after seven and decided to pass by Vaksala Square to pick up some groceries.

As so often happened after she had been working long and hard, she was struck by a feeling of unreality as she stepped into the completely ordinary surroundings. The canned goods, grains, and health food on the shelves in the ICA store seemed foreign, as did the other customers who pushed their carts around, discussed dinner plans, and disciplined their children.

Ann walked dispiritedly through the aisles and picked out a mismatched jumble of food. A vague feeling of hunger mixed with indifference made her walk in circles until she was able to decide what to buy.

She settled for some smoked salmon, a dessert cheese, some fresh pasta, four chocolate bars, a couple of cans of crushed tomatoes, and some instant coffee. Then her imagination and spirits failed her and she left the store with the unsettled feeling of not having bought anything sensible.

She was overwhelmed by a feeling of grief as she loaded the bag into the backseat. Is this how it was going to be? She sagged next to the car, with one hand on the sunwarmed roof and the other dangling limply by her side. An image of passivity. She heard laughter and saw four teenagers huddled closely together outside the display window of a furniture store. They were talking about a bed on display but quickly moved on, disappearing around the corner.

Thirty years ago in this place two young men—brothers—had died in a terrible car accident. An older colleague—one of the first to arrive on the scene—had confirmed the details. It had been very early in the morning, and the only witness was a taxi driver standing next to his car at the taxi stand some fifty meters away.

The story had been etched into her memory, and every time she passed this intersection she thought of the brothers and the third young man in the somersaulting car—the driver, who survived. Every place had its history and many times it involved both death and sorrow, but most people, ignorant of what had happened there, just unknowingly walked on by.

As a cop, you got to know too many sad locations. She had come to this conclusion as the years went by. Could no longer see normal life and people in the city without the images being darkened by violence, tragedy, and the strained faces of those chosen to remember and bear witness.

Ann stepped into the car and suddenly felt she had no choice but to call Edvard. No choice. There was no other way. Why leave the man she once loved and perhaps still did? How could she otherwise explain the strong feeling of agitation and also longing that she had felt when she heard Edvard's voice on the answering machine?

Her loneliness was eating into her, and although she wouldn't admit it to herself, she was afraid of ending up alone. She wasn't young anymore. If she wanted a child, this was the time. She had toyed with the idea of getting herself pregnant with Edvard, whether or not he wanted to, and then leaving him if he didn't want to become a father again.

Edvard had his moments, but he wasn't worse than anybody else. Quite the opposite. He had much of what Ann was looking for. She had to call him. Hear his voice, maybe meet up with him. Didn't he ever drive into the city? They could have a coffee together at the very least.

The first thing she did when she got home was to turn on the television. She half listened as she undressed. The weather report was promising more warm weather. She sniffed her underarms and immediately headed to the bathroom. The toilet had been leaking for a couple of weeks. She had removed the lid and stared into the tank, but that hadn't made her any the wiser. She decided to write an enormous reminder and put it on the refrigerator door. The property manager—if there was one—would be able to fix this in about five minutes, she was sure of it.

She showered for a long time, soaping every nook and cranny, allowing the warm water to spray across her body. She thought of Edvard. Could she perhaps spend a couple of her weeks of vacation at Gräsö?

She put on her robe with a strong conviction that her summer was going to be good. It was as if her repressed love for Edvard had been released by his message and the heat in the shower. Her face flushed, smiling at herself in the mirror, she brushed her hair with strong strokes. She tried to imagine what he was doing right now, how he would react if she called. It struck her that he might have gotten over his longing for her and was able to contact her now because he was sure of his feelings and wanted only to be friends. She didn't really believe this, but the thought was enough to make her lower the brush and stare at herself in the mirror. Then she resumed brushing. She knew him too well and was positive he would never call her to make small talk. It was his voice. He still loved her, she knew he did. I have to call him, she thought, and left the bathroom.

The bottle of red wine that she had opened the other day was still more than half full, so she poured herself a glass, busying herself in the kitchen by watering the flowers and wiping down the table before she took a first sip. Then another. The television was still making noise in the other room, so she walked out and turned it off. The evening sun shone through the blinds and created a striped pattern of dust across the floor. She vowed to vacuum the entire apartment, mop the kitchen floor, and clear off the balcony so that she would finally have time to set out her garden chair, if Edvard picked up and said he wanted to meet with her.

She went back to the kitchen, took a sip of wine, and picked up the phone. As she dialed the number, she realized she hadn't thought of Sven-Erik Cederén for at least a couple of hours.

He picked up on the second ring and Ann fumbled for her glass, but it was empty.

✦

Eleven

Jack Mortensen was basking in the strong afternoon sun. There was a strong smell of barbecue in Kåbo. His nearest neighbor—who was not visible behind the massive hedge—was having a party, which was growing louder as the day went on.

Mortensen leaned his head against the rough wall. The neighbor's party distracted him, but not so much that it prevented him from systematically reviewing the events of the past few days. The call from Málaga was what worried him more than anything else. The purchase of the land in the Caribbean had been the last step and the Spaniards were losing their patience. That Cederén's family had been obliterated and that Cederén himself was missing did not seem to concern them very much. De Soto almost sounded relieved. On the other hand, he had never worked well with Cederén and he had never met Josefin, much less Emily.

But wait a minute, hadn't he met her? Three years ago right here in the garden, as they were successfully marketing Cabolem. It was the profit from that launch that was right now being sunk into the Parkinson's project.

Then they had celebrated. He had taken care not to overindulge, as he was the host, but the rest had drunk all the more. He recalled how De Soto and his lady—or however one should refer to her—had downed their drinks, fondled each other, and ended up together in the hammock. It is said that Swedes have trouble holding back, but these Spaniards had put them to shame. One of them, the light-haired fellow from the Basque country who talked about ETA, had jumped into the pool fully clothed, and another—the head of lab two—had been blind drunk only an hour into the event.

Mortensen had felt embarrassed. If he felt irritated by his neighbor's noise level, what couldn't others have been able to reveal about that party? The following day he had bumped into one of his neighbors, the one who was known as professor although he was only a lecturer, and he had mentioned something about the carryings-on that went on long into the night. Mortensen had apologized but since then had always felt ashamed when they bumped into each other in the street.

Although the young police officer—Molin was his name—who had gone through the company papers had appeared young and awkward, Mortensen was convinced that he would discover the transaction from last December. This was not good. At first Mortensen himself had argued against it despite the financial and practical advantages, but had given his consent three days before Christmas. It was too late now, he realized. That operation would have been easy enough to conceal if only he had acted earlier.

The Spaniards were furious, but Mortensen had calmed them. The Swedish Financial Crimes division was overworked and lacked the necessary resources and knowledge, he claimed. It would take some time before the three million was unearthed, and a skilled business lawyer could punt it around as long as necessary. Perhaps it could be recast as an unfortunate misstep, intended only to strengthen the company's possibilities for expansion. They could blame their own amateurism and the fact that they had been so caught up in the medical research that they did not realize they had made themselves guilty of a financial crime.

More troubling than this was Uppsala-Näs, the purchase of the property, and Cederén's disappearance. The police would not give up easily. He thought of Lindell's visit. She had made a sharp impression, but also seemed strangely absent. Would she manage to uncover Gabriella? That depended entirely on Gabriella herself, if she could manage to stay calm. Mortensen had his doubts. She was weak. He had called, but no one had answered. That was not a good sign. Perhaps she was with Sven-Erik, but where were they?

On the other hand, Gabriella knew nothing that could tarnish Med-Forsk's reputation, unless Sven-Erik had talked to her. That was not inconceivable. Sven-Erik had grown increasingly soft in the fall, questioned the entire enterprise and his own role in it, slipped away to the golf course more frequently, lost his edge in the laboratory, and simply become unpleasant.

The argument that they had to succeed—and quickly at that—was one that he had waved away, snorted at. Which was hypocritical, in Mortensen's mind, because Cederén had been in on the plan from the beginning. Back then he had not protested—in fact quite the opposite. Mortensen remembered his enthusiastic introduction at the April conference two years ago, when the entire project was conceived.

Now he wants to discuss ethics, he thought bitterly. That's what they all do, come back after the fact, complaining when the problems start to pile up. If things go well, they grab all the glory. It had been the same thing at Pharmacia.

He felt deeply uneasy, could not escape the thought that the Spaniards were secretly pleased that Cederén had disappeared from the scene. And if the family had been wiped out—well, that was hardly something they could do anything about. De Soto's comments—about finally being able to work in peace and move forward—had appeared just as cynical as he felt their business ethics to be.

Mortensen gazed at his hand, the pulse under the skin in the fold between his thumb and forefinger. He made a fist so that his knuckles whitened. The neighbor must have gone inside because now the area was completely still.

Should he call his mother? She had already called him a couple of times that day, had been concerned and asked if he was managing. Mortensen smiled. That was just like her, he thought. Tomorrow she would most likely turn up in time for breakfast, with fresh-baked buns and fresh carrot juice.

He got up stiffly. How long had he been sitting against the wall? At least a couple of hours. Normally this was his primary mode of relaxation, these hours that he could steal to spend in the garden, but right now he felt no joy as he looked out over the profusion of flowers.

The telephone had been ringing off the hook since Cederén had dropped out of sight. The Spaniards aside, everyone at MedForsk wanted to talk to him about what had happened. Everyone had been upset and shaken, but a certain anxiety about the future of the company—and thereby their own—had also been evident.

Mortensen had calmed them all. We'll move forward regardless, he repeated.

If only he knew where Sven-Erik was hiding. Mortensen was convinced that Sven-Erik would eventually be in touch and had brought the cell phone with him into the garden, but the only caller was a reporter from the evening paper, *Aftonbladet.* A nosy type whom Mortensen had quickly brushed off, but in a polite and proper way. He did not want any trouble because he had been rude to a hack. There was enough bad press right now as it was.

Where on earth could he be if he wasn't shacking up with Gabriella? Mortensen had puzzled over this but had come up with no reasonable alternative. At one point he thought that Cederén might have gone out to Mortensen's cottage in Möja. Cederén was familiar with the place and knew where the key was hidden. Mortensen had called out there at least a dozen times, but there had been no answer. He had not mentioned this to Lindell. And why would Cederén want to hole up there? It was more likely that he had gone overseas. Had the police located his passport? Lindell had not said anything about that.

If Cederén was alive, he would attempt to contact him sooner or later. He would want to talk. He could manage to keep himself hidden and isolated for a couple of days, but Mortensen knew him too well to think that he could hold out any longer than that.

And if he was dead? Mortensen didn't want to believe it. They had been friends since they were in their twenties, when they were both studying chemistry. They had been roommates for a time, had backpacked through Europe, had fallen in love with the same woman—Sven-Erik the one who had won the fair maiden, of course—and had fallen out of touch but had been reunited at Pharmacia. The fact was that Sven-Erik Cederén was the person he had been closest to, with the exception of his mother. The one who knew his strengths as well as his weaknesses but who never abused this, never taunted him for his inability to keep a woman more than a month of two, never said a harsh word about his mother.

Mortensen had always trusted Sven-Erik. He was a person you trusted. Not a slick, socially adept charmer, but loyal as a friend and unusually honest at work in a way.

They had built up MedForsk—a huge risk at first—into a successful company with positive headlines in the business weeklies and a good reputation among their competitors and research colleagues. Now they were facing the largest step since the beginning, the public offering. Three hundred million. Everything was ready. They had hired a PR consultant to prepare the way, and he had succeeded beyond their expectations. The firm's results spoke clearly. Last year's profits had been almost fifty million.

Now all of this was threatened and Mortensen was not sure how he would be able to contain the damage. The Spaniards were furious, his head of research was in all likelihood a murderer and also nowhere to be found, the police were examining everything and everyone, and the mass media were on the hunt.

Mortensen shivered. He took the phone and went inside. After he had shut the door and turned on the alarm, he got a feeling of looming catastrophe. He closed the metal blinds in the textile room. The pale pieces of fabric displayed in glass and silver frames gave him no joy. Lately he had started to wonder why he had put so much effort into creating one of the foremost private collections of textiles from South America and Southeast Asia in the country. To what end? he thought as he closed the door behind him, locked it, and switched on the alarm. No one ever sees the collection, except for the occasional guest, who is only moderately impressed and interested.

Should he call that attractive policewoman? He had put the card with her home phone number on his bulletin board above his desk. He walked into his home office, turned on his computer, and looked up at the card.

What should he say? Should he tell her about Gabriella? It was tempting. He wanted to have something to offer her to get her to return, but revealing Gabriella's identity was too dangerous. The price could be too high. Ann Lindell's interest in him was probably only professional, and she would chew up Gabriella with relish and then it would be his turn.

He remained standing in front of his computer for a long time, wondering if he should put in a little work with the CAD program. He had decided to rip up a quarter of the garden, build another pond, connect it with the old, and also create a little woodland area for acidic-loving plants. The drawings on the computer were almost ready. Then all he needed was the listing of plants. Construction would begin in the fall.

He was just about to turn on the computer when the phone rang. He looked at the clock and picked up the receiver. Málaga. He had time to say only that Cederén was still missing before De Soto interrupted him. Mortensen was quiet, pulling over his chair and sinking down in it.

De Soto's long monologue paralyzed him. He hung up without saying another word.

✦

Twelve

Ola Haver lingered in the doorway. The terbutaline had kicked in and Gina appeared to be breathing more comfortably. He walked up to the bed and tucked the blankets around her, setting her stuffed animal on the pillow. Her eyelids fluttered and she coughed.

From the bedroom, he could hear the baby whimper before she found her way back to the nipple. Rebecka Haver called softly for Ola and he left Gina's room, casting a final glance at his resting daughter. Let's hope she can sleep for a while, he thought, and gently pulled the door until it was almost but not completely closed.

"Please remember to go by the drugstore," Rebecka said.

Ola had to smile. She was hoarse, had almost lost her voice—he could barely hear her—but she had not lost her ability to give him constant reminders.

"Of course. What a family. Happy almost Midsummer," Haver said and walked up to the bed.

Rebecka smiled and stretched out her hand to him. The baby snuffled contentedly at her mother's breast. Maybe she had fallen asleep.

Haver took her hand and squeezed it lightly. The bedroom lay in half darkness, with the blinds pulled down and only a single bedside lamp for illumination.

"Feel better soon," he said and bent down to kiss his daughter's neck. Her hair, which was still downy but dark and striking like her mother's, tickled his nose. He drew in her sweet scent and felt a vast joy.

———

He left Valsätra shortly after half past seven. He had an idea. Just as they had checked all of the restaurants that Cederén visited recently, they could methodically search out the gas stations he had been to.

On his way to the police station, he tried to imagine what Sven-Erik Cederén was like. The photos of him in the house had shown a man about his own age, not particularly handsome—at least according to Beatrice, but she was critical of most men. Short hair, tan, and in reasonably good shape. He reminded Haver of the real estate agent who had sold them their house. One of these thirty-five-year-olds lurching toward middle age who try to ward off physical deterioration with hair gel, gym visits twice a week, perhaps golf, and a confidence in their posture that did not always correspond to the state of their inner life.

Haver had been through all papers and documents that concerned Cederén but had not been able to add anything of substance to their understanding of him. Cederén was too much of a nonentity, too flat, too focused on his work and research. Even in his vacation pictures, he had remained a cipher. Of course in some photos he had looked fairly relaxed, laughing and perhaps striking an unexpected pose, but nothing there yielded more for anyone who wanted to learn more about him. Haver missed the voices and gestures.

At the Edenhof golf course in Bälinge, Haver had met with some of Cederén's acquaintances. All of them had maintained that Cederén was pleasant and easygoing but not particularly social. He was friendly but did not open up, rarely if ever talking about his personal affairs.

He played a decent game of golf, able to put in a concentrated effort without much trouble. If he ever missed a shot or a simple putt he never made much of it, other than perhaps an ironic smile. He played calmly and methodically. He was popular at the club, someone who could be relied upon, and he was a driving force in the tree-planting project as well as the youth recruitment initiative. Other club members said they would be happy to play a round with Cederén. He created a sense of order, as one member put it.

No one sensed any cracks in his facade other than the assumption that he was most likely cheating on his wife. How to explain this departure from his otherwise irreproachable behavior? Haver had fielded this question at the golf course, but everyone he spoke to had dismissed the idea of Cederén's having a lover as absurd. Most of them knew Josefin—admittedly not very well—and everyone had characterized the relationship as stable and even happy.

Haver drove past the Svandammen pond and cast a longing glance at the café Fågelsången. He had spent a lot of time there in his youth but nowadays rarely had an occasion to stop by. Perhaps he should take Lindell out for a cup of coffee and a vanilla custard doughnut. She liked hanging out at cafés. No, not a doughnut, they were reserved for him and Rebecka. The vanilla game was their secret.

The list of Cederén's purchases at the Hydro gas stations was not particularly long. He probably also frequented other stations. Most of the purchases were marked "Klang's Alley" and that made sense. A handful of transactions were from Råbyvägen and next to the E4 motorway as well as half a dozen stops along Öregrundsvägen.

Haver studied the list and realized that he would perhaps not get that far. Most of the gas purchases were self-serve transactions at a machine. The chance of anyone's being able to recall Cederén and any company he may have had were very remote, but on the other hand, they didn't have much else to go on.

Öregrundsvägen was the only station that stood out. What errand had Cederén had in that part of town? Something for his work? Hardly. MedForsk had no presence along that road. Cederén had no summer house. Perhaps he was visiting someone he knew?

Haver pulled out his phone and dialed the number to MedForsk. Sofi Rönn answered. Haver asked her if she knew why Cederén might have traveled along Öregrundsvägen so often. She had no idea and did not know of anyone he might have known who lived in Rasbo, Alunda, or any other area to the northeast.

Haver thanked her and hung up. The transactions had occurred with relative regularity. That was most likely no accident. Haver pounced on the explanation: Cederén's lover must live in the vicinity.

He stood up and walked over to the map of Uppland on the wall. It was like looking for a needle in a haystack. Haver took the road only on rare occasions, but he tried to visualize it in his mind. He had a vague memory of an unmanned gas station, but wasn't there a small shop nearby?

He opened the telephone directory and searched grocery stores. Just as he thought, there was a small grocery store in Vallby, Rasbo Allköp. He wrote down the number and decided to head out there right away with a photo of Cederén.

He called Lindell and told her his plans.

"How are things at home?" she asked.

"Rebecka sounds like Darth Vader, and Gina hardly slept last night."

"If you need to get back to them, you should," Lindell told him.

In spite of clouds sweeping in from the southwest, it was still a beautiful day. Haver drove out along Vaksalagatan, thinking of his little one. What should they call her? Rebecka had suggested Sara, but Haver thought it sounded too biblical. What about my name? she had objected. Doesn't that sound biblical too? But Haver had stood his ground.

Haver rooted around in the glove compartment for his sunglasses. He felt a great happiness that life had fallen into place. The anxiety during the pregnancy, his wife's constant spotting, the chaos and masses of overtime at work, and his own sense of having ignored his family—all this hung over him like a shadow all winter and spring. Now the sun was finally shining. He drove far too fast.

He could not manage to get his conception of Cederén to coalesce. A successful researcher and business executive, a well-regarded golf player, a man with an apparently stable home life. But also someone who had carried out a deception and perhaps even a murder. Haver had read extracts from Josefin's diary and seen her and Emily lying slain at the side of the road. What made Cederén tick? Haver wanted to catch up to him to find that out.

At Jälla, dark clouds drew across the sky, and at the exit to Hovgården, the rain arrived.

One of the store staff members was uncertain about recognizing Cederén, but two were able to identify him with assurance.

"He often shops here," one of them said. She was a young woman in her twenties and had piercings in her tongue and her nose. This, along with her lanky hair and drooping shoulders, initially gave Haver the impression she might be of limited intelligence, but he quickly revised his assessment when she turned out to be swift and assured in her answers. Occasionally she had to ponder on her answer for a moment, but on the whole she was a perfect witness.

She knew that Cederén drove a BMW—"that would be something"—and that he drove by regularly. She had seen the car drive past but also stop at the gas station; he had shopped in the store on multiple occasions. Once last spring he had bought all of the tulips in the store. She thought there were something like seven ten-packs in the store at the time.

"You remember a customer who buys seventy tulips," she said. "It's so romantic."

Haver smiled at her.

"Sounds like you wouldn't have anything against getting seventy tulips."

"I'd prefer roses," she said.

"Did he ever have anyone with him?"

It was the decisive question and she answered immediately.

"Yes, the time after that, he was with a girl. Blonde, around thirty, fairly pretty. Not beautiful, not a lady, if you know what I mean."

Haver nodded.

"I recognized her. She sometimes comes in."

Haver knew now that he was close.

"Does she live around here?"

"I don't know."

"When was the last time she was in?"

The young woman reflected for a few moments before she spoke.

"Last week. She bought some bags of seeds."

"Seeds?"

"Carrots and stuff like that."

Haver paused. He looked out of the window, watched the cars flying past.

"If she comes in again, would you write down her license plate? Could you do that?"

"Sure. Sounds exciting."

"I'll give you my number and you can call me right away."

"Is she dangerous?"

Haver shook his head and handed her his card. She studied it.

"Is she wanted?"

"No, we just want to talk to her."

"Do I get a reward?"

"Seventy tulips."

Ola Haver left the store in a good mood. He was almost certain that the young clerk would lead him to the woman, who was potentially hiding Cederén or at the very least would be able to shed some light on his disappearance.

As he unlocked the car, the phone rang. He checked the display and saw that it was Ottosson.

"We've found him," Ottosson said curtly.

"Where?"

"The Rasbo area. He's dead."

"Fucking hell. Suicide?"

"Looks like it. Where are you?"

"In Rasbo, or almost there."

Ottosson chuckled contentedly. Haver saw him in his mind's eye, his glasses pushed up onto his head and his hand in his beard, which was growing more and more gray and bushy.

Haver was given some hasty directions. Lindell, Sammy, Beatrice, and Ryde, the forensic specialist, were on their way.

The forest road was almost impossible to spot. It was partially concealed behind a thicket of willow. It was clear that it had not been used for a long time, because vegetation had almost completely taken over the entrance. Lindell's and Ryde's cars were already parked on the gravel road. Otherwise Haver would probably have missed it completely. He looked around attentively.

The many branches of a willow brushed Haver's head. A black woodpecker was frenetically working the heavily ridged bark. It hardly even looked up as he passed, simply casting him a glance as if to say: I was here first.

Fredriksson should have been here, Haver thought. He loved assignments in the country, especially in wooded terrain, and would take the opportunity to show off his knowledge of birds.

The overgrown tractor road lay in shadow. Logs strewn over the trail tracks, which were very likely sodden in fall and spring, lay like rotting cadavers. When Haver stepped on them, they collapsed in on themselves with a muffled crunch of decay.

To the left was an expanse of exposed rock laced with peat moss and decorated with the occasional twisted pine tree. Large blocks of stone had been heaved to the side and resembled mossy forest animals. The area had the feeling of a graveyard.

To the right was a bog, and Haver perceived a faintly sweet smell that he suspected came from the vigorous brushwood interspersed with emerald-green tufts.

Some thirty meters away, there was a clearing. On the far side of that was Cederén's BMW. The sporty car looked completely out of place, with the large spruce trees as a backdrop. Four police officers were hunched around the driver's side. Haver glimpsed a body in the car, draped over the steering wheel.

The clearing was around two hundred square meters, a little wooded area in which Sven-Erik Cederén had ended his life. There are worse places, Haver thought as he walked closer.

"That was quick," Lindell said and looked up.

"I was in the neighborhood," Haver said.

Lindell hardly registered his answer. She leaned back over the corpse.

"Oh, god, how he stinks," Beatrice said.

"Things go fast in a car," Ryde commented.

He was already wearing gloves. Haver saw that he was impatient. Lindell reached in and gently picked up a small piece of paper that lay on the dashboard. She straightened up.

"'Sorry,'" she read.

It was no example of fine penmanship. The five letters, written in capital letters, had been dashed down in a childishly uneven line.

"What an idiot," Beatrice said.

The ignition was on, but the engine was dead. A yellow plastic tube ran from the exhaust in through a narrow crack in the back window on the driver's side. A brightly colored piece of fabric had been stuffed around the tube in the crack to prevent the fumes from escaping.

Cederén's face rested on the steering wheel. One side of his mouth was pulled up so that it looked as if he were grinning. A sneer. "So long, I'm out of here," it seemed to say. He was tan, but an unmistakable gray patina completely destroyed the impression of health. He had been a handsome man, Lindell thought.

"I can't say I'm not disappointed," she said. "I would have wanted to have a few words with him."

"Who found him?"

"A farmer who lives in the house that you drove by," Sammy Nilsson said. "He was making preparations for the winter logging."

"Lucky us," Beatrice said. "Think how he would have smelled in another week or so."

"Yes, it is lucky for us. Now we don't have to keep looking," Ryde said.

"That's what I mean. It was a lucky break," Beatrice said.

"No one ever died of a bad smell," Ryde observed dryly.

The assembled officers fell silent. Haver suspected that the others were also thinking of Josefin and Emily. Somehow he wasn't able to feel upset. Not yet. He knew it would come. Maybe Cederén was a murderer, but the sight of his body, with his mouth wide open and his eyes closed, was so awful that it derailed his anger.

Suicide always affected police officers. All of them had toyed with the idea of taking their own life. Being confronted with the corpse from a suicide roused a heavy melancholy as well as a rare mixture of anxiety, disgust, and rage.

Haver walked to the front of the car. The right-hand headlight had a diagonal crack across the glass, but apart from that, the BMW looked undamaged.

He peered in through the windshield. Cederén was starting to go bald. There was a bare patch on the top of his head.

"Why here?" Sammy asked.

Lindell looked around, as if the answer were to be found in the clearing.

"You can hardly see the turnoff, and the road itself is rugged, to say the least. He must have been familiar with it," Sammy said, continuing along this line of reasoning.

"Maybe he's been mushroom picking here," Ryde said. "This is prime mushroom territory."

An image of Edvard picking mushrooms shot through Ann's head.

"Why were you nearby?" she asked and turned to Haver.

"I had dug up a lead on his mistress," he said humbly.

"Around here?"

"It's possible, but I'm not sure. We may be able to find her by talking to a girl who works in a store in Vallby."

"Why Vallby?" Sammy asked.

"The Hydro gas station. Cederén stopped there regularly."

Lindell gave him a smile and an appreciative look.

"All right then," Ryde said. "You done with your look-see?"

He bent over and fished out a bottle partially concealed under the seat.

"Gordon's," he said. "Five centiliters left, give or take."

He held the bottle aloft and smiled.

"Didn't you smell the alcohol?"

Ryde was triumphant.

"You think he downed an entire bottle?" Sammy asked in disbelief. "Seven hundred centiliters? Damn."

"This is a one-liter bottle," Ryde said, "but no one said he drank the whole thing. It is open and was resting on its side, so most likely some of it has run out onto the floor. We'll see."

He walked around the car, opened the back door, and picked up a briefcase.

"You can have this for now," he said and gave it to Haver. "Ask Jonsson to secure any fingerprints before you handle it too much."

He began by taking out his camera. Ryde was a highly skilled forensic technician, but he was also an excellent photographer. From time to time he put up small exhibitions in the conference room. The photos were usually extras from police investigations, but sometimes he surprised his colleagues by including scenes from his family life, of grandchildren and vacations. This humanized the otherwise gruff man. The Technical division voted on the best picture. The winning composition was always something from work. It was as if the officers couldn't bring themselves to vote for anything of a more personal nature.

Ryde's four colleagues left him to his work on the car. They walked slowly across the clearing. The sun peeked through the spruce trees.

"This is a beautiful place," Sammy said.

"Who is going to inform the parents?" Lindell asked.

The technicians had enough to keep themselves busy with for at least a couple of hours. The car, clearing, surrounding forest, and road all had to be combed for clues. Even though all signs pointed to suicide, this was a crime scene.

Lindell headed back to town in Haver's car in order to find out about the Vallby lead. Now that Cederén had been found, the search for his lover appeared most pressing. Perhaps she would even be able to shed some light on the motive for Cederén's final car ride and subsequent suicide.

Had he been to see his lover after his initial disappearance and taken his life sometime afterward? This was a question that gnawed at Lindell. If this was the case, what had been said? Had they quarreled? Had he told her what had happened? Why hadn't she called the police?

There was something murky in all of this, something that Lindell had to clarify. After Haver's report from the convenience store, it no longer appeared impossible that they would find her.

"If we assume that she lived in the vicinity, somewhere along the Öre- grundsvägen, and that he has visited her, there must have been many people who would have noticed his car," Haver said. "It stands out, and in the country it's the kind of thing people notice."

Lindell nodded. If this woman didn't come forward, should they publish a photo of the car to get some leads?

"What kind of person is she?"

Haver glanced over at Lindell. There was a tone of irritation in her voice—an impatience—that Haver interpreted as criticism of the unknown woman.

"You mean, it's her fault?"

"In a sense. Without her, the Cederén family would probably still be alive."

She paused. Haver waited for the rest, but she didn't speak again until they reached the turnoff for Uppsala.

"She must have loved him," she said, "and that isn't a crime. She can't be held responsible for his actions."

"Maybe she was pressuring him?"

"To run over his family?"

"Who knows? But I don't actually think she's like that," Haver said. "She bought bags of seeds in Vallby."

The evening of June 16, the preliminary autopsy report came in. Lindell regarded the fact that it came out that same day as a minor sensation. Combined with the forensic report, she was starting to piece a picture together.

Cederén had died sometime on June 14. "Around lunchtime" was the assessment on the report, with the official window of death estimated to be between eleven A.M. and two P.M. The cause of death was carbon monoxide poisoning by inhalation of car exhaust fumes. Shortly before his death, Cederén had consumed approximately fifty centiliters of gin. The brand was Gordon's London Dry. In his stomach there had also been remains of breakfast: yogurt, cereal, and coffee.

There were no signs of outward violence other than a discoloration on his right forearm consistent with the fact that the body had been found leaning against the steering wheel. He had been in good physical condition.

Lindell closed the folder with a sigh. Maybe he'd been in good physical condition, but he obviously was not in particularly good psychological condition. She did not know what she should think and did not like how the current situation appeared: a murder-suicide. It was now clear that the BMW was the vehicle that had struck Josefin and Emily. Fabric from Josefin's clothes had been found wedged next to the right headlight.

"Why?" was the question that recurred in Lindell's head. Perhaps the killing of his wife could be explained by a temporary state of confusion and hatred, but the child? Had Cederén intentionally killed Emily? Was that why he had written that pathetic suicide note and ended his life?

Had he stopped and made sure that the girl was dead or simply driven away? There were no witnesses to help them answer these questions. Despite persistent door-to-door work in Uppsala-Näs, they had not found anyone who had seen Cederén's BMW or any other car. The stretch of road where it happened was surrounded by fields, and there were no residential houses on either side.

He could have stopped, backed up, and checked to see if the girl was dead. But why drive all the way to Rasbo? Was he on his way to his mistress, or had he been there and then killed himself?

The questions on Lindell's pad grew in number. It was not clear if they would ever find answers. If they managed to track down the mistress, then perhaps a couple of the pieces would fall into place.

She was not as convinced as Haver that the woman would turn up again at the store in Vallby. A new sigh and then she stood up from the desk and walked over to the map. There were hundreds of residences in Rasbo, even more if one increased the area up to Upplands Tuna, Stavby, Rasbokil, and Alunda.

With her gaze fixed on the web of roads that branched through these districts, she was struck by a thought: Were there any public agencies they could consult? Anyone who might have records of single women in their thirties? Lindell dismissed the social welfare department outright. This woman did not seem a case for them. She had been well dressed and appeared financially comfortable. The church? Perhaps it was worth the trouble to call around to ministers in nearby parishes and ask if they had any ideas. Lindell decided to put Fredriksson on it. He was the right sort to call men of the cloth.

Lindell shut her door with unnecessary force. Ottosson, who never seemed to go home, peeked out of his office. When he saw Lindell, he smiled.

"Anything new?" Lindell shook her head. She walked up to him and thought how amazing it was that he managed to keep his spirits up.

"I'm going to go home, take a bath, have a glass of wine, and read some silly women's magazine," she said and stopped quite close to Ottosson.

"You read those? That surprises me."

"I go to the grocery store and ask what a gal in her best years should be reading and then buy something sight unseen."

"There's one called *Amalia*," Ottosson said. "Buy that one."

Lindell patted him on the cheek. *"Amelia's,"* she corrected him and smiled.
He smiled back. "I like you. You know that, don't you?" he said.

"I do. The feeling's mutual."

She saw that he was touched by her words. How sensitive he was, how much he cared about her. She didn't want to embarrass him any further, so she turned around and walked down the hallway. She glanced back before she went down the stairs. Ottosson was still there. He held up a hand. Under the pale glow of the fluorescent lights he looked like the kindly old gentleman he was. Lindell paused for an instant to reciprocate his greeting, then half ran down the stairs.

She felt happy for the first time in a long while. Lucky to have a job that she liked, colleagues and a boss that she respected; happy that Edvard had answered her. His voice had the same contented tone as it had had on her answering machine.

He had told her he couldn't work because of a knee injury. He had fallen five meters from a ladder. Lindell tried to imagine five meters and saw him fall helplessly to the ground. He admitted he'd had infernal luck. "I could have broken my neck," he had said in his calmest voice, and Lindell had been struck by his words, understood that she still liked him very much. Nothing bad was allowed to happen to him.

When she stepped into the Konsum grocery store, she realized how hungry she was and that she had been so for a while without thinking of it. She pushed the cart in front of her and quickly snatched up some items, driven by the desire to get home as soon as possible.

She wanted to hurry life along, she realized as she waited in the long line that reached halfway into the store. Couldn't people buy their groceries at another time? She wanted Midsummer to arrive. They had agreed that she would go out to Gräsö Island. They had planned out the food. She would get aquavit and beer. He would make a couple of dishes with matjes herring. She had the feeling that everything was as before, as if the six months that they had been apart had been only a seconds-long pause.

Now that the Cederén case appeared to have been solved—with the exception of the motive—things would hopefully calm down a little. No murders, no rapes, and no assaults, please. The time until Midsummer would pass, the beautiful weather would persist, and Edvard would be rested and happy. The sea would be more beautiful than ever. The narrow gravel road up to Viola and Edvard's house would be surrounded by wood-land geranium and Queen Anne's lace and—in the drier areas—yarrow and German catchfly.

Ann loved the pastures and meadows, the sea breeze and the buzzing of bumblebees in the flowers. Last Midsummer all three of them—Viola reluctantly at first—had picked flowers and made wreaths.

In the end there was neither a bath nor a magazine. Fatigue overcame her. She puttered aimlessly around the apartment as the rice cooked on the stove. She ate quickly as she flipped through the morning paper. They wrote about the hit-and-run in Uppsala-Näs, but she skipped past it.

She sat down in the sofa with a glass of wine. The television was on by force of habit. She felt an overwhelming sense of exhaustion. Her mind circled back to all of the people she had encountered over the past two days. She didn't want to think of work, but as so often happened, her thoughts churned unsystematically over recent events, a parade of words and facial expressions.

She tried to think of other things but couldn't think of anything that interested her. Why don't I have a personal life? she wondered. I'm married to my job. I drag my investigations home with me; everything else seems unimportant. What do other people do in the evenings? All the single people?

She realized that this was how bitterness set in. Even if she loved her job, there would come a day when all this would appear, if not meaningless, then of lesser importance. Work, all the papers, all the rushing—these would hardly count when weighed against her repressed need for love and intimacy. She feared that day when the scales dipped to one side, when her motivation fell to zero. Then there would be nothing there, at least if she went on in this way.

She had no countervailing ambition; that was the worst thing. No passion for long-distance skating, bird-watching, reading, or theater, bowling, dog training, or watercolor painting—everything that people did so easily and with such enthusiasm. She just had the feeling that she ought to do more than work all day and drink red wine at night.

If she didn't get herself out of the house, she wouldn't meet anyone except violent perpetrators and police officers. She thought of her last escapade with the girls. Too much wine, too little judgment. The man she had dragged home—or had he dragged her? The fact was, she didn't remember much from that night.

They had made love. That much she recalled. Nothing earth-shattering, but he hadn't been so bad. He had left before she woke up around ten the next morning. Her bed had smelled of a man and sex. She had lingered there and thought of Edvard.

He could have left a note—Bengt-Åke was his name—but he had simply sneaked out, satisfied. Beatrice had recognized him and claimed that he was a married man. She had denied that he had followed her up into the apartment. When Beatrice asked, she had maintained that he had only walked her to her door.

She heaved herself out of the couch. Her body longed to be close to another, but no more Bengt-Åke. She had decided that much that evening, the sixteenth of June. Edvard is the man that I will love. His hands will get to caress my body and his smell will linger in my sheets.

She pulled off her skirt and T-shirt, walked into the bathroom, and made a face at her mirror image. "No more Bengt-Åke," she said aloud, and sat down on the toilet and closed her eyes so she wouldn't cry. Why this melancholy, this teary sensitivity, now that she was about to go and see Edvard? Had fear come creeping in? The fear she had seen even in him and that she had stubbornly tried to break down for two whole years? She had been the one on the offense, the one who took the initiative, while Edvard had followed her lead. He had both appreciated her drive and passively resisted it, torn as he was between the past and the future.

Lindell pushed her thoughts aside, deciding to leave her melancholy, mechanically proceeding through her nightly bathroom routine and mentally preparing for sleep. This was a well-honed system driven by sheer self-preservation, by the necessity for sleep.

✦

Thirteen

In the next few days nothing else occurred that could shed any additional light on the Cederén drama. Lindell and the others felt that they had reached the end of the road. Fredriksson's rounds among the parish ministers had not yielded anything. In fact, most of them were pointedly unwilling to cooperate in the search for Cederén's mistress who—for lack of information to the contrary—was presumed to live northeast of Uppsala.

On a couple of occasions, Haver had called the store in Vallby and spoken with the clerk, but she had nothing new to report. The woman had not been back.

Lindell had held out hope for one final event, Cederén's funeral. It was held at Uppsala-Näs church one week after they had found him in the woods. Lindell guessed the woman might turn up, but it turned out to be a vain hope. Only a handful of people assembled in the pews. Apart from Cederén's parents, who mainly looked frightened, there were only a couple of colleagues from MedForsk: Mortensen and someone from the lab. There was also a fellow golfer from Edenhof golf course. Haver pointed him out to her. He had been questioned earlier. On this day, he had actually stood up next to the bier and said a few words. Cederén's parents shrank even further during this speech, and there was a painful silence in the church when he finished.

Lindell had lingered outside the church in the hopes that the woman she was looking for would turn up once the others had left. But it didn't happen. Lindell considered putting the graveyard under surveillance. Perhaps the woman would turn up at the grave site to say her good-byes. But they didn't have the resources to put an officer full-time in Uppsala-Näs. If the object of their search had been a suspected killer, that would have been one thing, but not simply to locate a grieving mistress.

Lindell did speak with the caretaker about keeping his eyes open and asked him to report to her if a blonde woman turned up at Cederén's grave.

He agreed but also informed her that he did not spend many hours at the church and so chances were slim.

Why didn't the woman come forward? Lindell wondered. But when she thought about it a little longer, this didn't seem so strange. The woman presumably had—even if indirectly—contributed to Josefin and Emily's deaths and her lover's suicide. Lindell was convinced that there was a story in all this, a drama of passion that no one was proud of, least of all the unknown woman. She had to grieve anonymously, alone with her despair. Perhaps she was ashamed? Perhaps she had ended the relationship and thereby set off Cederén's deranged actions?

Lindell wanted answers to her questions but realized that the chance of this happening was diminishing by the day. The unit had already started to consider the case solved. What remained were some suspicions about the financial crimes, but this did not fall to their division.

Mortensen denied any wrongdoing, in part blaming the Spaniards and in part the chaos surrounding the public offering, which now had been postponed. MedForsk had been shaken. They had put one of their best business lawyers on the matter and he had immediately charged headlong into the task of pushing the suspected transactions into the realm of legality. Many of the Financial Crimes officers were convinced he was going to succeed.

Life at Violent Crimes swung back into the old routine. That's how it seemed to Lindell after every extraordinary collaboration, where almost everyone in the building—Violent Crimes, Surveillance, Patrol, Forensics, and all of the other divisions—combined their efforts in order to generate a breakthrough. Many others experienced it as a hangover.

The old cases, the ones that had been pushed aside, came back to the fore. In some way they felt trivial. It would often take a couple of days until Lindell and her colleagues were back. Mentally they were still standing on the road in Uppsala-Näs or in the clearing in the woods in Rasbo.

Lindell wasn't satisfied. There were too many questions remaining. This feeling of dissatisfaction kept her from moving on for a while.

She had at least three investigations on her plate. Strictly speaking, she had even more, but she ignored the rest, moving the files far away onto a storage table in her office. From time to time she glanced at the stacks of papers.

Primarily she was working on an investigation involving drugs combined with threats and assault. The street dealer unit, which in spite of all the internal reorganization had managed to survive, had done a fantastic job and tracked the activities of a group of kids who during the past year had been supplying the market with Ecstasy. In the wake of the investigation there were at least three cases of assault, criminal threats, false imprisonment, and illegal possession of firearms. The investigation grew larger day by day, and Lindell had spent many hours sifting through the material, sitting in on interrogations, and participating in case reviews with her colleagues.

With the help of the prosecutor, they were preparing to arrest others while new charges were being brought. This appeared likely to grow into a case of enormous proportions.

But the Cederén family still came up in discussion, during coffee breaks and a couple of times in their regular morning meetings. Ola Haver especially found the whole thing hard to drop. He was still waiting for the call from the convenience store in Vallby.

Really the only new thing that had transpired was the fragment of a ripped-up letter in Spanish that had been found in Cederén's garbage can outside the house in Uppsala-Näs. It had been written by someone named Julio Piñeda, evidently complaining about something—that much they had been able to determine once it had been pieced together. The interpreter Eduardo Cruz had been called in again, but he had found it difficult to provide any additional context. Julio Piñeda wanted money, that much was clear.

It was also not certain which country the letter came from. There were a couple of reasonable assumptions about the country of origin. Most of them assumed it was Spain. Lindell had questioned Mortensen to see if he had heard the name Piñeda, but he denied all knowledge.

Perhaps an employee at the MedForsk branch in Málaga had been unfairly terminated or treated badly and was now turning to the person in Sweden whom he knew and trusted.

Mortensen had promised to check with his Spanish contacts to see if there was or had ever been a Julio Piñeda on their books.

The interpreter believed the letter came from the Dominican Republic. There was something about the handwriting, the quality of the paper, and perhaps above all the tone that suggested the Caribbean. He could not give any firm reasons, it was more of a feeling, he said, and Lindell believed him.

Now the letter had been pasted together as well as could be, copied, and archived. Perhaps Julio Piñeda would emerge at some point in the future. Lindell had driven to the site of the accident by the Uppsala-Näs church, and on one occasion she saw someone standing by the side of the road whom she became convinced was Piñeda.

That morning she had been poring over the letter with the interpreter and trying to understand it. It was as if the writer's words had sounded out across the valley. Lindell had learned the words in the letter by heart. It was written in a primitive, almost childish manner.

"*We have experienced so much suffering,*" the interpreter had quoted, "*and now we turn to you with a prayer for . . .*" The rest of the sentence was missing.

"'We have experienced so much suffering,'" Lindell had repeated as she stood by the side of the road. Josefin's father would be forced to drive by this site many times during the remainder of his life. And he would always be reminded. The unjust, almost unimaginable events that had occurred in this place would carve deep wounds into him. Perhaps he would start taking another way around?

What suffering had Julio Piñeda experienced? What role had Cederén played in all of this? Lindell walked along the road. A car went by slowly. The driver peered at her with interest and Lindell stared back grimly.

A few words from Josefin's diary returned to her. "Sven-Erik went out with Isabella. Was gone for two hours. Why does he drink so much? Jack says it is the stress, that he needs to rest. I don't believe him. Sven-Erik loves stress. He doesn't touch me anymore. He doesn't love me."

If Cederén no longer loved his wife, why run her over? Was there a financial motive? Lindell dismissed the idea. What had happened that morning? He had fetched the paper, had chatted with the neighbor as usual, and had driven away, apparently on his way to work. He had taken the dog. Where was it now?

Josefin had prepared for her annual pilgrimage to her mother's grave. No one saw her leave the house. She spoke with no one that day, either on the telephone or on the road. She did as she had planned to do, had taken her daughter by the hand and walked out the door.

Lindell could not understand it. And she hated not being able to understand.

✦

Fourteen

In fourth grade, Ann Lindell had played a mole in a school play. She had worn a fur costume—extremely hot and much too big—and a hat altered to look like the animal's snout and blind eyes.

She had stumbled when she made her entrance but had recovered by improvising and scoring extra points with her clumsy moves. When she took her final bow, she had bowed so low that the hat fell off, and as she fumbled for it, she had looked out over the sea of people in the audience and spotted her father, clapping wildly, as flushed as she was, enthusiastic, his mouth open and his eyes on her alone.

Everyone else in the school auditorium—parents and teachers—had faded away into a vague blur, still shouting and clapping but essentially faceless. Her father's face was the only one.

He had brought a case of soda for the entire cast to enjoy in the wings after the end of the show. Everyone had been talking excitedly at the same time. The costumes had come off and none of the sweaty ten-year-olds had yet recovered from the complete success that they now realized they had played a part in.

Ann's father had supplied soda and praise for the show. The teacher, Miss Bergman, had wept with joy. Ann had drunk Pommac. The crowded space behind the stage had smelled of sweat and happiness.

Viola was outside the chicken coop wearing an incredible mole-brown coat with a worn fur collar. On her head she had a knitted cap in a gray shade, and on her feet, the obligatory boots with the tops turned down.

Midsummer's Eve. The sun had just broken out from behind the clouds. Viola had been collecting eggs in the chicken coop. She had just stepped out into the yard and was standing completely still, watching Ann as she drove up in front of the house and parked her car. The sun revealed her gaunt frame. Viola smiled, not too warmly or too long, but enough for some of Ann's nervousness to pass. She stepped out of the car and walked over to the old woman.

They stood in front of each other. It had been six months since the last time. Ann resisted the impulse to hug her.

"Happy Midsummer!"

Viola snorted in reply.

"The hens have taken a vacation," she said sourly, and rattled the basket where a dozen or so eggs lay tucked into a bed of newspaper.

"We can make do with that," Ann said.

"Did you see Victor?" Viola asked. "He was supposed to come over this morning."

She always managed to make it sound as if her neighbor were a great imposition, but Ann knew that if there was anyone Viola wanted to have over, it was Victor. They had been born on nearby farms, had gone to school together, and had lived as neighbors on Gräsö Island their whole lives. Perhaps they had also once nurtured thoughts of living together. That is not how things had turned out, but Viola and Victor were the most touching and vivid example of a lifelong friendship that Ann had ever seen.

"It's only nine-thirty," Ann said.

"He's such a lazybones."

Viola took a couple of steps toward the house before she stopped and peered back at Ann, saying in an unusually kind voice that Ann should feel very welcome. Then she kept on walking.

Ann watched her go. Her feet slipped around in her boots and the worn coat looked as if it could fall apart at any moment. She appeared to have an endless supply of ragged old clothes from old trunks and cupboards. Ann guessed the coat had belonged to Viola's mother. It looked as if it was as old as she was.

Viola banged the veranda door shut and left Ann alone in the yard. If she hadn't known the old woman from before, she would have felt unwelcome. In this case it was almost the opposite. Viola was her usual self; nothing had changed in the past six months. Ann had turned up as an old friend.

Edvard was still nowhere to be seen and Viola had not said a word about him. Ann had a feeling he was down by the water and walked around the side of the house in order to catch sight of him.

They had not seen each other since Christmas. Would he look the same? How would he greet her?

She pulled off her thin summer jacket and let the wind bring the sea to her. The sounds of the birds, the heavy scent of meadowsweet, the year-old alder cones scattered across the sun-warmed earth like large rabbit droppings. Gräsö Island. She breathed in its name, allowing it to fill her lungs and bring oxygen to her blood.

She closed her eyes. The cries of the gulls across the bay. Maybe Edvard was cleaning fish. These sounds belonged to her. Even if the nor'easter was going to push its violent hand into the sound and whip the water into churning dark-green ferocity, her life in this moment was smooth as a mirror.

She was simply here, in the force field between Viola's house—a wooden palace for Roslagen princes and princesses, her fairy castle—and the heavy mass of the sea. Edvard rowing, his hands moving across the gray-blue shimmering surface, his smile and the ripple of his muscles under the faded T-shirt as his quiet but powerful strokes transported her into ever-deeper waters.

The dinghy was one of the few occasions where she could watch him without his becoming self-conscious or averting his gaze. She thought it had to do with the fact that he was engaged in work. He had his own style of rowing. He leaned forward so far that he almost touched her knees with his knuckles, placed the blades of the oars far forward, and with an elegant motion leaned his body so far back that he was almost horizontal. For a split second, before his next stroke, he stared up at the sky and Ann saw the glint from the whites of his eyes.

Up with the blades, the start of a new stroke, the knuckles toward her knees, and then pulling on the oar. A half-circular motion that was propelling them out into the bay. Her desire to watch him did not wane.

He claimed to have learned the technique from the Vikings. That was how the Vikings in their easterly expeditions made their way, he claimed. Nothing halfhearted about it. From time to time he paused, taking a look at where they were going, and Ann could see the sense of freedom in his face.

In these moments he wore an expression of energy and happiness. He was working and she could watch him to her heart's content. His hint of a beer belly had vanished in Gräsö—whether it was from the rowing or the frequent jobs with Gottfrid, the builder he was assisting, she did not know, but his stomach had grown flat and muscular. His hands had always been strong. A country laborer's hands, a rower's.

He had also talked more in the boat, become chatty in a relaxed and nonchalant way that she wished he would be more often, even on land. Why did he have to sit in a boat in order to speak freely?

For the first time she understood Edvard's longing for the sea. She wanted to scream out her joy, that life could caress her, surround her in this natural, uncomplicated way. No riches in the world could make up for this, she thought, and suddenly felt dizzy, forced to make her way to the boulder where Viola liked to rest her aching legs. She pulled off her shoes and pushed her feet gently into the grass. It was still a little damp and the stalks tickled her shoe-pinched feet pleasantly.

He would gaze at her with love. She was beautiful and desired. She untucked her tank top and let a little air onto her belly.

She drummed her fingers against the stone, picking off some moss, looking out toward the water. Then she stood up, grabbed her jacket and shoes, and walked hesitantly back toward the house. The gravel in the yard stuck to her bare feet.

She walked to the car and fetched her bag in order to put her things upstairs, then changed her mind, dropped it on the ground, and instead went straight to the rickety bench next to the chicken coop. She sat down. The temperature had risen even more and she had the impulse to pull her top off completely. She felt pale. If Viola hadn't been there behind the kitchen curtains, she would have undressed and sunned herself against the warm wall.

What was he doing? Now the question no longer had the ominous undertone it had had when she repeated it to herself through the winter and spring. He was down by the water and would soon turn up. She stroked her belly, pulled the top up so that at least her navel would get a little color. Soon he would come around the corner and they would lay eyes on each other. Would he have changed?

She bent over and picked up a handful of gravel. "Loves me, loves me not," she said as she dropped the pebbles one by one.

Her stomach growled. She raised her gaze, thinking she heard something, and only now noticed the young birches that Edvard had arranged by the door. They stood in a red plastic bucket, surrounded by Viola's white plastic flowerpots. Red-and-white-striped petunias, some yellow flowers, and some pink ice begonias. Only Edvard and Viola could create such a combination, Ann thought and smiled.

Viola peeked out from between the curtains. She was sitting by the chicken coop. Why doesn't she go down? But she knew why. Ann preferred to wait for him. Edvard was taking his time for the same reason. He must know she had already arrived but was slow leaving the shore. Viola sometimes became aggravated and also anxious when he was late. It was the island woman's inherited sense of worry when the menfolk lingered too long on the water. Only Stockholmers did that, lolling on exposed rock or just standing and looking out at the waves.

Edvard was almost one of them, and yet not. He sometimes dreamed down by the sea even if he usually tried to think of a rationale to go down there. Sometimes she went with him. In the fall they had picked sea buckthorn together, something she hadn't done since the thirties. Between the two of them, they had gathered fifteen liters. Edvard had sold the berries to a physician who lived in the direction of Svartbäck. They had met at the mill and had apparently started talking about buckthorn. It was exceedingly healthful, the physician had told him. Edvard had come back with seven hundred and fifty kronor, and Viola had laughed the whole afternoon.

She didn't know what to think as she watched Ann pining on the bench like a lovesick hen. Viola had sat there herself many times. It was a good place to wait.

One thing she knew: Her time with Edvard as a renter had been two good years. They got along well together. He made her life easier, went shopping, handled all practical matters, and gave her life a meaning these last years that she had to live. Even Victor came more often to the house when Edvard was around. There was life in the house. She loved to hear him bustle about in the morning, his footsteps on the stairs, how he came in with the firewood or when he wound the clock in the parlor.

She had made him her heir. He would inherit all of her belongings except the grandfather clock, which was going to a second cousin in Stockholm. Perhaps she had written her will with a touch of calculation—anything to keep him longer on the island—but the more time that went by, the better she grew to know her renter and the more her generosity was driven by pure caring and love. He had become the son she had never had, the one that Victor should have given her.

Ann threatened all this and had done so since the first time she stepped across the threshold. She had created anxiety, trying to get him to move closer to Uppsala.

Viola had been relieved last Christmas when it seemed that Ann had disappeared for good. Now here she was again, leaning up against the chicken coop with her attractive young body. How would Edvard be able to resist her this time? And yet she found it hard to dislike the policewoman. She was a good woman, as Victor said, considerate and never intrusive. Ann was a positive influence on Edvard. He had become happier, more open. That was something he learned from Ann, and it was something Viola also benefited from.

Perhaps she could move out to the island? Viola watched as Ann dropped pebble after pebble onto the ground and sensed what was going on in Ann's head. She was here at Edvard's behest, she knew that, and Ann had showed up and that was answer enough as to what was on her mind. She wouldn't have come if she didn't love Edvard.

Viola took out the large tray. They would be sitting outside. Two couples. Victor and she had never managed to get together, had never even kissed each other. And then there were these two youngsters, who had bedded each other so the whole house shook. She had never said anything or indicated how thin the walls were, how the sounds of their lovemaking had traveled through walls and floors and kept her awake as she had thought of her life and her aches.

Viola scrubbed the new potatoes briskly and tossed them one by one into the pot. They had grown these potatoes themselves. Edvard had helped her make the rows and then covered them in plastic to hasten the setting of the tubers. This variety was called Rocket, and Viola was unhappy with the fact that it was so watery. They should have planted the variety called Puritan, which she had suggested instead.

Ann waited, couldn't make herself go up. Perhaps he would like it if she marched in as if she were taking everything for granted. I am still a guest, she thought. I wonder how he has made the beds? Perhaps he didn't have a thought of resuming the relationship? The fact was that she wasn't sure herself. This Midsummer celebration would have to determine how things would be. There were worse ways to frame a lover's meeting, she thought, and the ache in her belly returned.

Then he suddenly rounded the corner. He didn't see her, but he did spot the car and peered in through Viola's window. He took some hesitant steps toward the porch. His uncertainty made her smile. It struck her that he was as nervous as she was. He pulled his hand through his hair and tucked his shirt into his pants. In one hand he was carrying a bucket.

She called his name. Edvard spun around, saw her, but made no attempt to walk over.

"Hello," he said simply and put the bucket down.

Ann got up. They looked at each other. He walked closer.

"Welcome."

"Thank you."

He looked like he did before.

"I'm glad you could come."

She nodded.

"It's been a while."

He was tan, his hair longer than usual, and he still had the same self-conscious smile. She felt as though he was a stranger, and yet so familiar. She looked at him. Would she have fallen for this threadbare middle-aged rustic if she met him for the first time today? He smiled wryly, aware of her gaze, and made a gesture that could be interpreted as *What you see is what you get.*

He prepared to say something, but the sound of a tractor stopped him. They turned to the road and saw Victor's Little Grey Fergie tractor come bouncing along, Victor at the wheel. His three cousins—Sven-Olle, Kurt, and Tore—as well as Tore's wife, Gerd, were being jostled in the wagon.

"The whole gang's here." Edvard chuckled.

The entourage drove in a circle around the yard and Victor honked and waved. Ann saw Viola's face in the window. Sven-Olle tossed a kiss toward the house.

"I brought the entire congregation," Victor yelled and pulled up so abruptly that Gerd was almost thrown off the vehicle.

"Be careful of the herring," she screamed.

Gerd was known for her vocal resources. The ferrymen called her "Screamer-Gerd." She took the moped to Öregrund two times a week and always placed herself at the front by the boom, blocking the cars as they tried to exit. The ferrymen put up with her, happy to have someone who could frustrate the city folk.

Edvard laughed and Ann looked at him.

"We have home-brewed aquavit," Victor went on, and Ann guessed that the white plastic container on the back of the truck was filled with Gräsö Absolut, which induced dizziness and inspired festive encounters. Victor and his cousins had most likely already sampled their wares.

How many times had she had to turn a professional blind eye to the containers and bottles pulled out at these parties? Victor had been a little careful in the beginning, especially when driving the tractor after consumption of the gray liquid was involved, but little by little his inhibitions were lowered as he realized that she didn't care.

They had brought not only pickled herring and alcohol but also bags and boxes loaded with pots and dishes filled with leek casserole and various gratins. Fresh vegetables and beer were unloaded. Kurt and Tore lowered a laundry basket that turned out to contain six different herring dishes, new potatoes, beets, dill, store-bought aquavit, liqueurs, pork chops, salmon, and freshly caught Baltic herring.

Ann and Edvard took in this magnificence, with Gerd's eyes on them.

Victor glanced at the kitchen window. The cousins started to fetch and carry. Gerd hollered.

"Wonderful," Edvard said to Gerd with appreciation. "You've worked hard."

She pretended not to hear and yelled at Tore for being careless. Suddenly the kitchen window opened and Viola stuck her head out.

"Get that miserable tractor out of my sight," she said and quickly closed the window again.

Victor smiled and walked up to Ann, putting his hands on her shoulders.

"This is your chance to get some meat on those bones," he said.

Ann looked into his aging face and felt his alcohol-laden breath.

"You're just the same, Victor. It's nice to see you."

He smiled, then turned to supervise the unloading. Tore grabbed the container and Gerd was looking more and more dissatisfied, but everyone knew things would lighten up when they sat down at the table. Gerd was a food person. She showed her best side when she was cooking and when she was eating what she'd prepared.

"We've slaughtered the calf," Victor said and turned back to Ann.

She didn't really understand what he meant by this. Surely they no longer kept animals? He saw her uncertain expression and chuckled but instead of explaining himself turned to Edvard.

"Was that stupid?" he asked and pointed at the cousins and Gerd.

"No, no," Edvard assured him.

"Viola might be unhappy."

As if in answer to these thoughts, Viola stepped out onto the porch. The old coat had been replaced by a green dress with red flowers. It reached all the way down to her rubber boots. Her hair had been smoothed back into a knot. She saw their gazes and appeared to have some trouble deciding which expression she should assume. Victor shuffled anxiously in his SnowJoggers.

Ann's gaze went from Viola to Victor, and suddenly she burst into tears. Victor was alarmed and rushed over.

"What is it?"

Ann sobbed, apologizing, and looked markedly embarrassed. The episode was over as quickly as it had begun.

"I don't know," she said truthfully.

"You need some food," Gerd pronounced.

Edvard stood completely passive. Ann looked up and their gazes met.

"I'll put the tractor away," Victor said.

They went about setting up one long table. Viola took out some linen tablecloths. Ann carried the china. Gerd scrubbed more potatoes, boiled beets, dished up herring in all kinds of pickled sauces, and heated dishes in the oven. The cousins carried the chairs. Victor fried the Baltic herring and competed with Gerd for space in front of the stove.

At half past twelve they sat down to eat, Viola at one end and Edvard at the other. Midsummer's Eve. To the east, over the mainland, there were dark clouds, but the sun was shining on the island. Kurt expressed his joy at the fact that it was raining in Valö and Norrskedika.

Ann had picked flowers and decorated the table with them. A brimstone butterfly searched for nectar in the head of a harebell. Everyone at the table fell silent at the sight of the yellow butterfly fluttering above the summery bouquet.

From the water, they could hear the buzz of the powerboats as well as laughter and noise. It was as if the cousins were listening out to sea because they shortly fell into telling their tales. The stories, the humorous ones, of which many had been repeated throughout the years and at many parties, evoked much laughter and commentary. Soon the din from the bay was drowned out by the eruptions from around the table.

"When it was hot in the summer, his wife set the vacuum cleaner in reverse and popped the hose under the sheets. 'Air-conditioning,' Morin called it."

"He died, that one," Gerd observed dryly, still eating with gusto. She knew this because Morin had become a wiener cousin to one of her kin.

"But he was nice," she added.

"The hell he was," Tore said, as always fired up by the Gräsö Absolut. "He was a mean bastard."

Gerd gave him a look above the flower arrangement. In time she would have the last word, she knew.

Tore and Morin had both been employed at the Forsmark nuclear power plant and had never seen eye to eye. The gang told a number of Forsmark stories, followed by the usual bad-mouthing of the summer residents and anyone else with more than six years of schooling.

They did this even as they knew better. The old people around the table felt a mixture of awe and envy, respect and inferiority toward the city folk who had invaded their island. This was true even for those necessary outsiders such as veterinarians, public works officials, land surveyors, highway engineers, and others who effectively governed their island through their arbitrary decisions.

The old people simply bowed, obstructed, didn't give a damn, bowed again, sometimes yielding, but always with the inherent suspicion and envy of generations of islanders. They judged people as it suited them depending on the day and what they stood to gain.

That they had accepted Edvard so quickly had to do with the fact that he had worked with the land and with animals. Ann was with Edvard. She was also a decent sort and didn't poke her nose in anyone's business, and last but not least, she was a woman and therefore of no consequence, especially as seen from Gerd's perspective. Gerd railed against all "womenfolk" regardless of where they came from.

Gather a bunch of Gräsö islanders around a table with filled shot glasses and there's no risk of low spirits, Lindell thought. Apart from a feeling of satiation, she felt very thankful for being included at the table. Kurt launched into a drinking song about a swan. He had a decent voice and sang verse after verse until Tore made him stop.

Viola had had a couple of shots and smiled at everyone. For once it didn't look as if she was cold.

The dinner dragged on and Lindell started to feel some impatience. She had not had the opportunity to talk to Edvard. She found herself thinking about the Cederén investigation. In her thoughts, she returned to the road in Uppsala-Näs and saw the unknown Julio Piñeda before her. "We all carry a great sorrow . . ." She was suddenly convinced that the answer to the riddle lay there, in Piñeda's great sorrow.

Edvard noticed her serious look and he realized where her mind was. He whispered her name, and after a couple of attempts, she reacted and looked up.

"Where are you?" he asked.

"Here," she said simply.

She got up from the table. Edvard did the same and together they left the increasingly noisy group. Lindell felt that she had to guard her tongue. The shots and the beer had affected her more than she had realized while she was still sitting at the table.

They walked quietly, side by side, down to the sea. Edvard turned his gaze to the west. A mighty rainbow rose up from the horizon, but the sun was still shining over the island. They halted. Lindell wanted to touch him but hesitated. Edvard was the one who continued the walk. He did not choose the usual path. Instead they ended up walking through high grasses and herbs and arrived at the old boathouse.

"How have things been for you?" she asked.

"Good."

Touch me, she thought.

"How about the knee?"

"It's better."

He continued along the shoreline and came to the new dock.

"We built this one last winter," he said. "Me, Victor, and the boys."

Ann nodded.

"It's nice," she said and gazed at the massive construction, which by its enormous weight and new lumber stood in stark contrast to the old boathouse and the graying logs of the old dock.

Edvard took a few steps out, testing its stability with bouncing steps.

"This will last a long time," he said and turned to Ann.

"The boys helped you?"

He nodded.

"They slaved over those stones and boulders every day of their spring break. This stone coffin construction—that's the technical term for it—is the largest on the whole island, according to Victor. They really worked hard."

"Stone coffin—is that really what it's called?"

"Uh-huh."

"It's a little creepy," Lindell said.

"Victor spent two weeks on the couch after we were done. He was completely finished."

Edvard looked out over the water. Stood silently.

"What did the boys say? Did they think it was fun?"

"Yes, they liked it. It's the best thing that's happened since I got divorced."

What about me, Lindell thought, but she understood what he meant.

"Maybe it's genetic. I loved stone masonry, my dad was the same, and now the boys."

He talked more about the stone boulders, how they had gathered them and thought of various solutions in order to get them where they needed to be. Some had weighed hundreds of kilos. The tractor and an old winch had been needed in order to coax the boulders into place, but they had also had to strain with their hands and sticks.

As Edvard talked, it struck her that it was the dock that had been the destination for their walk. This was what he had wanted to show her.

She realized that the four of them had built a monument. Victor had approached it from his particular perspective. This was likely the last dock construction he would be involved with. He had overworked his old body and had had to rest for fourteen days. For Edvard, with his love of stone and physical labor, it was his first construction of a stone coffin, a task to his taste. Few projects were as archaic as this. And the boys could finally be united with their father in a shared undertaking. She could imagine their enthusiasm, their pride.

A monument resting in the bay, equipped with seven-inch-wide pressure-treated planks, protecting the boats. A place to anchor that could withstand a nor'easter, the power of the ice and waves.

Edvard kept talking. He showed her the plaque with their names.

"And it turned out to be a fine dock," he said as a concluding statement. Then he looked at her.

Lindell agreed. When the story of the dock was finished, it didn't look like Edvard knew what else to talk about.

Lindell sat at the very end and let her legs dangle.

"I left," she said suddenly. "I loved you, but I left anyway. It was too much."

She sensed Edvard's anxiety but went on. It had to be said, six months worth of dammed-up thoughts.

"It got to be too heavy. Partly the job and partly you. We just didn't laugh enough. Do you know what I mean?"

She wasn't sure how to go on. She wanted to do it right, not to hurt his feelings or say things that would shut him down. She wanted to get him to talk about himself, about her, in the same way that he had talked about the dock.

"You gave me so much. I was richer with you, saw things in a different light. I know you don't want to move away from Gräsö. That was what I wanted last Christmas: that you would bet on me, move in closer to town, meet your boys, start to live."

"I love you," he interrupted.

It was as if the dock swayed from an imperceptible wind. He sat down by her side and put his arm around her shoulders. It was a weight she had been longing for. He repeated what he had said. They sat completely still, staring out over the water.

"I've thought about moving," he said, "but it doesn't feel fair to Viola. But I know it. I know I have to move closer to you and the boys."

Go on, Lindell thought, keep talking. She leaned her head against his shoulder.

"I want to try with you," he said softly. "Maybe we can pull it off."

Pull it off. She smiled to herself.

The sun had set behind the alder trees when they got up from the dock. They strolled hand in hand like a pair of newlyweds. Not much had been said, and they walked quietly back to the house. We have to learn to talk again, Lindell thought. This time I won't let go. I will force him to let go, to talk, to express himself, to give his opinion on how life should be lived.

"I'm not letting you go," she said when they arrived at the woodshed.

The old people had gone inside. The bank of clouds from the mainland had come a little closer, but the air was still warm. Dusk enveloped the house and its surrounding area in an expectant silence. It was completely still. The calmness of the nature around them, the light clouds to the south that slowly sailed into one another in the sky, swiping a neighbor here and being pushed together there, spoke of a clear evening and night. The birds in the trees were celebrating the twilight. They weren't moving as quickly anymore. They were flying in lazy arcs between the old rowan and the juniper bushes in the pasture. Edvard had a notion that they might be visiting one another, that the worst of the spring and early summer frenzy was over. The territories had been meted out and defined, the eggs were under way, and now there was time for a little relaxation, a little chirping in the bushes.

They did not go directly into the main house. Instead they took the stairs up to Edvard's room. Ann peeked in the room next to Edvard's bedroom and saw that he had made up the bed.

"Did you think we would have separate bedrooms?"

"You can never be too sure of these things," he said. "The fact is, that little bedroom is always made up these days. Fredrik comes out sometimes and then the boys. It's become a bit of a hostel."

She snuggled close to him. She wanted to feel his chest against hers.

"Should we go down?" he said and gently loosened himself from her grip.

Their need for closeness and—at the same time—their shyness with each other meant that they simply ended up standing there with silly smiles on their lips. Lindell wanted so badly for him to squeeze her long and hard, but he only smiled tentatively.

The rest of Midsummer's Eve they spent in Viola's parlor. The cousins were starting to calm down, but Victor and Gerd were still in high gear and playing cards. The television was on, displaying images from Dalarna: the raising of a Midsummer pole, a choir singing, and a tug-of-war. Lindell looked around and for a moment imagined that they were in a nursing home.

Edvard told Victor that the dock received approval from the police, at which the old man laughed heartily.

Viola bustled around the kitchen, making the coffee. Lindell went out to her and stayed there. Edvard sat down in the sofa. He could hear the two women talking and the dishes clattering.

When the shadow of the rowan reached the roof of the chicken coop, the old people gathered themselves together and left in the tractor. Lindell, Edvard, and Viola stood in the yard and watched it disappear around the bend by the plum orchard.

"The air is a bit raw," Viola said and shivered. "But at least there won't be any rain."

She kept talking, chilly but unwilling to turn in. Lindell wanted to ask Viola what she thought about the fact that she had returned, but realized that she couldn't. For a moment she was struck by uncertainty. Was this really the way things were supposed to be? Should she and Edvard go up the flight of stairs and become reunited? Her choice was so close at hand. Longing mingled with worries for the future. The stairs up to Edvard's room constituted a path that felt decisive. She wanted in some way to have Viola's blessing, as if the old woman with her gruff wisdom could pass final judgment and say: Of course, this is right. You're going to pull it off. Or perhaps: Go home to Uppsala, Ann, Edvard isn't right for you. I know, I'm a woman and live with him.

Say something one way or the other, Lindell thought, and in the old woman's talk of the weather, she tried to discern something else.

As if Viola could sense Lindell's inner struggles, she suggested that they have a final snack before turning in. Lindell knew that she had trouble falling asleep and liked having company as long as possible, but Edvard said he was more than full.

"In that case," Viola said, "we should get ready for bed and dream sweet dreams."

The day after started with nausea. Lindell woke early. Edvard was still sleeping heavily when she got up, pulled on her clothes, and went outside.

It was a heavenly morning. The birds greeted her with a song she had not heard for a long time. She had hardly gotten through the door before she gagged and got an aftertaste of herring. Suddenly the morning was no longer as appealing. She felt terrible and quickly made her way around the corner of the house. Just beyond the corner, by the large rain barrel, she vomited. Brutally, violently, and abruptly. She broke out in a cold sweat and hardly had time to think before the next attack came on. She leaned forward and stared repulsed at the ground.

She moved her hand along the barrel and dipped her fingers into the

water. The nausea still came in waves. She spit and felt completely confused. Yes, she had drunk alcohol, but only in small amounts. It must be
Victor's home brew, she thought, and felt panicky. She had heard about bad
liquor and witnessed the consequences.

For a couple of minutes she stood completely still, splashing the water,
dabbing her face, and rinsing her mouth. Hopefully Viola hadn't seen her.
The old woman's window faced this way but her blinds were still down.

After a while, when she felt better, she straightened back up. She shivered and cursed herself, or rather her body, for ruining this beautiful
morning. The birds paid no attention to her troubles, the wind continued
its soft humming in the alder thickets down toward the sea, and—despite
the early hour—the sun was warm. But still she shivered uncontrollably.

She wanted to walk down to the shore but hesitated. If she went in to
get a sweater, Edvard would likely wake up. Then she remembered that
Viola had an entire collection of coats and sweaters in the hall. She walked
carefully across the gravel yard, opened the creaking door, and picked out
a red sweater, which she wrapped around herself.

The sea was almost completely calm. A slender band of mist hovered
like smoke along the inside of the bay. She felt better and smiled. The peace-
fulness of the water and the pastoral idyll of this early morning caused her
to swallow, deeply moved. So beautiful, so breathtakingly beautiful. Nature smiled at her and seemed to say: I envelop you in my finest clothing,
my beloved.

Lindell wasn't religious but felt an intoxicating sense of wonder. Her
shivering was replaced by a warmth rising up through her body. This
was what Edvard had seen, she thought. The faint scent of thyme and a
tidy little stand of goldmoss sedum emerging from a crack in the rock
brought her to her knees. A light spray of water rinsed the bun-shaped
rocks on the beach. A tendril of water snaked up toward her foot but
then retreated languidly. She stretched out on the rock and let the sun
warm her face.

She could hear noisy sea gulls carrying on in the distance. She knew
that they would soon appear, perhaps attracted by her presence. She lay
completely still, her eyes closed. One of her hands caressed the rough goldmoss. She mentally examined her recent interactions with Edvard. He had

been shy, hadn't said much. She had expected—perhaps because he had talked so passionately about the boys and the construction of the dock—that he would be more talkative and tell her about his hopes and plans for the future, but he had only gazed at her with loving eyes. That night they had made love as before, intensely and furiously.

She loved his hands, his chest, and the tender words he whispered when he was excited. Afterward they had finally talked. He did want to try again. He had longed for her but had tried to build his own life. I thought I was a loner, he said. Someone who can no longer handle close contact with another, with a woman. He paused, but Lindell had urged him on. He told her that the renewed contact with his boys had weakened these convictions. He wanted to live with her. The boys had awakened his desire to share his life with someone, and Ann was that someone.

"There is no one else," he had told her. "I knew that two years ago. That's why I called."

"I'm glad that you did," Lindell had murmured, moved by his declaration.

As she lay on the rock, surrounded by the most seductive scents of Gräsö Island, her resolve grew even stronger. The intoxicating lovemaking could be an illusion, but she knew now that it was Edvard and no one else. They would pull it off. Maybe she could move out to the island. Violent Crimes was her life, but there had to be other work opportunities that would bring her closer. Any job on the outskirts of Uppland would be a step down, she knew that. It would curtail her career possibilities, but that wasn't what worried her. She could handle that. She didn't really have the ambition to climb that ladder. But she would miss the collaboration with her coworkers. And Ottosson. Uppsala was a fast-paced district in the hands of bunglers, but all the activity in their building, the interactions with her colleagues, and the encounters with the people of the city stimulated her, kept her going.

She tried to imagine working in Tierp or Östhammar, but she knew too little about northern Uppland to imagine what it would be like. She would have a life with Edvard, but what about the rest? She would have the bay, the pastures, and the chicken coop, but would she be able to stand the peace and quiet? Edvard did. He was raised in a small village. She had fled Ödeshög for the big city.

She lay on the rock for over an hour. It wasn't nausea but hunger pangs that made her rise. As predicted, the black-backed gulls had come. They were sitting on the skerry, screeching and quarreling as usual.

Somewhere in the distance, a motorboat started up. Lindell walked slowly back to the house. The water clucked against the stone-filled dock. A gull sat at the very end of it, grooming itself. She thought of the small plaque with the names of Edvard, Victor, and the boys, and how important it was.

In some way she wished that the guests of last night's celebrations had put their name on a similar plaque, hung somewhere. The cousins, wonderful Gerd with her temper and her dry sense of humor, the increasingly frail Viola and her Victor, Edvard and herself. This collection, connection—that's what it's all about, she thought. To live your life with the hope that love can forge a connection to other people. In her work she had seen what the absence of this could lead to.

She stayed until Sunday night. Victor had returned, out of a concern for Viola, it seemed to Lindell. When Lindell was staying, Viola was a third wheel. They'd had lunch and dinner together the day after Midsummer, and he had also come by on Sunday with several freshly caught perch that Viola had fried up with plenty of cream.

Ann and Edvard had gone on long walks, talking carefully of how the winter and spring had been. They were testing each other and themselves. This must be love, she said to herself.

They agreed to be in touch later in the week. Maybe Lindell would spend a week or two of her vacation out on the island. Maybe they would travel somewhere together. Perhaps they would go to Ödeshög together. Nothing was decided, but both of them knew it would be a good summer. Then they would have to see. Summer was easy. It was in September that the true test would come.

✦

Fifteen

Ove Lundin sat in the Avid editing room, putting the finishing touches on a segment about the Akademiska hospital. He thought he had seen the images before, the politician who said the same thing that all the other county officials had said before.

He heard someone on the stairs and then Anna's voice. She was the studio host and was escorting Ann-Britt Zimén from the Liberal People's Party, who was scheduled to appear in the studio later. Anna turned on the television in the small space outside the control room. He heard Anna explain when they were going to go in.

Lundin left the editing room, greeting them both. Zimén appeared nervous. He joined the rest of his colleagues in the control room. There was Melin, the audio tech, the image editor, Rosvall, and the editor for the evening, Charlie Nikoforos. The writer, a new girl Ove had hardly even spoken a word to, was sorting out the exact spelling of Zimén's name. She typed it in and was then done with her work. She was in charge of all of the times and the names.

In the studio there were two cameramen and Anders Moss, who was going to lead the conversation in the studio. The newscaster had not come down yet. They had a quarter of an hour to go. They would start at 18:10.

There was no shocking news to deliver. Beside some health care issues, there was a segment about genetic research, a quick report on a situation regarding the detention facilities in Enköping, and one about the Pharmacia board meeting. The LPP politician was the "headliner" who was going to try to bring county politics to life for the audience. Ove Lundin was not expecting her to cause a sensation. She had looked almost frightened.

Birgitta Nilsson, who would be reading the news this evening, arrived in the studio and commented on the new backdrop on the wall. For the nth time, Lundin noted with exasperation.

She sat down, glanced down at the computer screen built into the desk, and exchanged a few words with Moss.

"You have a spot on your nose," he said, and even though she knew that he was joking, she had to get out her compact and double-check. She put on her lapel mike and checked the prompter she would be reading from. The intro was already on it, the lead that gave all of the program headlines before two minutes of advertising took over. She sighed, but if this bored her, she did not show it. In fact she looked markedly alert.

She pressed the earpiece in firmly and immediately heard the editor's voice.

"We've shortened Enköping by twenty seconds."

She quickly checked the screen.

"Okay," she said.

Anna Brink observed the female politician. She looked extremely nervous. The guests often were—studying their image in the mirror again and again, pulling on their hair, making tiny movements with their mouths, straightening tie or blouse, laughing in a forced manner, or simply standing without saying anything. Anna had seen all of these behaviors, and Ann-Britt Zimén managed to combine all of them into a sort of spasmodic pattern.

"It's going to be fine," Anna said.

She felt sorry for the woman. They just had to hope that she would calm down or Anders Moss would have a hell of a time of it in the studio.

All at once the woman's face twisted into a frozen look of horror. She stared through the window in the door and whimpered. Anna followed her gaze. On the other side was a young woman. Her hair was no longer blonde but red with blood, as was her face. The whites of her eyes glinted, her mouth was open, and she was pressing one hand against the glass.

Anna pushed the paralyzed Zimén to one side, unhooked the chain, and opened the door. The young woman tried to say something that Ann couldn't understand.

"What has happened?"

The woman quickly pulled the door shut, and before Anna had time to understand what had happened, three or perhaps four figures dressed in black rushed from the loading dock into the narrow waiting area. All of them were masked, and the first thing the bleeding young woman did was also to pull a mask on.

"Not a word," one of them said and laid a hand over Zimén's mouth.

Security was an issue that had been discussed at the station. A lock for the front door had been ordered but not installed, so in a couple of seconds they had been invaded by some gang. This was not a studio visit.

"We don't mean any harm."

Anna saw that they were all young. Slender bodies, thin hands, and youthful voices.

"As long as you keep your mouths shut and do as we say," said another.

Anna and Zimén were forced into the Avid editing room. One of the masked figures grabbed the telephone receiver and pulled out the cord.

"Give me your cell phones," he said, clearly nervous. "How many of you are there?"

"I don't know exactly," Anna said. "Six or seven. Some are in the control room and a couple are in the studio. What do you want?"

"None of your business."

Anna was surprised at herself. She was afraid at first, but felt no terror. Zimén, however, had collapsed, much like her party, and was sitting apathetically against the wall. She would not say anything coherent for a long time. Anna leaned over and told her that everything would be all right.

The door of the room closed. One of the masked men remained outside. The rest stormed into the control room and the studio, the element of surprise on their side. There were only two minutes until the broadcast was scheduled to begin. Charlie Nikoforos attempted to resist them, grabbing one of them by the arm, but the invader only laughed and shrugged him off.

"No one will be hurt if you do what we say," said the one who appeared to be the leader. That was what the audio technician said to the police afterward, that the others seemed to look to him for direction, to follow his instructions.

"We want to broadcast our message and you're going to help us."

He looked slowly around at the entire editorial team, all of whom had gathered in the control room.

"This bag," he said and held up an old-fashioned shopping bag, "contains an explosive massive enough to blow this studio to pieces. You see this thread—if I pull it out there will be only ten seconds until the blast. Some of you may get out in time but not everyone."

They all stared at the insignificant shopping bag. A plastic string stuck up through a gap in the zipper. The man held the bag aloft in his left hand and waved the other, visually suggesting an explosion.

"Who is the newsreader?"

"I am," Birgitta Nilsson said.

"Good. You'll be reading a text for us."

He glanced at the clock on the wall, which read 18:09.

"I want you to look normal, read from the paper, nothing else. Do you understand?"

Birgitta Nilsson stared at him but didn't say anything.

"What the hell," said the editor, "you can't do that!"

"What's this about?" Ove Lundin asked.

"You'll see. All of you should do what you normally do. No tricks. Everything calm and orderly. When our message has gone out, we'll be on our way."

For a brief second, the room was deathly quiet. The shock and the feeling of unreality that had gripped the editorial team started to give way to fear. What if something went wrong? What would happen?

"And no messing around. We have someone on the outside to call to make sure the transmission is going out, so don't try anything. Get it?"

The masked man shouted out his commands. The red marker on the clock was steadily advancing.

"Sit down in there. Look like normal!"

"Thirty seconds," the scriptwriter said and sent a pleading look to the editor.

"Okay," he said, "go to the desk."

Birgitta Nilsson stared at the paper she had been given but couldn't seem to bring herself to read a single line. They all took up their positions in silence. Mechanically, Birgitta picked up the mirror and looked at her pale, blank face. The editor sat down at the small table in the control room. He turned on the microphone that put him in communication with Birgitta.

"Are you there?" he said softly. "You can do this."

One of the cameramen made himself ready.

"Ten seconds," the editor in chief announced.

His gaze was fixed on the monitors. The broadcast began. The introductory music sounded completely unfamiliar.

"Should I do the usual bit?" Birgitta asked.

Anders Moss looked over at the leader, who took a step closer to the open door of the studio, peered in, and then nodded.

"Then there are ads for two minutes."

The masked man nodded again. He appeared to have calmed down.

"Why?" Moss said. "They'll put you away for this."

"Shut up," the man hissed.

Moss was suddenly exasperated with the whole thing. Why do we have to put up with such idiots? The ads were running. Two masked men were keeping watch at the control table, another was in the studio, and then there was the leader. We could take them, Moss thought and tried to make eye contact with the audio technician. But he was just staring dumbly at his controls as if he didn't understand what he was supposed to do.

The seconds slowly ticked away. Ten seconds, Moss thought. How far can we get in ten seconds? Maybe it's a bluff, but who wants to show their colors?

The ads were coming to an end. The audio tech was trembling with terror. His hands rested on the table and were audibly shaking against the surface.

"Ten seconds," the script girl said.

She was the calmest of them all. Birgitta was suddenly on the screen. She gazed nervously into the camera. Those who knew her and who saw the broadcast said afterward that they had noticed nothing, but she felt nauseated from anxiety and fear.

She looked down at the paper in front of her. It was printed in large type, perhaps fifteen rows of strange black letters.

"The Uppsala company MedForsk conducts illegal experiments with primates," she said and then paused.

"What the hell!" the leader yelled from the control room. "Keep going!"

A couple of seconds that felt like years went by before she was able to continue. At this point many of the viewers realized that something was wrong. Perhaps they had heard the wild masked man's voice; perhaps they thought that the text had become jumbled and was the cause of the confusion in Birgitta's face.

"These activities have been conducted for the past two years and are both against the law and a terrible injustice to the primates who are held captive under the most abject conditions. They live in tiny cages and suffer pointlessly. We, the Animal Liberation Front, are warning MedForsk: Put an end to the painful experiments or we will put a stop to your bloody experiments. You think that you can put yourselves above the animals and excuse your behavior by saying that it serves mankind, but the only thing you want is to make money. A final warning: Desist from your criminal activities or you will regret it."

Calle Friesman, who was hanging around waiting for the story on Akademiska that he had finished earlier that afternoon, realized immediately that something was wrong. The first sentence could have made sense, although he hadn't heard anything about a segment on apes, but there was something about Birgitta's voice and gaze. She was reading from a piece of paper, not the prompter, and that in itself was unusual. Admittedly all newscasters had papers in front of them that they occasionally pretended to read from, but that was simply to give a little more life to the presentation.

When she went on, he was chilled to the bone. What the hell is going on with her? he thought and stood up. He looked around the editorial office, but he was the last one there. Maybe someone in marketing was still working, but they didn't normally watch the broadcast closely. Had she lost her marbles?

When she had finished the text, Birgitta Nilsson simply stared helplessly into the camera. She heard Anders shout something about cutting to black. The cameraman collapsed on the floor.

The leader had been in touch with someone who was watching the program. He turned off the phone and gave a chuckle.

Why are they still here? Anders Moss wondered. Don't they realize the police will soon be here?

"You did well. Thanks for the help."

He sounded genuinely appreciative. As if on command, they all left the control room. Their comrade poked his head out of the Avid room. At that moment Calle Friesman came storming down the spiral staircase so fast that he ran straight into the arms of one of the masked men.

"What the hell are you doing?" he yelled.

He was struck on the back of the head, which sent him tumbling against the staircase railing and then in a free fall down the stairs. The pain from his back as he smashed against a step was indescribable. The leader bent over him and Calle noticed his bad breath. Then they all disappeared through the loading dock, the way they had entered ten minutes earlier.

The politician's screams from the Avid room echoed around them.

The alarm came in at 18:15. The caller was Cissi Andersson from the marketing division. She had been working on a quote, and as usual, she had the television on. She rarely watched the broadcast; it was more of a background accompaniment.

But this evening something wasn't right. It was Birgitta's voice. Cissi lifted her gaze from the computer screen, stood up, and looked out through the glass pane facing the studio one floor down.

Anders Moss wasn't in, nor was Ville, the other videographer. Also, the door to the control room stood open, which it normally never did. She listened to the strange report for a couple of seconds and realized that something was wrong. She leaned over and caught sight of a masked man standing close to the cameraman.

Berglund and Haver were on call that evening. Haver was in his office, preparing for a meeting the following morning. When he spoke to Olsson from the call center he immediately realized the gravity of the situation. There was a protocol for terrorist activity, so Haver asked Olsson to call both Ottosson and Wirén at the Swedish Security Service right away.

For his part, Haver called Berglund on his cell phone as he sprinted down the stairs. The patrol units had been notified, and Haver was going to follow their cars to the TV4 station located in the industrial area to the south.

Once he was in the car, he called Lindell. He had heard that the incident involved MedForsk and he knew that she would want to be involved.

It took the police six minutes to reach TV4. The staff was gathered outside the control room and on the loading dock. A few were teary. Calle Friesman was still lying on the stairs, unable to move his legs. The pain in his back had made him unconscious for a short while, but he had come back around. He was sweating profusely and his fingers were twitching. Anna, the studio manager, was leaning over him.

"Just lie still," she said.

The sirens from the ambulance could be heard through the open door to the loading dock.

Haver stopped by the paralyzed man on the stairs for a few seconds and noticed the sweat beading on his brow. He was pale as a corpse. Haver didn't manage to say anything to him.

Berglund raised his voice in order to get the group to gather around. "Did anyone see how they left?"

Everyone stared at the shouting police officers.

"They ran," Anna said. "They rushed out to the loading dock, jumped down, and disappeared around the corner."

"Did you see a car?"

She shook her head. At that moment the ambulance arrived with squealing tires, braking abruptly by the dock. Two EMTs jumped out. Haver recognized one of them.

"Looks to me like he's paralyzed," he said quietly to the driver.

"Damn."

The EMTs exchanged a look, then went in. Haver wished above anything else that the television employee would pull through. If there was anything Haver was terrified of, it was paralysis.

He called Ottosson, who reported that the entire building was up and about. The plan of action for terrorist attacks and hostage situations had been set in motion. Blockades were being erected around the city at strategic, previously identified locations. Special reinforcements were mustered, both for additional officers and equipment.

"Do you have a copy of the broadcast?"

"Yes, we can play it immediately. Do you want to see it?"

"Tell me your name."

"Anders Moss."

"Okay, listen up, all of you. I understand that you are in a state of shock, but try to recall anything you can about the intruders. How many of them were there? Was there anything unusual about their clothing or voices? Were they speaking a dialect? Did they have foreign accents?"

"All of them spoke Swedish," Moss said. "They were young, between twenty and twenty-five."

"How many?"

"Five or six. It was a bit chaotic in here."

Haver looked at Moss, who appeared reasonably collected. Do everything right now, Haver thought.

The EMTs had secured Calle Friesman's neck with a collar and were carefully moving him to a special stretcher. Friesman's eyes were closed. He was gently lifted up and carried out through the narrow door to the dock.

The rest of them were quiet, their eyes locked on Friesman's pale face. Someone sobbed. It was the politician.

"Did they have any weapons?" Berglund asked.

The TV crew members looked at each other, each searching for the answer in another's face.

"I don't think so," the audio technician said. "I didn't see any."

A couple of the others shook their heads.

"They had a bomb," he added. He would always, at every future broadcast, think of the masked intruders.

"A bomb?"

"Yes, that's what they said. They had it in a bag and were going to set it off if we didn't follow their instructions."

"Did you see the bomb?"

"No, it was in a bag. With a string that they were going to pull."

"Describe the bag."

"Brown, with handles. My dad had one like it a long time ago. The kind you had a lunchbox and thermos in."

Haver nodded. His dad had had one just like it.

"But no visible weapons?"

"No," Moss said.

"How did they get in?" Berglund asked.

Moss pointed to the door.

"They tricked me," Anna said. "There was a young girl standing outside, her face covered in blood. I thought she was hurt."

"No one is blaming you for opening the door," Moss said.

"It was fake blood, then?"

Anna nodded.

"She pulled on the mask as soon as she came inside. The only thing I noticed was that she was blonde. I'm going with Calle." She added the last part abruptly and left the room.

The ambulance pulled away and more police vehicles appeared. Haver glimpsed Lindell on the asphalt outside. Canine units had arrived. Police with safety vests and machine guns were huddled together, taking orders from their chief, Ärnlund.

Lindell walked closer and Haver took the stairs down from the dock to meet her.

"MedForsk" was the first thing she said.

"Yes, they've turned up again."

"Any connection?"

"This was about monkeys, about animal experimentation. It sounds like animal rights activists."

"Armed threat?"

"No, they claimed to have a bomb and threatened to set it off. Other than that, they appear to have been rather nice terrorists. The staff is in shock, of course."

"Is the bomb still here?"

Haver couldn't help but smile. "You think we would be allowed to stand here?"

Lindell glanced at the station staff on the dock. Some were smoking; one man was holding a sobbing woman.

"They need help," she said.

"I think it's on its way," Haver said.

They could hear the sound of sirens from the E4. She knew that there were blockades at the Stockholm roundabout, the northern exit to Gävle, and all other larger roads out of town.

"I'll give Jack Mortensen a call. We have to bring him in for questioning and see what he says."

A bus from Radio Uppland drove up. Soon the other media would also have arrived. Taking over a television station during a broadcast was something new, and the other reporters would probably stress their media colleagues even further.

Haver let Lindell know what had emerged from the brief conversations with the staff.

"We'll let Berglund, Wende, and Beatrice take the first interviews. Is anyone hurt? I saw the ambulance."

"One of them banged his back pretty badly. He may be paralyzed."

"Damn," Lindell said. "I'll catch up with Security. They must have a whole database full of animal activist types."

"What should we think about MedForsk?"

Lindell had been thinking about this since she heard the news. Could these same activists have attacked Josefin and Emily?

"I don't know," Haver said. "To run people over is one thing, to save animals another. This doesn't seem to have been particularly violent. There were no visible weapons and the injury could have been more of an accident. They may simply have collided on the stairs."

"But there's been violence in earlier incidents tied to these kinds of people."

"Yes, but I'm still skeptical," Haver said.

"Okay, but is there a connection between Cederén, the chimps, and the activists?"

"You have a lot of questions." Haver smiled.

"Like I said, I'll call Mortensen. I think I'll bring him down to the station. And a chat with the Security people before then."

"I'll stay here. Maybe the dogs will turn something up."

The activity around them was intense. The voices of radio reporters, information updates, and calls mixed with the sound of general chatter. Some patrol officers were busy cordoning off the area. Ryde and a forensic colleague came rumbling along in Ryde's old car.

Lindell drove back to the station. She smiled to herself as she thought about the Security Services chief, the one with the extra-large felt slippers. He was likely having a blast. Finally their laborious information gathering was being put to use. At last they would get to show off a little, not least to their colleagues. Many in the building made fun of Security. Now their time had come.

She felt a sense of anxiety in her body. The holiday spent with Edvard had more than measured up to her high expectations. He had been unusually open and relaxed. They had made love, taken walks, lain down in the meadow and stared at the clouds, and made love again. They had talked about the future only a little, mere hints at its being something that could be shared. Edvard had spoken in vague terms about possibly moving back to town or at least a little closer, and she had mentioned that new officers were always needed in Östhammar and Tierp. Her work wasn't everything, or at least it shouldn't be.

And yet she felt a creeping discomfort. There was something that wasn't right. Later that evening she would understand.

Sure enough, the chief of the Swedish Security Service, Frisk, was very much in his element when he, Lindell, Sammy Nilsson, the head of KUT, and Ottosson had a review session the evening of June 26. He devoured a cheeseburger with chips as he volubly expounded on Security's files on vegans, animal lovers, and other enemies of the world order. Lindell watched his jaws smacking. Frisk had a large mouth and he smiled in a wolflike fashion. She didn't have anything against him but felt nauseated by his frenetic chewing.

"We have a good overview of the situation," he said and popped a handful of french fries into his mouth. "You'll have to excuse me, there was no time for dinner."

Ottosson nodded impatiently. He and Frisk did not get along well, and this was common knowledge.

"We have the Animal Liberation Front as well as AFA," Frisk went on. "Both with known activists."

"What does AFA stand for?" Sammy Nilsson asked.

Frisk looked markedly pleased.

"Anti-Fascistic Action," he said quickly. "They have some twenty members in town."

"Isn't it more likely that this is the work of an animal rights organization?"

"Perhaps," Frisk said and finally wiped his mouth with a napkin, pushing away the remains of his meal. "DBF has a dozen or so more or less active members—we can regard them as the core—and then there are about fifty sympathizers."

"That many?" Lindell asked.

"Yes, if one counts them fairly loosely."

Loosely, she thought. I wonder how that count was taken.

"It could be acquaintances, siblings, school friends, and others."

"Sounds like you've got these kids in your sights. I take it most of them are fairly young?"

"Completely in our sights," Frisk said.

"Can we have a list?" Ottosson said calmly.

"It's not that easy," Frisk said, and now the felt slippers came back on. He tiptoed around the subject, talking about integrity and leaks. It became a long lecture.

"We have to have names," Ottosson interrupted. "You understand that, don't you?"

Frisk's face took on a disapproving expression mingled with an ill-concealed delight.

"We can collaborate," he said, as if this were a historic compromise from Security's side.

"Bullshit," Ottosson said, to the others' surprise. Ottosson was not someone who usually took a hard line. "We need names and that's that. If you think the Violent Crimes division will leak the information, you're just wrong."

Frisk looked insulted. "I'll see what we can do," he said.

"Start with that core group of animal lovers. We'll start there. And we want those names tonight."

Lindell smiled inwardly. Sometime Ottosson astonished them. That's why he was so well liked as a boss.

Frisk stood up. Ottosson did the same. They stood like two roosters on either side of the table. When Frisk left the room, Ottosson took the packet of french fries and the greasy papers and threw everything into the trash.

"He leaves nothing but garbage in his wake, that one."

"Okay," Sammy said, "stuff this for now. Have you tracked down that Mortensen?"

"Yes, he's on his way in. He was in his summer cottage in the archipel-ago, but got in his car right away. He was shaken, of course. I asked about the primates, but he didn't want to say anything."

"Is he coming here?"

Lindell looked up at the wall clock, which read half past eight. "In half an hour, maybe."

"You look tired," Ottosson said. "Was it a difficult Midsummer?"

His anger had completely washed away. Lindell smiled and shook her head.

"I was hungry but lost my appetite," she said.

"Sammy will check Frisk's list and you can take Mortensen. I'm going to go home. Gullan isn't doing too well. She's got a bad summer cold. Is that okay? I'll be back later."

"Completely okay," Sammy said.

Jack Mortensen was tan, but that was the only sign of health he dis-played. He looked pained. He sat down in Lindell's office and looked around anxiously, as if he found himself in a torture chamber. Lindell fetched some coffee—probably her seventh cup—and sat down at her desk.

"An unpleasant incident," she began. "Do you take sugar?"

Mortensen shook his head and made no attempt to drink from his cup. It was as if he didn't even see it.

"Primates," Lindell said. "Do you have any of those?"

Mortensen flinched. He tried to smile but failed. Now he picked up the cup and brought it to his mouth while looking nervously at her. She waited, looking back with a neutral expression.

"Most people who research Parkinson's disease have to turn to animal trials," he said after putting his coffee down.

"And . . ." Lindell prompted.

"We have conducted animal experiments."

"The activists called them illegal. Is that true?"

"No, these were approved measures. We have had several series of trials. Everyone conducts research on primates. There's nothing unusual about it. Those people don't know what they're talking about. They've never seen anyone with Parkinson's. The only thing they're after is attention."

"Where do you keep them?"

"Various places," Mortensen said. "Ultuna is one."

"At the agricultural college?"

"Yes, exactly. They have ironclad controls."

"Who is in charge of these controls?"

"Independent veterinarians. There's an organization for it."

"So there's no basis for the activists' criticism?"

"Of course not," Mortensen said vigorously.

His confidence was returning. He took another sip of the coffee. Lindell felt as if she were sitting across from a politician.

"Then why do you think they would take this kind of step?"

"I told you—for the attention. They want to appear heroic."

"Have they ever paid a visit to your company?"

"No."

"Wouldn't it make sense for them to protest there?"

"I don't know what makes sense to these people."

"Did Sven-Erik Cederén come into contact with any activists?"

"No, not that he mentioned."

Lindell sat for a while without saying anything else.

"Do you see any connection between Cederén, the primates, and the incident at the television station?"

There was a flicker of pain in Mortensen's face, as if he had been stung. He squirmed in his chair, glanced very quickly at Lindell, and then leaned forward.

"I don't know what's happening," he said softly. "Sven-Erik was my friend, everything was going well. Now everything is collapsing. The entire company is faltering. Everyone is wondering what's going on. People are calling. Why should we have been targeted like this?"

"Maybe because you appear to have squirreled away a couple of million under the table, you conduct experiments on primates that animal rights activists—and perhaps others—believe to be unjustified torture, and your head of research recently ran over his family and took his life. Of course people are wondering what exactly is going on at MedForsk."

Mortensen did not answer.

"Clearly we're going to look into the matter of these animals. We may even have to reevaluate Cederén's death."

"What do you mean?"

"There may be a connection." Lindell made a note on her pad.

"I don't know what got into that devil!"

"You said he was your friend. You should know."

Again Mortensen didn't answer, sitting collected but grim on the other side of the table. His face had grown paler during the course of the conversation. He had a slightly indignant expression, as if Lindell had betrayed a prior agreement.

The conversation was over. Mortensen got up without a word while Lindell made a point of staying put.

"Let me show you out," she said finally.

She knew they were not going to get any further. She was convinced that a check on the primates at Ultuna would result in a report that all was in order. Perhaps not a pretty sight but very likely in accordance with the regulations. The man in front of her conjured up a feeling of distaste in her. The earlier sensation of relaxed intimacy from the garden was nowhere in evidence. She hated pathetic men, pathetic witnesses. Mortensen was trying to play a martyr, and the claim that Cederén was his friend was nothing more than an act and a bad one at that.

They walked in silence through the corridor and Lindell ushered Mortensen out with a sense of relief. She wanted to be alone. The nausea had come and gone all night and she felt exhausted. She had not been so smart in her conversation with Mortensen. She blamed this on her distaste. The feeling of having reached the end of her rope irritated her. Investigating an attack on a television station was not a task to her taste. She was the first to give primates their due, but it wasn't the same as solving human problems. She was a little ashamed of this feeling, because she had in fact become enraged by images of chimpanzees and other animals pierced with tubes, needles, and god knows what, but it was the image of Josefin and Emily by the side of the road that always forced its way to the front. Most of all she wanted to know what had happened to them, but she also knew that they were unlikely to get any further. Sven-Erik Cederén had taken the explanation for the drama with him to his grave.

Maybe it was Frisk's pose of confidence that had irritated her. She didn't have much faith in his lists of vegans and other similar groups. She suspected that pretty much anyone could end up on a list like that. A sense of arbitrariness radiated like an aura from Security, and not least from the division head. Where this feeling came from, she didn't know. Perhaps the source of it was the investigation of Enrico Mendoza from a couple of years ago. That was when she had realized how extensive their mapping of the left had been and that Security was still keeping an eye on completely harmless types such as Rosander, a middle-aged entomologist. They knew what newspapers and magazines he read, where he had been published. Massive resources were expended on these mental ghosts: There were many more Rosanders all over Sweden.

She walked back to her office. She knew that Sammy was still in the building, but she wanted to be by herself. It had been a long day. What will happen if I'm going to live with Edvard? she wondered. Will he accept that I'm gone so much? She tried to imagine Edvard in an apartment in the city, hanging out in front of the television or reading a book, as she was down at the station or chasing around the countryside. It was hard to believe that he would put up with it for any length of time.

The nausea came over her in an instant and she barely managed to get to the trash can before she vomited a thin green-tinted soupy liquid. An image of Frisk's greasy hamburger floated before her eyes and she crouched over the bin again. Please don't let anyone come by, she thought before the next wave.

There, her brow sweaty, crouched over on shaky legs, she suddenly realized what was wrong. She should have realized it long ago, but only now did it dawn on her. It spread through her body like ice. She felt as if her body temperature fell by several degrees and she shivered. So wrong! So damned wrong!

She stared down at the bottom of the trash can, where the scrunched papers—the result of the day's clever deductions—lay in a paste of vomit. So wrong, she screamed inside, and she knew that life was laying down its cards.

She should have realized. Her period was supposed to have come at least ten days ago. She remembered that she had wondered about it in the middle of her vacation week, had reflected that it would be a pity if it came when she headed out to Gräsö Island. Then she had put it out of her mind. That her period was late or even skipped a cycle was not unusual in times of high stress. She rarely bled very much or for very long. Her cycles were irregular, and she was never very aware of the days or weeks involved.

But now she was suddenly painfully aware of her body. She should have understood the signs. The nausea that came and went, how she had been sick to her stomach both at home and at Gräsö the morning after Midsummer. She had blamed this on her irregular meals, on the herring and the schnapps, but not this.

She suddenly recalled her recent cravings for sugar and salt. She had seen pregnant girlfriends reach for chocolate coconut balls, mustard sandwiches, licorice, and all kinds of candy. But she hadn't connected it to her own snacking habits these past couple of weeks.

Contempt was what she felt first. Contempt for herself. She—an investigative detective—hadn't been able to keep track of her own body. Then came the anger. Why go to bed with a boring engineer? Then fear. Now she would lose Edvard, the man she loved. And last, doubt. I can't be pregnant. I'm on the pill. This is just stress.

Her inner monologue was like a swarm of angry bees stinging her. The nausea had passed, but it had been replaced by something far worse: a throbbing sense of worry that she knew would hold her in its iron grip for the foreseeable future.

How was it possible to get pregnant on the pill? It simply couldn't be. It couldn't be!

The telephone rang and Lindell shot up from her crouch. She stared at the appliance. Four signals. Immediately thereafter, her cell phone started to ring.

She fished it out of her pocket and did not know if she should answer. The display read "Private Caller."

She pressed the talk button and said her name.

"Is this Ann Lindell?"

"Yes, as I already stated."

Her voice wobbled. The woman on the other end took a breath so deep that Lindell heard it.

"I have certain information regarding Sven-Erik Cederén."

It's his lover, Lindell thought, suddenly convinced.

"I see," she said.

"He didn't take his life."

"Who are you?"

"That isn't important."

"It's very important to me," Lindell said.

"No, it doesn't matter. What matters is that you don't believe that Sven-Erik ran over his family and then took his own life. He would never do that."

"Are you his female companion?"

The words sounded silly, but she couldn't bring herself to say lover.

"I'm a friend of the family."

It was clear that the woman had now used up her store of courage and strength. The line went dead. She had hung up. Lindell put her phone down with a feeling of great defeat.

She sank down on her chair. Who was the woman? I'm pregnant. Edvard. It was as if the events of the day had paralyzed her. She couldn't move, couldn't think clearly, could hardly breathe. She simply sat there with a single wish in her head: not to lose Edvard.

I should call Sammy, she thought and observed her hand that moved unbidden across the shiny surface of the desk.

"Hell," she said aloud. "But what about the baby? Am I willing to lose it?"

She stood but immediately sank back onto the chair.

"Take it easy, call Sammy, go home."

It was as if the sound of her own voice calmed her and she continued a dialog with herself. She talked incessantly like a very confused person, gathered her papers on the table, tied the stinking plastic bag from the garbage can, grabbed her coat, and looked around the office as if she were about to leave it for good.

She walked into the warm evening air and wanted to cry. I'm carrying a life inside me, a child that I've wanted so much earlier but that I now hate. Who was he, the father? She was hardly able to formulate the word "father" in her mind.

She would recognize him if they met in the street. As a trained police officer of course she would, if need be, be able to identify her temporary guest, whose sperm had outsmarted her. He had tricked her. No, she had wanted it. She hadn't been so out of it. She had wanted him in her home and in her bed.

She lingered outside her car. The feeling of low-level functioning was similar to a state of intoxication, and she was suddenly unsure if she would be able to drive.

"Idiot," she said aloud and unlocked the door. "Get ahold of yourself."

She dialed Sammy from the car and told him about the call. In turn, he told her that Frisk had presented him with a handful of names of the core members of the animal rights activists. They agreed to meet early the next morning. Lindell knew without saying that Sammy would spend the evening giving the names on the list a little more substance. Where were they? Addresses, jobs, if they were enrolled in courses, if they were already in the police register—all questions that it was possible to find answers to, if only you were logged in to the right databases.

Lindell had only one thought as she drove home and parked the car. To pour herself a glass of wine, lie down on the couch, pull the blanket over her, and sink deep into her own thoughts. The investigation of MedForsk that would normally have dominated her ruminations flashed past like speeding cars. Single words, a phrase she had heard the past week, the image from Uppsala-Näs, and the forest clearing in Rasbo. The woman whom she believed to be the lover had sounded nervous, her controlled voice an effort. She knew more than she had said, and Lindell believed that she would call again. The woman was apparently convinced of Cederén's innocence and would not be able to sit on her information. She would do anything to make Lindell believe her version.

But what was it that made her so certain? Lindell guessed it was love. To come to grips with the fact that one's lover had committed both murder and suicide was something that took time.

The wine didn't have much taste. Campo Viejo was the kind she almost always drank. She was a regular at the wine store on Skolgatan. It was almost to the point where the clerk put three bottles on the counter when Lindell stepped into the store. Recently she had been going to the store at OBS. It was self-serve and she could be more anonymous.

Do I want children? She had asked herself that question many times, and the past few years she had always answered yes. She had wanted them with Rolf, the man she was together with before she met Edvard. She had wanted them with Edvard, although she had been less certain. She was approaching forty and knew that it soon would be too late.

Why a child seemed so important, she didn't really know. As she lay on the sofa, staring into space, she reviewed her situation. She calculated that she would give birth in February of 2001. She was a March child herself. She thought of her parents in Ödeshög, their patient longing for a grandchild. What would they say? A child without a father in its life.

She reached for the wineglass, perched on her elbow, and took a sip. She shouldn't be drinking. She sank down on the pillow, pulled the blanket more tightly around her, and felt sorry for herself.

After ten minutes she was asleep. Her last conscious thoughts circled around the fact that she should have contacted Haver and told him about the woman's call. In some way this was his territory.

✦

Sixteen

Gabriella Mark stopped by the door to the earth cellar. Like Lot's wife, she stood paralyzed. For a moment she had looked back and that had been enough. She had seen him right here, his hand on the stone wall of the cellar. The lady's bedstraw had been in full bloom; she never touched it and had made a narrow path to the thick door. "My lady," he had said, "my beautiful flower," and he had gazed at her with loving eyes.

The scent of the bedstraw intoxicated him. Gabriella believed in the healing powers of plants. She knew that he was in the force field of this yellow flower, defenseless, stripped to his skin—no, the sweet smell went even deeper than that. It was the flower that brought the smile to his face, looking at her.

He loved her. Why, she could never understand. She wasn't particularly attractive. Not like his wife.

It was in the garden that she appeared at her best. Her body was delicate but with wide hips made to rest seed boxes against and with muscular legs and shoulders from digging, from loosening dirt, from crouching in dirt. Her arms were so slender that he could easily encircle them with his hands.

She had become a new person the day she had bought the house. Years of desperation, of searching for a life of meaning, had been replaced with a deeply felt sense of peace. Her period on disability after the accident that had cost her husband his life had been long, and she had feared for her life. Not physically—the doctors had fit her back together well—but her equanimity had been shaken. She found herself bumping against life, having to take detours and lean on pills, on sleep. She never woke up feeling happy.

And then she bought the house. It was by instinct, as if her body and soul were in charge. Dazed, she signed the sales contract and loan documents. Already after only a couple of days—that was also at the time the bedstraw was blooming—she felt her body slowly start to work again, as if her limbs were regrowing. Things she held in her hands took on a sense of weight and meaning. She fumbled for the poker, opened the door to the wood-burning fireplace in the kitchen, saw the glowing embers, and drew in the heat.

She stood there for a long time in the doorway of the old shed, peering into the half darkness, picking up raw and earthy smells. Then she stepped inside and found some rusty shovels, a garden fork, a wheelbarrow with a punctured tire.

The birds, enlivened by their guest, flew in wide arcs between the bushy thickets, chirping and tending to their little ones. A cat turned up after a couple of days, first keeping to the edge of the property, slinking around the shed and hiding in the nettles, but creeping closer.

The creaking doors were greased, the paths cleared, the firewood that had stood stacked for years received her with muted voices. She stood on the sawdust-strewn floors of the woodshed and smiled at the sawhorse and the chopping block.

Slowly but surely she had floated up to the surface, grown more beautiful and stronger, and taken up her place in the house, the garden, and the landscape.

She hired carpenters, painters, and electricians. The money from her husband's insurance was enough to make a lovely home out of the old cottage with its addition. Contact with the workers energized her. She looked forward to their voices and hands. She became the perfect client who baked, cooked, and brought home cases of beer. Rarely had they been as well looked after on a job. They thought of her as a jolly woman, eager and honest.

The fact that they were men—a couple of them attractive—meant that she gave more attention to her appearance. Not that she wanted anything to happen, but she noticed that they looked at her, that they probably made comments about her and her appearance. All men do, she thought, and in spite of herself she liked the fact that she could attract their gaze and innocently flirtatious comments.

Then Sven-Erik came along. He had known her husband, had found out that she had moved to Rasbo, and had called her. There were some photos he wanted to show her. He had found them in a box when he was cleaning up and throwing away some old junk. The photos were taken some fifteen, sixteen years ago by a guy in the group of boys he associated with as a teen. Nils, her husband, was also in that gang.

Sven-Erik had thought she might want a couple and that was why he had called. After the first visit, he had returned, and Gabriella had seen him change each time. She started to long for him to come by.

Now he was gone and she didn't know how she would be able to live. The memories of him were everywhere. He spoke to her in the darkness of the night, he caressed her in her dreams, and she wept with grief and sorrow when she woke up.

She knew that he could never have killed his wife and child. Not that he still loved Josefin, but he was not a murderer. He wanted to divorce her—that was something he had talked about with increasing frequency over the past year—but not in that way. And then there was Emily, his greatest love. He had talked a great deal about Emily and had shown her pictures. Never.

She had followed the reports in the papers. Each line pained her, but she had to read everything in order to understand what had happened. She had seen the obituary. She would visit the grave too, but later.

At first she had accepted the idea that he had become confused, committed the murders, and then taken his own life. There was no other explanation. After a couple of days she had spoken with Jack Mortensen, who had supported this theory and told her about Sven-Erik's worsening temper. He had asked her not to reveal her identity. He thought of Sven-Erik's family, he said. Things were bad enough as they were.

She had promised him that. He had called her several times, and in some way that was a comfort, to have someone who knew, someone who could acknowledge her grief.

After another couple of days her doubt had started to grow. Sven-Erik couldn't possibly have done this, not the man she loved and had come to know as a sensitive person whose values were changing during the time they spent together. He had become critical of his work, complained of the stress, of the constant need for money for the development of the company, of the demand for quick results from the Spanish investors. Most of the time he didn't want to talk about work, but sometimes it came up, and she sensed that he would soon break free of it. There was no other way. Sven-Erik was not the type of person who could take things lightly, simply push concerns aside and go on for the sake of his career or the money.

It was clear he enjoyed spending time in the house with her. He had peace here. Laughed. They played, they weeded the beds together. He had never gardened before. Isabella, the dog, lay in the shade and watched them.

And now he was dead. Disgraced in the memories of those who lived. She was the only one who could still speak of him with love. Not even his parents, whom she had called in order to offer comfort and perhaps to win the confidence of, could see anything to redeem their son. They had rejected her, had been merciless in their judgment.

It was when she called them for a second time that she received the information that had convinced her of his innocence. It was a relief, but also so sensational and upsetting that she couldn't quite grasp it. She had not been able to continue the conversation with his sobbing mother and had had to put the phone down.

It took two days before she resurfaced, before she realized the enormity of what she had been told.

She rested her hand on the handle. The door that was normally so stiff had dried out in the heat and slid open. She had forgotten what she was planning to get, but remembered as she stood there that it was strawberry jam.

She had called the police and spoken with the woman who was in charge of the investigation. She had read her name in the papers. She had sounded upset and unfocused and, which surprised her the most, angry. Gabriella was extremely attuned to other people's tone of voice. She could be reduced to tears by a single remark, lose her steam, retreat. She had not been able to continue the conversation, but she knew that she had to call again.

The jar was cool and she held it up to her forehead, following the narrow path back to the house. She glanced at the vegetable garden. She feared the worst. She had not watered it for two days and now she couldn't bring herself to go there. Much of it would have died, she knew that. Especially the cabbages and perhaps the lettuce. She had to pull herself together in the afternoon.

✦

Seventeen

The prosecutor hesitated but finally gave in. If it had been anything else, he would never have approved the warrants for the seven people. There was no clear indication of criminal activity other than the fact that they were vocal animal rights activists, and even that information was rather shaky.

Media had made a big thing of the attack on TV4. This news dominated the local and national channels. The TV4 morning news had been broadcast direct from the studio and included interviews of its own staff. The morning broadcasts of the daily news program *Rapport* had fixated on the terrorist angle and run a series of pieces on earlier attacks on researchers, stealth releases of foxes and minks, slaughter trucks set on fire, as well as various interviews with Security Service officers and terrorism experts.

The station was bombarded with calls and surrounded by reporters. The fact that their media colleagues were targeted had made them particularly insistent. The prosecutor yielded to this pressure.

The seven were brought in during a coordinated operation at eleven o'clock in the morning. Five were at home and two at work. Everything went calmly. It was as if they had been expecting company. All, however, protested the legality of the warrants.

They were led into private holding cells and led to understand that there were others. None of them were questioned until late that afternoon. They had to spend the intervening time in the cells in total isolation, checked on two times an hour through a window in the door. Nothing else. No human contact, no offers of food or coffee.

Sammy Nilsson felt a pang of conscience when the first one was brought in for questioning. She was a young woman, Erika Mattson, nineteen years of age. She had just finished high school and had a summer job at a supermarket.

"Do you know why you're here?" Sammy asked.

Normally he would take it easy, chat a little and try to establish a connection. Now he adopted a purely formal stance, turning on the tape recorder without further comments.

"May I call my mother?" the girl asked.

"You can do that later. Do you know that one of the reporters will probably have to spend the rest of his life in a wheelchair?"

Sammy looked at the girl, who gazed wide-eyed back at him.

"I don't have anything to do with that," she said.

"We think you were there."

There was no basis for this claim, but Lindell, Berglund, and Haver had decided to take a tough line. Possibly one of the youngsters would become uncertain and start to talk.

"You are vegan," Sammy went on.

"Is there anything wrong with that?"

"Your room is covered with posters, magazines, and pamphlets that address the same thing: that animal experimentation is cruel and should be stopped."

The girl didn't answer. Her gaze was fixed on her hands, which were clasped in her lap.

"Should animal experiments be stopped at any cost, is that it? Even if people end up hurt? You were questioned about an attack on a kennel in Norduppland last year. Now you are sitting here again. That time you were only making threats. Now you are playing at being a terrorist and actually hurting people."

"Stop talking about hurting people! I have nothing to do with this. I want to call my mother!"

Sammy sat quietly for a couple of minutes.

"What did you do yesterday?"

"I was home almost all day. I went out for a coffee in the afternoon."

"Where?"

"At Hugo's."

"Alone?"

"No, with friends."

"Do they have names?"

The girl gave him three names. He recognized one of them. Haver was in the process of questioning him.

"When did you leave Hugo's?"

"At around five maybe. I went home. I had to do laundry."

"Were you alone?"

"Yes, my mom was working. She came home at ten. She's a nurse."

"Home alone. Are you sure you didn't take a trip to TV4?"

The girl started to cry. Sammy turned off the tape recorder.

Haver met with steelier resistance. Erik Gustavsson was smirking at him, answering the questions quickly and with nonchalance. He leaned back in his chair, to all appearances completely unconcerned.

He had been home during the day and gone into town at around three in the afternoon to buy a record and have a coffee.

"I take it that isn't a crime?" he said.

"Go on," Haver said.

"I went to Hugo's, if you know where that is. I hung out there for a couple of hours, and then I biked home again."

"I see. What did you do at home?"

"Went online, talked a bit with a friend on the phone, and in the evening I went to Katalin and had a beer. Great alibi, don't you think?"

"I think you knocked down a reporter at TV4 at a quarter past six yesterday. Then maybe you had a beer to celebrate."

"Prove it."

Haver leaned back and flipped through some papers that lay in front of him on the table and appeared to have lost all interest in the young man. After a while he reached for the phone.

"Can you come get a guy who's with me? He should go back now."

He turned off the tape recorder, did not look at Erik Gustavsson, and glanced at his watch.

"Now I'm going to go home and have a steak," he said and stood up.

A guard stepped into the room.

"You know what," Haver said as Erik stood up, "I talked to your dad on the phone. He's pissed. Isn't it a bit of a quandary for a vegan to be the son of a butcher?"

Erik Gustavsson stared back at Haver with an amused smile.

———

It was eight o'clock. There was a certain amount of tiredness among the assembled officers. Berglund was making faces, lost in thought. Sammy Nilsson went to get some coffee and returned with a tray.

"No, not for me," Lindell said when he offered her a cup.

Haver looked thoughtful. Wende was almost asleep, his head cradled in his hands.

"Maybe we took the wrong tactic," Lindell said as she began the review of the day's events.

No one said anything.

"What we have turned up so far is not particularly significant. Everyone seems to have fairly decent alibis, even if the two Hugo-goers could very well have fit in a brief visit to TV4. The girl's appearance matches the description of the one who had blood on her face. We'll test that further tomorrow. We're going to see if Anna Sundmark, the studio manager, can pick out Erika Mattson. We're also going to run voice tests on all seven and play them for the TV4 staff. They may be able to identify one of them."

Lindell was exhausted after this short review. She was tempted by the smell of the coffee but thought she would throw up if she had any.

"We'll have to let them go tomorrow," Berglund said.

"Have the searches of their homes given us anything?" Wende asked.

"Two complaints lodged with the parliamentary ombudsman, a gaggle of crazed parents, and numerous letters to the editor expected for the next few days," Sammy said. "We'll probably find that it isn't to everyone's taste that we go turn seven people's homes upside down."

"But public opinion should be in our favor," Wende said.

Lindell felt even weaker. Since when did they modify what they did to fit public opinion?

She said this too and was immediately contradicted by Berglund. As always when he talked, she listened carefully. Her older colleague rarely spoke nonsense.

After hearing his objections, she had to agree at least in part. If people didn't believe in the validity of their procedures, public trust in police and prosecutors would quickly be whittled away.

"Okay," she said. "We'll do the identification and the voice tests tomorrow, and then we'll let them go."

"Yes, since we have nothing to go to the prosecutor with," Wende shot in.

"Unless we uncover something of significance," Lindell went on.

Wende left first, then Berglund and Sammy.

Still seated, Haver looked up at the clock and said out of the blue: "My father died exactly twenty-five years ago."

Lindell looked up. "Exactly?"

"Yes, exactly. Twenty-eight minutes past eight, on this exact date twenty-five years ago."

Lindell waited for more, but Haver pulled himself out of his chair.

"I'm going home," he said.

"How did he die?"

"A bee sting. Silly, isn't it? We were sitting out that evening. Dad was having a beer and a bee was swimming around in his glass. It went down his throat and stung him. Dad turned out to be extremely sensitive, because his throat immediately swelled up and he choked in a couple of minutes."

"How come you know it was at exactly twenty-eight minutes past eight?"

"The window was open, and when we stood there around Dad, the clock in the living room rang half past nine. At that point, a couple of minutes had gone by."

"How old were you?"

"Thirteen. It happened so fast. We were sitting there on the patio and talking and then suddenly he was gone. It was a warm evening. I even re-member what we were talking about. Mom said once afterward that she felt so helpless."

"That's awful" was the only thing Lindell could think of to say.

"No one should have to die like that."

"Death is never pleasant."

"I think about it more and more," Haver said, standing in the middle of the room. "I've tried to reach back into my memories, remember how Dad was, what he said, how his voice sounded, but I can't. I hardly remember anything. Some people can recite their entire childhoods, I remember al-most nothing."

"You're a father yourself now."

"That must be why it comes up."

"What did he do?"

"He was a construction worker," said Haver and looked at Lindell, whose eyes teared up when she met his gaze.

"That's good," she said. "That sounds nice. Construction worker. He must have built a lot of wonderful houses."

Haver smiled. Lindell thought her last comment sounded ridiculous and regretted it immediately. It was something you said to children. "Built wonderful houses."

"I knew you would think that," he said, and Lindell realized that he had appreciated her words.

They were silent for moment. Haver looked at her one more time and seemed to be about to say something else, but he didn't.

"Give your family my regards," Lindell said.

As was often the case, she stayed behind as the others went home. She thought about the seven young people who had been brought in and detained on dubious grounds. She realized that both the prosecutor and the police had given way to the pressure. At a public briefing, the chief of police had said that a number of suspects had been apprehended and that he hoped there would soon be a break in the case of the "terror attack against an organ of so vital a public interest as television." This statement inspired undeniable hope, and the evening newscasters, assuming this optimistic view was based on actual investigative information, had praised the Uppsala police and had also interviewed a high-level member of the Security Forces, who had basked in the attention.

The hangover would hit them the next day, unless the morning's attempt to link one of the seven to the station attack led to something. Lindell didn't know what the final determination of the offenses was likely to be and decided to contact the prosecutor.

She should have gone to the drugstore and bought a pregnancy test, but had not had time and was no longer sure whether a test was necessary. Yesterday's certainty had turned to doubt. The likelihood of becoming pregnant while on the pill had to be very small, and why would it happen after only a single night's adventure?

She stuck her hand inside her T-shirt and squeezed her breasts gently. Admittedly, they were a little tender. But that could also be the result of her Midsummer's activities. Edvard could be rough, she had noticed that before.

She should have called him but had not felt like it. What should she say? During the morning she had toyed with the idea of a quick abortion. Then she would not have to say a word to Edvard. Suddenly she was struck by the thought that this proved that she could have children.

"If I am pregnant," she muttered aloud.

I have no one to ask, she thought. No close friend to share confidences with, to talk to, to get advice from. She could have talked to Beatrice in her unit. She was experienced and smart and would never say anything to anyone. But Ann hesitated to confide in her colleague. It would affect their working relationship. She felt that she would find herself in a position of weakness psychologically if she opened up to Beatrice.

She hated being distracted. She should be putting all of her might into the investigation of Cederén, MedForsk, and TV4 so that it could be cleared up by the end of the summer. The summer with Edvard. Now everything had been thrown into disarray. She bit her lower lip until it hurt. She was awash with anxiety about having gone to bed with an unknown man.

She had been enveloped in a diffuse sense of worry for a while. She knew that her social life was a catastrophe. Almost all of her time went to her work. Edvard had not been the most ideal partner, but you don't really get to choose, she thought. You fall in love and are thrust into situations that are hard to control. Now life was catching up with her. This was nothing unusual. She had seen similar symptoms in some of her colleagues, a kind of unfulfilled longing to work in peace and also to establish connections between the workplace and the private sphere. Everyone found this hard to achieve, not just those involved in police work. It seemed as if the country was becoming more and more splintered, both at the level of the individual and at large. There was never enough time, someone said the other day as they were complaining to one another in the lunchroom.

That it should be so damned hard! Some managed to make it work. Like Ola. Two children and a wife that he loved above all else. He was tired but often smiled, and there was a longing in his gaze. He seemed so loyal toward something—what, she didn't know. I don't know if I would recognize it if it turned up in front of my nose.

Edvard could have become this "something" if I am going to hang this on a man, and I guess I will. I can't manage to live alone. If I am forced to, my life will be an endless series of investigations, stress-filled moments, and red wine in the evenings. Maybe I'll make commissioner in a couple of years, in a black hole of a society of fried people.

Edvard had talked about a kind of breakdown. He had his union spiel, which she often found tiresome. Life wasn't just a struggle. Sometimes when he was calmer, but also sometimes when he started to talk about the cause, he could express some of what he meant. She could sense an inheritance of sorts inside him.

Like her, Edvard was searching for connection and trust between people, and he had found it in Gräsö among the older folks—Viola, Victor, and the cousins, a dying breed. This lack of sustainability troubled him.

Lindell realized that the child had set this internal monologue going. A budding life was forcing her to make a decision, placing markers in the ground for a playing field on which she would act out her life. Until now there had been no lines. Life seemed unstructured, and in a couple of years she would be forty.

She sighed, rose heavily as if she were already in an advanced stage of pregnancy, left the office, and walked down the empty corridor. She remembered the first time she came to the station and walked by all of the offices, reading the name tags and arriving at Ottosson's door. He had received her with great kindness and care. She had felt welcome and secure from the first day, and she still loved her workplace and respected most of her colleagues.

But now there was this thing called life.

✦

Eighteen

Lindell woke at half past five. Her body felt tender and she immediately became aware of her condition. There was no morning respite in which—for a couple of seconds—she could think and act as if everything were normal. Abortion was the first thought that came to her. She had no moral objections to this action, but now that it concerned her directly, she realized that it was not as cut-and-dried as she had believed.

She remembered the few times when she had discussed the issue with friends who were wrestling with the decision about whether to have the child or abort it. At those times she had talked dispassionately and objectively about a woman's right to choose.

Free choice, she thought now. There's no such thing. I am caught in my body, by my longing for a child, in the conflicts between my work and Edvard's and my new life. I could probably have an abortion without Edvard finding out about it, but what happens then? Won't the unborn child always be there between us?

She got out of bed. The sheets needed laundering. There was so much she needed to attend to. The sun shone through the crack in the curtains and created a track across the floor and the bed. She allowed herself to stand in the pool of light for half a minute as her thoughts swirled. She looked down at her naked body, with the sunbeams dancing on her belly.

"Do you know what happened this morning?" Haver asked.

No one said anything.

"I stepped in some dog shit. A huge fucking pile of it, right outside the main door."

Sammy looked up and grinned. "Was it soft and warm?"

"It was disgusting. Right outside the door. It would be one thing if I had been in a park or on the sidewalk, but this was right in front of the door."

"You live in a slum," Sammy said.

"Right," Haver said.

"Drop it," Lindell broke in. "We have things to do other than to talk about dog shit."

"Well, excuse me," Haver said in exaggeratedly polite tones.

Sammy and Haver exchanged glances.

"But Eriksberg *is* a slum," Sammy maintained.

"So tell me about the woman," Haver said.

He saw from Lindell's face that they couldn't tease her any longer.

"She called me last night. She sounded scared but driven by conviction. I know she has more to say."

"How do you know?"

"It was the impression I had," Lindell said.

Ottosson entered the room. He stopped for a moment, indecisively rubbing his beard. Everyone stared at him expectantly.

"The prosecutor has decided to release all seven. We don't have anything on them."

He sat down at the table.

"It's the right thing to do," he went on and turned to Lindell, looking at her. At first she thought he looked apologetic, but then she realized she was reading too much into it. Perhaps he was simply tired, she thought, and tried to smile but failed.

"Is there a connection?" Lindell said to no one in particular.

She didn't like Ottosson's look. How many times had she asked herself this question during these past twelve hours?

"I have trouble believing that the animal rights folk are willing to run people over," Haver said and repeated what he had said the night before.

"What about this woman's conviction?" Ottosson asked.

He picked his nose unselfconsciously and Lindell averted her gaze. Abortion, she thought to herself.

"That Cederén would never take his own life and even less be prepared to kill his family," he said and took out a checkered handkerchief.

"He wrote a note that said, 'I'm sorry,'" Sammy said.

His comment was almost drowned out by his chief's violent nose-blowing.

"It was written in his handwriting," Sammy went on. "Why did he write it if he didn't kill his family?"

"Perhaps it was an apology for taking his own life," Ottosson suggested.

"So perhaps he had learned of or even witnessed the fact that his wife and child had been killed and could no longer bear to live," Sammy said, picking up on this thread.

"Shouldn't he have become enraged or gripped by hatred, revenge, or whatever else?" Haver objected. "Not just gas himself. That seems oddly passive."

Lindell felt that Ottosson was waiting for her to respond, but she couldn't manage to think of anything insightful.

Haver suddenly got up and started to walk to and fro across the room. The others watched him pace. He stopped just as abruptly and looked at Lindell, as if seeking her support.

"We should do a general sweep of Rasbo," he said in a loud voice. "Knock on every door, and if we are lucky, we'll turn up Cederén's mistress."

"Rasbo is a sizable parish," Sammy observed.

Lindell, who was not a native of Uppland, had only a vague idea of that part of the district.

"All right," she said, mainly to move things forward, "let's take the clearing where Cederén was found as our starting point and knock on every door in a two-kilometer radius and hope we get something. All women between the ages of twenty-five and forty will be given additional scrutiny."

Everyone pondered this suggestion and—when no one said anything—she continued.

"It will be your task, Ola. We'll bring in as many additional resources as we can," she said and glanced at Ottosson. He would be the one who would have to fight for the extra manpower. He nodded.

"Then we have TV4," Lindell continued energetically, surprising herself. "The roadblocks gave us nothing—we know that—as have our searches. We have a gang of teenagers out there somewhere, maybe with explosives, even though I have doubts about the contents of that bag, but who are prepared to adopt tough methods. Sammy, you will have to maintain contact with Frisk and see what Security can produce. Let's put twenty-four-hour surveillance on the seven."

She again glanced at Ottosson, but he looked neutral. She took this as his acquiescence, although she knew herself how much manpower would be needed to keep seven people under surveillance.

"We'll borrow some officers from Surveillance. We'll do one more re-view of the names that Frisk is sure to be working on. He'll be secretive as usual but will probably take the chance to gloat."

Lindell wanted to end the meeting as soon as possible and was in a hurry to arrive at these decisions. She wanted to be alone. The others interpreted this as enthusiasm and decisiveness.

They broke up after a quarter of an hour, everyone pleased that the morning's deadlock was over.

Back in her office, Lindell forced herself to work. She called the pros-ecutor and told him what they had decided. As the pre-investigative lead, he was the one who formally made the decisions, but it was usually never a problem. Their collaboration was smooth and painless.

He had a wise gaze and a pleasant voice. The prosecutor chose his words with a great deal of deliberation, seemingly weighing every possible option before he carefully made his case. Sometimes Lindell would get irritated by his slowness, but she always appreciated his thoughtfulness and good judgment.

They ended the conversation in agreement. Lindell sat down at her desk and pulled out her notepad, which she had filled more than halfway with various jottings and doodles about MedForsk and the Cederén family. She went through it and studied the large question marks that she always wrote in after the questions she thought to be most significant.

The problem with the case was that all the original question marks re-mained and now new ones had been added. She put down the notepad. There was nothing new to be learned from it. Instead she took out the reports of yesterday's interrogations with the seven young people.

She thought she could recognize the various personalities behind the answers. Some were clearly frightened by the situation. Others were more nonchalant and confident. You could never be sure what the various atti-tudes stood to hide. Lindell tried to see something behind the words but found nothing. All of them had reasonable alibis. Beatrice, Wende, and a couple of others were busy checking the rest of the information that had been provided. It would surprise her if something of interest turned up.

She tried to imagine what it would be like to be let go after having been apprehended and held for one night. They had to feel triumphant, regardless of whether they had been cool or anxious in the sessions. Probably they would consider their having been interrogated and locked up in a cell as a feather in their cap.

The phone rang and interrupted her train of thought. Edvard, she thought, and the lump in her stomach that she had battled so successfully that morning returned.

"It's me again," said a woman's voice.

Lindell immediately reached for her notepad. "It's good that you called. I've been thinking about what you said."

"Do you believe me?"

"I have very little to go on. You have to tell me more."

There was a long silence. Lindell could hear the woman breathe. She thought she heard a faint roar in the background. Perhaps of traffic or from a dishwasher.

"Sven-Erik was my friend. I knew him very well, and I know that he wasn't capable of killing anyone."

"What makes you so sure?"

"His entire nature. Sven-Erik was a very caring person."

The woman's voice changed. "He didn't take his own life. I know that."

"How do you know?"

Lindell felt a growing excitement. She drew a few strong lines on the notepad.

"Sven-Erik hated gin. He never drank it."

"What do you mean?"

"He never drank gin," the woman repeated, as if it explained everything.

Then Lindell remembered the almost empty bottle that they had recovered from the car. Cederén had had a high blood alcohol content and must have been extremely intoxicated when he died.

"How do you know what kind of alcohol was found in the car?"

"That doesn't matter."

"Why did he never drink gin?"

"He had drunk it in his youth, when he was fifteen or sixteen years old, his first real binge, and it made him very sick. I think he was also beaten by his father."

Lindell thought about Cederén's father, so despondent and helpless. Had he beaten his son?

"After that, he never tasted another drop."

Lindell felt in her gut that the information was true.

"I like gin and tonics but could never drink them when Sven-Erik was with me. He even hated the smell."

"How did you know that we found a bottle of gin?" Lindell repeated.

"I know. That's the main thing."

"So what do you think happened?"

"He was forced to drink it. If he had wanted to get drunk, he would have chosen a malt whisky."

The woman now sounded almost irritated with Lindell's hesitation.

"Ask anyone who knew Sven-Erik."

"Maybe he chose gin in order to punish himself?"

The woman ignored Lindell's question as if it were not even worthy of consideration. "I knew him and you didn't."

"We need to meet," Lindell said. "Just you and me," she added quickly. "I need your memories."

A new silence. The breathing grew more heavy. Lindell searched for the right words. The woman hung up.

With the help of seven colleagues, Haver worked his way through the part of Rasbo that they had decided to search. Rasbo was not known for much. Haver thought he remembered that Strindberg had written about this parish and used it to express his venom. The church lay some distance from the highway and Haver had never liked it. There he and Strindberg were in agreement. It shone fat and white and was of a more modern style, perhaps 1800 or so. Haver preferred the low gray stone churches from the Middle Ages that almost blended into the landscape. They seemed less pretentious.

A two-kilometer radius from the clearing where they had found Cederén meant a number of gravel roads and perhaps a couple of hundred houses—everything from farmhouses to modern construction and summer cottages.

Frode Nilsson, on loan from Surveillance, was originally from Rasbo and entertained Haver with anecdotes and more or less true stories. Haver glanced over at him. He was driving jerkily, braking often, accelerating quickly only to have to brake again. Haver wished his colleague would talk less and drive better. But at least he was visibly energized by his childhood memories. In contrast to Strindberg, he liked Rasbo. And he should be a better judge, Haver thought.

They had only just come out onto Jällarkan right outside of town when Nilsson launched into his accounts of Rasbo. He spoke warmly of berry patches and mushroom picking.

"But the church is ugly," Haver said.

Frode Nilsson braked abruptly and violently behind a garbage truck from Ragn-Sells.

"Why doesn't it pull to the side?" he exclaimed and swerved to the left to see if there was oncoming traffic.

"The speed limit is seventy," Haver said.

"Sure, the church may not be a winner, but there's so much else."

"You should become an ambassador for Rasbo."

"I'm a member of the local preservation society," Nilsson said and overtook the truck in a risky maneuver. "We put out publications from time to time. *Glimpses of Rasbo*."

Haver nodded. It was getting to be a bit too much Rasbo talk.

"Frötuna is kaput. Have you heard? The count declared bankruptcy. He deserved it. He was a pretty dim bulb."

Nilsson was quiet for a while after this and also drove more calmly.

"My dad worked there for a couple of years."

He paused again.

"There were some modern versions of indentured farmhands out there on the count's estate. Related to the royal family, apparently. Such trash."

The bitterness in Nilsson's voice bothered Haver in some way. Perhaps it reminded him too much of his father-in-law, the old shoemaker. He tried to get Nilsson to drop the count by asking him about mushroom picking.

We should all have the kind of local knowledge that Frode has, he thought as they passed Vallby and the ICA grocery store, where his greatest hope—the young clerk—worked. He stared in through the window in order to catch a glimpse of her.

The officers were traveling two by two in four cars. Back at the station they had divided the district between them. Haver and Nilsson's area lay to the north, and they had started at the four-way intersection in Kallesta.

Haver gazed out at the landscape he bore no relation to. He was extremely urban, a city boy four generations back, and had an awkward relationship with forests, meadows, and fields. While he did make a mushroom-picking trip every fall, this was more in order to please his wife.

Nilsson unfolded the map and together they decided the best course. Haver read out the names of the villages and farmsteads. He was convinced that Cederén's mistress was out here somewhere. At one of these black dots on the map, there was a grieving woman waiting for a visit. For she most certainly wanted to be found. She wanted to talk, to vindicate Sven-Erik.

Nilsson drove the car to the first farm. Haver was going to check off the places and keep notes. First they saw a small cottage. There was a Höganäs pot filled with flowers on the front step; a peaceful silence enveloped the place.

"This was an old soldier's cottage," Nilsson said.

He walked gingerly across the yard, sizing up the exterior walls as if he were an interested buyer.

"Some ten or more people must have lived here back then. And it was a one-room cottage."

Haver peered in through one of the windows. A newspaper lay open on a table. A cup of coffee.

"Let's go," he said, but Nilsson had already disappeared.

Haver walked toward the car and glanced back, but his colleague remained out of sight. Haver drummed his fingers against the roof of the car. They were not out on a preservationist cataloging trip. Many more houses and cottages awaited them.

"I think the last soldier's name was Sandberg," Nilsson said when he returned after a couple of minutes.

"When was that?"

"Maybe a hundred years ago. Then the cycling society took it over it. That was in the fifties."

"You are like a walking encyclopedia," Haver said.

"A beautiful place," said Nilsson, with a final glance back.

They drove along the roads, stopping to knock on doors and greet people, explaining their errand: Had anyone seen anything that might be connected with the suicide in the clearing? This was their official mission.

There was a great deal of chatter. Nilsson asked about everything and shared his knowledge. Sometimes they encountered people who had known his father. He established an instant rapport with those they encountered. The people they visited were clearly cheered up.

It seemed to Haver that Nilsson's voice changed. He had a different dialect when he conversed with the people of Rasbo. This is how it ought to be, he thought. We should have a person from each district, someone who speaks the language. Then we could talk about neighborhood policing. He became less and less irritated.

They covered fourteen houses in one hour. At nine of them, they were greeted at the front door. They could eliminate all of these houses, Haver noted. Through their conversations they were also able to eliminate the other five. None of the owners matched what they were looking for. Retired couples occupied three of the five, and the other two were middle-aged.

Haver started to lose hope. Finding Cederén's woman had been his thing. He was the one who had found his way to the ICA store in Vallby from the gas receipts. He was the one who had through the clerk been told that the woman most likely lived somewhere along the Östhammar road.

He called the other three cars. No one had found anything. Fridman thought that he had caught a masked odor at one of the places and was convinced that they engaged in home brewing. Drop it, Haver told him, to which Fridman grunted.

The fifteenth house was a built-out cottage. It lay high up, pleasingly surrounded by old pastures. A small stream ran parallel to the road and they drove across a small stone bridge before they arrived at the house. A blue Opel, perhaps ten years old, was parked outside what looked to Haver to be the woodshed.

As they pulled into the yard, it started to rain. They caught sight of a figure, or rather, a movement, behind a bush. Haver nodded in that direction.

"This must be Södergren's old place," Nilsson said. "But it's been redone."

The woman, who must have heard their car, was standing with her back to them. She carried a green basket on her hip. Haver coughed and she turned around. Haver knew immediately that they were in the right place. She had been expecting them.

"Hello, I'm Ola Haver with the Uppsala police. We're in the area because of the unfortunate event in the woods over there," he said and pointed vaguely. "You may have heard about it."

The woman put down her basket and rubbed her hands against her pants. She was blonde, about thirty-five. She nodded but looked very reserved if not completely dismissive.

"You've been weeding," Nilsson observed and looked around.

"You may have seen something?"

"What do you mean?" Her voice was low and revealed that she came from somewhere in southern Sweden.

"Something unusual."

"I heard he killed himself."

"That's right," Nilsson said, "but we don't really understand why. You've probably read about it in the papers. And we don't like unanswered questions."

His tone was friendly, and when he kneeled next to a bed of sprouting plants, Haver was afraid that he would start to talk about gardening again.

"Maybe he didn't take his own life," Nilsson said and looked up from the radishes.

She did not change her expression, and for a moment she stared out over the meadow as if she had heard something.

"I don't know anything," she said curtly, in a definitive way that would have put a stop to most conversations.

"Lovely sweet peas," Nilsson said. "Did you make this trellis yourself?"

She smiled for the first time. "Salix," she said.

"I know. My old lady does this too."

Haver had to smile at his colleague. The old lady—Nilsson's wife—could hardly be more than forty.

"Perhaps he didn't take his life," Haver repeated.

"Do you mean that someone killed him?"

Haver didn't reply to her question. Instead, he turned to Nilsson.

"What do you say, should we keep going?"

"Can I have a radish?" Nilsson asked.

The woman nodded.

As they were backing out of the yard, she stood as if paralyzed in the same position that they had left her by the vegetable bed, but just as she dropped out of their line of sight, Haver thought he saw her raise her hand as if to stop them or perhaps to wave good-bye. He wanted to ask Nilsson to turn back, but there was a better alternative.

"You think it's her," Nilsson said.

"Yes," Haver said and opened both his notepad and his cell phone. He dialed a number. Maybe she was still in the store. Shops were open at all hours these days.

It was the store manager who picked up. The store was closed and he was the only one left. Yes, Ulrika Olsson—the clerk that Haver had spoken to earlier—lived nearby. Haver was given her number.

"Do you know where Karby is?" he asked Nilsson, who gazed back at him with amusement.

Ulrika Olsson was feeding the chickens when they arrived.

"You're quick," she said. "I thought you were calling from town."

She said that she was happy to accompany them back to the woman's house.

"I'm just going to change," she said and ran lightly ahead of them.

"Spunky girl," said Nilsson, whose mood kept improving the longer they spent in Rasbo.

They decided that she would wait in the car as Haver and Nilsson had another talk with the woman. The hope was that she was still out in the garden so that Ulrika could take a look and say yea or nay.

Haver felt a rising excitement the closer they got to the cottage. Nilsson chatted away and tried to clarify Ulrika Olsson's relation to another Olsson from Rasbokil. Haver turned his head toward the backseat and gazed anxiously at the thick tree trunks bordering the narrow gravel road.

The woman was still by the vegetable beds. It had been only forty-five minutes, but Haver was surprised. She was leaning over the beds and he couldn't help but study her buttocks and slender thighs through her green work pants. Nilsson glanced at him.

Haver coughed lightly. The woman jumped and turned so quickly that she almost lost her balance. She looked frightened but tried to hide this by moving her hand across her face.

"Well," she said coldly.

"We forgot something," Nilsson said. "We're taking the names and telephone numbers of everyone that we're talking to."

Haver did not think that she was naïve enough to believe this explanation.

"Gabriella Mark," she said. "But I have a private number."

She sat down on the wooden frame of the vegetable plot and looked expectantly at the two officers, as if she was waiting for more. Haver sensed that she was tired and somehow pleased at their return. Now she had a reason to take a break from her work.

Their car was only about ten or fifteen meters away, but some bushes partially hid it from view. Get up, he thought. Take a few steps.

"Here is my number if you think of anything," he said and held out a card, but Gabriella Mark made no attempt to get up. Haver walked over to her. She looked at him blankly and took the card, slipping it into the breast pocket of her overalls without glancing at it.

Haver thought she had been crying. Her whole being screamed loneliness. Here she was, digging and weeding alone. Who was going to eat all of these vegetables?

"It's her," Ulrika Olsson said when they returned to the car. "I'm completely sure of it."

Haver called the rest of the team and called off the rest of the search. The satisfaction at having found her was tainted by the fact that they now had to disturb her, question her, and perhaps force her to recall the memories that she had been trying to repress. He had felt this before. Many times it was a thankless task to dig into human misery.

"Gabriella Mark," Lindell said, testing its sound. "A beautiful name. How did she seem?"

"Fragile and strong at the same time," Haver said.

He thought about her body. An attractive body accentuated by the worn work clothes. Her hands had been powerful, black with earth, while her gaze was sorrowful.

"I liked that she was working with vegetables," he said.

"I wonder why she denies knowing Cederén?" Nilsson wondered.

Haver was not surprised.

"I think she wants to talk to a woman," he said.

Lindell looked over at him and thought he was right. When Gabriella made her anonymous call, it had been to her, and most likely not simply because she was the one in charge of the investigation.

They decided that Lindell should visit the house the next day. She felt too tired to leave right away. Maybe it was also good to give Gabriella some time to think. Haver was convinced that she realized she had been identified.

Lindell drove slowly through the city. It was a warm summer's evening. She looked with envy at the people around her. They strolled, sat at outdoor cafés, drank beer, socialized. Others were walking with determination toward destinations that Lindell could only guess. Probably to the Filmstaden cinemas or bars, or perhaps they were just on their way home from work.

There was a group of teenagers at the Nybro Bridge, not more than fourteen or fifteen years of age. They poured into the crosswalk just as Lindell drove up, and she was forced to stop. She tried to smile at them, but it turned into more of a grimace. One of the girls threw her a curious glance. When she had reached the other side of the street, she turned her head and their gazes met for a moment. What did she see? Lindell wondered. The car behind her honked.

She turned right and went across the bridge. She did not want to go home. At the foot of the Slottsbacken hill, there was a man leaning against a tree, reading the paper. There was a can of beer beside him.

Her city. Inhabitants she was paid to help and protect. A beautiful city when the mild breezes swept between the houses and the trees in the parks. She liked Uppsala. And yet she felt more distanced from it all than normal. It was as if the city had nothing to do with her. It was work, nothing else. This was the insight she had as she drove aimlessly through the central city blocks.

At Martin Luther King Plaza she noticed a colleague in an unmarked car. He raised his hand in greeting. Outside the Fyris cinema, there was a lone woman. A man came around the corner at Rundelsgränd. The two walked smiling toward each other. Lindell averted her gaze.

✦

Nineteen

Gabriella Mark put the last of the seed trays away and piled them carefully in the shed. It would be a while until the next round of planting. Almost a whole year. She ended up standing with the last tray in her hand, tracing her fingers along the bottom. Knowledge that the growing season was coming to an end now that the plants were in place and sprouting in their containers and beds alarmed her. It wasn't that the season was over—there were a few months left until the final harvest. Some plants would even be left in the ground until the first snow. But the most pleasurable phase—starting the seedlings and transferring them outside—was completed.

She put the last tray on the stack. The evening sun shone across the yard. The mournful song of the curlew could be heard from afar. This was the second season the bird had nested in these parts. Gabriella loved that bird. Its song was hers: melancholy and full of longing.

She walked slowly back to the house. She was drawn to linger, to stop and draw in the heavy scent of the sweet mock orange. She could hear a faint noise from a car or tractor, but it died away.

"Alone," she muttered.

She did not know if she would ever plant any more seeds. Maybe it was the last summer at the cottage. She could sell. The prices has gone up and she would earn a pretty penny. Why would she stay now that Sven-Erik would never be back?

She had hoped that he would stay for good, that he would get divorced, as he had spoken about the last time she had seen him. She knew that he had been serious. It isn't right, she thought, sitting down on the bench at the corner of the cottage.

Would the police be back? She had mulled on this all afternoon. It would be strange if they weren't. She sensed that they knew she was Sven-Erik's friend. What did they think of her? She didn't care anymore.

But she knew she had to call Ann Lindell again. During the last call there had been a kind of connection. Gabriella felt she could trust her. She was a woman, and there was something in her voice that told her Lindell would understand. You don't get to choose the person you love, she thought. It hadn't been rational to fall in love with Sven-Erik, a married man so unlike herself. That was perhaps what had been so exciting and fulfilling for her. He had seen her life with different eyes, new eyes. He had longed for a more peaceful existence. He had said so again and again, and he saw the cottage as a respite. Slowly he had changed. At each visit, she could see how his attitude was changing.

It was his job that killed him. It had to be that. It was the job that had killed his wife and child. She was deeply convinced of this, but how would she make Lindell see it? They probably wanted to make this a crime of passion, assuming he had no longer been able to stand his double life. But Sven-Erik hadn't been like that. He had become happier and more open as time went by.

Work wore him down, but the time with her built him up. Then why would he leave her? Or was this all simply her own fantasy, built on dreams of a life together with a man?

She couldn't live alone. She knew that. The gardening and work around the house were a way to spend her time, a kind of therapy, in waiting for a real life. At first she had despised herself for thinking that a man would save her, but she had come to realize that love would heal her. She needed the warmth of another person.

The oxazepam she had taken a couple of days ago made her movements heavy. Her thoughts returned like the sound of a music box. The melancholy song played over and over. Even in her state of sedation, she realized that this had to be brought to an end, but she didn't know how. She saw no relief.

She heard a faint crackling of leaves in the woods across the road. She imagined it was the elk cow with her lame calf coming to eat of the abundant vegetation at the edge of the little marsh. She peered into the leaves to try to spot the animals, but they must be keeping farther back. She did not believe the calf would survive. They could not move far because of its injury, and in the winter it would probably lose the battle.

She got up from the bench and walked down to the road. The meadow-sweet by the side of the road sent out a sharply intoxicating scent. She broke off a couple of pieces. The woods were quiet. Dusk was starting to fall between the alder trees and the old self-seeded apple tree, whose fruit had started to take shape and grow. Some stock doves could be heard in the distance. Something crunched under her feet. A snail's slimy body slithered in the gravel. One of the antennae was moving spasmodically in and out of the damaged head.

The fleshy mass revolted her and she hurried back to the cottage. A gust of wind buffeted her, pushing her forward.

Alone. Eight hundred meters to the nearest neighbor. The woods close by. The only other life was an elk cow and her calf.

She turned quickly and searched the edge of the woods. She heard the crackle in the leaves again. She stood completely still and tried to figure out what the sound was. Perhaps it was the owls that were nesting farther in.

Shivering, she closed the door. At that moment, the clock on the wall struck eight. She began to cry.

✦

Twenty

The signals mixed with the images of her dreams. She was loping along when the sharp sound of the telephone cut through the apartment. She turned around, but her pursuers were far away. She had managed to shake them off. Would she be caught now because she had to answer the telephone? She stopped, panting. It could be a call from the pharmacy.

Slowly she returned to consciousness and fumbled for the receiver, squinting at the clock.

Edvard. At once she was wide awake.

"No, you didn't wake me," she said and sat up.

"I just wanted to thank you for coming out here," Edvard said.

"I should thank you."

It was half past seven and she should be at work.

"How are you?"

Don't call me! Leave me alone!

"Busy," she said and got out of bed.

"I'm going to be in town this afternoon. I thought maybe we could see each other tonight."

She walked absently toward the bathroom.

"I don't know," she said weakly.

"We could get a bite to eat. It's supposed to be nice weather."

"I don't know," she repeated.

"Has anything happened?"

"No, there's just so much going on with a case right now. I have to work."

She heard from his voice that he was disappointed. She knew it had been hard for him to call. He wasn't the kind who took the initiative.

"Maybe," she said.

Her face in the mirror looked ashen. The dream had left its traces.

"Call me on my cell," he said.

She lifted the lid of the toilet.

"I want to see you," he added.

Lindell ate breakfast with reluctance. The cereal caught in her throat. Coffee was out of the question. She leafed through the newspaper without noting more than the headlines.

It was now fifteen days since Josefin and Emily had died. There had been no breakthrough. If Sven-Erik Cederén really was innocent, then their chances of catching the real perpetrator were rapidly diminishing. Each day that passed was also drawing her closer to having to make a decision about whether to have an abortion or give birth.

In some way it felt immoral to get an abortion. Emily had died, and Lindell had a feeling that her child would be a sort of replacement for a lost life, that the fact that she had become pregnant meant something.

"Ridiculous," she said to herself and folded the newspaper. She was late but could not bring herself to hurry. He wanted to see her. Would she tell him? It would mean the end for them. He would never be able to take this. Never.

Lindell walked into her office at nine o'clock. She had run into Sammy Nilsson in the corridor, who had said hello and looked inquisitively at her. Is it written on my face? she wondered as she brought her notepad onto the desk.

The phone rang. It was Haver.

"Are you heading out to see Mark?"

"In about an hour."

"I'll bring you directions."

They had agreed that Lindell would go alone to see Gabriella Mark.

Lindell could visualize her, waiting. Most likely in the garden, to judge from Haver and Nilsson's accounts of her substantial gardening efforts.

The slow start to the morning was starting to give way to a curiosity about how Mark was going to behave, what information she would be able to provide. How did she know that Cederén had consumed gin?

Lindell felt in her bones that this was a significant lead. If Cederén never drank gin, then this meant that someone else was involved. It meant that he had been forced to consume what was to him a distasteful drink.

Only now did Lindell absorb the full implications of this. Someone else had murdered Josefin and Emily. Somewhere out there was an unknown murderer. A merciless killer.

Maybe I'll catch sight of Edvard, she thought as she passed Jälla. But he had said he was coming in the afternoon. He had not mentioned an errand. He did not visit Uppsala very often, so perhaps he was coming in only to see her?

From Rasbo church to Gabriella Mark's house, she tried to focus her thoughts on the investigation and the woman she would soon meet.

Haver's directions were precise, so she had no trouble finding the place. The first thing she thought about when she arrived was the enormous contrast between this home and Uppsala-Näs and the house that Cederén had lived in.

She did not see anyone in the garden or among the vegetable beds. Lindell knocked on the door, looked around, and waited. She felt observed. She repeated her knocking, more forcefully this time.

Her cell phone rang, but she turned it off without answering. The door was unlocked. She peered in and called Gabriella's name. The house was quiet. Lindell went in. There was a small vestibule and front hall leading to a kitchen. A cup of coffee stood on the table. It was an orderly kitchen, sparingly furnished. Gabriella Mark had good taste.

Lindell glanced into the only other room on the ground floor and then walked up the stairs. "Gabriella," she called, but no one replied. She became convinced that the house was empty as she walked up the creaking stairs to the two rooms on the upper floor.

The car was parked in the yard and the door was unlocked, but there was no sign of life. I must have missed her, Lindell thought, and decided to leave the empty house. She stood on the front steps and carefully examined the surroundings.

She searched the outbuildings and sheds. No sign of the woman. She was starting to feel disheartened. Had Gabriella Mark lost her courage when she saw Lindell? Maybe she was hiding out in the woods?

Lindell paused at the vegetable beds. Her colleagues had not been exaggerating. This was a substantial effort. Lindell was no gardening enthusiast, but she realized that there lay a great deal of work behind the well-ordered beds.

She sat down on the edge of one of the plots. Maybe Gabriella Mark was running an errand nearby. Lindell looked around again. The woods lay quiet and there was complete stillness at the cottage. Lindell had passed another house about a kilometer away before she got to Mark's cottage, but if she had an errand there, wouldn't she have taken the car? That's what Lindell would have done. Maybe she was out walking a dog. Lindell thought of Cederén's pointer.

She lingered for half an hour before she understood that Mark was not returning any time soon. If she was hiding in the vegetation, it meant she was unwilling to meet with Lindell and that she was not going to come out until Lindell left.

She took out her phone and called Haver.

"I don't like this," she said, and he agreed.

"Do you think something has happened?"

"I don't know," Lindell said. "But she's lying low. She must have heard me and taken off into the woods. I think I'll pretend to leave and return on foot. Then she may come out."

On her way to the car she opened the lid of the garbage can and took a look. Empty. Her irritation over Gabriella Mark's behavior grew stronger. She didn't have time for this cat-and-mouse behavior. Clearly Mark possessed some information. It made no sense for her to be so eager for Lindell to believe her and then hide away when Lindell came to see her.

She drove down the road a kilometer or so, passing the neighboring house and turning onto a small forest road, where she parked. The walk back to the cottage took at least twenty minutes. It was a while since she had taken a walk through the forest. It must have been last year with Edvard.

The smells brought back memories, and when she returned to the cottage, she was in a melancholy mood. She felt almost unseeing. The cottage with its beautiful garden gave an impression of unreality. Was there really a person here who had something to do with the killings? It seemed preposterous.

But Lindell had the feeling that Gabriella Mark's life was anything but peaceful. She was consumed by grief and anguish—that much had been clear from her voice.

Lindell did not want to wait any longer. She was afraid of losing herself in her own thoughts. She did not want to become enchanted by the forest; she wanted to think clearly and act like an investigating detective. But still she stayed. If there was anything she was good at, it was waiting.

For almost an hour she stayed hidden before she once again walked up to the house, which was as silent and deserted as before.

Lindell stood indecisively in the middle of the yard. She called Haver again and they decided to put out an alert for her.

After she hung up, she decided to check out the earth cellar. There was a large key in the keyhole, and with some effort Lindell managed to force the door open. She was greeted by the raw smell of earth and old potatoes.

Shelves filled with jars and bottles bore witness to Mark's gardening. Lindell felt guilty because she was holding the door open and letting the warm air inside. There was no Gabriella Mark inside, nothing except juice and jam.

To the right of the earth cellar there was an old, half-collapsed barn. Through a large hole in the wall she could see the rotten feeding troughs. Nettles had made their way inside and were growing through the rough-hewn floorboards.

She walked behind the barn. One wall held a large number of horseshoes. Behind the back of the building was a heap of stones. It looked like an ancient monument. This was where the original cottagers had tossed stones from the fields.

"Edvard," she muttered. "You would feel right at home here."

She thought of him and the stone coffin dock that he had built over the winter. Here he had ample building material.

The monumental nature of the pile of stones appealed to her. There was also something slightly mournful in this testament to the cotters' labor and the massive weight of the stones, overgrown with moss and lichen. She knew her reflection was a result of Edvard's influence. He had talked about the landscape and the traces left by humans, all the labor behind the beauty.

As she rounded the mound, she saw at once that something was wrong. Many of the boulders had been shifted out of place. The moss had been peeled away and the meadow grasses in front of the pile had been trampled. Something had happened here only recently.

Lindell stiffened, her gaze flitting over the area. She didn't want to take in what she saw. Someone had moved the stones and replaced them but had not been able to restore the scene exactly.

Why? There were only two alternatives. Either someone had removed something from behind the stones or else they had hidden something there.

She called Haver for a third time. The fact that she called him was most likely due to the fact that Gabriella Mark had been his lead.

"We should probably bring Forensics out here before I start to root

around," she said. Haver agreed, perhaps mainly because he would then
be able to join them.

Gabriella Mark had been strangled. Ryde and Haver had removed
stone after stone and eventually uncovered her body. A little moss had
fallen onto her face. Her hands were curled into fists. There was bruising
around her throat. She had suffered a nosebleed.

"A stone coffin," Lindell said.

"What?" Ryde asked.

"A stone coffin," Lindell repeated and checked the time: 12:32, Thursday, June 29.

Haver watched her.

"What made you come back here?" he asked.

"Because of Edvard," she said.

She felt their puzzled looks but said nothing to clarify this statement.
She looked down at the woman. Yesterday she had been alive; today she
was dead. They should have been sitting together talking at this moment.
Someone else had gotten here first.

"She isn't wearing very much."

Haver found it hard to tear his gaze away from her almost bare body.

"What did she know?" he asked.

"She believed that Cederén had been forced to drink the gin," Lindell
said.

Ryde looked up, interested. Lindell told them about her conversations
with Gabriella.

"Why would someone force him to drink alcohol?"

Lindell hesitated. "To make a murder look like a suicide. I think it was
homicide," she said finally.

Ryde and Haver stared at her. Something hung in the air. Lindell could
see fatigue in Ryde's face. Behind his usual tough attitude were helplessness and despair.

He saw her gaze and turned back to the body.

"Murdered?" Haver said. "You mean that someone filled Cederén with
that revolting gin and then gassed him to death?"

Lindell nodded.

"How do you explain the traces of Josefin's clothing on Cederén's car?"

"He may have been driving or it may have been someone else," Lindell said.

"You mean that the killings in Uppsala-Näs were staged to look as if they were perpetrated by Cederén," Ryde said.

Lindell nodded again. She was getting tired of their pedantic questions.

"I don't know, but I think this is more complicated than we believed."

Together with Haver and Berglund, who had joined them, Lindell searched the cottage. As usual, Lindell started with the kitchen. Haver focused on the bedroom, and the veteran Berglund started with the living room.

The cupboards in the kitchen were of that old-fashioned variety that had been in Lindell's childhood home as long as she still lived in Ödeshög. Now her parents had replaced them with dark oak paneling and brass hardware, but Lindell preferred the old ones with their wooden knobs and roughhewn shelves covered in oiled paper, attached with tacks.

She searched through the stacks of plates and serving bowls, peered into every cup and pot. Parts of the china were old, early Gustavsberg, the remnants of a full service. Gabriella Mark had not been status driven. This was functional china without any finesse. Nothing newly purchased from the expensive shops. Most likely purchases from Ikea filled in where the old set was incomplete.

Every item had to be lifted and inspected. She had the feeling that this was pointless labor, but it had to be done. Perhaps something in a mug or behind a frying pan would set the investigative machinery in motion. Lindell felt a rising irritation over the routine procedure. She was convinced that the solution was somewhere outside of the cottage, that important time was being lost, and she wanted to leave the interior search to her colleagues. But what would she do instead? Where would she search?

The feeling of uselessness and wasted time had its roots in the fact that she should have come out to see Gabriella last night. She had been alive then. Lindell knew that she had known something important. She had talked with someone and learned the detail about the gin. Who else knew this?

As she continued her search in the cleaning closet, Lindell decided to try to map the spread of information.

After some thirty minutes of searching, she had uncovered nothing of interest—no notes, receipts, or letters that would help with the investigation. She heard Berglund pad around the living room. She assumed that he was leafing through books and checking the drawers in the secretary desk.

The only item of any interest was an empty bottle of oxazepam with the physician's name on the label.

The cell phone rang. It was Beatrice, who had checked into Gabriella Mark's personal information. She was thirty-three years old, born in Österlen, just outside of Simrishamn. Beatrice did not yet know if there was a next of kin. Gabriella had been a project manager at a consulting firm that had finally gone out of business. She had been on disability several times in the past couple of years. The consulting company had declared bankruptcy eight months ago.

She was not registered as having any debts or defaults on payments. She had a current passport. This was as far as the internal investigation had gone.

Lindell asked Beatrice to check with the telephone carrier to see if they could provide an account of the incoming and outgoing calls from the cottage as well as confirm if Gabriella had had a cell phone account. Beatrice also made a note of Gabriella's physician and said that she would look into whether she could get ahold of him.

She may have been on disability, Lindell thought, but she certainly worked in her vegetable garden. Which definitely qualified as work, she reflected as she gazed out the window. She saw some of her colleagues securing evidence. A wave of fatigue washed over her, not so much for herself as for her entire unit. They were engaged in a constant battle, a Sisyphean task in that the boulder always rolled back down.

Lindell looked in on Berglund and asked if he had found anything of interest, but he simply shook his head without answering or even glancing up. She continued to the second floor. Ola Haver was halfway into a large closet. Heaped on the bed was a mound of dresses and skirts, and he was clearly working his way deeper into the closet full of clothes and shoes.

"Women" was all he said as he heard Lindell enter the room.

She knew he meant the masses of clothing. She looked around. The bedroom was also sparsely furnished, with sharply sloped ceiling, light-colored wallpaper with a design of small red roses, and a large bed, tidily made up with a brightly colored coverlet. There was a bookshelf along one wall, a small table, and a peasant chair. That was all. She walked over to the bookshelf: gardening books and novels. Lindell read the titles. She never had time to read herself and was somehow suspicious of those who read a lot. She imagined it was something that she had inherited from her father, who disapproved of those who wanted to stick their nose in a book at any opportunity.

There was a slender book on the nightstand: *Asian-Style Gardens*. Lindell picked it up and leafed through it. One chapter was called "Japanese Leafy Greens."

Haver extracted himself from the closet.

"Find anything?" Lindell asked.

"No, just a lot of clothes."

"Anything that stands out?"

Haver shook his head. He sat down on the edge of the bed.

"It's a blur," he said, and Lindell realized that he was suffering from the same feeling she was.

"What do you think?" she asked and sat down in the chair.

The sense of intimacy between the two colleagues was intensified by fatigue and frustration. Few outside of those in their unit were able to comprehend the pressure of their constant exposure to violence and human misery. They didn't want to force their way into all of these bedrooms and kitchens, snooping in people's things. Perhaps at the very beginning of their careers all of this had felt exciting and new, but now they mostly harbored vain hopes for normalcy, a life where they could meet people unaccompanied by violence and death.

"I think that Gabriella was lonely out here in the woods. She chose this isolation, but she also loved Cederén."

Exactly right, Lindell thought, who recalled Gabriella's voice and her conviction that Cederén was innocent.

"Can her dependence on Cederén have blinded her judgment?"

"Maybe," Haver said.

"She was taking tranquilizers and had been on disability. Maybe that affected her."

"But you can't forget that she was murdered," Haver objected.

He got up abruptly. Lindell sensed his displeasure. Gabriella Mark had been his lead, his idea. Her death immediately after they had finally found her was a considerable setback.

"Keep going," Lindell said, but she remained sitting.

"There's the question of a motive," she went on thoughtfully. "There has to be a strong one."

"Money," said Haver, kneeling to search the area under the bed.

"Yes, I don't think the animal rights activists would strangle a young woman," Lindell said. "But there may be a connection."

"How?"

"If their accusations are on target, if the primates are being mistreated— that is to say, if MedForsk is involved with animal abuse—then there is a lot to fear. Public opinion could quickly turn on them if this was the case. MedForsk is a company riding high, and they don't want to sully their reputation."

"But killing people to do so is a little extreme," Haver said.

Lindell sank into thought and Haver resumed his searching. He was in the process of taking out the books one by one and shaking them to see if there were any papers stuck between the pages.

"I'm going down," Lindell said. "We can let Ryde loose in a bit. I'm going back to town. Will you call me?"

"Sure. I think Bronkan's team has arrived."

This unit was trained to secure leads outdoors and had started combing the area.

Lindell had just stepped into the car when Edvard called. She felt some relief at being able to say that she was busy with a fresh murder when he suggested that they meet later that afternoon. If he was disappointed, he didn't show it. He wished her good luck.

"Maybe we can see each other over the weekend?" he asked.

"Maybe," Lindell said.

Even though she would have been able to take the time to talk to him, she led him to believe she was in a hurry and they ended the call.

"Coward," she muttered.

Lindell gave the house a final glance as she started the car. Out of the corner of her eye she caught sight of movement in a window upstairs. It was Haver, gesticulating. He was struggling to open the window. Lindell turned off the engine and climbed out of the car at the same time as the window shot open.

"Wait!" Haver shouted. "I've found some notes."

"I'm coming up," Lindell said and shut the car door. Notes, she thought, finally something personal. An image of Josefin Cederén's diary flashed in front of her eyes.

When she reached the bedroom, Haver was sitting on the bed, thumbing through the pages of a small light-colored almanac decorated with flowers. It was a kind that Lindell had not seen in many years and that she did not think was sold any longer.

"Come here," Haver said and held out the almanac, which was open to June 29. There were two sentences on the page: "What role does Pålle play? Can I trust him?"

Lindell looked at Haver.

"Yesterday," she said, and Haver nodded. "Where did you find it?"

"In the box under the nightstand."

"Are there any more notes?" Lindell asked, turning the pages and seeing for herself brief notations on roughly every other page. All were written in pencil and—from what Lindell could tell—in Gabriella's handwriting.

"Pålle," Haver said. "Who is that?"

"Pålle," Lindell said slowly. "It's a nickname."

She had not come across it before anywhere else in the investigation.

"He knows Gabriella, is agitated, and wants to see her. He has most likely been here before. For some reason she doesn't want him to come," Haver summarized.

"Is he mentioned anywhere else?"

"Not that I've seen so far," Haver said.

Lindell was quiet and tried to imagine Gabriella with the notebook in front of her.

"It must be a person that she has a relationship to, a person who means something," she said. "Who is called Pålle?"

"A Paul, Peter, Per-Olof, Petter," Haver began.

"Pålle, Pålle," Lindell repeated.

Lindell looked at a couple of more pages at random. It was not a diary in the traditional sense, more a collection of comments. Some were about the planting of vegetables, others about the weather. Sven-Erik's name appeared in many places. "Sven-Erik is coming" from May 20, and "Sven-Erik in Spain" on February 14.

"Okay," Lindell said. "Why don't you finish checking this and write up all of the notes that may be of interest. Skip the plants and the weather; take down all the names and their frequency."

"Pålle," Haver said musingly, as if he were trying to visualize this acquaintance of Gabriella's.

Lindell continued to turn the pages. On May 28, Gabriella had noted something that baffled her: "The calf is looking worse. Poor thing." She showed it to Haver.

"What calf?" he said. "Did she have cows?"

"I don't think so," Lindell said. "Maybe there's a neighbor who has some."

Lindell felt more satisfied as she got into the car to leave the cottage for a second time. Gabriella had been given a voice, even if only a few words in an journal. Who was Pålle? Lindell felt certain that he was a close acquaintance; otherwise Mark wouldn't have used this nickname the way she did.

Was Pålle the killer? It sounded like the name of a horse, Lindell thought, and imagined a large Ardennes draft horse with enormous hooves, a generous mane, and a long, rough tail.

✦

Twenty-one

Uncovering the details of Gabriella Mark's life and circle of acquaintances was a simple enough task, but frustrating nonetheless. She had been a very lonely woman. This was the conclusion Lindell arrived at upon reading Beatrice's report.

Born in a little village outside Simrishamn. Her father was a dentist and her mother a dental hygienist at the same practice. Both dead for five years: her mother from cancer and her father by drowning off the coast of Sri Lanka. Lindell's colleagues in Simrishamn had gathered a half page of information. There was nothing of a sensational nature.

Mark had no siblings. Her closest relatives were three cousins, one in Ystad, one in Tomelilla, and the third in Malmö. The first two had never had any real contact with Gabriella Mark. The third was the only one who had been in sporadic contact with her through the years. They wrote and called each other, according to the cousin in Ystad. They had not yet been able to get ahold of the Malmö cousin. The Malmö police had gone to her apartment, but no one had opened. A neighbor had said that she left for vacation a week ago and planned to be gone for fourteen days. She was hiking in the Dolomites.

The last time the four of them met up was three years ago. The meeting had been in regard to an inheritance from their grandparents. Gabriella Mark had traveled to Simrishamn and selected some decorative items.

Gabriella had always been a little unusual, as one of the cousins put it. Not unfriendly exactly, but reserved. Neither of them had ever heard of Sven-Erik Cederén.

The company that Gabriella had been working for most recently had gone out of business. Beatrice had managed to trace the former owner to Holland, where he was now involved in real estate transactions. He had sounded genuinely distraught when he was informed of Mark's death.

"She was a wonderful person," he had said on the poor connection from Boskoop.

Lindell thought it was comforting that someone had said a positive word about anyone in the investigation.

"She was also a very fine project manager," he said. "She had good ideas and was able to implement them, which is more than can be said for most people. She was hard to discourage, as stubborn as a mule, and very single-minded."

"Why did she quit?" Beatrice had asked.

"She didn't. She went on disability after the car crash that killed her husband. She never really rebounded from that blow."

The man had paused, and Beatrice thought she had been cut off, but he had then made a comment that Beatrice and Lindell later discussed the significance of.

"Gabriella always wanted to be fair. She hated injustice, whether it was whose turn it was to make coffee or something that she had read about in the morning paper. I think she got this from her father, who had been a bit of a do-gooder and truthsayer. She often talked about him."

Beatrice had thought it was refreshing to speak with a real estate swindler who was so adept at discussing personal relations.

"She lost everyone who meant anything to her," Lindell said as she and Beatrice went through the facts about Gabriella Mark. "Her husband died, her parents, and then this with Cederén."

"It's no wonder she was taking oxazepam," Beatrice said.

"She hated injustice," Lindell said thoughtfully.

She had liked Gabriella. Too bad we didn't get to talk more, she thought.

"She would have made a good police officer," Beatrice said.

"Yes, we are also project managers," Lindell said. "Project Justice."

The physician who had prescribed medication to Mark did not have much to add. They had not had any extended contact. Apparently she had not confided in him, just turned to him as a way to get tranquilizers and sleep aids.

Financially she had been comfortable. The cottage was paid off. She had inherited a certain amount from her parents and could be characterized as financially independent even though she had been on disability for such an extended period. Her monetary assets had been close to eight hundred thousand kronor. She was saving for her retirement and had no debts as far as they could tell.

"So she wasn't after his money," Beatrice said. "She had enough of her own."

"I wonder if she knew about Cederén's affairs in the Dominican Republic? Did she know that he had bought land out there? Maybe it was a joint project?"

"I don't think so," Lindell said. "Although you have a point. Do you remember the fragments of that letter we found? That Piñeda who wrote that they were suffering? Could that have been from the Dominican Republic? With Mark's sense of justice, it's not hard to imagine she would have wanted to put things right."

Their meeting was set to begin in fifteen minutes. The Cederén investigation was now being viewed differently. Lindell closed her eyes and tried to find some kind of logic in all of these loose threads. Where did Piñeda's letter fit? The attack of the animal rights activists at TV4? What had Gabriella known that was so dangerous she had to be silenced?

When she opened her eyes, Beatrice was watching her with an expression of both concern and curiosity.

What does she see? Lindell wondered. Their eyes met for a brief moment. They were not particularly close, even though they were the only women in the unit and should therefore have felt a certain kinship. Was there perhaps a streak of competition between them? Beatrice was not easy to get close to. That was probably necessary in this line of work. She could be acerbic. Many of their male colleagues thought of her as a bitch, and even Lindell sometimes wished she were a little softer.

"At least the guy who was injured on the stairs at the television station is going to be okay. The paralysis in his legs is gone," Beatrice said.

"That's great," Lindell said. "But our paralysis is increasing."

"Is it a man?" Beatrice asked.

Lindell nodded. "Yes. I think a woman would have trouble strangling another woman."

"He must have known her."

"I think so. This is definitely no maniac who appeared out of the woods and choked her to death for the fun of it. He knew her and wanted to keep her from talking."

Lindell felt the nausea come on in waves and stood up. Her lack of concentration bothered her. How long was she going to feel this way?

"If we assume Mark's theory that Cederén was murdered, what would the motive be?" Beatrice went on.

"Perhaps financial," Lindell said.

With an effort she managed to repress the nausea and turned back around.

"Maybe," Beatrice said doubtfully. "But MedForsk was doing well. They had consistently great results and new medical breakthroughs. They were at the brink of a significant expansion."

"The point at which things are starting to go well is often when desperation becomes the greatest—if there's something wrong with the picture. Maybe Cederén was the problem?"

Lindell felt suddenly close to tears. Again she had to turn her back to Beatrice. Images of Josefin's and Emily's bodies by the side of the road in Uppsala-Näs flashed before her. Above all, the girl's dress and her little hands that had been picking flowers.

"How are things?" Beatrice asked. "You seem a little down."

Lindell nodded weakly toward the window.

"I'm thinking of Emily," she said quietly.

"Little kids dying is the worst," Beatrice agreed. "I've also been thinking of her."

They were both quiet for a while. Lindell sensed that Beatrice would like to continue. She both wanted and didn't want Beatrice to ask her more about how she was feeling. She realized that she needed to talk to someone. Her mother was out of the question, in part because their discussion would have to be over the phone and because the situation of finally getting a grandchild but without a son-in-law would be so confusing for her mother. She would not be able to provide any sensible or comforting words.

Beatrice was the only woman who was somewhat close to Lindell, but only because they saw each other daily, not because they had very much else in common.

"Don't take this personally," Beatrice said. "I know that sounds absurd, but—"

"I can handle it," Lindell interrupted.

The morning meeting was a somber affair. Everyone was affected by the new homicide and the fact that the Cederén case had to be taken in a different direction. Sammy Nilsson was the exception. He seemed to be stimulated by the fact that the situation had grown more complicated.

"Gabriella Mark is the key," he said enthusiastically.

The rest of them pondered this for a few seconds, but no one found anything revolutionary in the pronouncement. There were plenty of keys. A new lead could be found by accident. Stating that solving the murder of Gabriella Mark could break the entire MedForsk case was hardly a revelation, but his colleagues let the comment stand. It was good that someone was positive. Perhaps they would even find a hint of value in his lengthy commentary.

"I have been checking her calls over the past few months," he continued. "She has not made very many, but a couple stick out as more important than the rest. A couple actually complicate this whole thing even further."

He paused dramatically. Now the others realized that perhaps he had a reason for his optimism and waited for him to continue.

"Four times she has made calls to Jack Mortensen, the CEO of Med-Forsk. And once to Cederén's parents."

Lindell's head jerked up. "Mortensen?" she said. "He denied all knowledge of Cederén's having a lover. When were the calls?"

"The last one was the day before yesterday," said Sammy Nilsson. "Fourteen-ten. And before that, on three separate occasions. The first call took place the day after Cederén's death."

"Damn," Lindell said in spite of herself.

"The call to the parents was made a week ago and was about eight minutes long. Her call to Mortensen was about fifty-two minutes long."

"Fifty-two minutes," Haver echoed. "They must have had a lot to talk about."

"Let's bring him in," Ottosson said. "Let him sweat a little. Ann, why don't you talk to Cederén's father again and see what the call with Gabriella was all about."

Lindell could see the old couple in her mind's eye. What did Mark have to say to them? Perhaps they knew one another from before.

"We know that she was strangled between nine and ten the night before last," Ryde said. "There are indications that it happened in the kitchen. A throw rug was scrunched up in a strange way. Since the rest of the kitchen was tidy, the state of the rug seemed significant, but of course we can't be sure. There were no fingerprints apart from hers and Cederén's. Nothing in the garbage, nothing under her fingernails. No other indications of injury on the body and no bruises."

"We have the journal," Berglund jumped in. "It doesn't give us more than the name Pålle. We also have some chicken scratches on a little notepad, not exactly a diary, but a series of writings that appear to stem from the time that her husband died. Sad reading. The address book had about forty names, which has to be characterized as relatively few. There is no Pålle anywhere. I'm still in the process of reviewing the list."

Ottosson looked appreciatively at him and nodded.

"Her shoes were still in the house. As you know, she was found barefoot, which corroborates the theory that she was killed inside. Her heels are dirty, consistent with the body's having been dragged down to the stone pile," Ryde said, and Lindell had the impression that he and Berglund had staged their participation.

"Have any of the neighbors seen anything?" Ottosson asked.

"No, not anyone we've talked to so far," Haver said. "Nilsson—our Rasbo expert—is in charge of that. But there are some indications that someone has been lurking at the edge of the woods. Bronkan's team found some evidence, but he didn't want to jump to conclusions. There's elk shit, to be sure."

"Okay," Ottosson said. "Someone came to the cottage, most likely someone that Mark knew. He entered, either invited or uninvited, strangled her, and then took off. There's no sign that anything else was touched or stolen."

"Hard to say. We don't know what was there before," Berglund pointed out.

"That's true," Ottosson said. "But nothing appeared messed up or searched through, I mean."

There were a couple of seconds of silence before Lindell took over.

"There's the question of motive. Gabriella Mark talked to me on the phone twice. The first time she sounded bewildered and upset, but the second time she was more collected and convinced that Cederén was innocent. She also thought it was completely unbelievable that he would have committed suicide. As her strongest argument, she raised the issue of the gin. What do we think of that?"

"So Cederén had been forced to drink gin and then been gassed to death?" Ottosson said skeptically.

Lindell nodded.

"It's not completely out of the question," she said. "Mark was very sure of herself. We're looking into Cederén's background to see if he ever drank gin."

"Who could have told her that detail? It wasn't in the papers."

"I've been wondering that too," Lindell said.

"Did we tell anyone?" Haver asked.

"I have," Beatrice said and everyone's faces turned toward her. "I talked to Cederén's parents, and when his mother asked me if I thought her son had suffered very much before he died, I said no. I said that he had been heavily intoxicated when it happened and probably hadn't felt a thing."

No one said anything.

"I said it to comfort her," Beatrice added.

"Did you mention that it was gin?" Lindell asked.

"I don't know. Maybe. That may have been wrong," she went on when no one said anything.

"Right, wrong," Ottosson said. "I understand what you were thinking. Let's just ask Cederén's mother," he added, trying to lighten the situation.

The meeting wrapped with Lindell summarizing the current findings and assigning tasks. This wasn't strictly necessary, since all of them were clear on what they were doing, but it was helpful for her own sake, to negate her own passivity. Ottosson smiled at her and rubbed his beard. Beatrice glanced at her from the side. Haver just looked impatient.

Afterward, Lindell went straight to the bathroom. She wanted to see herself in the mirror, to check if her inner confusion was visible from the outside. She drew one hand tenderly across her cheeks and forehead, as if in a lover's caress. The wrinkles around her eyes had deepened, and what was even worse was that her eyes had lost their sparkle. They stared dully out of a stranger's face attached to a stranger's body.

She left the bathroom in a state of despair and had to force herself to take the fifteen steps to her office. Once there, she pulled her notepad over and looked up Jack Mortensen's number. He wasn't at MedForsk and he also didn't answer his cell or home numbers. She left a voice mail on each line.

Haver was poring over passenger lists from Arlanda. This project had begun the moment that Cederén had disappeared. The goal then had been to find Cederén's name. Now the search had been widened to include a number of incoming and outgoing flights from the Dominican Republic and Málaga. There were thousands of names. He had ruled out most of the charter flights and was concentrating on the regular routes.

His idea had been that somewhere along the line he would see a name that he recognized from the investigation. Either Cederén or someone else at MedForsk. Now he was eyeing the lists to try to find the killer's name.

Cederén had traveled frequently to Málaga over the winter and spring. His secretary had noted some twelve trips to that city.

The company's offices and factories there had been expanded, and that was where most of the production took place. Perhaps Cederén had had company. Haver did not know exactly what he was looking for, but something could be hidden somewhere among all these names. In particular, he was watching for the name Piñeda, the person who had written the letter. Had he possibly traveled to Sweden to make his case? But so far Haver had not found anything of significance.

Mortensen returned the call after fifteen minutes.

"I don't have my cell phone on," he explained. "People are constantly calling."

Isn't that why you have a cell phone? Lindell thought to herself.

"I want you to come down to the station immediately," she said without any polite small talk.

"Right now?"

"Yes, now. We have things to talk about."

"I see."

Mortensen sounded as if he was having trouble getting the words out, but also as if he was gathering himself for some kind of protest.

"Now," Lindell repeated.

She did not have to wait more than twenty minutes before she received a call from reception and was told that she had a visitor. She walked down to get him and escorted him quietly back to her office.

He had stopped pretending to be baffled, which Lindell appreciated. She hated assertive types who became nervous teenagers with the police.

"You lied to my face," she began without introduction.

"What do you mean?"

"Cederén's lover. You knew about her existence and you knew where she was."

Mortensen looked back at her and she thought she saw a faint smile on his face. Was he mocking her?

"Yes, I know Gabriella."

"She's dead," Lindell informed him, though she regretted it immediately.

"That isn't possible."

"Why did you lie to me?"

"What happened to her?"

"Answer the question."

"I . . ." he started but immediately faltered. He stared at her as if he thought she was bluffing.

"You could have saved her life if you had told us where she was."

"Did she kill herself?"

"Tell me why you lied to me. No more shit."

"I wanted to protect her," he said quietly. "She has suffered enough. You may not know everything she's had to go through."

"Instead you contributed to her death," Lindell said sharply.

Mortensen looked as if he was reflecting on this statement but offered no rebuttal. He gazed down at his hands, lifted his head for a moment, and met her eyes, but then looked down again at once.

"She talked to me before she died," Lindell said.

His head jerked up with a look of astonishment that was also mixed with something else. Fear, perhaps.

"What did she say?" Mortensen said hesitantly.

"That doesn't matter. She wanted to talk about Cederén."

"How did she die?"

"She was strangled."

Mortensen swallowed.

"How well did you know her?"

"Not very. I knew that she and Sven-Erik were together. I met her several times. Who did it?"

"Tell me about their relationship."

Mortensen collected himself somewhat and launched into a more or less coherent account of how she and Cederén had met and how he had gradually started to change. Gabriella Mark was the reason for much of this change in his personality, he believed. Cederén started asking different questions, became more distracted, lost his focus on the company mission. He started to question his work, even the fundamental concept behind MedForsk.

"Was it the animal experimentation?"

"No, not that. Perhaps a little bit, but we've worked with test animals our entire professional careers. Working on animals is necessary in medical research, and we know the role that it plays in advances."

"So he was not a militant animal rights supporter?"

"No, definitely not," Mortensen said.

"Then what was it?"

"I think he was having some kind of life crisis. It must have had something to do with Josefin as well. I think they had grown apart."

"That's often the case when you start something on the side," Lindell said.

"I took it as a sign that the relationship wasn't doing well. That it was with Gabriella was more of a coincidence."

"Did Cederén see a future with her?"

"I don't know."

"Had his purchase of land in the Dominican Republic anything to do with her? Were they going to move there?"

"I don't know," he repeated. "That purchase is a mystery."

Lindell was starting to make peace with the thought that Mortensen had lied to her. He had regained some of the reasonable tone she remembered from their first meeting. Perhaps it was the satisfaction of being able to talk to someone who had known Cederén well that was lightening her mood.

"When you say that you were protecting Gabriella by not revealing her identity, weren't you also thinking of the company?"

"What do you mean?"

"There was some attention generated by the deaths of the Cederén family. If the information that he'd had a mistress had gotten out, the story would have become even more sordid."

Mortensen appeared to want to wave away the word "sordid."

"No, not like that," he said in a low voice.

"Who could have wanted to see Gabriella dead?"

The question hung in the air as the telephone rang. Lindell picked up the receiver but kept her eyes on the man across the table. Haver was on the other end of the line. She asked him to call back later, hung up, and repeated her question. Mortensen appeared to have gathered new strength and launched into a rant about the violence in society.

"It may have been revenge from someone who was close to Josefin," he said in closing.

"Was there anyone close to her who was prepared to kill for her?"

"What do I know? People seem capable of anything these days."

Lindell had to agree, but was less convinced by his theory.

"You talked to Gabriella for almost an entire hour. What did you talk about?"

"It was that long? Mostly about Sven-Erik, of course. I was wondering how she was getting on. I knew that she had been through a great deal. I know a number of physicians—if she was in need of any additional assistance, I mean."

"What did she say?"

"That she was planting vegetables. I thought that sounded crazy."

"And what did you do the night before last, on the twenty-ninth of June?"

"I was digging a pond," he said. "I'm working on the garden and have rented a small digger."

"You're doing it yourself?"

"A small machine like that is like a toy, every boy's dream."

"What time would you say you were out there in the garden?"

"I probably started around six o'clock and kept going as long as it was light out. You have to get your money's worth."

"You were alone?"

"The guy who rented it to me came by shortly before six o'clock. He instructed me on how to use it before he left. That was probably around seven. Then I got started."

"Did anyone come by?"

Mortensen thought about it. "No, but the neighbors can probably confirm that I was out there."

Lindell stood up suddenly and Mortensen shot back in his chair in reaction to her unexpected action.

"Is there anything else you're not telling me?"

He shook his head. "I'm sorry . . ." he began but was interrupted by Lindell, who thanked him for his time and held out her hand.

He grasped it and made a rather awkward motion with his other as if to say: Excuse me, I didn't know.

Lindell wrote down their exchange in her notepad. She wasn't sure what to make of Jack Mortensen. A tricky type who was probably used to adapting to new situations. His tone and gestures were a bit too obvious at times, a bit theatrical, but she also knew that some people chose to play a defensive role without having sinister intentions. They just wanted to meet the expectations of others. There was a number of indications that he was this kind of person.

She called Haver, but now he was no longer in his office. She dialed the number to Cederén's parents after finally locating the number in the mess on her desk.

It was his mother who answered. She immediately acknowledged that she had spoken with Gabriella Mark. Mark had presented herself as a friend of Sven-Erik, but she had never heard of her before. Her reason for calling was to extend her condolences and to say that she didn't believe that Sven-Erik had run over his family.

"She seemed very sweet," the mother said. "It sounded like she was crying."

She also acknowledged that she had told Gabriella about the gin. She had heard it from another woman police officer.

"I guess I told her that to comfort her a little," the mother said.

Lindell thanked her for her information and was getting ready to end the conversation when the mother stopped her.

"Who was she?"

"A friend of the family," Lindell said.

Mortensen's words about how it could have been a friend of Josefin who was getting revenge by strangling Gabriella came back to Lindell after she hung up. Could there be such a friend? Mortensen had put Josefin on a pedestal and on several occasions had referred to her as a "fantastic woman." Perhaps he was Josefin's friend? Had he been in love with his partner's wife? Gabriella would most certainly have let him into her house.

But Lindell dismissed the idea. She saw Mortensen's fragile hands in her mind and thought of his somewhat fussy emotionality. He was not a man who committed murder. Not with his hands, at least. He could probably be tough enough when it came to business, or at least that was the impression Lindell had from the comments at MedForsk. But he wasn't a killer.

She did have to check with the neighbors to verify Mortensen's claim of digging in the garden. She had also been given the name of the man who had rented out the equipment, Gustavsson.

Passions, she thought. Our lives are driven by strong emotions. Some don't make it. Others find love and sometimes happiness. Mortensen's strongest passion appeared to be his collection of textiles. Or rather, his mother's collection. Successful businessman that he was, he was still a mama's boy. That much had been clear.

Lindell dropped Mortensen. She became aware she was hungry, and that realization led her to thoughts of the little life inside her body. How big was it now? She had no idea how an embryo grew. She drew a hand across the top of her pants. She wasn't showing yet. The only change was that her breasts were somewhat enlarged. Hadn't Sammy stared a little too long? She stood in front of the small mirror and tried to catch a glimpse of her profile.

She could have gone down to the kitchen and grabbed something but decided to leave the station and walk quickly toward the center of town.

I have to think, she repeated to herself. She felt that she had a small window of opportunity in which to come to a decision about her own life, but then Gabriella's murder had happened and she was forced to push her personal concerns aside. She did this with a practiced routine but also with a certain half-conscious sense of relief. Now she didn't have to make up her mind and could instead direct all her attention to her work. She knew of course that she had to deal with this problem. It was literally growing and becoming an ever-increasing threat to her peace of mind.

It was hot outside and Lindell was sweating after only a couple of minutes. If only I would have a miscarriage, she thought, but regretted it immediately. Maybe this was her only chance to have a child. And maybe this was the way it was supposed to be. Usually she was a rational creature who did not think much about fate, but now her customary ways of coping were collapsing.

She tried to imagine herself as a single mother, but saw only the problems: having to be home, nursing the baby and changing its diapers, sitting with the other mothers at the volunteer preschool in her neighborhood. She had noticed the flock of mothers and only an occasional father and had always thought it looked deadly boring. When her child got older, there would be the constant stress of getting it to day care, and an ever-present feeling of guilt both at home and at work.

This was not the way she had imagined being pregnant and having a child. She wanted a husband and a father to share her daily life with. Just think if this had been Edvard's child! She stopped on the sidewalk, overwhelmed by this thought. She had decided to be with Edvard after the Midsummer holiday, but what was that decision worth now?

She walked faster and faster. Within a week I have to decide, she thought. How long can you still have an abortion? She had a faint recollection that it was something like twenty weeks. That would be five months. Was that possible? You were big as a house at that point.

"One week," she muttered softly to herself as she pushed open the door to the Elaka Måns café.

The only other notable thing that happened during the rest of the day was that Bronkan came by and told them that they had managed to secure a footprint outside Mark's cottage, about five meters into the woods. It was from a size 42 shoe, made in somewhat marshy terrain.

From this particular spot, you had a clear view of the house and yard but were shielded from sight by a few ragged spruces. There was elk dung next to the footprint. Haver joked that perhaps these were size 42 hooves, but Bronkan did not seem to appreciate the humor in this. He stared angrily at Haver and Lindell. Lindell knew that they had put a lot of time and labor into this work, so she was quick to congratulate him on his find and thank him for a job well done. Bronkan lit up, but this did not conceal the fatigue in his face.

Prints had been made and would be added to the as-yet-nonexistent forensic evidence in the Mark case. This wasn't to say that the footprint had anything to do with the murder. They could only hope that time would yield another piece to the puzzle.

The interviews with Mark's limited circle of acquaintances and former colleagues were completed. Most of these had taken place over the phone. In only one case had Berglund gone to a person's house. This was to interview a retired teacher who had been Gabriella Mark's neighbor on Geijersgatan and who had maintained sporadic contact with her over the past few years.

This person, Hedda Ljunggren, a lady of seventy, had more or less functioned as a counselor for Mark after her husband had died.

The last time they were in touch was in May, and then Mark had seemed very happy and positive.

"But she was always up and down," Hedda Ljunggren said. "She could suddenly collapse when everything looked wonderful. She was unstable."

Back then, in May, they had gossiped about old neighbors and Mark had naturally talked about her gardening and that she felt happy in her cottage. Ljunggren had had the impression that there was a man in the picture but hadn't wanted to ask her outright. It was a sensitive topic.

At the end of the conversation they had for some reason stumbled onto politics. Perhaps it was something that had been in the papers. Mark had spoken of some kind of international relief project. She was frustrated by the fact that so many people in the world were suffering while in Sweden everyone was doing so well. Ljunggren couldn't remember what organization was behind it or whether it was restricted to a certain country, but she thought it was a project to aid children.

Mark had sounded enthused and Ljunggren had sensed that this was in part compensation for the fact that she did not have her own children.

Nothing in the cottage indicated that she had been involved in any kind of project. There were no brochures or receipts or anything else to indicate this kind of engagement.

Ljunggren's account gave them the impression of a young woman who had been slowly but surely making her way back to the surface. She had in large part done this by herself, as she had always mistrusted psychiatrists. This pointed to both persistence and strength, qualities that Ljunggren assured them Mark had. In the midst of her grief, Mark had been certain that she would make her way out of her depression and create a new life. The cottage, which Ljunggren had visited several times, had been a first step.

She was so beautiful when she was happy, Ljunggren had said. She became simply radiant. She had also had a gift of generosity that few possessed. It could be a matter of a few words of appreciation or a bunch of carrots.

Berglund summarized his impression. He had liked the old teacher, had seen in her a knowledge of people and a consideration that Berglund sometimes wished he saw in many of his younger colleagues. Ljunggren was obviously greatly attached to Mark.

He found himself missing Gabriella Mark. He wanted her to be alive again. There were too few out there, he thought, who were radiant and gave away carrots.

He walked into Lindell's office and told her about his conversation with Hedda Ljunggren. Haver came in while he was still talking and the three of them ended up discussing Mark. They were trying to re-create an image of her.

"I think she was someone who was much more than a lover to Cederén. She must have been very different from the others that he knew."

"She softened Cederén's sense of duty and exacting demands on himself," Berglund speculated. "Everyone has commented on this, on how hard Cederén worked, how driven and goal-oriented he was. Life is not simply about producing a birdie and lowering your handicap or winning glory and money. I think she made the ground shake under his feet."

Lindell gazed at her older colleague, whose opinions she valued greatly.

"I know this is cheap psychology," Berglund said. "But life is often cheap and banal."

"I think it's clear that she changed his regular path," Lindell said. "He became unfocused, as many people have said. This may have had to do with her."

"Maybe he was also starting to doubt his work," Haver said.

"I'm not sure about that," Lindell objected. "We have to remember that he was a professional researcher and had devoted his life to developing new medications."

"I think you may have an overly idealized idea of the pharmaceutical industry."

"Let's talk about the Dominican Republic," Lindell said.

The room fell silent. No one wanted to talk about this because nothing new had emerged about this topic. Plans to send someone to the island to investigate the extent of Cederén's affairs had been shelved. The local police had provided all necessary information. It was simply a real estate transaction. There were no other connections between Cederén and the island, at least as far as they could tell.

They had questioned the builder with the contract, and he had had only professional dealings with Cederén. He had received a small advance in order to purchase the building materials and to be able to hire workers. Now he did not know what he was going to do with the cement or the money that was left over.

"It's strange to be building something on the other side of the world without being there," Haver said.

"I don't think it would be a problem as long as it was other people's money," Berglund said. "He was using the company's accounts. Maybe he had hired someone else over there to manage the whole thing."

The Swedish police had also asked their colleagues in the Dominican Republic to search for anyone named Piñeda who might turn up in connection with the construction project. To date they had not received any answer, however.

At that moment there was a knock on the door and Sammy Nilsson came in.

"Oh, good, we were just reviewing where we stand," Lindell said.

Sammy sat down in the only armchair.

"I know how this all hangs together," he said, stretching out. He paused.

"We have Josefin's father. He is the only one with a strong enough motive to revenge himself on the woman who was an indirect cause of his daughter's death."

Lindell conjured up an image of the old man from Uppsala-Näs sitting at the kitchen table, scratching at the open sores on his head, completely baffled by what had happened to his daughter and grandchild. Granted he had lost the big love of his life, but was he really capable of murder?

"Maybe he went there to talk to Gabriella, got angry, and strangled her," Sammy went on.

"How did he find out about her existence and where she lived?" Berglund asked.

"Josefin may have known about her husband's mistress. How many did she confide in? I bumped into Magnusson in the garage and he mentioned that he had called the waitress at the Wermlandskällaren again to see if she could remember more details from Cederén's visit. She mentioned that she had gone out to Uppsala-Näs to visit Josefin's father. She wanted to give him her condolences because apparently they'd had a good relationship when she was working as a home assistant. In other words, the father knew that we were looking for an unknown woman who had accompanied Cederén to the restaurant. He knew who she was, but instead of talking with us, he may have decided to look her up himself. Perhaps it wasn't to murder her, more to look her in the face and bawl her out, I don't know. People operate in such different ways."

Lindell couldn't help but smile at Sammy's final words. It was the only conclusion in his long and speculative account that she could agree with.

"Go on, laugh," he said. "But can you come up with something better?"

He pulled himself out of the chair, reached for the thermos on the table, and shook it, only to discover that it was empty.

"No one's laughing," Lindell said. "But you have to admit that you're an imaginative type."

"This is about motive," Sammy said. "Strong motives. And what is stronger than a father's grief at his only daughter's death? He couldn't revenge himself on Cederén. Gabriella was the only one left."

"I think this is messier than that," Haver said. "I mean, everything is connected. There is not only familial grief in this drama. There is also MedForsk, primates, and activists."

"Okay," Sammy said and got up. "Then I guess I will go think up a new theory. Are you here for another half an hour?"

"Another theory in half an hour is about right," Lindell said. "Then maybe we'll catch the killer in a couple of days."

"But I do think we should interrogate the father," Sammy said.

"I'll do it," Lindell said.

"Check his shoes," Haver said.

Lindell decided to drive straight out to Josefin's father. On her way there, she stopped at the church to visit Josefin's and Emily's graves. But she immediately regretted it and simply stayed in the car gazing out over the beautiful landscape.

A pastoral landscape, she thought. Very fitting next to a church. She lingered for ten minutes, toying with the idea of calling Edvard, but what would she really say? Would he call again or had he changed his mind? That would be good in a way. Then she wouldn't have to decide if she was going to tell him about the child. Then he was the one who had made the decision.

She decided that if Edvard didn't try to contact her again, if their Midsummer night had only been a nostalgic game, she would have the baby.

She drove on, noticeably more at peace, and passed by Cederén's house, which lay empty. It would be sold, and as far as she could tell, Sven-Erik's and Josefin's parents were the heirs.

Holger Johansson was sitting in a garden swing with his neighbor, Vera. He showed no surprise at Lindell's appearance.

Lindell couldn't help but check his scalp to see if the sores were still there, but she didn't see any. Vera went to fetch her a cup of coffee.

Johansson had aged during the weeks that had gone by since they last saw each other. He seemed slightly lost. He must be on medications, Lindell thought.

She told him very briefly that they had found the woman that Cederén had been seeing. Johansson did not look particularly surprised. He raised his eyes and gazed at Lindell as if to say: Of course, all this was Cederén's fault. It was his infidelity that killed my daughter and grandchild.

"Cederén's girlfriend is also dead. Murdered."

He put his cup down with a clatter and stared at her in amazement.

"How?" he managed as Vera returned. In one hand she held a cup, in the other a plate with slices of Swiss roll.

Lindell repeated what she had said. Vera froze where she stood.

"Was she the one who was written about in the papers?"

Lindell nodded.

"Coffee," Johansson said. "Give her some coffee."

Vera poured her a cup.

"It didn't say that it had anything to do with Sven-Erik," she said.

"No, we never told the media."

"How did she die?" Johansson asked.

"She was strangled."

It felt strange not to be able to say that Gabriella Mark had been a good person. Someone who had been beaten down by life but was finding her way back.

"How terrible," Vera said and shot Johansson a quick look as if she had said too much.

"So I have to ask what you were doing the evening of the twenty-ninth."

She hated asking the question, and in her next breath she explained that it was routine inquiry.

"I understand," Johansson said. "I was home as usual. Since Jossan died, I've hardly left the house."

"I can vouch for him," Vera inserted swiftly.

"I believe you," Lindell said. "I have to ask two more questions: What is your shoe size?"

"Forty-four," Johansson answered with surprising alertness.

"Thank you," Lindell said and took her first sip of coffee.

"You had two questions."

"Yes. The second may seem a little strange . . ."

"As if the one about my shoe size wasn't that already," Johansson interrupted.

Lindell had to smile.

"My second question is, was there any kind of alcohol that Sven-Erik didn't like, that he couldn't drink?"

"I don't know, but he mostly drank whisky. Without any ice or water. How many evenings haven't we sat here with a drink."

Holger Johansson sank into thought and Lindell gave Vera a look.

"Never a schnapps or a cocktail," he went on. "Is that enough of an answer?"

"Thank you," Lindell said.

She stayed for another fifteen minutes. When she stood up from the table she asked yet another question.

"You had a home assistant for a while, a Maria Lundberg. Have you spoken to her since she stopped working here?"

"No," Johansson said, puzzled. "Should I have?"

"We met her in another context and she mentioned that she recognized you. But you haven't seen or spoken to her?"

He shook his head.

"This is an odd conversation," he said. "But I guess it must be normal for you."

Vera got up and followed her out to the car. When they were almost there, Vera grabbed her arm.

"You'll have to excuse Holger," she said. "But he forgets things. Maria, the home assistant, has definitely been by to visit."

Lindell nodded.

She left Holger and Vera, feeling oddly disconnected. Was it because the couple in the garden swing reminded her of her own parents? The same stillness that seemed to inhabit the air around them, the same clatter of coffee cups and a slightly pathetic passivity. The garden swing swung back and forth. It was most likely Vera who occasionally gave it a discreet push with her foot. That was probably how it was—she was the one who supplied the motion. Holger swung along, perhaps unaware of the motion at all.

That was how it was back home in Ödeshög. Growing up with her father, she had learned that her home would fall into complete stillness without these little pushes. Her mother would probably not sign off on this assessment. She was able to keep her home in motion as a matter of course, so pointing this out would be received as a sign of familial disloyalty.

"It's not easy for him," she often said when Lindell pointed out that her father could be more active or help out with the housework. Lindell had never understood what she meant but viewed her mother's self-imposed tasks with a mixture of tenderness and contempt.

All this talk, she thought. It doesn't lead anywhere. "Monotony" was the word that came to her. She saw herself driving the same way an endless number of times. Somewhere along the road were the violent criminals, murderers, drug dealers, and rapists. In her mind's eye she saw her and her colleagues dashing back and forth, making notes, talking on their cell phones, and discussing the cases with one another. The perpetrators smiled confidently, smirking at the dull police officers.

Only once or twice did they make an unplanned turn from the main road, driving onto a side road that no one had paid any attention to earlier, and suddenly the investigation took on a new life. New landscapes and people emerged.

That's how we should work, she thought. We should do the unexpected. Which side roads have I overlooked? she wondered at she turned onto the 55 toward Uppsala by Skärfälten.

She drove quickly, much too quickly, and it did not take her long to reach the edge of the city, but instead of going back to the station she drove toward Rasbo.

She walked toward Gabriella Mark's house with a strange feeling in her body that was difficult to define. Dead land, a dead house, dying vegetable beds. There was nothing left of the cottage idyll. Instead, the property and the surrounding forest were draped in anguish.

She walked around, feeling sad. The cabbage plants in their beds lay like used, wrinkled gloves that had been thrown to the ground. A couple of days of sun had ruined them, and nothing could be done to revive them. Death leads to death, she thought darkly. The light glinted in the glassed-in beds. To what end did you labor with all this?

Lindell avoided the stone coffin, the mound where they had found the body. In a way she felt that Gabriella was still there. Once beautiful and warm, with an inviting body, but now cold, twisted, and besmirched. The soft skin no longer evoked caresses and kisses. It seemed perverse in its corpse-gray nakedness.

The stock doves called from the woods. Lindell walked along the road. At the edge of the property there was a very old pear tree, and on the ground there were piles of unripened fruit that the tree had released. She crouched down and picked up one of the rejects. It was shaped like a small pear but completely unripe.

The doves sang their melancholy song. At least they are a couple, she thought. Suddenly there was a faint rustling sound from deeper within the woods and Lindell immediately stood up. The unripened fruit fell from her hand. She strained her senses to their full capacity and took a step closer to the old tree trunk as if to win an ally. The knotty trunk of the tree with its deeply notched bark was the only comforting presence in this landscape of death.

The rustling came again. Lindell stared between the spruce and alder. She sniffed like an animal to pick up the scent of the new element. She glimpsed something between some trees. What it was, she didn't know. Terror came over her abruptly and she pressed herself close to the tree as if for protection. She tried to control her breathing and stood completely still, with only one thought: not to die like Gabriella Mark.

Curse the day I applied to the police academy, she thought. I want to walk in the forest, press my cheek against the massive weight of a pear tree and feel its warmth, but not with death as my companion. I want to live like a normal woman, not mingle with the dead, rummage through their homes, wander across blackened lands. I want to love, see life around me. I want to have children, she screamed inside.

Footsteps in the forest. Movement between the branches. It was as if the woods concealed everything inhuman and violent. It was all there, rustling, perceptible but invisible to the eye.

The stock doves called out. Lindell spun around and gazed back at the house. Where could she take cover? Had the murderer returned? Was there anything of significance left in the house? Something he had missed? There were always details that were visible only to the evildoer.

She considered running back to the car but couldn't see herself rushing back like a victim. Whatever was out there, regardless of whether it was the murderer or not, it was her job to investigate it. She had to deal with her terror as best she could. Whether that meant wine or sleeping pills didn't really matter.

It was Gabriella's terror that she was experiencing. Suddenly the murderer seemed like a kinsman, someone very dear who had desperately been searching for the truth. Mark had loved and lost everything, not once but twice. Death had come from the forest. It had slain her and the tender shoots in her garden. Lindell pressed her body against the tree, peering out to see if she could catch sight of whatever was moving through the thick vegetation.

She glimpsed a large body. An animal. Suddenly an elk cow appeared. It raised its large muzzle into the air and stared toward something unseen that she knew was there. She could not have been more than ten meters from Lindell. She had never been so close to a large wild animal before.

The cow took a couple of steps, then looked back. Behind her was a calf that now dared to emerge into the small clearing. It had to be the calf that Gabriella had written about in her almanac, Lindell thought.

The calf was moving with great difficulty. Its right hind leg was injured. A large, red, open, and infected wound. Lindell saw the flies buzzing around its hindquarters. Every step had to be an effort, she thought. The elk cow turned its head and looked at its child. Did she know that it was lost? She shook her sturdy head a little as if to express dismay at her little calf. Lindell thought there was only sorrow in her gaze.

They were keeping to this place because they couldn't move any real distance. The calf looked half-starved and weak. Marked by death, it picked at a few leaves.

Lindell stood as if turned to stone next to the tree and watched the patient cow wait as her badly limping calf tried to follow her. They disappeared into the greenery again. The tragedy in the mother's tenderness and the courage of the calf, the inevitable death that awaited the little one, almost caused her to burst into tears.

"So damn cruel," she muttered.

✦

Twenty-two

The morning meeting began with a brief review of what had been found out the day before. Three tips had come in from Rasbo. Two could be dismissed immediately, but the third—from a woman who had called the station late at night and been transferred to the Criminal division—was of significantly greater interest.

The woman lived about a kilometer from Gabriella Mark, and on the evening of June 29, around eight o'clock, she had seen a car she didn't recognize. There were only five houses including Mark's past the woman's house, so she normally recognized the cars that went by.

That evening a red car had driven past. It had a small area in the back, like a little van. She didn't know anything about makes, but she had never seen it before.

The car had gone by quickly, "much too fast for our little gravel road," and she had not been able to see who was in the car. The strange thing was that it had not driven back again. At least not while she and her husband were still up, which they were until half past eleven. She also claimed that they would wake up when a car drove by. "We are unused to cars, so we always wake up if we hear one." The report was taken down ten minutes before midnight.

"We'll have to check up on it," Ottosson said. "This is a job for Nilsson, who was born in this district where they aren't used to cars. Then I think we'll have to send someone to Spain," he said and made it sound as if it was a punishment.

Four hands immediately shot into the air. The interested parties were Wende, Beatrice, Sammy, and Jonsson from Forensics.

"Send Nilsson to Rasbo and me to Spain," Sammy suggested.

Ottosson smiled his kindliest smile. Sammy was due to have gone on vacation a couple of days ago but had suggested that he stay on for another week, so this alone pre-qualified him for an international assignment.

"We'll see," Ottosson said and couldn't help glancing at Lindell, who realized that she was the one who was going to make the decision.

"I think we'll send Ann," he said.

"No," she exclaimed. "I can't."

"You think you're irreplaceable on the home front, of course," Berglund said, and he was the only one who could make a comment like that without seeming uncollegial. The banter of the group was open and even raw, but Lindell's colleagues held back from joking too much with her. There was a streak of humorlessness in her, a certain unpredictability. Sometimes their jokes were appreciated, but occasionally she became offended.

"Of course you can," Ottosson said. "Things here will go on as usual."

"Maybe you'll meet a handsome flamenco dude," Sammy said, testing the limits. He could tell he'd overstepped his bounds by her furious expression.

Beatrice laid a hand on her arm.

"Go to Málaga," she said in a low voice. "It's probably thirty degrees there. You need it. They're just jealous."

"I can't," Lindell said.

That morning she had decided that she would contact the ob-gyn center to get some expert advice and perhaps simply discuss her pregnancy with someone. Every day that went by felt a little less like a catastrophe. She was swelling more and more, she thought, though when she examined her body in the evenings she could honestly not see that there was anything there.

The indecision pained her. She had to take ahold of the issue as swiftly and effectively as she did with her investigations. Traveling to Spain would waste even more time.

Perhaps I can take a couple of days and have an abortion in Málaga, she thought. Then no one would notice anything. But as she thought this, she became so angry with herself that her cheeks turned bright pink. The image of the elk cow and her calf floated up in front of her eyes.

"I suggest that we send someone else," she said, but there was no conviction in her voice. This was interpreted by the others as meaning that she in fact wanted to go but wanted to appear suitably resistant.

"I've talked to the boss and he agrees," Ottosson said.

Sammy grinned. He had a new joke in mind but kept his mouth shut after one look from Ottosson.

"To continue," Ottosson said, "Ystad has been in touch. The cousin has been located. His name is apparently Lennart and his last name must be Mark. He was hiking in Italy but fell and broke his leg and landed in the hospital. When he called one of his siblings, they told him about Gabriella's death. They are going to arrange a telephone number to the hospital in Bolzano."

"Gypsum is an Italian specialty," Sammy said.

They broke up and went off to their own offices. Lindell lingered a little, as she often did to get a moment with Ottosson. He was shuffling his papers; he looked at her and noticed her anxious expression.

"Go home and pack," he said kindly. "I asked Anki to check the flights. You can probably leave as early as tomorrow. All we have to do is give the Spaniards some advance notice."

"I really can't go," Lindell said. "For personal reasons."

"Is it your friend from Roslagen?" Ottosson asked.

Lindell shook her head.

"Or your parents?"

"No, not them either."

Ottosson's imagination could apparently stretch no further than that. He stood silent and watched her. She was about to tell him what it was when he got there first.

"Are you pregnant?"

"Can you tell?"

"No, and no one has suggested anything like that, but I've seen that you're more than worried about something."

He stuffed his papers into his bag and avoided her gaze.

"And . . ."

"Well, then I draw the conclusion that when a woman is as worried as you have been, then she is pregnant, most likely against her wishes."

He spoke quietly. Lindell stared at him without being able to think of anything to say.

"Have I said too much now?"

"No, I'm just at a loss for words."

In a way she was touched by Ottosson's words. Perhaps it was because it was the first time that she could talk about her condition. Perhaps it was the simpleness of his words that meant they went straight to her heart.

"You don't know what to do?"

"No. You're so sweet."

"So go to Málaga, talk to our colleagues there, check up on MedForsk's Spanish partner, and have yourself a think. Maybe you can take a couple of extra days and rest, get some sun and live it up."

"If I go, I want some company."

"We're sending Bosse Wanning from Financials, that much is decided. They have uncovered some interesting information but need to follow up on location. Maybe we can get some help from the Spaniards. I think there are EU funds in the picture, some kind of development money."

"I meant someone from our division," Lindell said.

"I see," Ottosson said, but he looked uncertain. "You know how the budget is."

If it had been up to him, he would have sent the entire team to Spain for a week or two.

"We're always two when we're out on assignments," Lindell said.

"And you will be two."

"But Wanning will be poring over the accounts. What good does that do me?"

"Okay, I'll see what I can do," Ottosson said.

Lindell went straight to her office. She hadn't asked Ottosson to keep quiet about her condition, but she knew she didn't need to ask. In a way it felt funny that a man was the one who had found her out, but then what did she know? Perhaps Beatrice and a few others had already guessed how things were.

Málaga was listed in the international weather reports—that was all she knew about the city. Southern Spain. It was probably forty degrees Celsius.

Ottosson had promised to handle all of the practical arrangements— that is to say, he would talk to Anki. Would Ola want to go? She had tossed out his name. He was the one she found the easiest to work with. Sammy could be a little too sharp sometimes, a little too macho as well. Ola was softer, though no softie. He could seem tireless when he was pursuing a lead. He drove forward like a hunting dog, not barking but tenacious. It was because of him that they had found Gabriella—admittedly too late, but still. No, not too late—she was the one who had botched the possibility of meeting with the living Gabriella.

She called Haver, who immediately stopped by.

"Spain," Lindell said as soon as he stepped into the room.

"What?"

"Both of us can go," Lindell said. "You can pack tonight. Sounds like it'll be warm."

Ola Haver looked bewildered, swallowed, and looked as if he was formulating an objection, but Lindell got there first.

"We need to be two. It's not a done deal yet, but I recommended you."

"I don't know. It could be complicated on the home front."

"It will be a couple of days. Come on. I'm not going alone."

"To be honest, I don't think Rebecka would be happy about it."

"I'm sure she wouldn't begrudge you a couple of days in the sun."

Haver stood up. He was visibly uncomfortable.

"That's not what she would mind," he said and walked over to the window. "It's the fact that it would be the two of us."

"What?"

"Rebecka is a little jealous."

"Of me?"

"Of everyone," Haver said, trying to make less of it when he saw Lindell's look of alarm.

"Do you mean . . ."

"I mean that you and I work well together, and the hours add up. You look all right and Rebecka knows that, so . . ."

"Thank you, Ola, but we haven't ever . . ."

"No, but she doesn't know that."

"Does she complain?"

"Not complain, exactly, but she makes these comments."

"Talk to her first," Lindell said, and Haver went back to his office.

Lindell felt a bit dazed after Haver's confession of his marital life and the effect she was having. She had never had a thought of Ola as a lover, not even as a flirt. He was good-looking and was nice, but there had never been anything more.

She smiled to herself. "You look all right" he had said, and it was probably the most extravagant compliment one could get at the division. Ottosson often praised her and made comments about her being fresh as a lily, but that was Ottosson.

She decided to call Edvard. Now she had a good excuse. She could blame her trip to Spain if he wanted to meet her. But when she dialed his number, his line was busy.

She wrote down her notes from the visit to Holger Johansson. It was as if the Málaga assignment had brought her back to life. Suddenly she felt full of strength and inspiration. She recognized the symptoms and knew she should take advantage of it.

She searched for the number to the owner of the landscaping equipment who had rented the digger to Mortensen. He picked up right away. The din in the background made it hard to understand what he was saying, so finally he turned off some of the equipment.

"I'll have to check the calendar in my car. The days run together. Why do you want to know?"

"Routine procedure," Lindell said.

"Sure thing," he said. "He was a unique type, that one. His mother too. She talked about how dangerous it was and didn't want her son to do the digging himself. Finally I told her to shut her mouth. I had to get to another job and didn't have time to stand there shooting the breeze. I could tell that Mortensen was blown away when I did that."

"What did the mother say?"

"She left without a word."

"Thank you for this information," Lindell said in a friendly voice. "One other thing: When did you come back for the machine?"

"Six-thirty the next morning. He wasn't very good at digging, but I guess he isn't used to it."

"Thank you," she repeated and hung up.

✦

Twenty-three

Lindell peered out the airplane window. No forest, was her first thought. Agricultural land was divided into sections, all with a red-pink tinge. Some fields were dotted, green little dots in ramrod-straight lines. Lindell thought they were bushes, maybe small trees.

All countries are beautiful from above, she thought as the plane swept over houses and office buildings and factories from a low altitude. She did not fly very often, so it was with some nervous anticipation that she had taken her seat on the plane. Haver was sitting next to her, and on the other side of the aisle there was Bosse Wanning from Financials as well as a Spanish-speaking data expert that Wanning's team had located at short notice.

When they picked up their bags and walked toward the exit, after first passing by an almost nonexistent checkpoint, the first thing they saw was a young man carrying a sign with her name.

"Welcome to Málaga," he said in English. He was dressed in civilian clothes and the car that they got into was also unmarked.

"I'm taking you to meet the commissioner for the Bureau of Criminal Investigations," the driver said.

"That sounds fancy," Haver said.

Málaga received them with tolerable warmth, some twenty-five degrees Celsius. The traffic into town was intense. Everyone sat quietly, observing the array of people.

For Lindell, this was only the second time that she had visited Spain. Many years ago she had spent a week in Mallorca with Rolf, the man before Edvard. She knew this would be something completely different.

She had never traveled internationally on assignment before and was curious how the collaboration with the Spanish colleagues would work. She had been forewarned about their bureaucracy and Berglund had made a comment about black shirts. She had asked him what he meant and he

had avoided her question, simply muttering something about old preju-
dices.

The criminal police headquarters were located at the Plaza Manuel
Azaña, which was not really a square as much as an intersection.

They were expected. The chief of the Criminal Division and the chief of
Public Relations were waiting for them in the foyer. Lindell looked around.
It was an airy space with a reception counter surrounded by a throng of
people. The noise level was deafening. It seemed as if the visitors moved
freely in and out, in contrast to the headquarters in Uppsala, where the
public was greeted by a relatively dreary setup of locked doors.

Antonio Fernández Moya was about forty-five, short and starting to
show a middle-aged heaviness. He was surprisingly pale, with intense
brown eyes. It seemed to her that his eyes went up and down her body before he grabbed her hand and shook it forcefully.

"Nice to have you here," he said and looked as if he meant it.

His colleague was older and looked considerably more buttoned up. He
muttered a name and took a couple of steps back. What function he filled
she did not know, but she imaged it was Málaga's answer to Liselotte Rask,
who was in charge of communications for the Uppsala police.

They were escorted up a flight of stairs. Antonio Moya spoke to them
the whole time. He chivalrously led Lindell by the arm. They were brought
to a small conference room.

"Coffee?" Moya asked.

All four of them accepted. A third police officer, also in civilian dress,
joined them and was introduced to them as Max Arrabal.

The room was bare and reminded them of an interrogation room, just
bigger. There was nothing here resembling a Swedish police conference
room with its heterogeneous mixture of functional equipment and efforts
toward coziness. Here the table and chairs were the main feature. The
country's monarch gazed out over it all from his position on the wall.

After some introductory words, as coffee was brought in by a uniformed
officer, Moya began an overview of MedForsk's Spanish partner firm, UNA
Médico. He was clearly in command of his material and gave a competent
impression. Lindell glanced at Haver and he smiled. They both felt excited.
It was possible that there would be an opening in the Cederén-Mark case.

UNA Médico had been established in Málaga eight years ago and quickly expanded. At first they had rented space in an old shoe factory, but after only a couple of years they had built their own office and laboratory facilities.

They had around fifty employees and were known for treating them well. They also had a good working relationship with the city authorities, and the mayor of Málaga had more than once expressed his satisfaction at the company's presence in the city. The pharmaceutical industry was a promising direction, he said. Moya also alluded to having an old school friend on the board of trustees of the firm.

Moya did not have many details regarding the partnership with the Swedish company other than that the Swedish flag would sometimes be hoisted outside UNA Médico offices.

Half of their employees were women, most of them in packing and warehouse. Although it was not a high-salaried workplace, there was no issue with retaining the workforce.

The fact that the Spanish police had been able to gather this much information in less than twenty-four hours impressed Lindell.

Moya went on to say that UNA Médico had managed their affairs without any problems. Earlier in the year they had received a development grant from the European Union of 250,000 euros for further investments. These had to do with making environmental improvements and developing international contacts. The pharmaceutical industry was becoming more internationalized, and UNA Médico, which was a small company, had to find partners.

If anything illegal had taken place with MedForsk, then this was nothing that the Spanish authorities knew about or had reason to investigate, although of course they wanted to assist their Swedish colleagues.

"It will be a pleasure for me to collaborate with you," Moya finished and let his gaze slowly travel around the table and come to rest on Lindell.

I wonder what his words are worth, she thought, but smiled politely. She opened her notebook, which was newly purchased for this trip, and gave an account of the reasons that MedForsk was an object of interest for her team. When she described how Josefin and Emily Cederén had been mowed down by an unknown driver, she heard a sigh, or rather a groan, from Moya. Lindell looked up and Moya's expression clearly communicated his anguish.

Lindell's prepared remarks took fifteen minutes. No one interrupted her, and when she was done, a rare silence spread in the room.

"More coffee?" Moya asked.

Lindell glanced first at Haver and then at Bosse Wanning as if to seek their support. Haver accepted the offer. Wanning stared down at his hands, which rested on the table.

"Very good," Moya said enthusiastically. "A very informative account, thank you."

Lindell felt herself blushing.

More coffee was brought in and Wanning immediately perked up. Maybe he's tired, Lindell thought. But he should still look more engaged.

"We have the following suggestion," Moya said as they sipped their strong coffees. "We have no clear cause to walk right into UNA Médico and start searching through their papers and affairs. We would need a warrant for this, as you understand. We are working on that. However, we can even now begin conversations with the company executives and hear their views on the irregularities of the Swedish company. We will then get a good sense of their willingness to cooperate."

"Have they been told that we are coming?" the data expert, Antonio Morales, asked in Spanish.

"Oh, my beautiful mother tongue," Moya exclaimed and smiled broadly. "What a surprise. No, of course they have no knowledge of anything.

"You hurt my feelings," he added and humorously adopted an aggrieved expression.

Morales inclined his head lightly and said something in Spanish. Moya answered his stream of words with a smile and a barely noticeable gesture of his head as he simultaneously moved one hand in a slow arc to the side.

Latin men, Lindell thought. Moya turned back to her.

"I suggest that you check into your hotel, rest, and perhaps eat something. Then—let us say at three—we can go to UNA Médico. Does that sound acceptable?"

"Shouldn't we try to go earlier?"

"No, here we work late," Moya said.

Málaga Palacio lay on what Lindell assumed was the main street of the city, Alameda Principal. Outside the hotel was a big park, and a couple of blocks to the north lay the grand cathedral.

Lindell had read a little of the city, its history and sights. She knew that it was over twenty-five hundred years old and had been in Arab hands for over seven hundred of those.

"Seven hundred years," she said to Haver as they sat on a bench in the park. "That's like if Uppsala would have been under Russian or German rule since the 1300s. That would leave traces on people, on the culture, on everything."

"Mmm," said Haver, who was studying the map.

"Picasso was born here," he added.

"Yes, well, there's that typical Arabic influence," Lindell said. Haver looked up and smiled.

"Are you feeling all right?" he asked.

"Do I feel okay? Yes, of course."

"You've just seemed a little down lately," Haver said and put the map down.

"There's been a lot going on," Lindell said.

She stared at the pigeons that were gathering en masse around an old man on the opposite side of the little open space where they were sitting.

"It's nice to get away for a little while," he said. "But I'm wondering what we're going to get out of it. If we can't review their accounts and correspondence, how are we going to find anything of value? We're completely in the hands of the company."

"I know, but I see it like this: The solution to the case is in Sweden—I'm convinced of that—but if we stir the pot down here, something may bubble up at home."

"That's a humble hope," Haver said.

A mother with a stroller walked by. He followed her with his gaze.

"I'm having a little trouble reading Moya," Lindell said.

"There's some of your Arabic influence right there," Haver said and nodded at the woman with the child. Her abundant hair swirled like dark smoke around her head.

At a quarter to three, a civilian car pulled up in front of the hotel entrance. It was the same driver from the morning. Lindell noted that he had changed his shirt.

Inside the car—a large Toyota—were Mora and Arrabal. The trip took them to an industrial area at the edge of the city, not far from the airport. Lindell thought she read "Guadalhorce" on a sign as they turned off from the highway. A train came rattling along the tracks parallel to the road. They took a right after a train station, went another couple of blocks, and then turned to the left. The car slowed down and glided past a row of police cars. Moya raised his hand in greeting as they moved to the front, like a presidential motorcade.

"That's quite a backup," Lindell commented and turned toward the smiling Moya.

"It's good to make a gesture," he replied. "So that they see that we are serious."

Lindell was struck by the thought that perhaps Moya was using his Swedish visitors and the coming strike for his own purposes. She glanced at Haver and was about to say something when Moya pointed and said something to the driver. He pulled in between some gateposts and up to a redbrick building. The row of police cars followed them like goslings.

UNA Médico was written in large letters on a copper sign, with Med-Forsk written in smaller letters underneath. An old man with a broom in his hand watched the invasion of cars with wide eyes. He pulled off his cap and in this way marked the spectacular nature of the event.

Moya walked confidently up to the front door. One of the civilian-clad officers took out a camera and snapped a photo of the chief as he put his hand on the handle. Now there was nothing pleasant in Moya's expression; he looked more like a field marshal.

Police chiefs are alike everywhere, Lindell thought. Soon our own little police chief will preside at all strikes, powdered and uniformed, as the camera flash blinds the gaping public.

The rest of the officers spread out and disappeared behind the corner of the building. About ten followed Moya and the Swedes through the main door.

The Spanish-Swedish delegation was met in the reception area by two middle-aged men. They were dressed in a way that in Sweden would have been categorized as extremely flashy. One of them was markedly short. This was the one who stepped forward and set his sights on Moya as if he already knew him or perhaps realized who was in charge.

"Welcome to UNA Médico," he said heartily and introduced himself as Francisco Cruz de Soto.

Had they been expected after all? This thought went through Lindell's mind when she could not discern a trace of surprise in De Soto's face. Instead he displayed a polite helpfulness, not effusive, but without any guardedness.

"We are here to investigate certain issues pertaining to your company activities," Moya said directly, and Morales translated for the Swedes.

"We have also brought some Swedish colleagues," Moya went on, and now he switched to English.

De Soto immediately walked up to the four northerners and shook their hands. He started with Lindell. It was not clear if this was because she was a woman or the leader.

"Pleased to meet you," he said four times, and each time it sounded genuine.

"We will need immediate access to your accounts, books, employee records, calendars, and correspondence," Moya continued and fished a piece of paper out of his inner pocket. "Here is the warrant," he said.

De Soto paid no attention to the document.

"We will cooperate with you regardless of the matter at hand," he said and turned to Lindell.

He knows what this is about, she thought.

Within a quarter of an hour, a handful of police officers were installed in the company offices. Moya, Arrabal, and De Soto plus a couple of UNA Médico employees and the four Swedes went into a conference room. Within a couple of minutes, coffee, soda, and beer appeared on the table.

Moya began with a long speech about the seamless and long-standing tradition of cooperation between the Swedish and Spanish police. He managed to squeeze in something about the European Union as well and how international police cooperation was developing still further, not least with the help of technology.

De Soto listened calmly to this lecture. When the police chief was done, De Soto repeated his assurances that they would not meet any resistance from the company.

Moya glanced at Lindell and she realized that it was her turn. She had prepared her statement and related the events that had occurred in Uppsala.

"We believe," she said as she wrapped up, "that certain answers to these events may be found here in Málaga."

"And which might those be?" De Soto immediately asked.

"Certain financial transactions that appear irregular," Lindell said, and now most of her nervousness had disappeared. "We have reason to believe that relatively large amounts of money have disappeared from MedForsk and possibly ended up here or in a third-world country. We also have some questions regarding the Dominican Republic. There has been a purchase of land there and possibly some other transactions that we find puzzling."

De Soto made an attempt to interrupt, but Lindell went on.

"Finally," she said, "I am sure that you are aware that the head of research at MedForsk, Sven-Erik Cederén, is dead, as are his wife and young daughter. The latter were brutally murdered."

"Yes, we have heard of this and are deeply saddened, but from what we understand this was a family tragedy that has nothing to do with Med-Forsk or us. Sven-Erik Cederén was an excellent researcher and friend, but apparently he became overwhelmed by madness—to put this plainly," De Soto said.

"Is the name Julio Piñeda familiar to you?" Haver asked abruptly.

A look of irritation flashed across De Soto's face, but he immediately answered in the negative.

"Have you ever been to the Dominican Republic?" Lindell asked.

"Yes, on two occasions. Both times with my wife and children. It is a beautiful country."

"You have no business there?"

"No, the political situation is too uncertain. Also, there is insufficient developed infrastructure and access to a well-trained workforce."

"So what did you do there?" Haver asked.

"Vacation," De Soto said curtly.

The hell it was, Lindell thought, and she could see the skepticism in Haver's face.

"And you have no plans of conducting any business there?"

"No, as I told you. The Dominican Republic is of no interest to us." Bosse Wanning from Financials had sat quietly to this point, but now he coughed and all eyes turned to him. Lindell was grateful for his initiative. It was challenging to undertake an interrogation in English and she felt pressure to be extra smart. In part because De Soto was so polished and in part because she wanted to make a good impression on foreign soil.

"We have identified a transaction from the Swedish firm to a country in the Caribbean," Wanning began. "I'm sure you are familiar with this affair."

He paused as if he was waiting for an objection from De Soto, who was calmly awaiting the rest.

"What comments do you have on this matter?"

"No comment, as is the standard phrase," De Soto said and smiled. "We simply are not familiar with it. Isn't that right?" he said and turned to one of his colleagues, who made an expressive gesture with his arms.

"But we have found a fax that contradicts your statement," Wanning said in a mild voice.

Lindell knew that he could be as sharp as a razor blade—quite mean—when he chose to be so.

"A fax from where?"

"From this office," Wanning said without looking up as he leafed through his papers.

"It was signed *Pedro*," he added.

"We have a Pedro, perhaps a couple, but they work in production and have nothing to do with the management," De Soto said, still calm.

"Perhaps it is a slang name?" Wanning said, at this point receiving help from Morales to find the right word.

"This is a company, not a soccer team. We have no nicknames here."

"We have certain statements from your Swedish friends," Wanning continued happily.

"Statements?"

Wanning pulled out a piece of paper that he quickly eyed before pushing it across the table.

"It has been translated into Spanish," he said.

De Soto did not pay any attention to the paper and simply passed it along to his colleague.

"Perhaps there have been questionable actions, what do I know, but not due to a deliberate will to disobey either Swedish or Spanish law. We are in a particularly expansive period. I repeat, very expansive, and it is conceivable that small mistakes have been made. In which case we would of course correct this mistake."

A few seconds of silence followed as if to give those present a moment to evaluate this first admission from the head of UNA Médico. It was the same argument that Mortensen used, Lindell thought.

"We can not afford any illegalities," he went on. "The business is going so well that all resources are needed to develop the products and break into new markets. We have a promising new medicine that will be approved by the American FDA any day now. You understand that we would never risk this for a few paltry pesetas."

Lindell realized that they would not be able to get any further. De Soto was well prepared for their visit. Was that what Moya knew? Was that why he had been so willing to dispatch the cavalry?

She coughed. That appeared to be the way to get a word in edgewise in the assembled group.

"Can we get a list of your employees? And not just the ones who are working here right now. I would also like to see the names of those who worked here, let's say a year back in time."

"Of course," De Soto replied.

"Thank you," Lindell said.

"When was Cederén here last?" Haver asked.

The two men from UNA Médico exchanged glances. This was apparently a question they had not prepared for.

"We will have to review our records," De Soto said finally. "But I seem to recall it was sometime at the end of May."

"Did he mention anything about the Dominican Republic?" Haver continued.

They could detect a certain irritation in De Soto.

"As I said, we have no reason to discuss this country."

"But did Cederén bring it up?" Haver insisted.

"Not that I remember. He may have spoken about the Caribbean in general, and he must have known that I vacation there. He may have asked how it is for vacationing."

"When were you last in Sweden?"

Lindell wondered where Ola was going with this, but sensed that he was simply peppering the Spaniard with questions to wear him down.

"In May. We were both there in May," and nodded to his colleague. "It was a productive visit. Only good results."

"Who is the chief owner of the two companies?" Wanning broke in.

Switching off, Lindell thought, pleased.

"Cederén. Jack and I own a quarter each. The rest is spread across some twenty or so investors."

"Are they actively involved?"

De Soto shook his head. "They see the stocks as a good investment."

"What will happen to Cederén's portion?"

"According to our contract, Jack Mortensen and I have the right of preemption on Cederén's shares. If we are not interested, they will be offered to the rest of the stockholders according to the proportion of their current investment."

"And are you interested?" Haver asked.

"I have not considered this yet," De Soto answered.

Nonsense, Lindell thought. That was the first thing you thought of when you heard that he had died.

"Can you see any financial motives for the tragic events that occurred?"

"No," De Soto answered quickly, clearly somewhat off-kilter at the barrage. "Jack has told me that he has been deeply worried about his friend and business partner."

"We have some information that indicates that he did not take his own life," Lindell went on.

De Soto raised his eyebrows. "How is that possible?"

"We do not have all of the details," Lindell said and leafed through her notepad.

"Do you know if Cederén drank gin?" Haver said, jumping into the fray.

"No idea."

Now the irritation was very apparent. There was nothing left of the servile smile. He continued to answer politely but showed in his expression that he felt they were completely irrelevant.

Moya, who had long been quiet, suddenly leaned forward.

"Señor de Soto," he said, "I too have some information."

A tense silence followed. Moya resembled a tiger about to pounce.

"According to a secure source, or more precisely two sources, you have consorted with known criminal elements. Individuals that we from the police know very well. What do you say to this?"

This was a complete surprise to the Swedish detectives, and they realized that Moya had been waiting out De Soto. The Spanish commissioner was also not a novice to interrogations.

"What should I say? There are always rumors about successful companies and their leaders. That is probably also true of successful police chiefs, I imagine?"

Moya immediately countered this. Lindell observed with fascination that he appeared to feel right at home in the thickening atmosphere.

"Jaime Urbano," he said.

Lindell felt the reaction from Haver against her arm. He flinched but immediately took control of himself and pretended to hold back a sneeze. Well done, Lindell thought. She now knew that Haver had come across this name in his investigations.

"No," De Soto replied. "Is this one of your acquaintances?"

Moya sank back against his chair and gazed at De Soto with eyes that now had a completely different sharpness. Lindell understood the undertone of De Soto's comment. It was a veiled suggestion that perhaps Moya had connections that could not stand up to the light of day.

"He is an infamous killer," Moya said calmly. "From the beginning he was a simple thief and troublemaker, but now he is a fully accomplished killer. I believe that you have met. It may just be the case that you do not remember his name. He was paid four million pesetas by an unknown admirer only four weeks ago."

De Soto's gaze was unsteady. Lindell was enjoying herself immensely and Haver was feverishly jotting notes in his book.

"Urbano does nothing for free," Moya added. "In a way he is also a successful enterprise with possibilities for expansion. This is at least the view of his mother."

"I don't know anything about that," De Soto muttered. "I guard myself against associating with his type."

There was a knock on the door and one of Moya's men appeared at the door, looked at his boss, and nodded.

Moya stood up, excused himself, and walked up to the young officer. They conferred in whispering tones and after a while left the room.

Moya returned after half a minute. He sat down again without giving any explanation for his departure. Everyone was now waiting for his word. He resumed his relaxed stance, turned toward Lindell, and smiled encouragingly.

How can thirty seconds feel so long, she thought, and smiled back.

"I am afraid that we will have to inconvenience you and your company for another couple of hours," the Spanish commissioner announced.

Lindell looked at Moya and saw that he liked the situation, not least the fact that he had surprised his Swedish guests. This could have been irritating, but Lindell was happy to give him this. She wanted him to enjoy this, and if he was acting unpredictably, then why not. This only added spice to the whole thing.

"We do have our production to consider," De Soto said, but it was an empty objection. He and Moya both knew this. The latter did not bother responding to it.

"We thank you for your cooperation," he said politely. "We will leave some ten officers here for a few hours. If we need to remove any materials from your company, then we will of course present the required legal documentation to facilitate this."

De Soto knew that Moya had the upper hand and played along. He said something in Spanish and Moya cast an amused glance at him.

"Thank you for everything," Lindell said and grasped De Soto's hand energetically.

Haver shot her a look. "That's what it says on funeral wreaths," he said in Swedish.

"It may be a funeral we're witnessing," she answered.

They returned to the police headquarters in Plaza Azaña in silence.

Moya appeared thoughtful. Lindell knew that he was reviewing his performance, perhaps testing his arguments and the solidity of the effort. She recognized this. The afterthoughts. Should we have done this a different way? What will the prosecutor say?

She had not understood all of the implications in the exchanges between Moya and De Soto. There was something more in all of this that Lindell did not grasp. She was irritated at not being fully briefed but calmed herself with the thought that this was only the beginning. It was a game. She and the other Swedes were only pawns.

Had Moya used them for reasons she did not understand? What lay behind this massive response from the Spanish authorities?

When they stepped out of the car at the station, Moya suggested that they eat dinner together. Lindell was exhausted. Trying to follow everything, to speak English and be smart, had taken its toll. What she wanted most of all was to stretch out on the hotel bed.

"With pleasure," she said and smiled her nicest smile.

They moved into the same conference room that they had been in before. King Juan Carlos on the wall looked far more satisfied now, Lindell thought.

"I have to ask you why you held back so much in the beginning," Lindell began. "You gave us the impression that you did not have the formal warrants necessary for a larger action against UNA Médico."

"I did not want to create all too great expectations," Moya said modestly. "It is better to be able to provide positive surprises."

"I recognize the name Jaime Urbano," Haver said.

Everyone looked at him in astonishment.

"That's why you reacted so strongly," Lindell said in Swedish.

"We have reviewed the passenger lists to both the Dominican Republic and Málaga," Haver continued. "There are thousands of names, but we removed all of the ones that we thought were tourists, Swedish retirees who live on the Costa del Sol, and those traveling for health reasons. It was a little subjective, but we had to proceed in some manner. And still there were a thousand names left. Among them was Jaime Urbano."

"Why do you remember this name?" Moya asked.

"My neighbor's name is Urban," Haver said. "I thought it was a little funny that there was someone with the name Urbano as a last name. That was all it was."

"And Urbano traveled to Stockholm?"

Haver nodded.

"I don't remember when it was, but he is on the list," he said. "But perhaps there are many Urbanos?"

"Probably around one hundred in Málaga alone," Moya said. "But not so many Jaime Urbanos. Are you sure of the first name?"

"Very," Haver said.

"Do you have the lists with you?"

"No, but if I can borrow your fax, we can get them shortly."

Arrabal recited his fax number.

Haver glanced at the clock, picked up his cell phone, and dialed.

Lindell feared that the dinner Moya invited them to would be at a fancy restaurant and eyed the clothes she had brought with her critically. But to her surprise they ended up at a casual joint in the shadow of the great cathedral. Because it was an outdoor café with a large number of people around the many tables, the noise level was high. Traffic on the narrow street sometimes made it hard to hear what was said, but Moya appeared to think that it was quite normal to take care of police matters in the midst of the noise and bustle.

Lindell stared up at the cathedral. She thought the building looked heavy, as if it was pressing down on the observer with its imposing, almost frightening facade that most resembled a fortress. She imagined that it gave a completely different impression from the inside.

Moya ordered food and drink as he chatted about Málaga and asked about his Swedish colleagues' family lives. When Lindell explained that she lived alone, he gave her a look that was difficult to interpret but that she understood to be one of commiseration, as if she had confided that she suffered from a severe illness.

"We now know with certainty," Moya said when the food was on the table, "that Jaime Urbano—and it's very likely that he is our man—flew to Stockholm two days before Cederén's wife and child were killed, more exactly on the twelfth of June. Three days later he returned. On this trip he was accompanied by a certain Benjamin Olivares. A lowlife that we are also well acquainted with."

Lindell felt a rising excitement. For each hour that they spent in Málaga, she was becoming more and more convinced that Gabriella Mark had been right: Sven-Erik Cederén had not killed his family, nor had he committed suicide.

"For what it's worth, Olivares is a small-time crook who doesn't appear in connection with any more substantial violent crimes, but in Urbano's company, anything can happen," Moya went on. "We have been searching for Urbano for a while, but no one seems to have seen him for several weeks. We know that he received a large sum of money in the middle of June. This is confirmed by several independent sources: a drug dealer whom Urbano owed money and also a prostitute for whom he was a regular."

"How did you manage to gather all of this information in so short a time?" Haver asked.

He was tucking into the octopus with gusto. Lindell wished he would use his napkin on his greasy mouth.

"We've had our eye on Urbano for a while," Moya said. "Or rather, we've been looking for him."

He put down his knife and fork, rested his chin on his hand, and gazed up at the cathedral.

"He is a cop killer," he said darkly.

Moya took a sip of his wine, put his glass down, and let the words sink in. Lindell glanced at Haver. That's why he had struck with such force, she thought. He had already uncovered a connection between Urbano and UNA Médico, and when we came to him with our questions, it fit perfectly into his plan to take a torch to the company.

"What worries me is how Urbano has been able to travel in and out of the country under his own name without us discovering it," Moya said.

"Do you want to tell us what happened?" Haver asked.

Moya nodded and poured himself some more wine before he started. Lindell was done eating and waited for him to continue.

"It was in the beginning of May. A colleague from the local police had pulled over a car to the north of the city. We don't know why, but he guided the car to the side of the road. It was a white Honda, according to the only witness—a young car mechanic who was waiting for a bus some fifty meters away."

A car went by at high speed and Moya made a face.

"The witness saw the driver step out of the car and take something out of his pocket—it turned out to be a pistol—and immediately opened fire on the police officer. The officer had only just made it out of the car when he was struck by four shots, of which one should have killed him immediately. But he lived for a couple of minutes."

Moya looked down and paused.

"The whole thing went very quickly," he said. "The driver of the Honda calmly got back in his car and drove away. It was as if he had stopped only to aid an animal that he had struck on the road and put it out of its misery. He smiled as he drove past the witness, who then ran straight to the scene of the crime. Our colleague had time to say a few words to the witness before he died. He gave us the name Jaime Urbano. We know that he recognized Urbano from before. Why he stopped Urbano, we have no idea. It was admittedly a foolish thing for him to do on his own, but the punishment should not have been death."

"And you have been searching for Urbano since then?" Haver asked.

"Day and night. We quickly found out that he had been in contact with UNA Médico. This surprised us. The company had a good reputation and had never previously been involved in illegal activities. Not as far as we know, at least. We did not know the nature of the connection, but when Urbano is involved, it is not a regular business agreement."

"So you began to take a closer look at UNA Médico," Lindell said, seeing clearly the parallels to her own investigation.

Moya told them about the efforts that both the national and local police had made to locate the police killer. The name Olivares had turned up early. The intensified police efforts had roiled up Málaga's underworld, and there had been widespread gossip about the two men. Many passed this information along to the police, perhaps to secure some peace and calm for themselves.

"We received a tip that Urbano and Olivares had been spotted in Ronda, which is a town some distance up into the mountains. That was a week ago."

In some way Lindell knew what was about to follow.

"Olivares is dead, isn't he?" she said.

If Moya was taken aback by this statement, he did not show it.

"You are a good detective," he said and smiled. "Yes, he is dead. A half hour before we arrived here, our colleagues in Ronda called and said that a body had been recovered in a ravine outside of the town. It was Olivares. He had taken three shots, one behind the ear."

"What will you do now?" Haver asked. Between the questions, he was still chewing his octopus.

"There is some information that Urbano may still be holed up in Ronda. It is a little town and the gossip travels quickly across the bridges. One of my old acquaintances—a check forger who now spends his time picking the tourists' pockets in his bar—often gives us tips about his old buddies. He saw both of the men as recently as yesterday."

Lindell felt a sense of gratitude. All of her suspicions of a corrupt Spanish police had come to nothing.

"We have arranged a trip to Ronda early tomorrow morning," Moya said. "Perhaps you would like to join us?"

"Claro," Haver said, and Lindell had rarely seen him look so pleased.

They stood up from the table after having agreed that Lindell and Haver would be picked up at four-thirty in the morning. Lindell checked her watch and quickly calculated how much sleep they would get.

In spite of her tiredness she had trouble winding down.

"I'm going to walk a bit," she told Haver.

They parted ways. Haver walked toward the hotel and Lindell decided to visit the cathedral.

"I deserve to do a little sightseeing," she had said to Haver, but it was actually a desire to be alone that drew her to the church.

A pair of beggars slouched outside the door. One of them—an older man with gray hair—uttered a few unintelligible words as Lindell went by. She stopped, fumbled around in her shoulder bag, and pulled out five hundred pesetas, about as much as a beer had cost at the restaurant they had just left. She placed the coin in the man's hand and received a gurgling sound in thanks.

Inside the cathedral there were preparations for an evening mass. Some fifty people were sitting in the pews. A custodian was walking around and lighting the candles in front of the altar. He looked bored and his movements were lackadaisical. It irritated her because she herself was overcome by a feeling of awe. She was in no way a believer but still felt that the area inside a church was conducive to peace and reflection.

The candles on either side of the sanctuary were put out one after one. An older woman in nun's clothing stepped forward and tested the microphone by tapping on it with her finger. Lindell sat down. The nun launched into something that Lindell thought sounded like a hymn of praise. "Dios," she heard the nun sing with a clear voice. The congregation rose to its feet and Lindell felt compelled to follow their lead.

The priest and his assistant—whom she had mistaken for a custodian but who was now dressed in a long coat—walked in and the mass began.

The congregation inserted a few words in the priest's recitation. Why was I pulled into this? she wondered. She sat at the very front and did not feel that she could leave during the ceremony.

The nun burst into song again. She looked pleased, almost humorous, as if she did not take all this too seriously, but Lindell thought she was probably just happy to be able to express her unwavering faith.

The congregation sank down with a sigh, and Lindell sat gratefully. The priest took up where the nun left off and Lindell was captured by his voice, allowing herself to relax into a state of melancholy restfulness. She realized that what she was feeling was grief—a sense of sadness that she did not belong to any group with which she could share her beliefs. In a way, the police force was her safety net, but this did not get her very far when troubled thoughts overwhelmed her mind.

She wanted to leave the church while at the same time retain this feeling of worship. Perhaps this is where I will make my decision, she thought, only to find herself in the next moment cursing her own volatile emotions.

She stood up quickly but took her time to leave the church, in order to show proper respect to the mass in progress. The nun's voice followed her, and as she came out onto the front steps, the beggar greeted her with a smile on his dried and cracked lips.

It was still very warm in the air—probably twenty-five degrees—and she walked slowly back to the hotel. She tried to think about the investigation and the more or less sensational turn that it had taken.

✦

Twenty-four

Edvard pulled up the boat with a jerk. A few fish scales that still adhered to the railing after the late spring herring fishing caught on his hand. He picked them off with a thoughtful expression.

He knew that Ann was in Spain, but it didn't matter. She might as well be in Uppsala; the distance would feel as great. It had been two weeks since they last met. The joy he had felt at seeing her again and actually being reunited with her had been replaced by the old sense of doubt.

His uneasiness was in part due to his knee. It ached, and occasionally his leg would give way, producing a lot of pain. Viola had told him to see a doctor.

Viola herself had not been completely well herself. Right after the Midsummer celebration she had contacted a severe cold with a high fever and a barking cough. Edvard could see that it had left its mark. She was still noticeably low and sluggish.

While they drank their morning coffee, the radio played songs from the fifties. Lily Berglund sang about "let a little sunlight in my mind." They had looked at each other and laughed.

The sunshine had mostly been absent this summer, but today it had broken out in the afternoon and Edvard had decided to set some nets in the evening. He would surely snare a perch or two.

He had decided not to turn on the engine and had rowed out into the bay instead. The sea gull that spent so much time on his dock had followed him. Now it was back on the dock.

Viola had been unusually irritable before he set off. Something was bothering her. Sometimes she saw signs and got notions about things. She had suggested that the wind might pick up and that he should be careful. When he told her that he was only going some hundred meters out, she had calmed down a little.

He took her concerns seriously. Many times her somewhat vague predictions about the weather turned out to be true, though today she had been wrong. The bay was almost completely still and Edvard lingered on the shore.

Ann was fishing for bigger fish than he. She had told him very briefly why she was going to Spain. Was he jealous that she got to travel? Or simply jealous, period? He knew that she met many people in her work, and he felt more and more like the isolated islander that he had to look like in comparison to the other men she met.

What kind of life could he offer her? A feeling of helplessness overcame him. How could he leave Gräsö and establish a new life? If he did, he would have to feel certain that it was somewhere he could remain for a long time. He was no nomad, despite his longing for new horizons. This realization had come to him during his two years on the island. He was not going to run anymore. Either stay on the island and focus on his island life and bachelor existence or start a new family with Ann and perhaps have children with her.

The wind picked up somewhat. Had Viola been right after all? Sometimes a wind picked up in the evenings and it didn't die down again until morning. That was what Viola had worried about, he realized. She must have thought a little further ahead.

The gull took off, made anxious by the wind. Edvard walked indecisively up to the water's edge. Fredrik Stark, his old friend from the farm labor union days, was going to come up for the weekend. Edvard didn't know what to think about this. Of course it was nice to have company, but most of all he wanted to be here with Ann. He wasn't sure how long she was staying in Spain. Should he call her cell phone? A sense of longing mixed with his completely unfounded jealousy ached in him. He was unable to describe it in any other way. An ache in his knee and an ache in his heart. He smiled to himself.

✦

Twenty-five

The streets of Málaga were deserted when Haver and Lindell climbed into the Toyota to drive to Ronda. Moya looked tired. Likely he had gone back to work after their dinner the night before.

They drove in silence. Moya told them nothing about what to expect. They drove inland, and after half an hour—when they had left the coast and arrived at the mountains—they could see the Mediterranean spreading out behind them. Blue and inviting. Lindell thought about another sea—the Sea of Åland, which Edvard looked out over.

After several hours they came to Ronda, which resembled a fortress on a cliff. An unmarked police car was waiting for them at the main road into town. Moya exchanged a few words with the officer in the car before they continued into the center.

"We have an address," Moya said and turned to Lindell. "According to our sources, Urbano is there."

He was interrupted by a call on his cell phone and listened for a few seconds.

"Our colleagues have prepared a strike. Unfortunately you cannot play an active role. You will have to follow the events from a distance."

They drove past the old bullfighting arena that Lindell had read about in the guidebook and entered an older residential area. The car slowed down and stopped at a street corner.

"On that street," Moya said tersely and pointed. "That's where Urbano is supposedly to be found. Stay here."

Lindell nodded. Moya left the car and disappeared around the corner while the driver remained in his location. She really wanted to tag along. Instead she tried to strike up a conversation with Haver, who seemed both tense and uninterested at the same time. She knew that he wasn't a morning person, but couldn't he have tried to put on a slightly happier face?

It was a long wait. Lindell knew that the Spanish police were approaching

Urbano's supposed location with great care. Perhaps they were working in conjunction with plainclothes officers who were going to perform duties such as garbage collection or something else that fit into the everyday picture. She tried to imagine the scene but had trouble because the environment was too foreign.

Half an hour went by without any change. She was starting to become impatient. The driver's cell phone rang, and he listened without saying anything to the caller, whom Lindell believed to be Moya. Then he hung up and started the engine.

"There's nobody there," he said.

They drove around the corner and then another hundred meters. The street was now full of police cars. Curious onlookers hung out the windows. Moya was standing in front of a building with a cracked facade. The closed shutters made it appear boarded up.

"The bird has flown the coop," he said as they stepped out.

Lindell glanced up at the building. Outside a door that had been painted green hung a small handwritten sign: *Camas.* She knew that this meant beds.

"This was a very simple hostel," Moya said.

A woman of about eighty was standing in the doorway. She was draped in black. Lindell's thoughts went to witches. The woman's tiny eyes in her wrinkled face glared with both fury and curiosity at Lindell. Behind her there were voices, and she turned and screamed something.

"Let's go in," Moya said.

Reluctantly, the woman let them pass. Lindell heard her muttering. The hall was dark, with only a naked bulb in the ceiling for lighting. A man of about fifty was standing at the foot of a staircase. He said something to Moya. He had a speech impediment and seemed extremely stupid. He smelled of the stable and was gesturing wildly with his large hands.

Moya turned to them to interpret what was being said. "He is the son of the house," he said. "He has been in his barn about a kilometer outside of town, milking the cows."

Lindell had seen a moped leaned up against a wall, with stainless steel containers in baskets on the back, and realized it was his.

"Mother and son rent out three rooms on the upper floor. We can go up," Moya said.

The son followed him and his speech impediment made Lindell shiver. He sounded agitated in an unpredictable way.

The first room, the door to which was open, was very simply furnished. A bed, a chair, and a wardrobe, that was all. Next to the bed there was a chamber pot. A man with sunken cheeks lay on the bed, his thin gray hair standing on end. He had a coughing fit and immediately spit into the chamber pot, which was filled with gray-green mucus. The man coughed again, spit, and seemed completely untroubled by the fact that Lindell was standing at the door.

"He has bad lungs," Moya said apologetically. Lindell had the impression that he was ashamed of this image of his country.

Lindell continued walking. A man on a bed occupied the next room as well. He was short, almost dwarf-like, and was missing part of his leg. It had been severed just below the knee.

"He sells lottery tickets," Moya said. Lindell was struck by a feeling of unreality at the sight of these human wrecks.

The man nodded at Lindell and reached for his prosthesis, which lay on the bedcovers.

Urbano's room was considerably larger than the rest.

"The suite," Lindell said to Haver.

The floor was tiled in black and white. A print of Jesus during his long-suffering journey to Calvary dominated one wall, and on the wall opposite this was a double door that stood open to the street. When she walked up to it and leaned out, she became dizzy even though they were only a couple of meters above the ground. She grabbed the wrought-iron railing and closed her eyes.

Some children were playing noisily in the street, and Lindell opened her eyes again. The dizzy spell passed. On the other side of the street, in an equally dilapidated building, all of the windows were open. A woman was walking around in one of the rooms. What Lindell noticed most distinctly were the pink slippers she was wearing and her incredibly beautiful hair, which flowed all the way to her waist. A child of perhaps two was clinging to her robe. For some reason this was the image that she would remember. The woman, the child, the slippers, and the hair. This everyday scene in what to her was such a foreign land, plunked in the middle of a dramatic phase of this investigation, not to mention at a turning point in her life—this was what became etched in her mind's eye.

Moya pulled her back to the matter at hand by placing a hand on her shoulder.

"The woman claims that Urbano left the house very early this morning. The son, whom I have trouble understanding, claims that Urbano left a couple of minutes before he arrived. That is to say, at around five o'clock."

Too late, Lindell thought. We were still sitting in the car. She was going to ask if the house had been under surveillance, but Moya anticipated her.

"It seems he managed to escape despite our precautions," he said. "He may have used a back exit. There is a door that opens into a narrow passage between the buildings. There one could force oneself between the wall and an old chicken coop and reach an alley."

The son of the house gurgled and stammered in the corridor, the man in the first room continued to cough, and the noise from the street grew louder. She heard laughter and the sound of an accelerating Vespa.

The surreal nature of the entire situation meant that Lindell was less upset than she would normally have been. She had been looking forward to putting her hands on this Urbano. He would—if he chose to cooperate— shed light on the Cederén investigation. So close, she thought, so damned close, and now the anger struck her with full force.

They left the building. Two policemen stayed behind in case Urbano returned. Lindell and Haver speculated about the possibility that he had been tipped off and decided to flee. They did not want to trouble Moya with questions. His body language indicated that he was ashamed and upset, and they did not want to add to his burden. He spoke quietly and tersely to his staff and colleagues from Ronda, but when he got into the car, his rage broke out. The officer from Ronda who had swaggered down the street was given an earful. Moya barked incessantly for a couple of minutes and then slammed the car door shut.

Lindell and Haver flew home the following day. Wanning and the data expert were staying on for another day or so. The good-byes between them and Moya were warm. Lindell again invited Moya to visit Sweden and Uppsala. Moya smiled and assured them that he would very much like to travel to Scandinavia, not the least so that he would see them again. Haver thought that Moya was really talking to Lindell.

On the plane on the way home they conversed in low voices, summarizing their visit and wondering how best to make use of the information that they had acquired. They had already faxed home the facts about Urbano's and Olivares's trip to Sweden, and Lindell had called Ottosson on several occasions in order to keep him informed.

She knew that digging into the two Spaniards' trip was already under way. The most pertinent questions were where they had stayed and how they had gotten around. Had they rented a car or was there a Swedish contact with whom they had stayed? The hotels in and around Uppsala would be checked as well as all of the car rental companies.

Overall, Lindell was pleased with the visit, despite the fact that Urbano had slipped out of their grasp.

✦

Twenty-six

"So let's see where we stand," Ottosson said cheerfully.

He was standing in front of the flip pad that was hardly ever used in meetings but that now he seemed to feel was necessary in order to illustrate the current situation.

It was Lindell who should have given the overview, but she had asked him to step in, claiming a headache.

"Two Spaniards with criminal records, Urbano and Olivares, travel to Sweden and stay here for two days. During this time the Cederén family dies. Two of them are the victims of a hit-and-run, and the third dies in a most perplexing fashion," Ottosson went on.

Sammy Nilsson gave Berglund an amused look. "Dies in a most perplexing fashion," he wrote in his notebook and pushed it over to Berglund so he could read it.

Both of the names were written across Ottosson's flip pad in big letters.

After Olivares's name there was a black cross. Ottosson had been in full pedagogical gear as he set up the meeting.

"We believe that they contributed to Josefin and Emily's deaths. It may have happened thus: They picked up Sven-Erik Cederén somehow—we still don't know how—take his car, drive to Uppsala-Näs to kill the first two, return to the forest in Rasbo, get Cederén drunk, and gas him to death."

"But what about the note that says 'sorry'?" Riis objected.

"It's very possible to force someone to write a note like that," Ottosson answered calmly. "Keep in mind that he had fifty centiliters of gin in his veins."

He looked at Riis, who did not pursue this any further.

"But why did they do it?" Ottosson said.

"Cederén was the primary target in the trip to Sweden," Haver said. "I don't think we have to speculate too much about that."

"How did they know that Josefin was taking a walk that day?" Ottosson asked.

"They drove out to Uppsala-Näs in order to kill Josefin and Emily in some way, intending to frame the husband. Perhaps they saw the mother and child leave the house and followed them to wait for the right spot."

No one could understand why it had been so important to kill Sven-Erik Cederén to the point of murdering his wife and child and making it look like a family drama. What interests had Cederén posed a threat to?

A large part of the morning meeting was devoted to various lines of speculation. Everyone assumed that the actions had been directed from Spain, but nothing new had been heard from Málaga and Urbano was still missing. The murder of his companion Olivares was still unsolved, but everything pointed to Urbano being behind it. Perhaps Olivares had become shaky and started to pose a risk to Urbano.

Haver tossed out the theory that perhaps someone had intended to silence *both* Urbano and Olivares, but that the former had gotten away. In this case, there was another force to be reckoned with. Perhaps UNA Médico was the party that had the most interest in keeping the whole thing quiet.

In other words, the investigators were frustrated. The scrutiny of hotel and car rental companies had not yielded any results. The group was slowly becoming convinced that someone in Sweden had assisted the Spaniards.

Lindell was having trouble maintaining her concentration. She participated only sporadically in the discussion. The experience outside Gabriella Mark's cottage had left an impression. Her thoughts kept circling back to the injured elk calf. What was going to happen to it? She had even thought about trying to get someone to catch the calf and take it to the animal hospital in Ultuna but realized that this was impractical. Who was concerned about an injured elk calf?

But it wasn't simply the sight of the animal that had shaken her. She had experienced some of Gabriella's terror in the brief time that she had spent at the cottage. Lindell had no trouble identifying with her. They were almost the same age and were both single, and there was an aspect of deliberate isolation to Gabriella's life that both attracted and repelled her.

The source of her uneasiness was probably the fear of loneliness, but it was also the thought of the life that Gabriella had created for herself: the process by which a woman with significant problems had slowly transformed herself into a strong and solitary figure. The vegetable garden seemed to Lindell to promise a way out. Did she herself want to flee to the country and carrots? Not really, but perhaps in another form. To choose a life other than the one she was currently living was becoming her goal.

She tried to pull herself together and listen more carefully to the comments her colleagues were making, but she soon realized that the discussion was faltering. Ottosson had also seen this, and his previously optimistic commentary had switched to the occasional words of encouragement to get the team to engage in creative thinking.

The meeting ended after three-quarters of an hour. Lindell, who did not want to hear any comforting words from Ottosson, hurried to her office.

On the desk there was a note from Fredriksson. He had been working for about a month on a stabbing case that was starting to unfold into an unpleasant chain of events with connections to the so-called Uppsala mafia. Lindell had hardly seen him for the past two weeks.

"Call Adrian Mård," the note said, accompanied by a telephone number. "Animal lover," Fredriksson had added at the very bottom.

Lindell stared at the note and wondered when Allan had dropped it off and how he had come across this "animal lover," but she decided not to worry about any of this. She dialed the number.

Adrian Mård picked up on the first signal as if he had been waiting for the call. Lindell introduced herself.

"I'm glad you called," Mård said.

From his voice, Lindell judged that he was in his mid-twenties.

"I have some thoughts about MedForsk," he went on. "Isn't that what you're working on?"

"Who are you?" Lindell asked.

"I work at a publication called *Alternative Animal*. We cover information on animal factories, the food industry, and alternative lifestyles."

"I see, and why do you want to talk to me?"

Mård eagerly started to describe the typical living conditions of the most common household animals. He spoke a great deal about chicken farming, which he had apparently given a lot of thought to.

"You mentioned MedForsk," Lindell interrupted. "Perhaps we could meet and talk about that?"

"Sure," Mård said. "That was why I reached out."

They decided to meet up in town. Lindell suggested the Savoy, but Mård had no idea where that was, so they agreed on Hugo's instead.

Adrian Mård was close to forty and did not match any of Lindell's expectations. He was short and portly—if not outright fat—and had unruly red hair.

He was sitting at the very back of the café, chain-smoking. Alternative lifestyles indeed, Lindell thought.

"Cheers," he said, smiling widely and holding out a chubby hand.

"Hi," Lindell said, finding it hard not to like this unusual character.

She sat down after she had bought herself a cup of coffee with milk. While she was busy getting herself settled, Mård took out a stack of papers.

"Here is a little information on what we do," he said and pushed it over. The magazine that he had mentioned lay on top.

Lindell shoved the stack into her bag and sipped her coffee.

"MedForsk," she said.

"I have a good friend in Save the Animals. It doesn't matter what his name is. I wouldn't reveal his name even if I was tortured."

"I don't think you need to worry about that," Lindell said.

"Well, he's worried. Ever since the business at TV4, your friends have been on him like hawks. They're pretty shook up even if they're trying to look cool. A lot of them are kids who aren't completely clear about what they're doing. It's fun to save foxes and hamsters, but now things are starting to feel uncomfortable."

He lit a new cigarette. Lindell was starting to get more interested. It's when things get uncomfortable that we come into the picture, she thought.

"My contact says that they have evidence that MedForsk is engaged in illegal animal experimentation."

"Where is the evidence coming from?"

Mård looked at her appraisingly. "From inside the company," he said finally.

Lindell tried not to reveal her excitement. She took another sip of her coffee and adopted a neutral expression.

"Who was it?" she asked.

"I don't know," Mård said, but Lindell could see that he was lying.

"Who was it?" she repeated.

Mård looked disappointed, as if she hadn't lived up to his expectations.

"Please respect what I'm telling you," he said. "What is important is the information my contact received."

His voice took on a sharp note that Lindell did not associate with his almost jovial appearance. She always found herself assuming that heavy-set people would also be friendly and communicative, but it was clear that Adrian Mård knew how to stand up for himself.

"Okay," she said and smiled. "Keep going."

He returned her smile and resumed his narrative. The leak inside Med-Forsk had apparently come across a document proving that experiments had been carried out on primates. What tests these might have been, it did not specify. When Lindell asked if the tests could have been conducted abroad, Mård said that the document neither proved nor disproved this.

The test results had been difficult to evaluate. A group of test animals had reacted in an unexpectedly positive way, while others had actually suffered damage. The effects in question pertained to altering internal systems, and some of the animals became extremely aggressive.

"And these were illegal tests, you said?"

Mård nodded.

"How can you be sure?"

"We just know."

A group of teens came into the tiny café and sat down at the table next to them. They were talking loudly and immediately lit cigarettes.

"Maybe we should go somewhere else," Lindell said.

They left Hugo's, and when they came out onto the street, Lindell gratefully drew in the fresh air.

"Let's go to the Linnaeus Garden," she suggested.

They had to crowd through the narrow door with a group of Japanese tourists before managing to get inside. On either side of the gravel path leading up to the orangery there were beautiful flowers in blue and pink. A few vibrantly colored peonies were now wilting on their stems.

It turned out that Mård knew something about plants.

"These used to be called Linné's daughters," he said and pointed to some pale pink blooms planted along the path. Between these there were patches of wolfsbane and daylilies.

They found a bench in the shade under a linden tree. Lindell's gaze swept across the garden. If it hadn't been in this context, she would have appreciated this pocket of fresh air in the middle of the city a bit more. She enjoyed the sight of the neat rows of plants marked with handwritten signs as well as the happy tourists who sat at the café tables in front of the orangery. They reminded her of another life. Even though she had lived in Uppsala for many years, this was only the second time that she had visited the world-renowned garden. The first time she had come here was with Lundkvist, a former colleague who had moved away.

He had also liked plants, and they had slipped out here during a lunch break. There had not been a lot of talk of flowers that time either. Lindell recalled that Lundkvist had talked about a murder—now subject to the statute of limitations—that had taken place in the city.

Lindell brushed these thoughts aside and asked Mård to continue his narrative.

"Okay, illegal testing, I'll buy that," she said.

"In addition to this, there was a document that we couldn't understand. It was in English."

Lindell felt a physical sensation in her body. Now, she thought with a sense of relief. This is the pebble that triggers the avalanche.

"Have you had it translated?"

Mård nodded.

"What makes it so difficult to understand?"

"In part it's the medical terminology. It was about Parkinson's research. We got that much. But the document was formatted so strangely that we couldn't make heads or tails of it."

"Is it about primates?" Lindell asked.

"To be honest, we don't know," Mård said. "What made us more curious was a comment written in Swedish at the very bottom. Someone had written a note in large letters that said, 'I recommend not proceeding further. Insanity—may involve great risk and suffering.'"

"Was it signed?"

"No, it was just a scribbled comment," Mård said.

"And where is this document now?"

Mård looked worried. His fleshy face twisted into a grimace and he gazed out over the garden. Lindell followed his gaze and saw the Japanese tourists gathered around a small pond. They were wearing similar red hats and their heads moved obediently in the direction indicated by their guide.

"It's gone," Mård said. "At least as far as I can tell."

"Gone?"

"After the research director at the company died, our contact got cold feet. The person in question now refuses to talk to us and the document has been destroyed."

Lindell noted that Mård had not said "he" but "the person in question." Did that mean it was a woman?

Mård explained that his contact at MedForsk no longer wanted to talk to his friend in the animal rescue organization. He or she had said that the matter was now closed. The document had been shredded and the contact would deny all knowledge of its existence.

"You don't have a copy of it?"

"No, we never got one."

"Do you remember anything else?"

Mård shook his head. A dead end, Lindell thought with frustration, and tried to think of a way out.

"Do you think it described illegal activities? Do you know if your contact at MedForsk felt threatened?"

"I don't know anything more than I already told you."

It suddenly occurred to Lindell that the contact may have been Cederén, but Mård immediately dismissed this.

"I have to admit that I feel a bit nervous myself," Mård said.

"Why are you telling me all this?" Lindell asked.

"To help my friend. When they did the thing at TV4 they didn't have the whole picture. They were just protesting against the primate experiments. Now they're being squeezed. I think they're being watched pretty closely by your side."

"Of course they are," Lindell said. "It's a serious crime to take hostages. And they also injured one of the employees."

"Yes, I heard about that," Mård said in a low voice. "But they didn't mean to do that. They didn't even have any weapons. The whole thing with the bomb was something they had made up, an empty threat."

"I suspected as much," Lindell said.

The Japanese tourists left the garden, talking animatedly. They streamed out of the exit like liquid pouring out of a bottle.

Lindell and Mård remained on the bench, lost in reflection. Mård's initial cheeriness and enthusiasm had given way to thoughtfulness and perhaps also fear. He had seen Lindell's gaze and intense interest in the document and realized—if he hadn't already—that he was in a minefield.

"You don't think . . ." Lindell began.

"No," Mård broke in. "My contact is going to deny everything. I'm sure of it."

"Fear?"

"Yes. Even terror, I'd say."

"Have you met your contact?"

"No, only my friend did."

"What was their relationship to each other? I mean, why did the contact reach out to your friend?"

"I don't know," Mård said, and this time Lindell believed him.

"You said that after Cederén died, the contact got cold feet, but the document probably came into the light of day after the TV4 event, which took place after the death. How does that all hang together?"

"I may not have expressed myself in the best way. What you're saying is right, but clearly something happened that shook up our contact."

"What were you working on earlier?" Lindell asked.

Mård smiled before he answered.

"I was an investigator at the National Food Administration. I wrote my dissertation on free-range hens."

Lindell smiled. Free-range hens, she thought. That's me. I'm a free-range hen.

"Wild birds?" she asked.

"Not really, but free to wander a floor. There was a law passed at the end of the eighties that outlawed caged hens, but since then, there has been exception after exception. I know what the food administration is capable of, and that's most likely also true of the pharmaceutical companies. Nothing is more important than profit."

"That's why you're involved in this?"

"Profits," he repeated simply and nodded.

"What does the name Gabriella Mark mean to you?"

"Should I know her?"

Lindell was about to say that she was dead but decided not to scare him further.

"What about Julio Piñeda?"

Mård jumped when she said his name, and he stared at her with bewilderment.

"Have you heard the name before?"

"Not heard, but I have seen it," Mård said. "His name was in the document with a number of others."

"Can you remember any of the others?"

"No, but when you said his, I remembered that I had seen it," Mård said. "What is this all about?"

"We don't know," Lindell answered honestly. "But so far it has cost five people their lives, maybe more."

"Five people," Mård said breathlessly.

Lindell let this sink in. Where should she go from here? She believed Mård's insistence that the animal rights activists had nothing to do with the death of the Cederén family, as well as that the event at TV4 had been highly illegal but had not constituted a threat to people's lives. If Mård was telling the truth, the activists would lay low for a long time to come.

The answer lay in the document that had disappeared and also in Spain. She was more and more convinced of this. She should get in touch with the prosecutor to figure out how to proceed.

Lindell's thoughts were interrupted by Mård.

"If this case is as serious as you say, that five people have died, then our contact at MedForsk is in grave danger, isn't that right?"

Lindell nodded.

"That's why we need to get in touch with him or her," Lindell said. It suddenly struck her that Gabriella Mark may have been the contact and that she may have paid with her life for having poked around on her own. There was nothing to say that the information had remained within Med-Forsk. It might have been Cederén who had written the comment across the bottom, shown Gabriella the document, and expressed his concerns about what the company was doing.

"I want to meet your friend," she said. "He can remain anonymous if he wants. But it's absolutely necessary for me to speak to him."

Mård shook his head.

"It can help to solve the murders and may prevent more," Lindell urged. "Just talk to him anyway. Try to get him to understand the seriousness of the situation."

"I think he understands that," Mård answered quickly.

"One of the murder victims may have been his contact," Lindell said. "And he could be next."

She hated having to paint such a threatening picture, but if they were to get any further, they would first have to crack the question of who the source was, the leak at MedForsk.

"I'll talk to him," Mård said.

There was nothing left of his cheeriness. He sat leaning forward, staring down into the gravel. A flock of sparrows swooped down and landed in front of his feet.

Mård turned his head. He was sweating profusely.

"It's incomprehensible what people will do for gain," he said. "When I started to get involved in this, I thought that we could change things, that human beings were fundamentally reasonable."

He fell silent again and turned to study the sparrows. His gaze turned reflective, as if from these small creatures he could discern some wisdom.

"Dialogue was what we called it. We were going to create a dialogue, but how do you talk to murderers? Is it so strange that teenagers become desperate and burn slaughtering trucks and release minks? I started as a field biologist, studied to become an agricultural expert, and imagined a future in research, making the world a better place."

"But," Lindell prompted when Mård paused again.

"But," Mård resumed, "there are structures we are powerless against. You see, there is an invisible network of power mongers, politicians, industry and finance people, researchers and journalists who steer our thoughts. This happens in the shadows. We think that we live in an open and democratic society, but these people control us. You probably do a good job, but you're only skimming the surface. The real criminals go free."

"Are you thinking of environmental crimes?" Lindell asked.

She had read statistics about how few cases were prosecuted and how only a small number of these led to sentencing.

"Yes, in part, but the really large crimes, I would prefer to call crimes against humanity. Those criminals receive honorary doctorates and even the Nobel Peace Prize. Who works for justice?"

The question hovered in the air. Lindell had no answer. Normally she would have replied that it was the police and the judicial branch, but she realized that this would carry no weight with Mård.

"Talk to your friend. I gave you my card. Ask him to call me. Tell him that it could save a life. We may not be able to change the world, but we can solve this together," Lindell said and put a hand on his shoulder.

He looked up at her and smiled for the first time in a long time, nodded, stood up, adjusted his wrinkled pants, and left without saying a word.

Lindell stayed behind for a couple of minutes. Did they already have their eyes on Mård? Was even he in danger?

She looked around the garden.

She called for a cab, which was not something she did very often. It would have taken only a quarter of an hour to walk back to the station, but she felt drained after the conversation with Adrian Mård, and the feeling that she was one step behind made her want to hurry back.

Ottosson, Lindell, and Fritzén, the prosecutor, had a long meeting in the afternoon to review the current state of the investigation. All three agreed that they should question all the employees at MedForsk as soon as possible, as well as inform the Spanish police of their developments.

They decided to bring in everyone in the company at once, with the exception of any essential personnel who would keep the basic functions going—feeding test animals, answering the phones, or whatever.

There would of course be protests from Mortensen, but the prosecutor was convinced that they would reach the best results by taking this approach and that all complaints would be ignored.

"What you have to do is to shake up the employees," Fritzén said. "Maybe we'll rattle them so much that one of them will let something slip and will give us something to go on."

They planned the interrogations and decided who would play what part. Berglund would take on Mortensen. Lindell would be the spider in the web and walk between the various sessions. After a while all of the interrogations would be suspended and the detectives would assemble to compare results and decide how to proceed from there.

They would focus on three things: if anyone had had contact with or heard anything about the two Spanish men; if they had any comment about the allegations of illegal animal testing; and finally if they were aware that by withholding any information, they were making themselves an accessory to the crime.

"We need to frighten them a little bit," Ottosson said. "Lay it on thick."

"Should we make them think they will be detained at the station?" Lindell wondered and glanced at Fritzén.

When he didn't reply, she continued. "We could just say that it is for reasons to do with the investigation."

Both Fritzén and Ottosson knew very well what she was referring to.

"You'll have to make that determination yourselves," Fritzén said finally. "I'm not going to rule it out."

✦

Twenty-seven

The nor'easter had grown stronger in the night. When Edvard woke at five, he heard it whine above the roof tiles.

He lingered in bed for a couple of minutes and thought about Viola's last words of the preceding evening, when she had predicted a strong wind, even though they hadn't heard anything about it on the late night weather report. It was remarkable how that woman could read the sky and the signs of pending bad weather.

The morning light shone in under the blinds. He tried to see if it was raining. If so, he would ditch the idea of seeing to the nets. He had cast three of them close to the reef in the middle of the bay. The catch would probably be poor due to the weather.

Viola was already up and about. He heard her rattling around in the kitchen. Her weakness after her cold did not prevent her from getting up at dawn and making his breakfast. She did this every day that he went to work. Now he was going out to take up the nets, so it was her duty to make sure he got something in him before he headed out. That was how she felt. "It's my duty," she had told him when he tried to convince her to take it easy in the mornings. However many times he told her that he was used to fixing his own breakfast, the old woman always got up to do it herself.

This morning she tried to convince him not to set out. Viola was a tough old woman, but if there was anything she feared, it was the powers of nature.

"Forget about those nets" was the first thing she said to him when he came down the stairs.

Only rarely was she so direct. He sat down. The coffee thermos was already on the table and Viola was making three sandwiches. Always three, two with cheese and one with roe spread.

"It's not so bad," Edvard said.

"It's near gale at least," she said, turning to him and fixing him with her eye.

She had used a sash that didn't match—Edvard thought it was a curtain sash—to fasten her fringed robe, revealing a glimpse of her nightgown and gaunt body underneath. He felt uncomfortable. If he had been alone, he would very likely not have gone out that day, but in a way this was his duty. If according to the traditional gender roles Viola's task was fixing the meals, then it was his job to go out and haul in the nets. This was instilled in his unconscious, even though he saw the old-fashioned and irrational aspect of his belief.

"I'm going out anyway," he said and started to eat.

Viola grunted in displeasure. She poured him a cup of coffee but did not sit down to join him. Edvard interpreted this as her protest at his decision.

Near gale force at least, she had said and that was true enough. Fresh gale, he thought as he rounded the grove of alder trees and the bay came into view.

The sea was boiling, and out at the reef, white cascades of foam were whipped into the air with a ferocity that Edvard had rarely seen. At this point he should have turned around and returned to the warm kitchen, but instead he decided to go down to the boats and check on them. Granted, the new stone dock was stable and could handle the worst, but you never knew. He could at least test the mooring lines.

At least a third of the little boat was filled with water and Edvard jumped in and started to bail it out. After a while he looked up, out of breath and with a pain in his knee, and he stared out over the water. Hadn't the wind calmed somewhat? He stood up and looked out at the reef. Yes, a little, he decided.

When the little boat was emptied of water, he went to work on Victor's

Uttern and then ended up standing on the dock. The wind shook his rain-coat. He closed his eyes and turned to the north. In a way it was freeing to expose oneself to the raging elements. All the morning grogginess left his body and he felt cleansed by the wind.

"Jens and Jerker," he muttered almost inaudibly.

He repeated the names a little louder and then louder still, finally screaming their names out over the stormy seas.

He imagined that the wind would carry the names from the island and the waters of Öregrundsgrepen and then out across the mainland all the way to Ramnäs farm where they lived.

The wind was no longer whipping as hard against the dock as before. He turned and stood in front of the little boat as if it would be able to make the determination as to whether he could go out or not. It was bobbing fairly peacefully, shielded by the stones and heavy timber. He could take Victor's boat, which would stand up better to the waves and had a covered wheelhouse for a little protection. Victor wouldn't mind, but Edvard felt it wasn't right to borrow a boat without permission.

He loosened the ropes and stepped into the little boat. As he punted his way out of the calm and protected area created by the stone dock he thought he saw something moving back on the shore. Perhaps Viola had come down, but he couldn't tell. He also knew that a great deal was required to bring her all the way to the shore. Even if she had some doubts about his endeavors, she would be hesitant to show her concern so clearly. Instead, she would nurse her fears in the kitchen or maybe the parlor, with its windows facing the sea.

He rowed a couple of strokes before he turned on the engine. The seas were rough enough that the engine was lifted clear out of the water from time to time. He steered almost straight into the waves and they washed in over him and the boat. His plan was to hold this course for a while, then turn and follow the waves more diagonally toward the nets.

He searched in vain for the buoy marking the location of the nets. It must have drifted away, perhaps along with the nets themselves. Damn it, he thought. Now there will be a lot of seaweed and shit in the nets.

The engine struggled in the hard seas, the boat slowly chugging its way forward. Edvard was drenched through but also felt free, absorbed in the interplay between him, the boat, and the sea. He brushed a hand over his face and tasted salt. The southwesterly threatened to blow him over, but he managed to stay on his feet by hanging on to the straps.

When he changed course, he finally spotted the buoy. As he suspected, it had drifted in toward the reef. The vivid red-painted plastic container bobbed in the water, disappearing sometimes, but now he had a target and steered the boat toward it, the waves now diagonally behind him.

He felt the boat pulling toward shore and had to straighten its course. A large wave suddenly appeared and washed over the boat. Was the storm getting worse again? He grabbed the bailer, leaned forward, and started to scoop the water out while using his other hand to try to stay on course.

Yet another wave filled the boat with water once more. Now there was ten centimeters of standing water in the boat and Edvard felt it get heavier.

The buoy was fifty meters away, but he could not take a straight path there because of the rocks just under the surface of the water between him and the marker. He turned and tried to keep the boat so that the waves would not wash over it again.

It started to rain hard and Edvard quickly glanced up at the sky. Black clouds had piled up in the opening toward the Sea of Åland. They must have traveled at a furious pace because when he was standing on the dock he had thought the sky was lightening toward the north.

Then he arrived at the buoy. The first attempt to grab the red marker was unsuccessful, so he had to turn about-face and come in for a second pass. He hauled it into the boat and pulled on it appraisingly to get a sense of how the nets had moved. The large loops of the net disappeared into the dark water. He pulled. A sudden gust of wind caused the boat to careen and he lost his grip as he tried to parry with his body and twist the rudder while grabbing the buoy again before it went back overboard.

Now he had his first serious pangs of doubt about setting out to sea. The rain grew heavier. The water level in the boat rose, so he had to bail more water. He held on to the nets, planted his feet, and managed to get a little shelter from the reef. The first flash of a perch calmed him a little. It landed in the boat, and then there were two more, but mainly there was only seaweed in the nets.

He had to stop bailing water and squeezed the nets between his knees as well as he could. It hurt his bad knee and he clenched his teeth so he wouldn't scream with helplessness, rage, and pain.

The first net resulted in eight fish, but now the perch were the least of his concern. There were two more nets. The boat whirled around as he grabbed at the nets, which exposed him to the bucking waves.

When he had managed to reel in net number two, a powerful wave struck, shortly followed by another. The boat reared up like a circus horse and then dove down into the sea, dipping the bow into the water that rushed in. The rain pelted down without ceasing. The boat wrenched to the side and Edvard was forced to drop the nets, which immediately started to slither over the side like angry serpents.

He considered tossing out the grapnel so that he would have time to bail and gather his strength but didn't have time to do more than think that thought before the next breaker came. The boat was thrown starboard and Edvard had to grab hold of the thwart in order to prevent himself from being pitched overboard. The nets slipped out, the fish disappeared into the sea, and the boat dipped precipitously downward along with them.

The next wave finished the struggle. He had now drifted out of the small area of calm that the reef had afforded. The boat suddenly came under the full ferocity of the bay. A heavy wave struck and waterlogged the boat immediately. Edvard was thrown forward and hit his legs on the thwart but felt no pain as in the next second he found himself in the sea. The boat spun around.

When he came back up to the surface he fumbled around instinctively for something to hang on to and managed to grab an oar. The boat was drifting aimlessly back and forth, bottom up, a couple of meters away. Edvard had time to see that the hull needed a coat of paint before the next wave came and crashed over him with such force that he took in a mouthful of water. He let go of the oar and, with a couple of forceful strokes, tried to swim over to the boat. This was his only chance. If he were forced to swim farther than that, he would quickly run out of energy. He was a good swimmer but wasn't wearing a life vest.

He managed to reach the boat with one hand and could therefore pull himself closer and rest for a moment on its side. He tried to see how far he had drifted from the reef but was not able to see anything through the forest of waves.

This is where I die, he thought, and leaned his head back on the boat.

I'm supposed to die here. This was where his longing for the sea had led him. Is this my punishment for leaving Marita and the children? he had time to ask himself before the next big wave came and dragged him under the water.

He thought of Viola and renewed his efforts to clamber onto the boat. Perhaps he would be able to hang on, and if he didn't return in half an hour, Viola would walk down to the shore to see what was happening, and she would give the alarm.

He tried to pull himself up further but failed and realized that he should save his energy. The thought that he should simply let go flashed through his head and paralyzed him. How many times had he stood on the shore these past two and a half years and wished himself dead, buried in the deep? The sea had always fascinated him. Even as a child he had nursed a desire to live close to it. Was it fate that had steered him to Gräsö, not in order to live, but in preparation for his death?

He clung to the side of the boat. The water pounded him, grinding down his resistance. The cold crept into his limbs and his body now felt heavy, as if it signaled that enough was enough, that it wanted to sink.

He thought of Ann but without sadness or grief. She had fluttered past in his life, given him a little bit of hope and human warmth. What was she doing now? Eating breakfast, reading the paper, showering or getting dressed. He tried to imagine her face but couldn't manage it. Instead he recalled how her shoulders, back, and hips gleamed in the light of the candles they used to light.

✦

Twenty-eight

Lindell woke with a start. The alarm clock read 6:03 A.M. She sank back against the pillow. She had half an hour left until the alarm was set to go off.

The sheets were sticking to her legs and she pushed the blanket off, but regretted it when she immediately began to shiver. She heard the wind blow outside and feared that it would be another blustery day. Indeed, every-one complained that this particular summer had been cloudy and cool.

She pulled the blanket back over herself and curled up under it. She vainly tried to recapture the images in the dream that had so rudely awak-ened her. The only thing she remembered was that it had been about Ed-vard. He was on the island but not at the house. He was in surroundings she didn't recognize. There were fishing cabins and reeds. Edvard had been standing out in the reeds. Ann had shouted at him, but all his attention had been directed toward the sea.

This was all she recalled and it bothered her. What had Edvard been looking for? She could not even remember what she had been shouting, but it had been important.

She stayed in bed and one hand automatically found its way to her belly. She stroked it slowly as if to calm either herself or the embryo growing within her. The alarm rang and she quickly turned it off.

Today they were going to turn MedForsk upside down. Lindell was looking forward to it but wasn't certain how fruitful it would be. They had so little to go on. They had only a few vague, uncorroborated pieces of in-formation from an animal rights activist, and these were secondhand. The document that Mård had talked about had most likely been destroyed. So what was its value? In terms of a future court case—absolutely nothing. She understood that. But perhaps it was worth something as a point of entry for questioning the MedForsk employees. She wondered if it was possible to use it at all.

Someone who should know about it was of course the CEO, Mortensen. She had to discuss tactics with Berglund, who would be conducting the interrogation.

She dragged herself out of bed and got in the shower. As she soaped up, she wondered if her sense of her own body had changed with her preg-nancy. Earlier she hadn't paid it much attention. Certainly she had studied herself in the mirror, had searched for signs of aging such as wrinkles and cellulite, but her overall attitude had been relaxed. She knew she was at-tractive. Her proportions were fine: While no wisp of a thing, she had fine full breasts and was not too stocky in the thighs or rear. She knew that men looked at her with appreciation. In his own simple way, Edvard had assured her that she was beautiful. This had been hard for her to accept at first, but then it had made her happy, even lyrical, when she had realized how he regarded her. He had raised her up with his hands and his mouth. Had made her aware of herself.

With Rolf, it had been different. He had taken her for granted and they had been younger. Then both had assumed that their outward appearances should be, if not perfect, then at least free of major flaws. Edvard had a different kind of sensitivity that had brought out her own sensuality and sense of self-worth. In Edvard's presence, she had never felt like a woman approaching middle age. Instead she had matured and started to discover and appreciate herself for who she was and how she looked.

Once he had said something about her being as beautiful as a field of wheat. She had started to cry because she had realized the meaning and depth of this metaphor. He was a farmworker who read beauty in the landscape, that which could not be put into words, that which could be perceived only as a joyful intoxication or a peaceful gratitude for the gifts of life. That is to say, love. She wanted to be his ripened field of wheat.

She had observed Edvard at the edge of a field, by pastures and meadows, perhaps a few steps into the crops, among the plants. That gaze, the calm that came over him at these times, fueled her love. "Sun-ripened" was the word that came to her in the shower.

Now her body took on another significance as the bearer of new life. She realized that she should stop drinking wine, live more healthfully, and not tax herself too much. Her awareness that she was responsible for another person was growing stronger.

What she wished was that Edvard could join her in the journey.

A group of frustrated individuals were assembled for interrogations and questioning. They had to leave their desks at short notice. The prosecutor, Fritzén, had even joined them at MedForsk, something that Lindell had never experienced before. Earlier he had taken a passive role, but his very presence at this scene testified to the seriousness with which the action was regarded.

Some had protested, among them Jack Mortensen, but all their complaints had been ignored. When the group filed into the lunchroom, Berglund and Haver had patiently explained why they were impelled to act so forcefully.

"This is about murder," Berglund had intoned.

One of the researchers had stood up halfway as if to say something but had immediately been interrupted by Berglund.

"Murder," he had repeated, his voice harsh, and the researcher lost his nerve.

Now the eight people had been dispatched to separate interrogation rooms. One of the employees, Lena Friberg, had been allowed to stay at her station to answer the phones and explain that no one at the company was available for the moment.

Jack Mortensen had glared at Lindell when she entered the room where he and Berglund were sitting. Berglund had just started, and Lindell paused by the door for a moment before she continued in.

Beatrice was sitting in the next room with Teresia Wall. Lindell nodded in greeting. Teresia's belly had grown in the interim since they had last met.

She was clearly nervous. Lindell stayed for a couple of minutes and observed Beatrice draw on her best side in order to get her to relax.

"Is this your first child?" Beatrice asked.

Teresia nodded.

"Isn't it hard to be pregnant in the heat of summer?"

"It's not too bad," Teresia said hesitantly, as if she had trouble evaluating this informal conversation.

"I always made sure to time my pregnancies for the winter," Beatrice said. "What does your husband do?"

"He works at Ultuna," Teresia said.

"And he's a researcher?"

"He's a vet."

Lindell left the room and went up to her own office.

Eight people, she thought as she poured herself a cup of coffee from the thermos. Are any of them going to crumble? She had her hopes pinned on Teresia or Sofi Rönn. Not because they were women but because Lindell had questioned them herself and it was easier to imagine someone who was already familiar becoming talkative and cooperative.

As far as Mortensen was concerned, she held out little hope. His gruff manner indicated that he was going to be uncooperative. Lindell considered returning to his interrogation room but decided to let Berglund continue on his own.

There was a knock on the door and Lindell called out, "Come in!" She knew that it was Ottosson. The rest of the unit just walked in after a brief knock. Her boss always waited for an all clear.

"We have a fax from our Spanish friends," Ottosson began, waving a piece of paper. "I'm so bad at English that I don't understand very much of it."

Lindell quickly eyed the fax. Jaime Urbano had not yet been found. Moya wrote that the search would continue unabated. In their review of UNA Médico's accounts and correspondence, however, they had found something that Moya believed would be of interest to her. In the fall of 1999 one of the company's researchers had traveled to the Dominican Republic on three separate occasions. In all he had spent three weeks there. Moya had made a note of the dates.

Ottosson tugged at his beard and looked thoughtful.

"Didn't these clowns deny all connection with the Dominican Republic?" he asked.

"Yes. De Soto claimed he had only been there on vacation," Lindell said. "Let's ask Haver check the dates. Perhaps Cederén was there at the same time. That's what I have been led to believe. There's something up over there, but what?"

"Animal experimentation?" Ottosson said.

"Probably."

Lindell thought of the document that Adrian Mård had mentioned, the descriptions of various experiments and the handwritten notes that had been added. Was it Cederén who had made those notes and who had advised the company not to continue?

"Julio Piñeda," she said. "That's a name that appeared in Mård's document. He remembered the name when I mentioned it. I'm willing to bet that he is the company's man in the Caribbean."

"But how do you explain his letter? It's only a fragment, but still. It made it seem as if some people were suffering or however it was that he put it."

Ottosson sat down in her visitor's chair and Lindell realized this meant she would have him for a while.

"Piñeda could be a man with a conscience," she speculated. "Perhaps he tried to talk his way to extra benefits for himself or others."

Ottosson looked unconvinced.

"Well," he said, "I don't think he would have formulated himself in that way. Think about being a representative for a European company. You would want to be assertive, not appear as if you were whining."

Lindell didn't answer. There was something she had heard that nagged at her. Very recently. Was it Mortensen or Teresia Wall who had said something?

"Maybe you're right," she said. "But we'll have to keep working on the mysterious Julio. Has the contact with the Republic given us anything?"

"No response so far," Ottosson said. "It must be a little hard to get things done over there."

Lindell had trouble imagining how her colleagues on the other side of the Atlantic worked. There must be constant sun and summer, hordes of tourists.

"Maybe there is a siesta every day," Ottosson said but did not elaborate further on the Caribbean when he saw Lindell's expression.

"How do you think your scare tactics are working?" he asked, changing tack.

"We'll see," she said. "I think Mortensen will be hard. Some of the researchers looked very nervous. I took a peek at the rats they keep, and I have to say it can't be a pleasure to sit in a cage with a needle in your back. I know the researchers must justify the animal experimentation to themselves, but they are also probably aware of public opinion."

"You didn't see any primates?"

"No, only mice and rats."

Ottosson slowly got up out of the chair. Lindell could tell that there was more he wanted to say and had an idea that it was about her condition. She did nothing to help him, only turning the pages of her notepad to a clean page as if she were getting ready to write something.

Ottosson rocked back and forth on his feet for a couple of seconds and then left her office.

✦

Twenty-nine

As Julio Piñeda approached the outskirts of the town, his heart skipped a beat and he became so agitated that he thumped on the roof of the car. His nephew reduced his speed and pulled over to the side of the road just as a truck loaded with construction materials roared past and brushed the side mirror of the pickup.

"What is it?" Antonio shouted, without getting out.

"I saw him!" Julio answered. "Back up!"

Antonio snorted but obeyed and began slowly backing up. The car bounced on the uneven road. More trucks overtook them at insane speeds.

"A little farther!" Julio shouted from the back of the pickup.

A few seconds later, he was disappointed. It wasn't him. Why do these gringos all have to look the same?

"Do you see him?" Augusto, another nephew, asked.

"Keep driving," Julio said despondently. "Head to the Baker."

That was his last hope. The Baker might know where "El Sueco" was and if he had been around recently.

In his village, Gaspar Hernández, they had given up hope, but Julio refused to. He wanted justice. He had told the villagers this, but they had only laughed. Not openly, but behind his back. He knew it.

Antonio made a U-turn and parked in front of the Baker's store, which was also a bar. This was where Julio had met the Swede for the first time. That was almost exactly a year ago. Julio knew that he frequented this place. The Baker and the Swede got along well and Julio thought the Baker had found women for him, although he denied this.

"El Sueco is a fine man," he had said the last time Julio came looking for him.

A fine man, Julio thought as he climbed down from the bed. He had given up hope but was still looking for justice. If the Swede really was a fine man, he would understand.

The Baker had already opened three bottles of beer when they walked in. They helped Julio sit down at one of the tables. The Baker placed the beers on the table, greeted Julio and then the two youths.

"How is it going?" he asked and wiped the table with a rag.

"As usual," Julio said. "You haven't seen him?"

The Baker shook the rag and then his head.

"Damn it," Julio muttered.

He put the bottle to his mouth. The first sip was always the best. That was true of everything in life. The first time you made love with a woman, the first banana from the bunch, and the first bite of breakfast in the morning. The same was true of the Swede. The first meeting had been happy. The stranger had offered him food, beer, and rum, made jokes and laughed.

"I don't think he'll be back," the Baker said, and Julio noticed the hesitation in his voice.

"Yes, I think you're right," Julio said quietly.

The tone of his voice caused his nephews look at him. Their minds had been clear from the beginning: Julio's expedition was doomed to fail. They were making this trip so that the old man would stop carrying on so much and also because they liked him, because they felt sorry for him.

Julio took another sip. He felt betrayed, he was betrayed. People laughed at him and the others who had been taken in. It was fortunate that Miguel, his older brother, was no longer alive. He would have laughed himself silly; he had never had a sense of justice. His sons were better. Julio lifted the bottle but did not immediately bring it to his lips. He looked back at his nephews. They lifted their bottles too and together they drank a toast to confirm that the world was unfair and that life for the poor was hell.

The Baker stood behind his counter. He gazed at Julio sympathetically before he delivered his news.

"I believe that the Swede is dead," he said.

He knew that this was the case but did not want to completely obliterate the old man's hopes by sounding too certain. The trio at the table stared at him, and the Baker now saw the family resemblance more clearly than before. They all had the Piñeda nose, broad across the top with nostrils that widened to gaping holes with every breath.

"The police have been here," he said. "They asked questions about the Swede and wanted to know everything about the purchase of the property. I said that I didn't know anything and that the Swede came here only to drink."

"Why do you think he is dead?"

The old man did not reveal any stormy feelings. The Baker assumed it was the beer that made him calm. Some became aggressive and talkative when drinking, but Julio had never raised his voice in the bar, no matter how much he had had.

"It was my impression from their questions," the Baker answered.

"What else did they ask?" Antonio wondered.

"I said nothing about you, Julio, but they said they would go to the village."

"No one has been there," Julio said. "God has forgotten about us."

His hand shook as he reached for his beer. There is no justice, he thought as the beer slipped down his throat.

✦

Thirty

It was shortly before eleven o'clock when the interrogations of the MedForsk employees were halted. Ottosson decided to order food for those being interrogated as well as for the police.

There were several protests. Mortensen, above all, was extremely agitated. He talked about a breach of civil liberties. So call your mother, Lindell thought when she heard his angry voice. Ottosson responded in a calm voice that additional issues had to be resolved, but that first everyone needed some food.

Lindell smiled to herself. He sounded like a day care teacher who was explaining something to impatient children.

They had decided that the employees would eat separately in their individual holding rooms, so after the brief meeting they were led back to their original locations. The detectives, however, all ate together.

"How is it going?" Ottosson asked cheerfully to his assembled colleagues.

The resulting discussion was lively. The main impression so far was that the majority of the employees were shaken. In part because of the Cederén drama and Gabriella Mark's subsequent death and in part because they and the company were now under such close scrutiny. Mortensen had been duly informed that the Swedish police had visited UNA Médico in Málaga, but this was news to the rest of the company.

"Teresia Wall's jaw dropped," Beatrice said. "At first she couldn't even get out a single word."

"Same thing with my guy," Haver said.

"Mortensen referred to an internal investigation that the company is allegedly going to undertake," Berglund said. "Until we got to that point, he had claimed he had nothing to add to what had already been said."

"What did he say about our Spanish excursion?" Lindell asked.

"He had clearly been briefed by De Soto and the tactic is apparently that each blames the other. Whatever irregularities we might find, they will be the other one's fault. 'We're clean,'" Berglund echoed.

"They're hoping that we're going to jump into their books and intricate affairs and drown in the paperwork," Ottosson said. "But we couldn't care less about their money and the various transactions."

The prosecutor entered the room. He nodded a greeting to the group.

"Would you like a bite?" Ottosson asked, and Beatrice and Lindell exchanged looks. Ottosson was in his sunniest mood.

Fritzén declined the offer with a smile and sat down.

"I think my girl has something to contribute," Beatrice said. "She's more than a little edgy."

"She's pregnant," Sammy said. "That makes them all shaky."

Beatrice glared at him and was on the verge of taking him to task for this but kept going instead.

"She asked a lot about Gabriella and was surprisingly curious. When I asked if she knew Gabriella or had heard about her before, she talked around her answer."

"Something she said struck a chord in me," Lindell said. "But I can't remember what it was. It bothers me."

"You weren't in more than two times," Beatrice said.

The rest listened. They had enough respect for Lindell's intuition to sense that there might be something to this.

"When I came in the second time you were talking about primates," Lindell said slowly.

"What about the first time?" Beatrice asked.

"That was social chatter," Lindell said. "Social chat," she repeated more softly.

"No one has any idea who Pålle might be," Ottosson said. "That indicates that he isn't in immediate contact with MedForsk. Otherwise someone should be familiar with the name."

At that moment one of the secretaries, Anneli, came in, turned to Lindell, and indicated that she wanted to speak with her.

"An older woman called and she was very upset," Anneli said. "She's looking for you."

"I see. What was it about?"

"Her name is Viola and she lives in Gräsö Island," the secretary said, and Ann caught the look of empathy in her gaze before she really understood what she had said.

"What's happened?" she managed.

"You're supposed to call. She said you had the number."

Lindell left her colleagues without a word and ran to her office. Edvard, she mumbled. Edvard. The dream from the morning returned to her as she dialed Viola's number with shaky fingers.

The old woman picked up immediately as if she had been waiting by the phone.

"This is Ann. What's happened?"

She heard Viola's labored breathing.

"It's Edvard," Viola said and was interrupted by a fit of coughing.

"What is it?"

"He was at sea and went by the board and . . ."

Lindell swayed, fumbled for something to steady herself on, and struck a heap of reports that tumbled to the floor with a thud. Then everything went black for a moment. She fell on top of the papers on the floor.

She was conscious, but her legs wouldn't hold her. Nothing could hold her. She pulled the receiver to her and heard Viola shouting.

"But he's alive, my dear girl, he's alive."

In that moment she hated the old woman, but this feeling disappeared as quickly as it had come. She pulled herself into a sitting position. The cramp in her stomach receded somewhat and she sobbed from pain and anguish.

"Tell me," she said and saw an image of Josefin Cederén's father when he received the news of her death. So close, she thought.

"He was taking up the nets and went by the board," Viola began.

Why is she using that wording? Lindell thought and her anger returned.

"He hung on, and after an hour we were able to get him with the boat. It was Victor, the old man," Viola said, and now Ann heard that she was close to tears.

"The old man," Lindell repeated mechanically and burst into tears.

After a long while Lindell managed to collect herself enough so that she felt comfortable rejoining her colleagues.

They were cleaning up the remains of the meal when she returned. The room went completely quiet and everyone's gaze went to her. She saw the worry in their eyes and struggled not to start crying again.

"It was Edvard," she said. "He fell out of his boat this morning. It was blowing hard and the idiot went out to pull up some nets."

"How did it go?" Ottosson said and took a step closer.

Right then she did not want him to touch her or put his arm around her shoulders and say something nice as he usually did when he saw that she was concerned about something.

"He broke his leg, but that was when he was picked up from the reef. Apparently he slipped."

She saw the relief among her colleagues. They think I'm fragile, she thought. That I wouldn't be able to handle Edvard dying.

She tried to pull herself together and said something about the ongoing interrogations, but it was as if the others no longer cared. A gust of cold air had swept through the room. Death had showed its face. One of them had been close to losing a loved one. Even though they worked with violence, death, and grief, the message from Gräsö touched a nerve and revealed their vulnerability. So close, they all thought, and their own loved ones came to mind. Lindell felt as if the group of detectives drew closer. She saw the seriousness in their faces. Never before had she felt as strong a connection with them as at this moment, in these few seconds during the transition from the personal to the collective.

She lingered in the room. More than half of the food on her plate remained but she was no longer hungry. Beatrice was waiting in the doorway and watched Lindell as she gathered up the remains of her meal.

"Do you think you can go on?"

Lindell turned around.

"Of course," she said but her thoughts were of Gräsö.

Edvard's leg had been set and he had now been admitted to a clinic in Östhammar. She tried to imagine him in a hospital bed, but it was difficult. How would Edvard with his impatience deal with being hospitalized? Lindell had told Viola that she would try to drive out to Östhammar that evening.

The interrogations continued after lunch. Lindell walked around, listened, and tried to build up her knowledge of the MedForsk employees. Teresia Wall, whom Beatrice was questioning, really did look terrified. Lindell tried in vain to remember what had been said when she was there before time but could not think of anything out of the ordinary. There had simply been normal conversation.

Berglund, who was now focused on trying to get Mortensen to elaborate on his relationship to Cederén, looked more and more exhausted as Mortensen explained that he and his research director's quarrels over the past winter and spring had arisen from differences regarding the future direction the company should take. He assured Berglund that it had had nothing to do with any supposed experimentation with primates.

"We were in complete agreement on that point," Mortensen claimed.

"Sven-Erik was a serious researcher who would never allow himself to cross the line into ethical misconduct."

"Was that something you argued about?" Lindell inserted.

Berglund shot her a quick look and she had the feeling that he resented her intrusion.

"If you're implying that I have a different opinion on the matter, you are mistaken," Mortensen said emphatically. "We were, as I said, in complete agreement."

Lindell left and sought out Haver's room next.

After an hour, Lindell and Ottosson decided that the sessions should be ended. Nothing of substantial value had been uncovered. It had been easy to slide out of the grasp of the police.

"We simply had too little to work with," Ottosson concluded.

The employees were shaken up and had become visibly nervous over the broadly coordinated action, but when it was revealed that Lindell and her colleagues did not have more substance to their assumptions, the whole thing came off sounding hollow. They could not corroborate Adrian Mård's claims in any way, much less refer to a document that they had not even seen.

Was it financial issues that had led to the deaths of Gabriella Mark and the Cederén family or was it something to do with the alleged illegal animal experimentation? This question remained unanswered.

The investigation was simply marking time, and this left its mark on the detectives as they met to review the situation.

"Mortensen is slippery," Berglund said. "He acts friendly but glides away in an underhanded way. He knows that we don't have anything."

Berglund didn't like the CEO, and Lindell had seen it as soon as she had seen the two men in the interrogation room. The normally mild-mannered Berglund had appeared irritated and given an almost unprofessional impression in his attempts to get in under Mortensen's skin.

The wind was blowing hard when Lindell stepped out onto the street a little after five o'clock. She felt extremely dissatisfied. As she got in her car, the tears suddenly came. It was as if all the tension and hopes for the interrogations made her defenseless now that she was no longer at the station. As long as the interrogations and discussions with her colleagues had been going on, she was able to retain a facade, a facade that was now collapsing. The uncertainty in her existence presented itself as an insurmountable obstacle, both in her work and as a future mother.

"Pointless," she muttered.

Earlier, she had made up her mind to drive out to Östhammar but was becoming increasingly unsure of what she should do. She both wanted and didn't want to see Edvard. She longed for his voice and hands but realized that things would never be as before. She could not keep him in the dark for very much longer. The story of Edvard and Ann was almost at its end. Deal with it, she thought, and the thought left a bitter taste in her mouth.

She drove home and entered the quiet apartment. Everything felt unreal. Had she really lived here for several years? The refrigerator was empty, the sink was full of dishes, the laundry basket was full, and she was almost surprised that the water still came out of the shower. Something was working. She watched the water whirl down the drain.

She wanted to pour herself a glass of wine and settle herself on the couch but she was out of wine and had decided not to get any more. Not for several months. How long did you have to breastfeed?

It had been raining heavily in Östhammar, and when Lindell stepped out of the car in the clinic parking lot, she breathed in deeply. The air was very fresh.

With every step she took she felt increasingly tense. She had brought nothing. No chocolate or flowers. She came empty-handed with a single hope: that he would hug her like before.

A staff member came to greet her. She had a name tag that read *Maria. Nurse.* Lindell explained why she had come and the nurse pointed to a bed at the far end of the corridor.

"We've put a cast on," Maria said with a smile, but Lindell saw that she was tired.

"Will he stay here?"

"No, we send them home as soon as the plaster dries."

"Is he in pain?"

"He was given painkillers back in Öregrund. I don't think it's so bad."

That's what you always say, Lindell thought.

"Thanks for the help," she said, and again had the feeling of gratitude that she often had around hospital workers.

Lindell walked up to the bed. He was sleeping. There was a bruise on his right cheek. Apart from that, he looked fine. The cast was hidden under the blanket. She studied him, the thinning hair, the wrinkles in the tanned face, and the large hand resting on the covers. The large white scar he had from before.

If it hadn't been for the rise and fall of his chest he could have been dead, so strangely peaceful was this energetic and restless man.

Ann gently stroked his hand. Let us stay here, she thought. Can't we freeze life right here? Let's pretend, Edvard. I stand here as your beloved. You are dreaming about me. You wake up and I am here by your side. I love you. I know that now.

When she lifted her gaze from his hand, he had opened his eyes. He looked at her and smiled a crooked, almost shy smile.

"Just look at me," he said.

He twisted his hand and took hers. Your hands make me defenseless, she thought.

"How are you?"

"Well taken care of," he said and smiled again.

She nodded. He moved clumsily to the side so that she could sit down on the edge of the bed but Ann went and fetched a chair.

"What happened?"

He told her briefly about his fishing outing. He praised Victor's courage. Edvard had seen the old man as he must have been thirty or forty years ago, forceful and with an assurance in managing the boat that he himself would never possess. The old man had skillfully maneuvered between the reef and the underwater rocks and tossed the anchor at exactly the right moment. It was as if the sea itself grew calmer.

"It was slippery on the rocks," Edvard finished.

"It scared me half to death when Viola called. She said that you had gone by the board and I thought you had died."

Edvard didn't say anything.

"Why did you set out in such bad weather?"

"It was Victor's nets."

"Who cares about some silly old nets?"

She saw that Edvard didn't want to keep talking about it. He stared straight ahead. The slightly embarrassed but open expression in his face was gone.

"You wanted to test the limits, didn't you? Isn't that right?"

"No," he said, but Lindell heard the hesitation in his voice.

"I'm pregnant," she said.

He had no reaction. He simply turned his head, looked at her, and nodded.

"Did you know?" she asked.

He shook his head.

"I love you," he said quietly and she saw tears in his eyes. "I knew it without a doubt when I lay there in the water. I can't live so far away from you."

"It's not yours," she said and she didn't understand where she found the words or the strength.

Lindell saw the doubt and then the pain that drew across his face like a thundercloud. It was as if she had whipped him. Edvard collapsed in front of her eyes. He didn't want to believe her. For a few seconds he had experienced joy and uttered the words that she had longed for.

"I'm sorry," she sobbed.

His body became rigid and he closed his eyes. The color in his cheeks had been replaced with a sickly gray pallor.

"Forgive me. I love you."

He started as if she had given him another blow.

"Go," he said curtly.

"I love you," Ann said.

"Just go. Go, for the love of god!"

Lindell staggered off. She cast a last glance at Edvard. He was watching her and their eyes met. It was a desperate hate that she saw. She could walk. He was bedridden and she sensed his emotions. He who always fled when the questions became too many or too difficult, who dove into work when darkness threatened to take over. Now he was laid out, fettered to his own anguish.

She regretted having spilled the truth so baldly. It was as if she had taken advantage of his vulnerability, newly rescued from the sea, exposed not only to the waves of the Baltic but to the swell of emotions. He could interpret it that way.

Their shared life was now over. The trust between them would never be reestablished. Suddenly she was standing at the clinic exit. She had noticed his hesitation when she had asked why he had gone out in such bad weather. Had he intended to take his life? She gazed up at the outside of the building, where the windows gleamed in the slow evening sun. He was capable of it, she was sure of it.

If she had had an abortion, would he have wanted her then? She turned as if to go back through the entrance, run down the corridor, and ask him. Straight out. Not care about her shame or his unspoken questions. She knew that he would never ask who the father of her child was. Would she be able to explain, win back his confidence enough that they could at least try again?

She shook her head. Not Edvard. His melancholy nature put a stop to any such thoughts. Simply the knowledge of her brief affair would lie like a boulder in their path.

Her cell phone rang, and for a moment she thought it was him, but it was Frenke at the call center.

"Hi, Ann, sorry for disturbing you, but I received a call and I thought I recognized the name. Mortensen, does that ring a bell?"

"Yes, of course," Lindell said quickly.

"His neighbor, who seems to be a nut case, called and complained about Mortensen's making too much noise."

"Too much noise?"

"Yes, apparently he's operating some kind of machinery in his yard and the neighbor thought it was too late. He's been firing it up a lot lately, he says."

"I see," Lindell said.

"I know, I know," Frenke said, "but since I recognized the name Mortensen, I thought I would let you know. He's involved in that MedForsk investigation, isn't he? I asked the neighbor to give you a call tomorrow morning."

"I appreciate it. Thanks for calling."

"Have a good one," Frenke said, feeling a little better after these parting words.

In this abrupt way, Lindell was returned to life without Edvard. She checked her watch. Mortensen is at the end of his rope, she thought. Sits in an interrogation all day and then goes home to dig up his yard at night. What had he said? "You have to get your money's worth."

The way back to Uppsala was long. The brief moment with Edvard had frozen her movements and thoughts. She drove past Börstil and it occurred to her that perhaps it was the last time for a long while that she would drive by the white church. It had always been a journey marker for her. Once past it, she was in Roslagen. The church for her marked the entrance to Edvard's kingdom, and she remembered all the times that she drove past it with a tingle of excitement.

Now her insides were tingling from other reasons. Deep inside she despised herself, but she always repressed this feeling. In time her self-disgust would grow even greater. Instead she managed to distract herself so she would feel some relief. It was cowardly, but she swallowed it out of pure self-preservation. She had to keep herself together. She had to solve the case.

Through Gimo she kept to the speed limit for the first time. Skäfthammars church. Next it'll be Alunda, she thought. Then Stavby and then Rasbo. From the cathedral in Málaga to this parade of country churches in Uppland.

The guilt she felt at hurting another person threatened to overwhelm her, but she forced herself to think of the investigation. What was it that Teresia Wall had said? Granted it had been social conversation, but Lindell could not come up with what it was that had caught her attention. It could have been a single word, but what?

At the exit to Tuna she finally remembered. It was Teresia's comment about her husband, who worked as a veterinarian at Ultuna. Adrian Mård had a degree in agricultural science and had most likely also gone there. Maybe they had met? Maybe they knew each other? Maybe it was Teresia's husband who had supplied Mård with the information about the illegal animal experiments?

A lot of maybes, but Lindell had followed her intuition before, and this lead wasn't any worse than the others. She checked the time. Edvard, what are you doing? A sense of loss and sadness came over her. She fumbled for her phone, which had slid down between the front seats, and dialed Beatrice's number.

It rang five times before she answered.

"Were you sleeping?"

"No, we're playing Kubb in the garden," Beatrice said cheerfully. "I had a feeling that it was you."

"I had an idea . . ." Lindell began.

"Teresia Wall," Beatrice filled in.

"Exactly."

"I realized when you said that part about the start of the interrogation, when we were chatting to get her to relax a little."

"Her husband works at Ultuna and most likely got his education there. Adrian Mård did too."

She didn't need to say anymore. Beatrice understood.

"Should we bring her in again tomorrow?"

"Can you arrange it?" Lindell asked.

Karl-Göran Wall had received his degree from Ultuna in 1982, the same year as Adrian Mård. Lindell had uncovered this fact with the help of a cooperative staff member at the university.

Granted, the two men had different specializations, but the probability that they knew each other was still fairly high.

"Do you remember a man by the name of Adrian Mård?" Beatrice asked.

Teresia Wall answered in the negative, but her eyes gave her away.

"Maybe your husband does?" Lindell suggested. "We can call him and ask."

Teresia pushed out her lower lip in an expression that was hard to read. Perhaps it was anger. She said nothing, and both Lindell and Beatrice knew they were on the right track. Teresia was smart enough to realize that their questions were part of a series. They were weaving a net in which she was gradually becoming snared. Some reacted with relief, others with passivity, and still others with anger when they realized that they were like a fly in a spiderweb. But however hard they struggled, it was in vain. The conclusion was a given.

"Okay," she conceded, "I know Adrian Mård. What about it?"

"He has shared certain information with us," Lindell said.

Teresia started to cry, the tears slowly trickling down her cheeks.

Beatrice gave her a tissue. Teresia blew her nose loudly and then started talking. Lindell made sure that the tape recorder was on. Now, De Soto, now we've got something for you.

"It was last fall," Teresia said. "Sven-Erik had been down in Málaga and had come back very upset. He wasn't like himself at all. He was curt and off-kilter, and the atmosphere was strained. He and Mortensen were fighting more and more. They slammed doors and there was just a bad feeling. Everything had been so good before. The business was going well, we were on top. Everything got turned upside down."

"What did they fight about?" Beatrice asked.

"We didn't know. Sofi confronted Mortensen and asked him, but he wouldn't say. We thought that it was money at first. That's often why people fall out, but it was something else. I went into Sven-Erik's office once to get some documents. I couldn't find them and started to look through the files stacked on his desk."

She paused for a moment and looked at Lindell.

"I wasn't snooping," she said. "It was important to get a copy of the report I was looking for."

Lindell nodded.

"In the middle of the stack there was a document that caught my eye. It looked like all the others, but at the very bottom Sven-Erik had written 'Jesus Christ' in capital letters. Of course I would be curious. And then it said that he recommended against something and that it could cause great suffering. It was those words 'great suffering' that had the biggest impact on me."

"Was he the one who had written this comment?"

"Yes, I recognized the handwriting," Teresia said. "It was about a clinical trial that was going to be undertaken. We had been running primate trials for a couple of years. Liiv and Södergren had been responsible for them, and they had been moderately successful."

"Was there any truth to the animal activists' claims?" Beatrice asked. "They maintain that the animal trials were illegal."

Teresia hesitated.

"I think they did parallel trials," she said. "One series was approved. Every trial has to be reviewed. The other was probably not official."

"Probably? You think that they conducted two series of trials, one of which was illegal?"

Teresia nodded.

"You think this or you know it?"

"I know," she said quietly.

"Why didn't you raise any alarms?" Lindell asked.

Teresia Wall took a long time to answer.

"The company's future was hanging on the Parkinson's project," she said finally.

"You knew it, but you kept quiet," Beatrice said grimly.

"Did Cederén know about it too?"

"Of course. He was the head of research."

"What was the difference between those trials and the new ones, the ones that Cederén was so upset about?"

Lindell's question brought Teresia to tears again. She stared down at the floor, her hands folded on her large belly.

"What were the results?" Lindell asked.

"They weren't so good," Teresia said. "Something went wrong. The trials were stopped because there were too many side effects."

"And those trials were conducted in the Dominican Republic?"

Teresia nodded.

"Why there?"

"I don't know. Maybe the controls aren't as strict."

Teresia told them how she had first been beset by doubt and then disgust. She had also been afraid and nervous and did not know what to do. Her husband had noticed the change in her. At first he thought it had to do with her pregnancy, but finally she hadn't been able to keep the information from him anymore. She told him about her discovery.

Together they had then reached out to Adrian Mård, who they had known for fifteen years. They trusted him. They knew that he would be able to get the word out without involving Teresia and her husband.

She assured them that she had not talked to anyone else at the company about the document that she had found. She had been planning to discuss it with Cederén but had not done so in time.

Lindell left the room and immediately walked over to Ottosson's office. He noticed her look of agitation and gazed back at her with concern but was interrupted by Lindell, who told him what Teresia had said.

Ottosson listened without interrupting and sat quietly for a while with a look that Lindell could characterize only as abstracted.

"What pigs," he said finally.

He stared at her as if he thought that she had come to him with a fictionalized story.

"Can it be true?"

"I am sure that Wall is telling the truth," Lindell said. "Why would she be making this up?"

Ottosson left the desk and started to walk to and fro across the floor, only to stop, grab the telephone receiver, and dial a number.

"This is Ottosson. Can you come here?"

He listened to the answer before he went on impatiently.

"No, it can't wait," he said and hung up.

"Fritzén?" Lindell asked.

Ottosson nodded. A great calm came over her. It was as if Ottosson drained away the anger. She sat heavily in the chair and couldn't really think straight. Ottosson said something that she didn't quite catch before he left the room and set off down the corridor.

When he returned, Lindell saw that he had rinsed his face. His hairline and beard were still damp.

"How do we proceed?" he asked in a tired voice and sat back down at the desk.

"We bring in Mortensen," Lindell said.

She walked back to her room. The exhaustion was starting to get to her as well, but she forced herself to reach out to Adrian Mård. He seemed to have been swallowed up by the earth. He did not answer at any of the telephone numbers that he had given her and had not returned any of Lindell's earlier messages.

She ended up sitting with the phone in her hand. How cruel I was to Edvard, she thought. Barge into his sickroom and let drop that I am carrying someone else's child. If I had just approached this in a different way, maybe I could have reasoned with him.

Did she love him? She believed she did. She didn't dare let herself test this fully. Since she was denied the joy of living with him, it didn't matter in the end. The sense of having thrown away all possibilities of a future with Edvard only stoked her self-disgust. A single night's thoughtless escapade ruins everything, she thought bitterly. But what do I know about what Edvard might have been up to during the six months that we didn't see each other? He may have taken the opportunity to spread his wild oats. But if this thought was meant to comfort her, it failed. Her intuition told her that he had not been with anyone else, and anyway, what would it have meant? Nothing. This was about her and Edvard.

She leaned over the desk. Should she call him? He would hang up immediately. Driving out to Gräsö was senseless. Viola was caring for Edvard, and his head was most likely filled with hatred and a sense of betrayal.

The phone rang and she automatically reached for the receiver, saying her name mechanically.

"My name is Eilert Jancker and I live in Kåbo, right next to Jack Mortensen, if that rings a bell."

"Of course," Lindell said and recalled Frenke's call from the night before. "What can I assist you with?"

"I am completely fed up with the noise level in the neighborhood, and Mortensen is the one who causes most of the disturbances."

"I see. Go on," Lindell said when Jancker made no attempt to elaborate on this statement.

"I've registered a complaint about this before, but now I'm at my wit's end. There has been no improvement—in fact, quite the opposite."

"Can you tell me in concrete terms what this is about?" Lindell said and felt a growing sense of impatience.

"Work machinery noise," he said.

"I'm in the Violent Crimes division, so this isn't really my turf."

"I was connected to this number," Jancker insisted.

"Then let me hear it."

"A couple of days ago, Mortensen operated a digger long into the night. As my neighbors and I understand it, digging should be undertaken during business hours only. I believe I speak for all of us."

Why do they have to be so long-winded? Lindell thought tiredly.

"What I would like to know is what you are planning to do about it?"

"Have you tried to speak to Mortensen directly about this? That's often a good first step . . ."

"I have tried," Jancker interrupted her. "I went over the other day, when I was completely beside myself, to discuss the inappropriate nature of his behavior. And what did I find? A machine that was on full bore but no Mortensen."

Lindell became more alert.

"The digger was on and making noise, but you didn't see Mortensen, is that what you mean?"

"Exactly," said Jancker, pleased that he had been able to make his point.

"When was this?"

"The evening of the twenty-ninth, between six and ten o'clock."

"You entered Mortensen's garden in order to speak to him?"

"I know this may seem forward, but what was I to do?"

"And you did not find him?"

"As I said, no. I even rang the doorbell, but no one opened. Don't you think it's reprehensible? To turn on a piece of machinery and then leave the property?"

"You are absolutely convinced that he wasn't there?"

"Absolutely. The car was gone. He came back at around ten. I noted the exact time: 10:05 P.M."

"And then he turned it off?"

"Yes."

Lindell recalled the words of the man who had rented out the digger: that Mortensen had not been particularly good at it, that he hadn't been effective in his efforts. This statement now took on added significance. The machine had not actually been working.

"Is it possible for you to come down to the station and file a complaint? We can send a car to fetch you."

"I have to say," Jancker commented, "that it's a relief to find a person who understands the importance of peace and quiet. Of course I will come in. How about if I come down in half an hour?"

"That will be absolutely fine," said Lindell.

The digging had been Mortensen's alibi for the evening Gabriella was murdered. He had said that his neighbors could vouch for the fact that he had been working the digger all evening. Now this alibi had been discredited. The neighbor's statement blew holes in it.

Lindell could not sit still. She stood up and paced. As she passed her desk she removed the telephone receiver from its hook and walked up to the window.

✦

Thirty-one

Jack Mortensen was brought into the police station that afternoon. He smiled at Lindell and Ottosson as he walked up to them, accompanied by Berglund.

"This is becoming quite a habit," he noted and calmly sat down.

"It seems so," Ottosson agreed grimly.

Mortensen's smile stiffened when he saw Ottosson's expression.

"Gabriella Mark was murdered on the evening of June twenty-ninth," Lindell began swiftly, but she stopped almost as soon as she had begun.

Mortensen didn't react at all to her words. He simply stared down at his folded hands.

"You said that you had been digging in your garden the whole evening, isn't that right?"

Mortensen looked up. "Yes, that's correct."

"No, that's wrong," Lindell said.

She gave him a few moments to reflect on her statement before she continued.

"We now have information that your digger was simply idling for large stretches of that evening. What do you say to that?"

"It did idle for a while, that's true. I went out for a snack."

"Why didn't you turn it off when you left?"

"I was afraid it would be difficult to restart," Mortensen answered.

"It can't be that difficult. You had been given instructions by the man you rented it from, hadn't you?"

"I'm not well versed in machinery."

"No, he did tell me that. He thought that you had managed to dig very little, and I guess that can be explained by the fact that it was idling most of the time."

"Where are you going with this? I told you I went to get some coffee."

"You also left the house that evening. Where did you go?"

"I didn't," Mortensen said, but then reversed himself almost immediately, stating that he had driven to the office to get some papers.

Lindell sat quietly for a while.

"Papers," she said finally. "What kind of papers? You leave a machine that you have rented for a lot of money so that you can go and get some papers? It must have been some very important documents."

Mortensen nodded.

"And it wasn't because you took a drive out to Rasbo?"

"You're accusing me of murdering Gabriella Mark. Why don't you just come out and say it?"

"I'm just trying to clarify what you were doing that evening," Lindell said calmly. "What cars does the company own?"

Mortensen pushed his chair back from the table, crossed his legs, and pushed his hair back with his hand.

"We have two cars," he said. "A Fiat van and a Škoda."

"What colors?"

"One is blue, the other red."

"No company logos, decals, or anything like that?" Lindell asked.

Mortensen shook his head.

"I think that you took your car, drove to MedForsk, changed to the red Škoda, drove out to Mark's cottage, and strangled her," Lindell said.

Before Mortensen had time to reply, she went on.

"I think we'll take a break here for the moment. There are some things we have to check."

She stood up and Haver followed her lead. They left the room without giving Mortensen a second glance.

"We'll let him sweat for a while," Lindell said.

"That he left the house was news," Haver said, and Lindell detected a note of displeasure in his voice.

After ten minutes they returned to the interrogation room. Mortensen was sitting in the same position. If he had been sweating, no one could tell.

"I want to get this over with now," he said as soon as the detectives sat down and Haver had turned on the tape recorder.

"That's fine with me," Lindell said.

"I'm sick and tired of your accusations. I actually have a business to run, and if you don't have anything more than these vague assumptions, then I'd like to leave."

Lindell disregarded this.

"Is there anyone who can corroborate your claim that you went to get some papers from the office and then returned to your home?" she asked.

"No, I was alone there. We don't have an evening shift, if that's what you're asking."

"You spent a lot of time talking to Gabriella. What did you talk about?"

"All kinds of things, but mostly of course about Sven-Erik and everything that happened."

"Did you call her on June twenty-ninth?"

"I'm not sure but I don't think so. Most of the time it was her calling me."

"Does the nickname Pålle mean anything to you?"

"No."

"Did you ever visit her cottage?"

"No."

"But you met?"

"A couple of times."

Lindell paused. Mortensen watched her attentively as if he were waiting for the next quick question.

Instead Haver jumped in. "What size shoe do you wear?"

Mortensen looked at him with surprise. He glanced down at his feet, and strangely enough his face turned red, as if it were an inappropriate question.

"Forty-two," he said. "Why do you ask?"

"I was just wondering," Haver said.

At that moment Lindell's cell phone rang. She picked it up quickly and answered.

"Send her up," she said after listening for a while.

An ominous silence fell in the room. Lindell looked appraisingly at Mortensen, who immediately lowered his gaze.

Haver was on the verge of saying something but held back. This was the moment of truth. The answers were here in this silence. Personally he was convinced that Mortensen was lying on one or even several points. Was he the killer? If so, they would have trouble proving it. The fact that he had misrepresented the extent of his digging was nothing that would hold any substance in court. He could very well have gone to the office that night. It was up to the police to prove that he had gone out to Gabriella's cottage. The fact that MedForsk had a red Škoda van didn't prove anything either. There were many of those around town. Lindell had asked Ryde to drive out to MedForsk and take the Škoda to the garage to be searched, but neither Haver nor Lindell held out much hope that it would yield anything.

There was no forensic evidence from the crime scene either. The only thing was a footprint. Haver did wear size 42 shoes, but that didn't make him a murderer.

He shot Lindell a look. She could probably guess what he was thinking. She smiled. At that moment there was a knock on the door.

It was Riis accompanied by an older woman. When she entered the room, Mortensen jumped out of his chair as if stung by a bee.

"What are you doing here?" he shouted.

"I could ask you the same question," his mother said forcefully and looked around the room.

Riis hurried to bring in another chair and placed it on the other side of the table. Mortensen watched in disbelief as his mother sat down with an ease that astonished even Lindell. She knew that his mother was an iron-willed woman, but the way that she had sailed in and taken her place demonstrated an unusual degree of strength.

"What have you gone and done now?" she asked and fixed him with her gaze.

"Nothing," he said.

"Sit down," she said and he obeyed.

"We were talking about the murder of Gabriella Mark," Lindell said. "We think your son may be withholding additional information."

"What do you mean by dragging my poor mother into this? It's unbelievable. You're capable of anything, aren't you."

"Your mother came of her own free will," Lindell said calmly.

"You don't have anything to do with this, do you?" he asked and turned to his mother.

She looked at him with a pitying gaze. "You could use a little help," she said. "You always have."

"He isn't very strong," she went on, and for some reason turned to Riis, who was leaning against the wall. "To lose two of your best friends isn't easy."

"You mean Sven-Erik and Josefin?" Lindell said.

"Josefin." Mortensen's mother snorted. "There was never much to that woman. I couldn't for the life of me understand why you were once interested in her. No, I mean Gabriella."

Mortensen raised his eyes and stared at his mother.

"Did you know Gabriella?" Lindell asked.

The mother stared at Lindell.

"Know her? Of course. She and Pålle have been best friends since they were little."

There was hushed silence. Jack Mortensen stared at the floor.

"Who is Pålle?" Lindell asked.

"My son, Jack," his mother said. "We've called him Pålle ever since he was little. He and Gabriella were inseparable when they were little. We were neighbors in Simrishamn for at least ten years. Look at Pålle's teeth! It was Gabriella's father who straightened them so nicely. Before that, he looked like a rabbit."

She stopped suddenly. Mortensen was shaking.

"What is it?" his mother asked, and now for the first time Lindell heard a softer tone in her voice.

Everyone looked at Jack "Pålle" Mortensen. He sat with hands raised in front of his face, sobbing.

"Pålle, what is it?" his mother repeated and placed her hand on his arm.

"Let go of me, you old bitch," he yelled and jumped up from the chair.

Riis reacted in a flash, throwing himself forward and grabbing Mortensen.

"Calm down," Riis said in low voice but with a smile on his lips. Lindell saw his muscles tense up under his shirt. Mortensen's mother sat completely frozen.

"Sit down," Lindell ordered.

Riis lightened his grip and Mortensen sank heavily and helplessly back in the chair.

"You knew Gabriella well, something that you denied earlier."

Mortensen let out a sob. His mother stared at him in disbelief.

"You did go there that night, didn't you?" Lindell asked again.

He said nothing, staring down at the floor. Beads of sweat formed on his brow. Lindell shot Haver a look.

"Answer them," Mrs. Mortensen said. "What's the point of denying that you knew Gabriella."

Mortensen's cheeks twitched. Riis stood behind him, prepared to jump in.

"I did know Gabriella," Mortensen said hoarsely. "I liked her very much."

His mother stared at him with an astonishment mingled with what Lindell took to be disgust, an impression underscored by her aristocratic appearance. She was watching her son being interrogated by the police as well as suffering inner anguish, and her facial expression indicated no empathy.

"I liked her," he repeated and looked at his mother. "You didn't know that. There's so much you don't know."

Mrs. Mortensen was about to say something, but Mortensen gestured for her to keep quiet and continued.

"She lied to me. She told me when she became a widow that she would never be with another man."

"You knew that she and Cederén had a relationship?" Lindell asked.

Mortensen turned to her with what appeared to be a great effort. His labored movements matched the slowness with which the words were leaving his mouth. She had seen this before, the paralysis that came over some people in stressful situations where lying was no longer an option. They slowed to quarter speed, and it could be incredibly frustrating for an interrogator who wanted to hasten toward their goal, but Lindell knew to remain patient.

"Yes," he said finally, "of course I did. I came across them, saw them in Stockholm by chance."

His mother laughed unexpectedly.

"Poor Pålle," she said. "First Josefin and then Gabriella."

"Shut up," Mortensen said harshly, and she looked as if she had been struck in the face.

"Did you go to her on June twenty-ninth?"

Lindell put her question to him in a low voice. Mortensen nodded.

"Can you please answer so that I have it on tape?"

Mortensen smiled sarcastically, leaned over the desk, and clearly enunciated "yes." Then he shut his eyes and fell back against the chair.

"Did you fight?"

"Answer her," said Mrs. Mortensen, who appeared to have recovered.

"Get rid of her!" Mortensen screamed and pointed to the door.

"It may be best if you wait outside," Lindell said and turned to Mrs. Mortensen, who got to her feet without a word. Large patches of sweat had appeared under the armpits of her light-colored summer dress. She stared icily at her son.

"You damn devil-bitch!" Mortensen screeched. "You have always ruined everything. Your fucking textiles that no one cares about. Who is interested in rags? And your damned breakfast rolls that you come in with every morning. Just to check on what I'm doing. You hated Gabriella and you hated Josefin. You stuck your nose into my business, talked shit, and schemed."

He sank down, and the silence felt like an icy wind flowing through the room. Lindell saw Riis start to hold out his hand as if to place it on Mortensen's shoulder, but he stopped himself. She had the impression that he felt a certain sympathy for Mortensen. She, on the other hand, simply felt drained by the emotional turbulence in the room. Forty years of ac-cumulated hatred that had been held in check by nothing but a kind of dependence. Mrs. Mortensen had taken advantage of his weak personality and bent him according to her wishes. Now he was striking back.

"Fuck it," he said and banged his right hand on his knee repeatedly as if he had realized that he had spoken up too late—much too late.

"You poor thing," she said before she left the room, followed by Riis, who stopped in the doorway and gave Lindell an approving look.

As soon as the door closed, Mortensen launched into his confession. He had driven out to the cottage on the evening of the twenty-ninth. Gabriella had again been threatening to go public with the truth about MedForsk's illegal experimentation. She had hesitated because she hadn't wanted to smear Cederén's memory, but she had decided to tell the police everything.

"And she died because she wanted the truth to come out?" Lindell asked.

"She hated me," Mortensen said quietly. "She accused me of Sven-Erik's death."

"But you weren't guilty of his death."

"I wanted to support her after he died. She was alone again. But all she did was go on and on about Sven-Erik and the experiments. I thought she liked me."

He paused and looked down at his hands. His breath was the only sound in the room.

"We knew each other so well!" he exclaimed suddenly.

The sharp odor of sweat emanating from him made Lindell have to stand up. Haver looked at her with a watchfulness in his gaze betraying his inner tension. His words fell like heavy stones in the bare interrogation room.

"I strangled her," Mortensen mumbled.

"Where?" Haver asked.

"In the kitchen."

"What did you do with the body?"

"I buried it in a pile of rocks. At first I was going to put it in the car, but I got scared."

"Scared of what?"

"Everything was calm, but I thought I heard sounds in the woods the whole time. I got scared. Gabriella . . ."

He broke off. Both Haver and Lindell waited for a continuation. He began to cry softly and stroked his hand over his face. A murderer's hands, Lindell thought.

"Did you kill Josefin and Emily?" Haver asked. He sat down where Mrs. Mortensen had been sitting earlier.

"No, never," Mortensen said loudly. "I would never have hurt her."

"But you hurt Gabriella. You killed her."

"But it was different with Josefin."

In what way, he did not specify. Lindell let it go for the moment. There would be time enough for him to explain later.

"Who killed Josefin and Emily?"

"I don't know," Mortensen said.

"I don't believe you," Haver said calmly.

"It's true! I don't know! I would never have allowed such a thing. An innocent woman and a child."

"You murdered Gabriella," Haver pointed out.

"Do the names Urbano and Olivares say anything to you?" Lindell asked.

Mortensen denied any knowledge of them, saying he had never heard their names, much less hosted them during the two days that they had been in Sweden. Lindell believed him.

"Josefin was pregnant when she died. Was it your child?" Haver asked.

Mortensen looked alarmed but shook his head.

"Did you have a relationship?"

Another shake of the head.

"We only talked," Mortensen said. "Josefin wasn't happy."

"But you knew that the destruction of the Cederén family was planned by your colleagues in Spain?" Lindell asked.

Mortensen sat quietly as if weighing his answer.

"They called me afterward," he said finally.

"Who?"

"De Soto."

"What did he say?"

"He said that it was necessary for Sven-Erik to disappear."

"Why?"

"Because Sven-Erik wanted out."

"The purchase of the land in the Dominican Republic, how do you ex-plain that?"

Mortensen now looked completely exhausted. Lindell heard rapid foot-steps in the corridor and then Riis's voice. Perhaps Mrs. Mortensen was still out there. Mortensen stared at the door as if he expected or feared that she would come back in. His gaze was glassy. The former impression of boyishness was completely gone, and Lindell guessed that he would break down completely at any moment.

"Did it have anything to do with the illegal animal experiments con-ducted there?"

Mortensen looked up with surprise.

"Yes, I know that you conducted illegal experiments there," Lindell said.

He gave her a look of amazement and a half smile.

"Why are you smiling?"

"You've done your homework," he said.

"That was why Cederén wanted to get out, isn't it?" Haver asked. "He couldn't stand the thought of the apes suffering. Some of them died, didn't they?"

"Maybe some of them," Mortensen said.

"And what do you think?"

"It isn't very pleasant, but sometimes things go wrong."

"Why did Cederén want to get out if the experiments had already been stopped?" Lindell asked.

"I don't know. He was so changed. I think Gabriella changed him."

"You called down to Málaga and told them?"

Mortensen nodded, then directed a clear "yes" at the microphone.

More than this, Mortensen was unable to manage. He leaned forward and closed his eyes. Lindell and Haver exchanged glances. There was both relief and a kind of hopelessness in their eyes. Haver gathered together his notes. Lindell reached over to turn off the tape recorder after first explain-ing that the session was over. The room grew quiet. Mortensen looked as if he had disappeared into his own world. He straightened his upper body and stared at the wall with an empty gaze.

A murderer had confessed. Lindell was wiped out. Her muscles ached from tension. She checked the time, stood up, and went off to call a guard, who would escort Mortensen to a holding cell. Haver stayed behind. Lindell thought he was probably thinking of his children. That's what he always did when he had that dreamy look in his eyes. He used his thoughts as a shield against all cruelty and evil.

Once Mortensen had been led away, Lindell and Haver went to their offices, Haver in order to call home and Lindell in order to contact the prosecutor.

The rumor spread quickly in the building, and many of her colleagues came by to congratulate her. The chief of police called and Lindell passively received his praise. She was unable to feel any real joy. There was far to go in the investigation as a whole. Mortensen and others at MedForsk would have to be interrogated many more times, forensic examinations would have to be carried out, Mortensen's home would have to be searched, and Moya would have to be informed of the latest developments. The search for Jaime Urbano—the most likely killer of the Cederén family—would continue, but during their last conversation Moya had not sounded very optimistic. He speculated that Urbano might be dead. In any case he was nowhere to be found.

De Soto would be brought in for questioning, but Lindell thought the probability of his being charged with being an accessory to murder was small. It would depend on what Moya could dig up. She discussed the matter with Fritzén and he was of the same opinion. If the Spanish police didn't find Urbano, then De Soto would slip out of their hands.

When Fritzén had left, Lindell continued to sit at her desk. Thoughts of Edvard returned with a regularity that alarmed her. As soon as she left the realm of work, if only for half a minute, he was there.

She was ashamed of the rough way she had treated him. She would always remember his calm gaze after she told him that she was pregnant and his subsequent assurance that he loved her. Those were big words coming from a man like him. What was it that he had said? That he couldn't live so far away from her. For over two years she had longed to hear those words.

Now it was all behind her. She sat as if turned to stone. She ached with disgust at having destroyed their life together. Nothing like this could be undone. If she had only kept her mouth shut and given herself another week to think it over.

"Edvard," she said softly, almost inaudibly.

She knew that she would have imaginary conversations with him for a long time to come.

Lindell was brought back to life by the phone signal. It was Ryde. The red Škoda from MedForsk had been examined. Everything had not yet been analyzed, but Ryde did not think they would turn up anything significant.

"There was just one thing," he said. "A tiny unripe fruit, probably a pear, that was caught in the tread of the right front tire."

Lindell remembered the pear tree along the road to Gabriella's cottage and the unripe fruit on the ground. She told him about the tree and he chuckled.

"Congrats," he said.

"Thanks for your help," Lindell said.

The phone rang again, but she didn't answer.

Vacation, she thought. Two or three days of interrogations and writing the reports, and then it would all be over. This time.

The telephone rang again. She stared at it as if it were a foreign object. The phone kept ringing. On the sixth ring she grabbed the receiver, but at that moment there was a clicking sound on the other end. The dial tone came on and Ann felt close to tears.

✦

Thirty-two

Lindell asked Berglund and Haver to search Mortensen's house. She didn't have the energy. It was as if all the air had been drained out of her. She sat in her office unable to think of anything but Edvard. Could he have been the one who had called? Perhaps he had thought about it. Perhaps his love was so great that he could look past her infidelity and cruelty.

She had lost everything. Even though she had solved Gabriella's murder, she was unable to feel any satisfaction. Gabriella was dead. If she had only gone out to see Gabriella right away, she might still have been alive today.

If. If only she hadn't jumped into bed with that Bengt-Åke. If she hadn't done this and she had done that.

The phone rang. This time she picked up. It was a reporter from channel 4 who was looking for a comment about the solving of Gabriella Mark's murder. Lindell didn't understand how he had heard about it so quickly but sensed that someone at the station must have told him.

She explained that they had apprehended a suspect who had confessed. She said nothing about the illegal animal experiments. When the reporter asked if she could come down to the studio in thirty minutes, she said no. She did not want to see herself on television.

After she hung up she thought of Adrian Mård. It was his information that had led to Mortensen's arrest. She dialed Mård's number but no one answered. Suddenly she became nervous. Why wasn't he answering? Why didn't he return her calls after listening to her messages?

Josefin and Gabriella, two women her own age, murdered. So too Emily, a little girl. Josefin pregnant just like herself. Images from the investigation whirled through her head and left her no peace. The vegetable beds at the cottage. The elk mother with her injured calf. Every new case left new impressions, new memories to add to the old. The evil put away. In the midst of this she had to be strong and rational.

Never before had she missed normalcy as much as now. The appeal of a normal life with a normal man was greater than ever in the gap between the MedForsk mess and the new cases she knew were coming. In the midst of all her turmoil, suddenly she realized that some of her colleagues did enjoy a normal life. Haver did. As did Ottosson and maybe even Beatrice. They could shut their folders and drive back to a home worthy of the name.

There was a knock on the door and Berglund walked in. His face was grim. He held a piece of paper in his hand.

"I think I'm going to get a dog," she said.

Berglund looked at her with surprise. "A dog?"

He sat down and tossed the paper onto her desk. Lindell paused for a second before picking it up. At the same time she gave Berglund a look.

"Yes, a dog," she said and started to read.

The first thing she saw was Julio Piñeda's name.

"What is this?" she asked and looked up.

The document was written in Spanish.

"We found it at Mortensen's."

Lindell scanned the document. She could guess the meanings of some words, but the context was unclear. Piñeda, the mystery man who managed to stay just beyond their ken, appeared here with eleven other names.

"I talked to Riis," Berglund said. "He knows a little Spanish. At first he thought it was a staff listing, but then he wasn't sure."

She read the names again and then looked up.

"So who are they?"

"Riis thought it was some kind of health report."

"Many have suffered." Piñeda's words floated up into her mind.

"The Dominican Republic," she said and Berglund nodded.

Suddenly Lindell was gripped by a frightening thought. What if they weren't experimenting on primates, but on humans? That would explain Jack Mortensen's smile. When they had started to talk about experiments on apes he had realized that the police had no idea what they were really up to.

"Could this be human experimentation?" Lindell asked.

"Fuck, that can't be possible," Berglund said. He took the page back from Lindell and stared at it.

"Call our interpreter, the Chilean. Ask Beatrice to bring Teresia Wall back in."

Berglund immediately stood up and left the room.

Eduardo Cruz grew pale as he painstakingly translated the entire document. He sat across from Lindell and looked at her, then at the page, with an expression that indicated he assumed the whole thing was a bad joke.

He stumbled over some of the scientific terms and explained that he did not know what all the words meant, but the context was nonetheless clear. There was no personal commentary. Everything was presented in crisp precision. It was a medical report of twelve men between forty-four and sixty-eight. The state of their health was described in blunt, concise terms. Three of them, Piñeda among these, had suffered terrible side effects. There was talk of palsy, paroxysmal attacks, and seizures.

"What cruelty," Eduardo said quietly. "What cruelty."

"It is like the Nazis and their experiments," Ottosson said. He was standing by the window.

"My father had Parkinson's," he said. "He would stop in mid-motion and simply stand there, unable to go on. He started to shake and became hoarse. By the time he died, the medication was giving him hallucinations and nightmares."

Ottosson turned around and looked at Lindell. He had tears in his eyes, and Lindell felt a great admiration for him in that moment because he dared to show his emotions so openly.

"It's genocide," said Eduardo and his accent grew stronger with his agitation. "They think that poor people don't have a soul."

Ottosson turned to him as if he had said something very odd.

"Just a body that the researchers can play with," Eduardo went on.

"It's the money," Ottosson said. "Money decides. The soul is much lower on the totem pole. If you can gain a dime or a peseta by another's suffering or death, there is your justification."

"But they are supposed to be saving lives," Eduardo said. "They are doctors and researchers. But it's true what you say," he added, as if correcting his idealistic statements. "I saw this in my country when Pinochet came into power."

"Palsy is the same as paralysis," Lindell said.

She reviewed the names on the page. Ottosson was right. They were only numbers in a list. Who was this Julio Piñeda? What was his profession? What did he and his family look like? He had written a letter to seek justice, but perhaps he would never get it.

That evening Lindell called Antonio Moya in Málaga and told him about Mortensen's confession and their discovery of the human trials. He listened to her account without trying to interrupt and didn't say anything after she finished. At first Lindell thought the connection was broken, but then Moya coughed.

"I am ashamed of these people," he said.

He did not show any great surprise at the macabre turn of events, and Lindell almost had the impression that he had already known of the experiments in the Dominican Republic.

He promised to bring De Soto from UNA Médico in for questioning in the morning. Lindell repeated her invitation that he visit his colleagues in Sweden. Moya thanked her but without enthusiasm, and they ended the call.

He had sounded tired and somewhat reserved. Lindell guessed that his work was at least as difficult as hers, but she was still irritated by his muted reaction.

On the way to the car she bumped into Beatrice.

"How are you?" Beatrice asked, and Lindell didn't like her searching gaze.

"Tired," Lindell said curtly.

"Can I ask you something, Ann? Are you pregnant?"

Lindell felt the mask that she had been wearing crumble quite literally as the tension in her muscles relaxed and she showed her true face.

"Yes," she said, and in that moment she felt enormous gratitude toward her colleague.

"I had a feeling," Beatrice said. "What does Edvard say?"

Lindell started to cry.

"Doesn't he want a baby?" Beatrice said.

"It isn't his."

"Oh, fuck."

It wasn't often that Beatrice swore. She took a step closer and grabbed Lindell's arm as she saw her anguished expression.

"Are you sure you're pregnant? Have you done a test?"

Lindell shook her head. She hadn't even managed to do that, but Beatrice looked as if she understood.

"Do that first," she said. "Then at least you know."

Lindell nodded and felt like a teenager.

"You have to take care of yourself," Beatrice said. "You have only one body and one life."

"I know," Lindell said hoarsely.

They parted and Lindell got in her car with mixed emotions. She wanted to keep talking, but at the same time she wanted to be alone. She watched Beatrice put up her hand in greeting, drive out of the garage, and disappear.

They following day they conducted new interrogations with a pale Mortensen. He denied all knowledge of human experimentation and also all knowledge of the documents that had been found in his home.

"I've never seen this," he stubbornly maintained during the first two hours, finally he become completely silent.

He repeated his confession that he had killed Gabriella but refused to cooperate in any other way. He had been assigned an attorney, but the latter mainly sat quietly as if he had trouble understanding why his client was involved in such serious crimes. The last thing Mortensen said was that he did not wish to have any visitors.

After lunch Moya called.

"We discussed everything this morning," he began, speaking in the same tired voice as he had on the day before. "It has been decided that we will not proceed further."

"What are you talking about?" Lindell asked breathlessly.

"We are going to intensify our search for Urbano, but we will do nothing about the Dominican Republic."

"But why?"

"I can't comment further," Moya said. "Since this matter is in regard to another country, it is out of my jurisdiction."

"That's unbelievable," Lindell said. "That means that the whole thing will be buried in silence."

"That may not be true," Moya said, but she heard in his voice that he shared her opinion.

"I am very sorry," he added. "But there is nothing I can do. At least no one has died."

They concluded the call in a formal way. Lindell promised to send translated copies of the interrogations with Mortensen, information that the Spanish police could use in their investigations, and for his part, Moya promised to be in touch if there were any new developments.

Lindell went in to Ottosson's office and told him about the conversation with Moya. After a moment of silence, he called the chief of police.

Three hours later there was a fax from the National Police Board. It was full of superfluous words as usual, but the gist of it was that the Spanish police had the formal responsibility for the investigation in the Dominican Republic. Any illegal activities that might have taken place had been undertaken by a Spanish company. The document was signed by Chief Superintendent Morgan at the National Police Board.

Lindell tried to get ahold of Adrian Mård but was unsuccessful and subsequently left the police station without talking to anyone. It had started to rain. The temperature hovered at around ten degrees Celsius.

In Gräsö, Edvard Risberg sat leaning against the chicken coop, his legs outstretched. Viola was harvesting the first new potatoes. Out across the sea of the archipelago, a strong nor'easter was brewing. He could already feel the first raindrops on his face.

✦

Thirty-three

The chickens were peacefully pecking at the ground under the mango tree. Half dozing, Julio Piñeda watched them. His daughter-in-law had placed him in the shade under the trees. Two of his grandchildren were playing noisily. Julio thought they were helping to pour out honey into bottles.

The Swede was dead. He knew that now. The police had come around and told him. The project of a house for the affected had fallen by the wayside. But it no longer mattered in his case. Death would soon be paying him a visit. He had already started to smell, he felt. His limbs no longer obeyed him, and he had trouble making himself understood. His grandchildren watched him with wide eyes when he tried to speak.

Death will be here soon, he thought, now without fear, but it would have been nice to have had a few more years. Now that the trees were yielding a proper harvest and they had gathered enough building materials to erect the little stand by the road where the tourists could stop to buy fresh fruit and honey.

He had been planning to walk around among the trees, telling the amazed Europeans, Japanese, and Americans about his plants, showing them how to crack and peel a coconut. An old man with worn trousers and a stained shirt, but with a machete in his hand. The grandchildren were to have followed him, helped him, and then asked for money.

Now others would have to take over. He had been paid to participate. They had given him almost half a year's salary. Hauled it out as if it were change left on a bar counter. They had bought Julio and eleven other villagers. Now the Swede was dead and Julio would soon follow. Perhaps they would meet on the other side. There everyone was equal. Perhaps there were also mangoes, papayas, and bananas.

Or was it more like the land of the Swede: cold and sterile?